COMBO

TALONS

by

JOHN DeCHANCIE

A TERRIBLE BEAUTY

by

JOHN J. MILLER

ibooks

new york

www.ibooks.net

DISTRIBUTED BY SIMON & SCHUSTER, INC.

A Publication of ibooks, inc.

Originally published as separate volumes.

An ibooks, inc. Book

Distributed by Simon & Schuster, Inc.
1230 Avenue of the Americas, New York, NY 10020

ibooks, inc.
24 West 25th Street
New York, NY 10010

The ibooks World Wide Web Site Address is:
www.ibooks.net

ISBN 1-4165-0405-2
First ibooks, inc. printing February 2005
10 9 8 7 6 5 4 3 2 1

Edited by Steven A. Roman and Karen Haber

Cover art by Greg Land

Cover design by Brandon Diaz

Printed in the U.S.A.

TALONS

JOHN DeCHANCIE

ibooks
new york
www.ibooksinc.com

DISTRIBUTED BY SIMON & SCHUSTER, INC

PROLOGUE

VIENNA, AUSTRIA, 1986

Demel's coffee-house was not crowded that afternoon. In a far corner, directly under a painting of the youthful Franz Josef, Horst Pfordmann sat sipping coffee with whipped cream, and drinking in the *Gemutlichkeit.* The German word does not translate easily: coziness, congeniality, a feeling of belonging. However one defines it, Demel's had it. It had good coffee, too.

And pastry. A table near the counter was piled with confections the like of which only Vienna could produce: vanilla crescents, Congress doughnuts, Sacher tortes, endless varieties of cookies, lady fingers, and more, most fattening in the extreme, all looking absolutely mouth-watering. But Horst wasn't hungry.

He looked around at the customers: a bespectacled old Frau writing a letter; an elderly couple in the opposite corner drinking melange—half milk, half coffee; a pretty waitress in the back on break, sipping a soda; a man in a dark suit reading a paper. Horst wondered what would any of these people do if they knew what he knew. If what fell into his lap would fall into theirs, what would they do? That frump of a *gnadige Frau*, there, scribbling a newsy missive to her sister in Munich, what would she do? Who would she turn to? To whom would she divulge the secret?

Whom do you trust? Good question. Horst reached inside his jacket and fingered the padded envelope again.

In the envelope was a floppy disk, and on that disk was a file. The file had come in over an international bulletin-board network, but the accompanying e-mail note had not been coded, and the note had let on what was contained in the encrypted file. Why Dr. Pastorius had done it that way, Horst did not know. Perhaps he did not fully understand the workings of computer networks, a fairly new phenomenon. Sometimes even Horst forgot that two people communicating on net was like shouting into bullhorns on opposite sides of a crowded public square. Anything one did on a public network could be monitored by anyone in the world. Every intelligence-gathering organization on the planet routinely patrolled cyberspace for anything that might be a threat . . . or an opportunity.

But only Horst had the key to the encrypted file. It was in his pocket, on the disk with Dr. Pastorius's file. Only Pastorius could decipher Horst's files and messages. It was the same code, and it was unique. And that code could not be broken by any means known at present.

The code was, in principle, unbreakable. Neither ordinary complexity nor subtlety was its guarantee of secrecy. A thousand supercomputers working in concert for a thousand years could not unscramble the data. Of course, Horst had no guarantee that Pastorius did not send the same file, under a different encryption, to someone else. If so, Pastorius had not let on. The possibility that someone else had the file comforted Horst a little, but not much.

He got up. The *gnadige Frau* smiled at him toothily as he left the coffee-house.

Walking through the elegant commercial clutter of the Kohlmarkt, Horst got a sudden urge to do something, to make a decision. He had to communicate with somebody. This thing was too big for him alone. He saw a mail kiosk, stepped up to it, took out the small padded envelope, and slipped it in the slot. He sighed. Done. Now it was out of his hands. But had he done the right thing? As he walked away from the kiosk, doubts arose. Was Pastorius simply the crank that most of his colleagues around the world thought him?

Was he crazy? Was that file and its purported secret simply a delusion? Pastorius was eccentric; was he also stark staring mad?

He wanted to forget about the whole thing. There was no way he could gain any professional recognition out of merely relaying Dr. Pastorius's findings to the proper experts.

Then there was Kenneth Irons in New York. He was an amateur, of course, but he seemed to know more about the artifact than anyone. In fact, Irons sometimes sounded as if he already was in possession of the artifact, and was simply trawling the professional field to see what others knew about it. Curious. But how could he have it? No, he was just a well-informed amateur.

Well, now I *know possibly more about the ancient magical gauntlet than anyone else in the world,* Horst thought.

He turned into his apartment building and mounted

the two flights to his floor. Stopping just short of the door to his flat, a mild depression came over him. The good thing about living alone was that when you came back home, your apartment was always the same way you left it. But that was also the bad thing. A loneliness welled up in him, a loneliness that had been with him throughout his adolescence and his young-adult life. He had never had a steady girlfriend. Women had never taken to him. It wasn't that Horst was bad-looking. He was just painfully shy and fearful of rejection.

He was not a virgin, and, in fact, had had a few very brief affairs. But so far he had not managed to snare a steady mistress. He was lonely most of the time.

He suddenly decided to take the underground to Rotenturmstrasse and pick up a girl.

Or perhaps . . . he'd been told of a very good place on . . . now where had Franz said it was? He checked his wallet. Not enough money. He'd have to hit an automatic teller machine. But did he have his ATM card?

No, he did not. For a second, a sinking feeling hit him as he wondered whether he might have left the plastic card in the slot the last time he used an ATM. But, no. He'd never done that; no reason he should have started.

Wait. He remembered he'd done a housecleaning job on his wallet recently, generally slimming the thing down, throwing away old business cards and dozens of slips of paper with girls' telephone numbers on them (numbers he rarely had the courage to dial). He hated a bloated wallet; rather, one bloated with anything other than money. He might have left the ATM card in his desk drawer. Well, he'd have to go into the flat after all.

He got out his key and opened the door, and walked into darkness. And stopped. He distinctly recalled leaving a light on. Bulb must have blown out. As he edged cautiously toward the alcove that stood for his study, a curious feeling came over him, one he couldn't readily identify. Something was not right. He flicked on the light, and saw what was wrong. Two men were standing in opposite corners of the alcove.

They stepped forward. One was taller, and wore a black trench coat over a brown suit. The other had on an expensive-looking black leather jacket over a blue turtleneck. He had an ugly face but a pleasant manner.

"You're probably wondering," the toad-like man said in a Prussian accent, "who the hell we are and what we're doing here." He smiled.

Horst had frozen. His only thought was *police*. He could only stutter, "Who . . . who . . . ?"

"Relax," said the taller one. He was fairly good-looking, with dark eyes and a wide mouth. "First of all, you are Horst Pfordmann?"

Horst nodded.

"Graduate student, University of Vienna. Archaeology?"

Horst nodded again.

"Good, at least we have the right man. We're interested in the Witchblade code."

"The . . . the Witchblade–"

"I said relax," the man told him mildly. "Nothing's going to happen to you if you cooperate. Recently you received data from a Dr. Helmut Pastorius in Egypt, concerning the Witchblade. It was encrypted. We need the de-encryption code."

Horst finally drew himself together. "Who the hell are you?"

"Who do you think?" the taller man said, shrugging.

He had a symmetrical face with movie-star good looks that Horst knew women really went for.

"It's private information," Horst said, trying not to sound as frightened to the core as he was.

"Not any more. We need this data for our case files."

"Who are you?" Horst demanded. "What branch of the government?"

"My name is Erwin Strauss," said the toad. "We need the code. If we have to, we'll impound your computer and every floppy disk you have."

"I want to see some identification. I don't think either of you are Austrian."

"You won't give it up?"

"I must refuse. You have no right . . . no . . ."

Strauss reached into his jacket and drew out a .9mm pistol with a silencer.

Horst saw his death coming, and in the few seconds of his life remaining, as the numbed shock of realization paralyzed him, his only thought, a wild shouting in his mind, was that it could not possibly end this way, so quickly, with so little warning. Things like this did not happen. There was no way it could happen to him. Not to him. Not like this.

The small apartment resounded with a dull thud. Horst Pfordmann fell backward to the tile floor, a single, oozing hole in his forehead. The two intruders cocked their ears for any reaction outside the apartment.

When nothing seemed forthcoming, the taller man sighed. "Nice shot, Strauss. Though I wish . . ."

Strauss put the pistol-with-silencer back in his shoulder holster. He scowled. "It's better, cleaner, this way. You have any objection?"

"Forget it. It's just that the last time I was in Vienna, I got shot."

"I remember. You took a bullet in the chest. You didn't die."

"I lead a charmed life."

"Let's gather up this stuff."

The men made short work of it. In minutes they had cleared the apartment of every floppy disk, in all formats, that could be found in drawers and file cabinets, on shelves, and on the desk. In doing so, they methodically trashed the room, artfully littering the floor and misarranging furniture to make it look as though the place had been burgled. They accomplished these tasks making as little sound as possible.

"Get his wallet and his watch," the tall one ordered. Strauss obeyed.

"Telephone-address book?"

"Probably on his hard disk," Strauss replied.

"Check anyway."

"Right." As the ugly one rummaged through the desk, his leather-jacketed colleague dumped all the floppies into a plastic shopping bag.

"Got it," Strauss said after a few moments. "Telephone-address book. Let me plant the cocaine, and we'll leave."

"Does it need that?"

"Can't hurt. Drug deal goes bad, man's dead."

Strauss took out a small plastic bag filled with a white substance and lightly powdered the desk top with it. After sprinkling some on the floor, he folded up the bag again and pocketed it. "That ought to do it. Just traces."

The trenchcoated one stripped the computer's Central

Processing Unit of its peripheral components: keyboard, printer, mouse, external modem, joystick. He unplugged the power cord, and after hefting the CPU, he picked it up. "We just walk out, right? No guilty looks, like we own the place."

"Like we're repossessing a computer."

The thin mouth over the strong jaw turned upward wryly. "No one repossesses a damned computer. Practically no resale value."

"All right, you're the computer expert."

"Here we are in the age of science and technology, and we're running around chasing after ancient talismans."

"I wonder how long we'll have jobs at all, after *glasnost*," Strauss muttered. He groaned as the computer shifted in his arms. "This bastard is heavy."

The two men left the apartment. The tall one shut the door gently. It locked automatically.

No one noticed them, much less challenged them, as they left the building.

CHAPTER ONE

NEW YORK CITY, PRESENT DAY

Sara Pezzini came running around the corner of the alley and saw that the man she was chasing, a crackhead snitch who called himself "Kool Whip," was far ahead. It was dark in the shadows behind these old warehouses, dirty-bricked old hulks that would probably be luxury apartments one day.

I only wanted to ask you a few questions, is what she wanted to yell to the guy, but it sounded lame even to her. She'd no sooner got out of the plain-brown-wrapper police car than he'd bolted, athletic shoes chirping *squeak squeak squeak* against wet concrete. He was a streak before she got up to speed. The guy could run.

As she followed, the strange bracelet on her left wrist began to throb. Just faintly, just edging over the threshold of tactile sensation.

Faintly or not, the bracelet didn't throb often.

It was drizzling in New York. The sky was slate gray. It had been drizzling all day without ever adding up to real rain. Nevertheless, puddles had accumulated in gouges, potholes, and cracks, lay oily and glistening in plugged drains and odd depressions. Sara's sneakered foot splashed into a deep one.

"Damn it."

Then her *squish-slap squish-slap* went chasing after Kool Whip's annoying squeak. This operation was already turning into a Keystone Cops scenario. It wasn't much of an operation anyway, just routine questioning of an informer who was in the habit of supplying valuable info now and then, if it could be scared out of him. He was scared now, that was sure, but of what? He'd run at the very sight of Sara, and that could mean only one thing: Kool Whip was good for the clubbing death of a junkie down near East 29th Street and First Avenue last night.

He hadn't even been on Sara's list of usual suspects. Whip was not the violent type, but he was a little hot headed, and anyone can get riled enough at someone to pick up a length of two-by-four and cave in a skull. Now and then.

Slap-squish slap-squish . . .

Squeak squeak squeak . . .

That wet shoe was really vexing. And it was soaked, too, down to the sock.

An incongruous thought flashed: she wondered if she had a dry pair in her desk drawer somewhere. No, why should she? Wait, in her locker. Didn't she once come into work with a change of clothes to play racquetball, and wasn't that last week? No, two . . . three weeks ago.

Don't worry about the damn sock. Catch the suspect.

"Whip, wait up!"

Tearing around another corner, Whip didn't answer

"I just wanna ask–" She slowed, more disgusted than winded. She'd been slow to react.

Now he was lost in shadow. Gone.

Her cell phone tweeted.

"Rats." She stopped and took it off the hook on her belt and hissed an exasperated "Yes?"

"Well, excuse me all to hell."

"Jake?"

"Right. Your partner. Your bosom buddy."

"I'm the one with the bosom, buddy."

"Don't think I'm not aware."

"Sometimes I wonder if you're conscious half the time. Whassup? How's your flu?"

"It's not the blue kind," Jake McCarthy said. "I'm really sick."

"So am I."

"What, you catch it, too?"

"No, sick of chasing geeks through back alleys."

"Who're you chasing now?"

"I was. Kool Whip, a.k.a. Charles Morton Bromley, the Second."

"Are you kidding me? That's his real name?"

"I just looked at his file. He comes from a well-to-do Boston family."

"Get out."

"Nope."

"You lose him?" Jake asked.

"Yup."

"Excellent work, Detective Pezzini."

"Up yours. He ducked into a door. I'll find him."

"Call backup."

"I can handle it."

Jake coughed away from the phone.

"Hello?" Sara said.

"Sorry. Yeah, I think you can. You think he brained Smokey?"

"Why did he run?" Sara wanted to know.

" 'Urban anxiety' or whatever they call it. He's afraid of cops, the poor little tyke."

"They hung out a lot. We know they sometimes didn't get along. Whip has a short fuse. Ergo . . ."

"Ergo. One question, though. Why's he so stupid as to run?"

"Whip can't think straight when he's strung out."

"Okay, Pez," Jake said. "I'll go along with it. Wish I was there."

"No, you don't. Get rid of that bug. Wait a minute. Why did you call?"

"Seltzer phoned me about you. He's not what you call favorably disposed toward you, Pez."

"What other revelations do you have for me today?"

"Says you haven't returned his calls."

"I never return his calls."

"I know, and he knows. I guess he called the chief and asked about you, and the chief said to talk to her partner."

"What'd he want from you?"

"Asked if you had any friends in organized crime."

"He asked you that?"

"Yeah."

"Why the hell?"

"Dunno, Pez. I think he's got a new theory about you."

"What do you think it is?"

"That you're mobbed up in some way."

"Of all the . . . He actually said this?"

"Not in so many words, but that's what the whole conversation was noodling towards."

"He's crazy."

"He's Internal Affairs. They're all paranoid up there."

"Maybe I'll drop by your place today," Sara said.

"Don't. You'll get this crud I got."

"You California boys shouldn't ever come east. You belong on Zuma Beach getting a tan and hanging ten."

"Or hanging with surfer girls. I do miss the beach. Nothing like roasting marshmallows on a driftwood fire at night."

"Catch you later. I have to roast one of our East Side snitches. On a spit, if possible."

Sara flipped the phone shut and rehooked it.

Now, where the hell did Whip get to? Ah, a gouged and battered steel fire door hanging open, service entrance to a large abandoned building. She took out a small, slim but quite powerful lithium ion flashlight from her back pocket.

Beyond the doorway lay jumbled shapes in the darkness: hulks of dead machinery, piles of boxes, assorted junked equipment all over a debris-littered floor. Everything of worth had been stripped away. Pipes had been cut, plumbing fixtures removed, even some windows had been surgically excised, carried away and sold long ago. After some cleanup, the structure would be ready for gutting and renovation. On her salary, Sara wouldn't be able to afford the condos and apartments that would result.

Sara tiptoed through a vast ruined silence, listening. Coming to a stairwell, she looked up, playing the tight, focused beam of the light through creepy shadows. She didn't like the prospect of going up those stairs. Whip wasn't ordinarily dangerous, but he scared easily. And frightened little men are to be treated circumspectly, she had discovered in her career as a detective for the Police Department of the City of New York.

She turned off her cell phone and listened. The building

creaked and moaned. Sara cocked her head to one side. Maybe he didn't duck in here. But out in the alley his squeaking had stopped at about where the door was.

She began to tour the ground floor of the building, following a corridor lined with more debris, wreck, and ruin. Every door she came across was nailed shut from the inside.

She called out, "Whip! Come on, dude. I just want to ask you something."

Silence.

"Just a talk. That's all I want."

Nothing.

"I'm not taking you in."

Lie. She had to haul him in now.

She went on, "There's just a few things I need to know."

More creaking upstairs.

"Shit," she said to herself.

She turned to walk away. Maybe he got out some way. Well, she wasn't going to risk stumbling around in this wreckage.

"I got nothing for you!"

She stopped and whirled, then walked cautiously through an archway into an expansive open area surrounded by a tier of railed balconies. What kind of place was this? There were things here, hulking in the darkness. Strange-looking things. "Whip, that you?"

"Yeah. I don't have anything for you today, Pez." The voice echoed hollowly, coming from one of the galleries above the huge open space. She played the beam upward but couldn't see its source.

"I haven't asked you anything yet," she said.

"You wanna know about Smokey."

"Okay."

"I heard he was killed. He tended to piss people off. Someone got mad at him and hit him."

"Did you do it?"

"No. He was my friend."

"You two mixed it up a couple of times."

"Sure, we had a tiff now and then. But I swear, Pez. I didn't hit him over the head."

"How do you know how he was killed?"

"I heard."

"You hear a lot."

"That's what you always say. That's why you hassle me all the time."

"How many times have I hassled you this year?"

"Uh . . ."

"Come on," Sara wanted to know. "How often did I ask you for information on a case I was working on? This past year."

"Who keeps track?"

"Once, Whip. Once this year. I checked. I just looked at your file. Now, is that all the time?"

"How do I know how often you bother the shit out of me? It seems like all the time."

"Accuracy in media. Come on down, Whip."

What the hell was this stuff down on the floor? Jumbles of metal in odd configurations: grates and lattices, geometrical arrangements, juxtapositions and structures. It looked like . . .

"I didn't do anything."

"Why did you run?"

"I didn't run," Whip said.

"You walk faster than anyone I've ever seen."

"I saw you parking the car and I just had somewhere to go, so I went."

Sara had never noticed the Boston accent before. *Pahking the cahh* . . . It wasn't thick, just a trace, but it was there. Amazing what you don't pick up. "You were a little too quick. I gotta ask you about Smokey."

"So ask."

"When was the last time you saw him?"

"Christ, I don't know."

"When was it?"

"Don't know. Couple of days ago."

"Where?"

"How do I know where? On the street."

"When?"

"Two days ago."

"How about last night?"

"Didn't see him."

"Where didn't you see him?"

"On the street."

This was getting nowhere. Besides, she was distracted.

Sculpture. Suddenly she knew what she was looking at. She walked past an odd assortment of tall, conical, wickedly pointed shapes. Metal sculpture. Some artist was squatting here, using the place for a studio. The stuff looked pretty good. She was no judge but thought she saw talent sitting in the blackness.

Back to business.

"Whip, get your ass down here or I'm coming up to get you."

"Stay away from me."

Whip started moving as Sara walked back through the archway and went to the stairwell, which she mounted, taking each littered step carefully and letting the flash beam lance the darkness ahead. It looked clear to the second level. She came forth onto a wide balcony strewn with mountings for missing machinery. Apparently the artist's squatting rights didn't extend beyond the ground floor. This had been some kind of shop, probably a metal shop. Maybe the artist had worked here at some point, then came back to make art. She gave a glance downward, where the sculptures brooded in shadow. This guy—or gal, for that matter—could have quite a show.

"Where are you?" Sara demanded.

He stood by the rail running along the balcony. "Keep away, I'm warning you."

"Stay cool, dude. Nothing's going to happen." *Except now I gotta arrest you*, Sara thought.

Whip was telepathic, apparently. "You're not going to bust me," Whip said. "You can't. You don't have a warrant."

"Don't need one if you flee an interview. That means I get to take you in for questioning. You'd played it cool . . ."

"I'm telling you, I didn't run."

"Look, if you give up the truth about what happened, it could be Man One instead of murder. It could be something even less."

"I didn't kill him!"

Edge of desperation now, a cornered quavering to the voice that kept retreating as Whip bumped into things and sent debris skittering across the floor.

"Okay, so let's talk about it," Sara said in her best touchy-feely voice. "Smokey stole from you again, right? He took your money when you were sleeping. He needed a fix, he ripped you off. He'd done it before and you got mad, madder than ever before. So you picked up . . . what was it? What did you hit him with, Whip?"

"I didn't. Stay away from me, you."

"You stay right where you are."

He didn't, then suddenly began climbing, and Sara's sweep of light picked up a rickety ladder running between levels. Sara heard him clamber to the next balcony. She reentered her stairwell and went up another flight.

"Tell me what happened, Whip."

"Nothing happened. I haven't seen him in weeks."

"I thought you said you saw him a few days ago."

"Keep away."

Sara stopped. "Whip, I've never seen you like this. Listen, it's not so bad. You have a family, don't you? Your parents are well-off. They can help you. They can get you a good lawyer."

"*Stay away from me!*"

Sara stopped, letting the panicked echoes die. He was freaking out. Withdrawal symptoms? Probably. Smokey had stolen all his ready cash, and that was a tough position for an addict like Whip to be in.

"What's wrong?" she asked.

"You."

"What's wrong with me?"

"You kill guys all the time."

"What?"

"I know about you. You don't like someone, you think they're dirty, they've done something, you take 'em out. Guys get dead around you a lot, lady."

"It's not true." She winced saying it.

"You're some kind of witch. That's what I hear."

"Who says this crap?"

"Lots of people. You're a killer cop. You're a . . . I don't know what. You're a monster."

"Cut it out. Kool Whip, I gotta take you in. We have to talk, and you have to come clean. It'll be better all around. You can call your family."

Whip laughed maniacally. "You have no idea what you're saying."

"You don't talk to them?"

"They don't talk to me. They talk only to Lowells and Cabots, and maybe God once in a while, when they have time for him."

"You don't get along?"

"I haven't seen them in ten years. Not since I dropped out of Columbia."

"Well, maybe it's time for a reconciliation. But, look, this has nothing to do with Smokey's death. Just tell me where you were last night. That's all I want to know."

"Get away from me, Pezzini!" He was screeching now.

"Whip, calm down."

There was no more room for retreat. He suddenly turned and leapt upward. Balancing on the thin railing, he put one foot on a rung of the ladder.

The ladder suddenly collapsed under his weight, and he fell.

"Whip!"

There was no sound but metal clattering to the floor. But with it came a strange, muted sound, like a knife going into an overripe melon.

Sara came to the edge of the balcony and sent the flash beam down, trying to make sense of what she saw.

He had fallen on one of the sculptures. The beam illuminated his face, which bore a look of such shock and dismay that it made Sara's stomach lurch.

She rushed down the stairwell, came out onto the floor, and advanced toward Whip's still moving body.

He had landed on a metal spike. The man was impaled, skewered like so much meat, a huge spear of metal running up through his bowels.

She couldn't look. There was nothing to do for him. No 911 call would save him, though she got out her phone and punched in the numbers anyway as he made muted, gurgling noises deep in his throat and twitched horribly.

Mercifully, he didn't do either for long.

After she got off the phone she saw what the artist had spray-painted on one of the other sculptures:

USELESS JUNK

It wasn't a gang tag, not a graffiti vandal's comment. It was artfully done, a despairing wail of self doubt from the sculptor himself. He had given up, abandoned his squatter studio and its contents. His life's work, perhaps.

HOPELESS

The Witchblade made a dull drumbeat against her wrist.

CHAPTER TWO

She stood in the alley, watching the paramedics take the body out on a gurney. It had taken them a long time, an agonizingly long, horrid time, to get him off the sculpture. He'd died before they arrived, she guessed, but only the autopsy would make that clear.

The Witchblade was quiet now. She wondered what it had been trying to tell her, if anything. It had seemed mildly interested in the death of Charles Morton Bromley, the Second. As if it might be of some significance, but only in the abstract.

Footsteps up the alley.

"Pezzini!"

She turned. It was her boss, Captain Joe Siry.

Siry walked straight up to her and brought his haggard face up close to hers, close enough so that she smelled his sour breath. She wasn't particularly keen on monitoring his oral health.

"You have an explanation?" he demanded.

"Simple."

He backed up a little. "Well, now, if it's so simple, why don't you tell me."

"Okay," she said with a shrug. "Nothing special."

"Not what I heard. I heard you got a guy run through like a shish-kabob in there."

"That's not a particularly tasteful way of putting it, but, yeah. There was a freak accident as the result of the suspect's resisting arrest."

"This was a suspect?"

"Not exactly. He was an informant."

"And you were arresting him?"

"I tried to question him on a routine investigation. He ran. He had an accident. Fell and got impaled on some metal sculpture."

Siry turned at looked at the building. "Metal sculpture. This an art gallery?"

"In a way. Place is full of somebody's sculpture. Abandoned, looks like."

"What makes you say that?"

"Some indications. You'll get the report."

"So this guy wasn't even a perp. He wasn't a suspect at all."

"Not until he ran, Joe. Then it was pretty obvious . . ."

"What was obvious?"

"That he was good for the killing."

"Nothing's ever obvious. You have any proof?"

"Not a lot."

Siry began pacing. "Fingerprints?"

"No murder weapon yet."

"Christ."

"What's up?" Sara asked.

"We have an evaluation coming up. I'm trying to think of how to play this."

"What's there to play?"

"To quote you, not a lot."

"It was an accident, Joe."

He poked a finger at her. "That's 'Captain Siry' to you, Detective."

"Okay. A freak accident. That's all."

"Too many," Siry grumbled, still pacing.

"Too many what?"

"Too many freaky things happen to you."

"So I've been told."

He stopped and he fixed her in an admonitory stare. "Don't get smart with me."

"Sorry."

That vein was popping out on his forehead again. She always had trouble stifling a laugh. She looked away.

Siry was about to add something, but footsteps brought him around to look.

"Oh, Christ."

It was Seltzer, from Internal Affairs, trooping up the alley.

"Don't answer any questions now, Pezzini," Siry told her. "Write that report, and let me see it first before you send it to him."

"I always do, Cap."

"Good evening," Seltzer said as he approached.

"Any reason for this honor?" Siry wanted to know.

Seltzer's face could be described as pleasantly mean-spirited. It was pinched and narrow and smilingly thin-lipped.

"Only the honor of watching our department's men . . . uh, personnel . . . in action."

"What's up?"

"Heard there was a death of a suspect. Have to investigate."

"Really? Even if it was an accident? Even if our man . . . if she never laid a hand on him?"

"I can't judge before I know the facts. This is just routine on my part. I'd like to see where it happened."

"In there," Sara said, pointing.

"Sounds very unusual," Seltzer said, "the circumstances." He licked his lips. "Freakish."

"It was," Sara said.

"An impaling. Is that true?"

"You make it sound like an execution."

"Was it?" Seltzer said with a leer.

"It was an accident."

"Keep quiet," Siry told her. "Let me handle this." He rotated to Seltzer. "Does she have to answer questions right this very minute? If you're going to make a full investigation, she has certain rights, okay?"

"Captain, I'm perfectly aware of departmental procedure."

"Well, maybe you're not aware of this. I'd like to think that at least the dust can settle before you begin to make accusations against one of my best—"

"I haven't made any accusations."

"Well, what the hell was it I just heard?"

Sara walked away as her boss continued sparring. Two uniformed patrolmen strolled by.

"Right up the old kazoo," one of them said with a shudder.

"Man, what a way to go," the other said.

She shivered. The fool, running like that. If he'd simply played it cool, she never would have thought him a suspect.

Routine investigation. Routine murder. Victim less than nobody. What did it matter?

But, God, what a way to die. And for nothing.

What the hell was the Witchblade's interest?

The mind of Kenneth Irons was a vast and labyrinthine place. Thoughts raced through it in geometric patterns, crossing and recrossing. Behind him, the city was a panorama of power, light-studded shafts thrusting into a black sky.

He swiveled the chair slightly. His hands formed a pyramid on his chest, fingertips almost touching his chin. His eyes swept over the things on his desk. He had kept the same accoutrements over the years. That crystal paperweight, this clock. Knick-knacks here and there. Marble-based pen set. Gold cigarette lighter. Same objects. Same desk. Many, many years. They reassured him.

He was not easily reassured.

The door to his office cracked light.

"Mr. Kontra, sir," said a voice.

"Have him come in," Irons said.

Lazlo V. Kontra entered. He nodded and sat down.

"Excuse the dim light, Mr. Kontra," Irons said. "I find it necessary to rest my eyes now and then. Shall I turn on . . . ?"

"Don't trouble yourself," Kontra said. He eased his massive frame into a leather chair. He seemed comfortable. Perhaps a little self-satisfied. His face had a certain rugged symmetry. Women found him attractive, and he knew it.

Irons regarded him. One rock cliff regarding another. "We can do business."

Kontra nodded. "I think so."

"Computer business."

Kontra kept nodding. "One of my businesses."

"You have the foreign contacts," Irons said.

Kontra grinned. "You have financing to run big operations." His accent was thick but comprehensible. "Big."

"Yes. You can increase your staff, buy capital equipment."

"More computers. Everything today is computers."

"Indeed. Little bits of data flowing through the latticework of a massive grid. Pulses of light, throbs of electric charge. Instead of the jingle of gold we have the clicking of a hard drive. Registering dollar signs all over the globe."

"And what you do, you control the little bits," Kontra said. "You herd them like sheep, this way, that way, until they come into your barn."

Irons smiled. "Yes."

"This is new way of doing business. Forget profit."

"Rather tiresome thing to worry about, profit. The money left over after doing business. Why not just rake in the money and forget the business?"

"I like that," Kontra said.

"So do I." Irons's chair drifted to the left. "Increasingly, too many stumbling blocks in the way of making money. Too many leaks in the bucket. It's almost not worth conducting business any more. Why not herd those bleating dollars? There are flocks of them. Swarms. Trillions out in the electronic pastures. What does a few billion of them matter? Who will even notice they are gone?"

"Ah. It is even better. You don't even have to steal."

Irons chuckled. "I know. One can even indulge in the creation of money itself, *ex nihilo*."

"Eh?"

"From nothing."

"I see. Yes."

"Like God touching his finger to the center of the void. I've done it for years. I own banks. Banks can create money, within certain governmental limits. But the new ways are even easier and can yield a lot more."

"No limits."

"Right, Mr. Kontra. No limits. And as long as your . . . uh, experts . . . stay in—where are they again?"

"Just say eastern Europe," Lazlo Kontra said. "There they are immune from arrest."

"Arrest?"

An awkward silence fell.

Kontra sat and waited.

"Whatever would they be doing that they should fear arrest?" Irons wanted to know.

"Not a thing," Kontra said. "I still need people here. I have people."

"I understand the need for monitoring your employees. Difficult to maintain control long distance. What sorts of operations have you in this country?"

Kontra shrugged. "I have lots of businesses. Moving vans. Dry cleaning. Home heating oil."

"I mean the computer experts."

"They mainly develop software."

Iron raised his eyebrows.

Kontra's smile widened. "They study firewalls."

"Yes."

"And other things," Kontra said.

"Firewalls," Irons said. "I love these metaphors."

"They describe precisely."

"Why do you keep your R&D here in the States?"

Kontra shrugged. "More experience in software development here."

"Yes, the U.S. leads."

Kontra guffawed. "You always did. I'll tell you a joke."

"Do."

"Old Soviet joke."

"You're not Russian."

"I lived in Moscow for years."

"However, your name . . . ?"

"Romanian."

"Ah."

"I'll tell you this joke. Two guys meet in Moscow airport. One is pushing huge dolly across terminal, loaded with suitcases. The other says 'Hello, Ivan, how are you doing?' Ivan says. 'I've been developing Soviet People's Pocket Computer.' The guy says, 'We have a pocket computer? Ours?' Ivan says, 'Yes, it's ours. We didn't steal it from West.' He takes small computer out from pocket. The guy looks at it. Has nice screen, easy keyboard. The guy says, 'That's marvelous! I can't believe we did this.' Ivan says, 'I got to go.' He starts pushing. The guy says, 'What's all this?' Ivan says, 'Oh, that is power supply.' "

Irons's sudden laughter was genuine. His face cracked like a limestone palisade. "Hadn't heard that one."

"Funny, eh?"

"Very. You worked for Russian intelligence for years. Before you defected."

"First was with Romanian military intel, then went to civilian intel, and then to KGB in Soviet Union. I was with them long time."

"But you obviously had extracurricular activities."

"Yes. I did lots of things *na levo*. On the left hand. Underground. Black market. Only way you could make enough money to live well. Whole country was *na levo*, or you starve."

"Then you came to New York."

"I defect in New York. I like it. I stayed."

"Still a great city, despite recent tragedies."

"Yes. So, we can do business."

"I think so, Mr. Kontra." Irons's smile glowed in the shadows.

"Good," Kontra said.

"You will hear from me soon. Through intermediaries. Does that suit you, Mr. Kontra?"

"Certainly, Mr. Irons."

"It's been a pleasure."

Kontra rose and left the room.

Irons contemplated the silence for a moment. Then he got up and went to the window. He looked out on the city. Oblongs of light speckled a forest of tall shapes. Below, white lights approached, red lights receded. Glowing like a stormy sea, low clouds touched the tops of the highest buildings. At night the city seemed insubstantial and mysterious. The realm of another world.

His thoughts were not on business. They were on the Witchblade.

CHAPTER THREE

It was late when Kontra got back to Brooklyn and home. The apartment building was quiet. The murmurs of televisions and radios were muffled—insistent voices, barely heard, chattering away on the other side of the walls, as if the building's roaches had gathered for a political rally.

The hall smelled. The hall always smelled, though it wasn't a bad one. Faint odors of cabbage. Maybe it wasn't cabbage. *Somebody* had cabbage, he decided. It was one of those bad-good smells, cabbage. He had eaten enough of it. He liked it, in fact. But it was not so good in a hall. People should use their kitchen exhaust fans. He was used to odors in hallways. Even now, when he could afford it, he did not buy a single-family dwelling. In this city they were horrifically expensive, but he could have one if he wanted it. That wasn't the issue. Apartment living was habit, what he was used to.

His stalwart bulk mounted the stairs. He didn't like elevators. He remembered living in a six-floor walkup when he had a low post in the army.

He was big. There was some middle-age ballast on

him, but it covered a spring-steel mass of muscle. He was built like a stout tree, and his arms were long and thick. His legs were a little short, but that made him even more powerful.

Quiet. He stopped to listen. The late evening news? No, it was well after eleven. *The Tonight Show*? He wanted to sit and look at the *Tonight Show*. He moved up the stairs.

Ah, the sound was coming from his apartment. His wife was up watching the television. He fumbled in his pocket for his keys. The *tuica*, plum brandy, was a little sour in his stomach tonight. He wondered if there were any antacid in the bathroom cabinet.

"Good night."

A voice to his right, a visitor coming out of the neighbor's. He glanced, and the face was familiar. Ever so faintly . . .

Where was that door key? He wasn't drunk, but he had downed a few glasses. Just a few.

That man. He turned to look again. The man was aiming a silenced compact semiautomatic.

At him.

"What?" was all Kontra could say. Then a thought occurred: *Shit! The neighbors are in Europe.*

The pistol snapped once. He felt a poke in the chest, as if a buddy had landed a good punch on him.

The guy was trying to kill him! The rotten, no good . . . *"Bastard!"*

The gun went off again. Enraged, Kontra rushed the hit man, who by now had a puzzled look.

"God damn you!" Kontra roared as he lunged.

The man panicked and raised the pistol for a head shot. But he never got it off, for Kontra had the gun in both hands, twisting it upward. He had moved like a striking snake, like a demented bear. The gun fired again into the ceiling, then went flying off, bounced against wallpaper, and fell to the carpet.

Kontra had the guy trapped in the blind hallway, hands around his neck. He squeezed. He had always liked the feeling of a human neck in his hands. He could feel the arteries closing, feel the soft muscles collapse. Nothing could break Kontra's hold. No one ever had, for all that they beat and flailed and tried to come up between his arms. No routine judo countermove could work. Kontra was too strong.

He did it as he had done it to prisoners. The technique was to strangle them until they passed out, then slap them back to life. They did not expect to wake up again, and when they did, they were cooperative. It made interrogation a lot simpler. True, a few had never revived. But not many.

He would streamline the technique now. He squeezed and squeezed. The terrified man's face turned red, then changed to a dark shade of purple-green. He kicked at Kontra's shin. Kontra ignored it.

There was a bell ringing somewhere. He couldn't figure why a bell was ringing. Like a chime. He ignored it and kept up the pressure on the man's neck.

But damn that bell. Then he noticed that he couldn't see much. Everything in his peripheral vision was black. Only the man's discolored face was visible.

And then he realized that he was losing consciousness, and that, as bull-strong as he was, there was nothing he could do about it.

Sara lay almost naked on her bed. She was exhausted, and she hadn't done a thing all day. It was night. The apartment was dark.

She sat up on the edge of the bed. Then she rose and went to a television on an entertainment center on the far wall.

She halted as she moved to turn it on; instead, she switched on the compact disc player. The tiny red light seemed like a distant star. She ran a finger over the few CDs she had. No. The red star winked out.

Moving to the kitchen space, she opened the refrigerator: a lemon, a quart carton of milk, two bottles of water, and a long-forgotten Chinese take-out box. Shifting her attentions to the freezer compartment, she found a frozen diet dinner, low-fat fettuccine with clam sauce. A plastic tub of fake butter, filled presumably with leftovers she had frozen, sat beside the fettuccine.

She contemplated the contents of the compartment in a Zen fashion, then closed the freezer door.

Maybe she wasn't hungry after all.

No, she was, but she wasn't going to eat the frozen glop, and that Chinese had surely gone bad. And she couldn't for the life of her remember what was in the plastic tub. Go out?

Alone?

She sighed. "Wouldn't be the first time . . ."

The phone rang, and she crossed to it almost gratefully. "Yeah?"

"Sara?"

"Jake."

"Uh-huh. You okay?"

"Sure."

"You sound glum," Jake commented.

"I'm fine. Have you eaten?"

"Uh, kinda."

"Kinda?"

"Why, you wanted to go out?"

"Not really. I was thinking about it, but I'm too tired."

"I could use some coffee. And some cannoli. Want to meet me at Chez Nunzio?"

"Sounds good. Are you sure you're well enough?"

"I'm over it. It was a mild flu. Just starting to get my appetite back."

"Okay. Meet you in, say, half an hour?"

"Give me an hour, Sara."

"Okay. See you."

She put on a skirt, black and short. To hell with that. She tried her plaid one. Nope. Putting off the lower-body decision, she tried on some blouses. She had three that were nominally passable. All looked hopelessly wrinkled, hopelessly drab. God, when was the last time she ironed?

She ended up putting on jeans, black T-shirt, leather jacket. Gun. No purse. Badge. No bra.

She regarded her image in the mirror.

Let's face it, I'm butch.

She looked at her nightstand, on which the Witchblade sat. The stone seemed to glow.

Voices, tiny, distant voices babbled inside it. Or just behind it? Somewhere associated with it.

She picked it up and put it on her wrist. In this world, in its passive state, the artifact was a simple gold wire bracelet set with a puce stone. What it was in its natural habitat, nowhere in the known universe, no one knew. It was a strange manifestation, whatever the hell it was.

It was the Witchblade.

Should she wear it or not? The question always came up when she dressed to go out for a purely social occasion.

And this *was* purely social. It was her day off, and Jake was still officially out sick.

It was still on her wrist as she left the apartment.

Hospital rooms always have harsh florescent light. It shone right in his eyes. Wires and tubes connected him to various mechanisms behind him and at either hand.

Kontra looked around. Lots of machinery. Some of them beeped. Some winked lights at him. Others leaked fluids into his body. There was an oxygen hose.

He hated hospitals. But this was surely one, and he was here.

He remembered being shot at, but that was all he remembered. He had tried to do something about it. Run? No, he hadn't run. The memory was a blur. How long ago had he been shot? Yesterday? Two days ago?

Life had been a jumble since: Lights blinding him, the faces of nurses orbiting, doctors speaking, things beeping and humming. Needles jabbing in his skin. All a blur, a smear of memory.

"Hello, Mr. Kontra."

This was another doctor, he believed. Different from the one who had spoken before. At least he thought. This one looked a little older. The first one had been a baby.

"Yes."

"You're a lucky man."

"I'm going to live?"

"Yes, sir. You took two bullets to the chest. Fortunately, one of them only nicked an artery. The other collapsed a lung. You're very lucky to be alive."

"So I'll live." It was a statement.

"We still have some work to do in there. We got out both bullets, but we found something very strange."

"Strange."

"Yes. The bullets we took out were .32 caliber. They hadn't deformed much. But we found a third bullet. At least we saw it in the X-rays."

"Yes?"

"One that's been in your body quite a while. We can tell this by the tissue that's grown around it. It wasn't fired from the same gun that was used on you yesterday. It's an .8mm slug."

"Ah. Yes."

"You've been shot before?"

"Yes. Long time ago."

"Remarkable. You must have the constitution of a bull elephant."

He shrugged, and it hurt.

"Well," the doctor went on, "we couldn't get at it while we were extracting the others. We should go back in at some point and remove it."

Kontra shook his head. "It's been in twenty years. It can stay."

"Not a good idea to leave it in, Mr. Kontra."

"I will think about it."

"We won't be able to do further surgery until you've completely recovered, of course. But let's talk about it. I think we can release you in about a week and a half. Perhaps a little less, if everything stays stable. You're doing fine, actually. Remarkable. As I said . . ."

Kontra nodded. "Lucky."

"Um . . . the police would like to come in now and question you."

"Send my wife in first."

"Of course. I'm sure they'll understand."

"The man, he got away?"

"Man? Oh, the man who shot you? I think the police had better give you that information."

"I didn't kill him?"

"Not as far as I know. Your wife found you in the hall, called the paramedics. You lost a lot of blood, but they did a good job on you."

Kontra nodded. "This country has good medical system. Doctor?"

"Yes?"

"You can tell police I'm not well enough yet. I don't want to see them. Not yet."

"I wasn't enthusiastic about your undergoing questioning right now. I'll tell them to wait at least a day. That okay?"

"Fine. Thank you. You are good, doctor."

"I'll ask your wife to come in now."

CHAPTER FOUR

A candle flickered between them. Italian smells hung in the air: oregano, thyme, fennel, garlic. Jake attacked his vanilla cannoli. The dark chocolate flecks in it looked like dead ants.

"This is great. I hate the kind with candied fruit. This is vanilla cream. You only nibbled at your sandwich."

Sara wished that she smoked. It would give her something to do now that she decided to give up on the avocado, tomato, and alfalfa sprout sandwich. She hadn't been hungry after all. Surprise. She sipped her coffee.

Jake persisted. "You didn't eat."

"I'm aware of that."

"So?"

"Maybe I'm coming down with your bug."

"You look fine," Jake said.

"Thanks. Any particular reason you wanted to talk tonight?"

"I worry about you."

"I know," she said.

"You seem distant. Have anything to do with what happened yesterday?"

She regarded his cabana-boy good looks. "You've been talking with people."

"Yeah. I heard it was a freak accident, really freaky. You want to talk about it?"

She stirred her coffee for no particular reason. "No."

He chuckled.

She put the spoon down. "Oh, maybe. What's there to say?"

"How'd it happen?"

"Talk about freaking. Whip just absolutely freaked. He went buggy. Started screaming at me, and then he tried to make it up a ladder . . ."

"Ladder?"

"In that abandoned shop. The ladder broke–metal fatigue, I guess. Rust. It broke, and he fell, and for some reason this sharp metal stuff was beneath him."

"The sculpture."

"Yeah. Metal work. Welded together. The guy was impaled on a welded work of art."

"Weird."

"Not the first guy to die for art."

"It wasn't his."

Sara shrugged. "Maybe it was. I don't know. This wasn't a studio. It was a place that someone was using as a studio. Maybe it was Kool Whip's."

"Was he a sculptor?"

"Have no idea. He never let on."

"And you were chasing after him . . . why, again?"

She looked away. "God."

"Sorry."

They did not speak for at least a minute. Suddenly, Sara picked up the sandwich and took a bite, out of pure guilt.

She made a face. "Alfalfa tastes like grass."

"It *is* grass," Jake said.

"Oh." She smiled. "Yeah."

"At least I got a laugh out of you."

"Did I laugh? I didn't notice."

"You smiled. It's a start. I've seen you moody, but this . . ."

"Moodier than usual?"

Jake nodded. "What's the problem? By the way, what was Whip screaming about?"

"Besides something to the effect that he didn't clobber Smokey?"

"Besides that."

"That I was a witch. I went out and killed guys."

"Killed guys?"

"Yeah. I don't know exactly what he meant." She paused. "I guess he means the way people tend to die around me."

"Well . . ."

Sara shrugged in resignation. "It's true. I know."

"You've had some strange things happen. Things not easily explained."

"Sure have. You don't know the half of it."

"You'll have to tell me sometime," Jake said. "Sit me down and explain it all."

"Wish I could sit myself down and explain it all," Sara said.

"Anyway, I take it the accident has you down. Judging from what you say, it doesn't sound like your fault."

"It wasn't. It was just so senseless, so haphazard."

"Uh-huh."

"And it happened so fast, and there was no chance to save him, prevent it. No chance to help him after."

"Useless all the way around." Jake shook his head.

"Funny, that's what the sculptor said."

"Huh?"

"Graffiti to that effect was spray-painted on some of the best pieces. I think the artist wrote them. 'Useless junk.' And then, 'Hopeless.' "

"Maybe he was a better critic than artist?"

"Didn't look like it to me. Anyway, it was an especially senseless death. It just got to me. I'll get over it."

Jake smiled grimly. "You'll get over it. That was good."

Sara eyed him suspiciously. "You talking about the cannoli now?"

"Yeah," he said quickly. "You going to eat that sandwich?"

"You want it? I thought you had dinner. And you just had dessert."

"It looks good. I love alfalfa. I'm like a cow."

She pushed the plate toward him. "Graze away."

"Lazlo?"

He opened his eyes. Someone stood beside the bed. He got a familiar whiff of perfume. "Sophia."

"You were sleeping."

"Nothing else to do."

"They are putting you in another room tomorrow. Regular hospital room."

He gestured at the IVs and monitors. "Then I won't have these things on me?"

"Not so many. You can maybe sit up."

"Good."

She came closer. When his eyes finally focused he could see her face well enough to notice the lines. She was dressed well, as usual, bedecked with jewels. She liked diamonds, and wore them for almost any occasion. For all the make-up and miracle wrinkle cream and hair coloring, she was beginning to look a lot older, and he wondered why he had not noticed before. Or had he? He was getting old himself.

"The doctors say you are surprising them," she said. "You are getting well so soon."

"I always do."

"You are stronger than most men. But of course . . ."

"What?"

"You know," she said hesitantly.

Kontra rolled his eyes. "Oh, please."

"Baba has helped you."

He turned his head. "Again, this old nonsense."

"Do you remember the last time you were shot?"

"Yes. In Vienna."

"Baba helped you then, too."

"Baba is always helping me. She should mind her own business."

"If she did, you would be dead. This man now, he shoots you with three bullets."

"Two. Only two."

Maria looked at the ceiling. " 'Only,' he says. In your *heart*."

"They missed."

"They missed. They *didn't* miss. You had protection."

"Magic," he said with a sneer.

"You don't believe. You have never believed."

"Nonsense. Magic spells. Do you expect me to believe some old witch woman?"

"How else do you explain it?"

"Explain what?"

"That no one can kill you."

"Luck. Strength. I killed that guy."

"What guy?"

"The hit man."

"You dreamed it."

He raised his head and looked at her intently. "They didn't find him?"

"I heard you yell. I was afraid, so I listen. Then I open the door. There you were, bleeding."

"No man running?"

"I heard someone running down the stairs. Maybe. I think so."

"Did you see him?"

She shook her head.

He lay back. "Then I didn't strangle the bastard."

"How could you strangle him when he was shooting you?"

"I rushed at him and I got my hands around his neck."

She laughed. "With two bullets in you. And you doubt Baba."

He had no answer.

"Your lunch is here," she said.

"I don't want it."

"You should eat."

"I'm not hungry. Leave me, woman."

"I'll leave. Try to eat, Lazlo."

"The food is bad."

She smiled. "What hospital has good food? Tomorrow, I will bring you something from the delicatessen."

"Good. If they let you."

"I will bring it anyway."

CHAPTER FIVE

Sara liked to walk at night in the city. She'd read something about Thomas Wolfe. Not Tom, but Thomas. He would write all day and stalk the city in the pitch of night, tramping from the Battery to the Bronx and back again.

A walk was nice, but that was a trifle extreme.

She was a little edgy tonight, and did not know why. The weather was exceptionally clear. No fog, no clouds. What few stars as could be seen from the streets of Manhattan were pinned to a velvet sky. They did their best to shine.

She stopped suddenly, and looked up, thinking she had heard something strange in the night. She searched the blackness between the buildings. Nothing moved.

She walked on. The nearest business district well behind her, she walked along a street lined with brownstones.

There it was again.

A shriek.

"What the hell is that?" she muttered. It sounded

unusually piercing, and its source seemed to be in the sky somewhere. A light plane with a loudspeaker? What?

No, it was the shriek of a bird. A screech, a caw. A cry. Like a seagull. Or maybe something else.

A plane with a loudspeaker broadcasting bird calls. Okay. Either that or a very, very large bird flying very high. A big gull?

A *really* big gull.

Whatever it was cried again. It had a particularly weird sound. There was something almost human about it. The *almost* is what made it unsettling.

She walked on, coming presently to an avenue. She stopped and looked up and down it. Was this Madison? Park? It was an unfamiliar part of one of them. Let's see, she'd started on Lexington. This should be . . . Madison. Wait. No, hadn't she passed Madison?

No traffic. Very little. Okay, it was late, but she couldn't see a headlight. Oh, wait. There's one, way the hell downtown. And a red light crawled on the horizon uptown. The cross street seemed deserted.

She looked at her watch. Okay, it must be wrong. It wasn't that late, was it? How long had she talked with Jake? She tried to remember chairs on the tables when she left. Okay, she did remember that. She thought. So tempis had fugited all over the place. But how late did that restaurant stay open? Not past eleven, surely. She wondered how long she had been walking.

Missing time?

Jeepers.

Screeeeeeeeee.

"Go away, bird."

What bird? What the hell kind of bird could be that loud and . . . and yet so high up there?

Scanning the sky, she continued on, and her footsteps threatened to become more hurried. So she willed herself to slow. Relax, take it easy.

Let's not completely freak out. There's absolutely nothing to be afraid of.

The Witchblade was telling her different. Its babble of voices crossed the threshold of hearing. They sometimes warned of danger. At other times they cackled with glee at the approach of something threatening. It was hard to tell whether they were for it or against it.

She stopped at the next corner, hitting a wall of confusion. She did not recognize this avenue at all. Lined with dark, faceless monoliths, it was no Manhattan thoroughfare she knew.

"What the hell?"

She stood unbelieving, casting eyes to either hand, north and south. No familiar landmark presented itself. The dark gathered between towering black shapes. They could have been buildings, but ones that offered no access to mere mortals. Their upper portions had protrusions of some kind. These were skyscrapers, but of a kind she'd never seen. Their bases were without openings, no entrances. Some towers sat on massive pylons and did not have ground floors.

Nothing made sense here. Was this some kind of housing project she had missed in the newspapers?

Something had happened to the streets themselves. They had narrowed, were now no wider than alleys.

Darkness hid any revealing detail. These presences seemed little more than geometric shapes. She was not even sure she was seeing something that existed. Only something that would exist. Or perhaps that could exist? She did not know. The images in her eyes flickered.

She closed her eyes and massaged them gently with her fingertips.

Screeeeeeeeee.

She looked up. A typical urban vista presented itself. Signs glowed reassuringly over closed shops a few streets down. Headlights crawled in the distance. The totally normal had magically reappeared. The mundane had teleported back from the alternate reality where it had been hiding.

She breathed again.

The sounds of fluttering wings made her resume her journey westward. She didn't balk at hurrying now. The Witchblade seemed disturbed, and that was enough motivation. Yes, there was a danger, but perhaps it wasn't immediate.

"Yeah," she told it. "So?"

No answer. No specifics. No guesses as to what she was facing.

At the sound of huge beating pinions she began to run. There came a rustling, a fluttering, a swooping, and the click of talons. Was she hearing it or was it in her mind? She sprinted across another wide avenue, fearful for her sanity.

The thing, whatever it was, sounded as if it had swooped close and passed directly overhead. She hadn't seen it, had felt only a strong presence, a manifestation of something strange, alien, and evil.

Evil.

Or perhaps just unknowably alien and strange. There came with this feeling a sense of intense curiosity and a need to satisfy it, to explore, to discover. To seek out and reconnoiter.

There was no fear, but there was a wariness, a caution. Nevertheless, this circumspection could not thwart a resolve to fulfill a destiny. To have what was wanted, to gain it, to keep it.

The sound of its wings filled her ears as she ran. The thing swooped and swooped again, getting closer, and she could feel the wind from its wings and hear the whistle of air as taloned feet flexed and clenched, eager to grasp, to claw, to tear her apart. To rend flesh.

Evil.

She hid in shadows and felt a transformation come over her.

Wings rushed and beat like a racing heart, a darkly malevolent heart. Hovering. Hovering.

She was ready to come out into the dim light. When she did, the metamorphosis was almost complete. A filigree of delicate metal work had crawled along her body, providing her full breasts and nether portions with cover but leaving little else unexposed. Her right hand and wrist, where the bracelet had lived, and part of the forearm, were now embellished with sharp, spiky gingerbread, covering her fist in an impossible gauntlet of swirls and arabesques. She was nude and yet somehow completely covered. These geometric flourishes bloomed along other parts of her body. Up and down her long legs, around her silky thighs, covering and protecting her knees, shoulders, spine, and neck. All vulnerable points buttressed against assault. Yet wide areas of smooth skin permitted the caress of air. She was a study in dress and undress. She was a paradox.

She was the Witchblade.

Striding boldly into a pool of spilled light, she looked up and regarded the thing.

It was an enigmatic shape in the sky between the

buildings. A menacing outline, an abstract intelligence embodied in a suggestion of an avian configuration, monstrous wings flapping impossibly fast. And in the center of the phenomenon, eyes like diamonds.

She lifted the gauntlet skyward and pointed an imperious finger.

"You!" she shouted. Her voice bruised stone, made windows rattle their mullions.

The thing hovered and observed. Coolly.

She flung a question at it with resounding contempt and annoyance: "*What?*"

It continued to hover, its raptor's eyes cold and dispassionate.

Time perched somewhere else, but nearby. It waited, and watched. At some point it decided that enough eternity had occurred, and began to tick off the seconds again.

And the thing above, the indeterminate shape in the sky, began to lift, the sound of its immense wings growing into the militant beating of war drums. Its vast obscene bulk rose and receded. And with a final rustle and flutter, it disappeared into the dark sky whence it had come.

Sara stood in the middle of a deserted New York street.

She ran her hands over her leather jacket. Checked her pistol, her badge, the money in her pocket. Jingled the change. She found a piece of lint and flicked it away.

Back to good old Sara.

Old. She felt a little older after each manifestation of the Witchblade, a bit longer in the tooth. A stiffness and ache came as additional residuals, but overall it was not altogether a bad feeling. It felt a little like the afterglow of a good, vigorous gym workout, albeit one she had overdone a bit.

She walked the rest of the way home at a steady pace, not minding the shadows, unafraid, but thoughtful.

CHAPTER SIX

It was a miracle of rare device, but it wasn't a pleasure dome. Merlin Jones's pad was more than a place to crash, having some nice stuff in it. Widescreen high-definition television, state of the art sound system. Both had fallen off trucks. Merlin had bought them at a fence's warehouse for a few hundred dollars apiece instead the thousands they cost retail. There were a few nice pieces of furniture; the couch, for one. It came from a cache of household items retained against failed payment of criminally inflated moving costs. A few other appointments around the one-room apartment were anomalously opulent. Like that massive oak bookshelf, filled to capacity.

Otherwise, the place was pretty much a mess. Stacks of books lay piled around the room, along with boxes filled to the brim with CDs, DVDs, video tapes, floppy disks, and other tech bric-a-brac. There were dozens more boxes stuffed with stolen procedure manuals from phone companies, Internet service providers, on-line brokerages, and other concerns.

Basically, the place was a dump in the Bedford-Stuyvesant section of Brooklyn.

One of the *Die Hard* movies was playing on the HDTV, running through the DVD deck. Merlin wasn't watching. He was doing what he usually did, typing on his keyboard.

The sound system crashed and banged with alternative rock of some esoteric kind. Someone was screaming obscenities.

He found it distracting. He picked up a remote and clicked it until the system breathed a sigh of relief and settled down to Mozart on the piano.

"K. 525," Merlin said to himself, still typing. It was a piano and orchestra piece.

The apartment door burst open and two big guys walked in. Merlin looked up. He knew them: Anton and Sergei. Two Russians, both wearing expensive leather jackets, shiny brown and shiny black.

"Jones," one of them said.

"Yeah," Merlin said.

"You come back to work?"

Merlin put his eyes back on the screen. "No."

"That's not good."

"Sorry." Merlin wasn't very sorry.

"You have to come back to work. Mr. Kontra is angry with you."

"I'm pretty angry with Mr. Kontra."

"He got shot, you know."

"I didn't shoot him," Merlin said.

"We know," the big Russian said. "But you refuse to work. We need you."

"Uh-huh," Merlin said, unconcerned.

"We pay you lots of money."

"Not enough. I'm putting in sixty, seventy hours a week. I either need time for my own projects or more pay for the work I do. I told him that."

The other one, the blond one with the black jacket, spoke. "You better come back to work."

"Can't. Have my own projects. Interesting stuff. It won't pay immediately, but I need to work on them."

"What can we say? What can we do?" The brown jacket sauntered over.

"Not a lot, Boris."

"How come you call me 'Boris' all the time? My name is Anton."

"Not a lot, Anton."

"Too bad," Anton said. "He needs you to work. Credit cards."

"I must have given him ten thousand good numbers. Corporate accounts. If you keep charges below a hundred bucks apiece, they'll never even know the numbers have been stolen. They might never find out. They're all big companies."

Anton shrugged. "Too many transactions. Too much bother."

Merlin sighed. "You guys." He shook his head.

"We need more numbers. More accounts."

"Yeah, well . . ."

Anton turned to his partner. "Okay, Sergei."

Sergei tipped the bookcase and half the books slid off and hit the floor.

Merlin regarded the mess casually. "What do you think you're doing?"

"He's clumsy," Anton said. "Don't do that, Sergei. Let that go."

Sergei let the bookcase crash to the floor.

"The downstairs neighbors are always complaining," Merlin said.

He kept typing.

"You don't want to piss off Mr. Kontra."

"I thought he was already pissed off," Merlin said.

"He is," Anton told him. "Hey, you like *Star Wars*." He was standing in front of a poster.

"Yeah. May the Force be with you, and kick the shit out of you."

Anton laughed. "Hey, *we* kick the shit out of *you*."

"I have other friends," Merlin said.

"Yeah?"

"Yeah. Militant friends. They wouldn't take it kindly if you mess with me personally. They don't like it when white guys mess with black guys. Want me to call them?"

"We don't mess with you personally. Hey, Sergei, are we going to bother him personally?"

"Not personally," Sergei said before he threw the Boze against the wall with a lot of force.

"Hey!" Merlin said. "That was one expensive piece of equipment."

"We know." Now Anton was looking at a table filled with candles. "What's this?"

"I'm pagan."

"What's that?"

"An ancient Celtic religion."

"Oh, you worship devil, uh?"

He and Sergei laughed.

"Get stuffed, guys."

Sergei picked up the DVD player.

Merlin scowled. "Put that down, you fool."

Anton asked, "You coming back to work?"

"No."

The DVD didn't break the HDTV screen, but the impact made the screen go dark.

"Shit," Merlin said, jumping up. "Hey . . ."

"That's what it is," Anton said. "Now it's big piece of shit, that TV. You need to get it fixed."

Merlin crossed the room and picked up the DVD player. He shook it. It rattled. He looked for the TV remote, found it, and thumbed a button. The TV switched over to cable and showed CNN. He breathed.

"Next time we bust it," Anton said.

Merlin sighed. "Okay."

"Okay? You come back to work?"

"I'll metaphorically come back to work."

"Eh?" Sergei looked confused—not exactly out of the norm for him.

"I'll log on."

Anton smiled. "That's good. Let's go, Sergei."

The two Russians left, neglecting to close the door.

Merlin threw the busted DVD into a corner and closed the door. He went back to his computer desk. They wouldn't touch the computer. They knew that would put him out of touch and out of business.

He sat, dumped out of what he was doing, and called up another file. Fingering the mouse, he caused the file to print. His ink jet printer whined and rolled out a sheet.

He picked it up. The white paper bore a brightly colored mandala of unusual complexity and design. He studied it.

"Magic," Merlin Jones said with a big grin.

They had put him in a private room. It was nice, and probably cost a mint per day. He could afford it. He wasn't worried. His man Anton had put some men on to guard the room. Good thing the waiting room was right across the hall. They could sit there and watch.

Anton appeared in the doorway.

"I was just thinking of you," Kontra said.

Anton walked in, hands in his pockets. "How are you today?"

"Pretty good. I must look like hell. I don't know when they will let me shave."

"You don't look so bad. You maybe should grow a beard."

"I'd look like Rasputin."

Anton chuckled. "We talked to Merlin."

"Oh? Did he see reason?"

"Yes."

"Good."

"He is a weird one."

"Ah," Kontra said, leaning his head back. He inhaled sharply, still feeling the aftereffects of the attack. "God damn this."

"It's rough," Anton said.

"Yeah. Rough."

"I wanted to tell you, the cops are here."

"Again?"

"I told the woman you didn't want–"

"Woman?"

"Woman cop from homicide."

"Homicide."

"Yeah, they sent her. I told her you were still feeling like hell."

"She went away?"

"No, she's talking to the doctor, but she's insisting on seeing you."

"Let her come in. I don't know why they bother."

"They probably know it was Italians."

"Shut up," Kontra snapped.

"Sorry."

"Maybe you want to tell them they want a piece of the moving business. Anything to do with trucks, they want their cut. You ought to tell her our whole business. Where is she?"

Looking sheepish, Anton peeked out the door. "Still talking."

"All right, send her in."

"I'll go tell her."

"Besides," Kontra said to himself, "it wasn't Italians."

The woman was surprisingly good-looking. Tall, thin, flowing hair, outstanding face. Big bosom. Dressed like beggar, though. He didn't like that. But he liked her.

"Mr. Kontra." Nice voice, too.

"Come in."

"I'm Detective Sara Pezzini, NYPD Homicide Division."

"Why Homicide? Do I look dead?"

"Well, you see . . ."

"Wait until I shave. I look a lot better." He immediately felt himself warming up to her. She looked magnificent. He took an instant shine.

"What kind of name is Kontra? Russian?"

"My mother was Russian. My father Romanian."

"So you're Romanian."

"I am an American."

The woman acknowledged the point with a smile. "Do you know who shot you, Mr. Kontra?"

"Somebody shot me?" He was all innocence.

She winced. "Wow, you are really going to make me work, aren't you?"

"Sorry. What was question again?"

"You took two .32 caliber slugs in the chest. Do you know who put them there?"

"A man."

"A man. Could you describe him?"

Kontra shrugged. "Medium height, about . . . oh, maybe thirty."

"Hair?"

"He had hair." Kontra's mouth twisted wryly. "Dark."

"Dark, like black, or brown?"

"There was no light in the hall."

"Really? I went up there. Lots of light, even at night."

"Okay, so there was light. I didn't get good look at him."

"What was he wearing?"

"A coat. Light."

"Okay, medium, about thirty, dark brown hair. Wearing a light coat. That's not a lot of help, Mr. Kontra. Could you describe his face?"

"No."

"You can't, or won't?"

"Can't. No memory. Bad memory."

"You're making it hard for us, Mr. Kontra."

"Can't help."

"What do you do for a living?"

"Businessman."

"What business?"

"Moving van and real estate."

"I see. Mr. Kontra, we think it was a mob hit."

He did his best to look shocked. "What?"

"Mob hit. An assassination attempt. You were lucky. They'll probably try again."

Kontra flipped over a hand. "This is new to me."

"Okay," the detective said with finality. "We just wanted to check it out. I suppose it's useless to ask if you recognized him."

"Never saw him."

"He was probably from out of town, anyway."

No, he wasn't, Kontra thought. He didn't rate that.

She took a stroll around the room. "We pretty much know your run-ins with the established crime families. The Sicilian crime families. You've had dealings with them in the past. And you've come into conflict."

"You know so much," Kontra said.

"Thanks. I don't know a lot of the specifics. It's not my line of work, organized crime. But I do know that you are a prominent member of what's called the *Organizatsiya.* The Russian version of the Cosa Nostra, call it what you will. You're a crime boss. Not a big time one, but one who's been up-and-coming for a long time. I read a file on you."

"They have a file on me?"

"A pretty big one. They think you've branched out into computer crime."

"I don't own a computer."

"But you are a crime boss. You still have ties to Eastern Europe."

"I have lots of relatives back there."

"And business associates. In Poland, Bulgaria, Hungary, Romania, Germany, and, of course, Russia."

"You really read this file?"

"I got a pretty good briefing this morning from the Organized Crime Task Force. These are nice flowers, by the way."

"Are you married?" he asked. This woman intrigued him.

"No. Are you?"

"Yes. Her name is Sophia. Tell me something."

She spun around. "Yes?"

"Why do you dress like a boy?"

She looked down. "This is boy stuff?"

"Or a bum's. You should wear a dress."

She raised an eyebrow. "And spike heels? I have to move when I work."

"Women today." He shook his head.

"Let's stick to the subject."

"You have a boyfriend?"

"Mr. Kontra, I know you're curious as to why I'm here, and I'm going to tell you."

Kontra shrugged amiably. "Okay."

"We were interested in a description of the hit man to see if it matched the few we have on file. We want to know if he was local or imported. And you've pretty much led us up a blind alley. I'm here simply because Homicide has to ask questions in a case like this."

"You have duty," Kontra said.

"Precisely."

"I can't blame you. Will you have dinner with me some night?"

She looked at him curiously.

He returned the stare; presently, he said, "Eh?"

"I was just trying to remember if I've ever been hit on from a hospital bed. I don't think so. I was never a nurse or hospital aid. No, I think this is a first."

"Do you like Rachmaninoff?"

"Why?"

"There is concert coming up, New York Philharmonic. There is new young soloist playing. I like him. I saw his first performance in St. Petersburg when I went back after Soviet Union fall. I want to go. You go with me?"

"Should I sit next to your wife or on your other side?"

He grinned slyly. "Whichever you wish."

"No thanks, Mr. Kontra. Nice of you to ask."

"He is playing the Second Concerto. My favorite."

"I actually prefer the Third."

"Oh, you know Rachmaninoff?"

"I have a few CDs."

"Then you should go."

She paused, seemed to consider the offer. "I might. When is it?"

"Oh, next Thursday night. I think"

"Ten to one the Philharmonic has a web page. I'll look it up."

"You like classical, then?"

"A little. Actually, my true love is alternative rock."

Kontra made a face.

"I used to be an advance person for a rock band. Before I went to the police academy. We toured Europe. It was fun. Anyway, I'll check the symphony web page."

"You do that." Kontra was amazed she showed any interest at all. He had naturally expected a cold refusal. This little sop she had thrown him was a surprisingly positive sign.

"You Russian guys are normally quiet about your business," she was saying. "But recently, there's been some bloodletting. Do you know how many unsolved gang-style homicides we have in our files?"

"Lots, I guess."

"Lots. And lots of cases have Russian names."

"Then you should go to the concert with me."

"Maybe I will. But you've been shot. Do you really think you'll be well enough in a week?"

"In a week I'll be doing gymnastics."

"You must be strong."

"You won't be able to tell me from Nadia Comaneci."

She grinned at him. "Let's hope I can."

CHAPTER SEVEN

Kontra woke up with a start, half expecting to see the policewoman again. My God, what had he done, asking her out? Was he crazy?

Yes, probably.

He kept falling asleep, jumping awake. He didn't have a clear idea of how long he'd been in this place. A week? Only three days? Time had become meaningless.

Crazy, asking her to go out with him. He must be mad. But she was powerfully beautiful.

Something loomed off to his left, just out of sight. A tall shape in the corner of his eye.

He jumped.

It was his grandmother.

"Baba," he said.

"How are you feeling?" Baba asked. "You look bad."

"I got shot, you crazy old woman."

"They tried to kill you."

"I think we can assume. Why are you hovering around like that, like some ghost in an old house? Come over here in front of me, please."

The old woman moved into view. She was tall and gaunt and had hair the color of fright—stark white, with hints of waxy yellow. Yet her face was still handsome, in a spooky, wrinkled way. She dressed in traditional garb, or as close to it as twenty-first century America would allow. Whatever she wore, it was drab, colorless, and had a tattered look, even when it wasn't tattered. And that babushka. Kontra hated babushkas. Always had. It made women look old before their time.

"They tried to kill you," she said.

"I think we've established that. Who do you think it was?"

"Should I know your business?"

"Do you think it was the Italians?"

"No."

He looked into her piercing blue eyes. She had no education, but she had a mind like a lighthouse. Like a beam that swept around and illuminated things far away. She was like that. "No? They don't want me out of the way?"

"They are not what they used to be. They would like to make trouble for you, but they have other problems. It was someone you know."

"That I figured. You mean in my crowd?"

"It was a rival."

"Ah. That is not a revelation from scripture. Who? That is the question."

"I will find out. I will tell you."

"Good. Bury a potato in the backyard at the full moon. Dance naked."

She glowered. "All the time you laugh at me."

"Your spells work. I'm not laughing. They shot me. For

the second time, the bullets didn't find my heart. Or anything. They cut them out, and I'm fine."

"Of course. You will be protected. You laugh at me, but I'm sworn to protect you. Your mother made me promise before she died, before the German bombs fell."

"Yes, yes." He had heard the story too many times. Suddenly his eyes shut. This sleepiness was getting out of hand.

"That woman."

He opened his eyes again. "What?"

"That woman," Baba said. "She is beautiful, do you think?"

"What woman? Oh. Yes."

"I know of her. She is a devil."

"What? Are you insane?"

"She is a demon-lover. She sleeps with incubus."

"Stop talking nonsense."

"Did you see the bracelet?"

"What bracelet?"

"The one she wore. It is so powerful it made my teeth hurt. She is demon herself."

"She is a policewoman."

"Perhaps. I knew of her before I saw her. She is a tool of the spirits. They use her."

"I thought she was a powerful demon," he said pointedly.

"She is, but she is also a tool of more powerful spirits. From hell."

"Oh, I see."

"You laugh again."

"I'm not laughing. Do you see me laughing?" Kontra shook his head. "Such an insane old bat."

"You were always disrespectful. You will believe anything but me. You believed the communists since you were a child."

"I was young. I think I stopped believing when I was about sixteen. After that, it was just a job."

"You believe anything but the old wisdom. What the gypsies know."

"You're not a gypsy."

"I am an old woman. I learned."

"What about this police girl? She is in league with the devil?"

"I must find out more about her."

"Find out. Please, Grandmother."

"You're going to do *what?*"

Joe Siry almost swallowed his cigarette butt. He spat it out, picked it up off the desk. It was out, so he threw it into the wastebasket.

"How many packs a day do you smoke, Joe?" Sara asked.

"Don't start with the smoking thing," he said. "What did you say you and Lazlo Kontra were going to do together?"

"He asked me to a concert."

"What, a rock concert?"

"No, classical. New York Philharmonic."

"And you're going with him?"

"Tickets are hard to come by. I haven't gone to a symphony concert in years. I figured it was about time."

"What, you've taken a fancy to gangsters?"

Sara smiled tightly. "We know next to nothing about the newest gangs. The ethnic ones. The Russian is the newest. Well, maybe not the newest. Maybe there are ones we don't even know about yet."

"What's to know about them? They all live in Brooklyn. They've been pouring into the country since the Soviet Union closed up shop."

"That I know. I was thinking about getting some deep background. We have at least six suspected contract killings unsolved that might be Russian-related."

"And you figure he's going to tell you something, what, over cocktails before, or maybe late supper after? He's going to turn state's? Gonna pull a Gravano?"

"We don't have any leads in any of those killings, Joe. Maybe I can tease one out."

He regarded her sardonically. "Interesting word you used."

She shot him an annoyed look. "You know what I mean. This is a unique opportunity. He came way out of left field. I've never . . . I mean, he just sprung it on me, and it took me a few seconds to see it as an opportunity. A Mafia don dating a cop. It's like *The Sopranos.*"

Siry scowled at her. "I never saw anything about . . . oh, you mean like it's being a security risk for him?"

"This isn't a thing you'd write in a TV script. No one'd believe it. But this guy is a wild card. If he's willing to get social with a cop, we should take advantage."

"Yeah." Siry appeared to be digesting it. "Maybe. But he's not a don. First of all, he isn't even Russian. He's Bulgarian."

"Romanian."

"Whatever. And he's ex-KGB. He's not like most of the Russian gangsters. Most of them are thugs with lots of prison time. This guy has education, and he was smart enough to bail when he got into trouble, way back in the Eighties. He's clean. He's a born criminal mastermind. He can't be dumb enough to spill something on a social occasion."

"I'm not so sure."

"Not so sure about what?"

"That I can't find out something useful. Few cops ever socialize . . ." Sara's voice trailed off. "Hmmm. I better not say anything."

Siry laughed. "Yeah, you better not. Seltzer might have a bug in here."

"I wouldn't put it past him. Anyway, I view it as a unique undercover opportunity, in a way."

"You make it sound as if he's going to show you his books. If he keeps any."

"I'm telling you, Joe, I want to do it."

"Okay. I don't know what I'm going to tell Seltzer."

"Why does he have to know?"

"You know he oversees undercover operations. Makes sure our guys don't get carried away with their role-playing."

"This isn't undercover. I'm not playing any role. I'm going on a date with the guy."

"Wait a minute. Where did I put that file . . . ?" Siry rummaged through the scrum of paperwork on the desktop, came up with a sheet. He eyed it a moment, then pointed at one line in particular. "Here. The guy's married. Hey, I don't know about this."

Sara glared at him. "Joe, I'm not going to *sleep* with him."

"I don't . . . jeez." Siry was nonplused.

She smiled. He was vein-popping again.

"What's so goddamn funny? Look, I can't tell you

what you can do on your own time. But there's such a thing as the appearance of . . . of . . ."

"Don't worry. There's not going to be an appearance of anything. He's not my type."

"I don't give a damn about whether he's your type. I'm worried about what it's going to look like."

"Yeah, so many cops have season tickets to the symphony."

"You are a wiseass, you know that?"

"Yes, sir."

The office door creaked open and Jake McCarthy stuck his head in. "Joe, did you want to see—Oh, hi, Pez."

Siry jerked his thumb at Sara. "Know she has a date with a Mafioso?"

Jake stepped in, his jaw hanging. "Huh? Sara, is that right?"

Sara ignored him. "The Task Force summary talked about another term—Russian, what was it? 'Chief Thief' is the translation. No, that isn't it. I have the brief on my desk."

Jake said, "What did you say, Joe?"

"She's going out with a gangster."

"Huh?"

"She's going undercover."

"Watch how you phrase that," Sara warned.

"Huh?"

Siry threw his arms up at McCarthy. "Are you going to keep saying 'huh'?"

"Huh? I mean . . ."

Sara rose. "I gotta go. The concert isn't for a couple of days, so there's no hurry about this."

"Pez, uh . . . how about a cup of coffee?"

" 'Thief-in-law,' " she said, snapping fingers.

"Huh?" Joe Siry said.

Jake looked at him.

"That's the translation of the Russian term for crime boss," Sara explained. " 'Thief-in-law.' I forget what the Russian phrase is. But Kontra didn't start out that way. The way I figure it, organized crime could only exist with high-level Soviet corruption. Kontra was probably a cop on the payroll, then became a player himself. But now he's *capo* of his own little family."

"Isn't that Italian?" Siry asked, frowning.

Sara shrugged. "I don't know any Russian."

"I'm really sorry I sent you for the interview," Siry told her. "I gave it to you because it was bound to be useless. I thought you couldn't get into trouble. But . . ."

Sara said, "But?"

"Since you're taking such an interest, I might as well loan you out to the Task Force temporarily. I put in a request for better coordination with the division. I don't know, though . . ."

"Are you still bothered by that accident?"

"Forget it," Siry said. "I backed you up."

"I know you did," Sara said. "I appreciate it. But there's still going to be some nosing around about it. I'm still facing a preliminary investigative interview."

"If it was an accident, it was an accident," Siry tautologized.

"It *was* an accident," Sara told him.

"Good. Remember that the Task Force is hooked up to the DA's office. You'll be working with the same people who might indict you for involuntary manslaughter."

Sara asked, "Do you know something I don't?"

"God, I hope not. Now get out of here and leave me to my misery. McCarthy!"

"What?"

"Don't you know that when you come back from being out sick, you're supposed to report to the Watch Commander that you've returned to duty?"

"Sorry, sir. I forgot. I've been meaning to do it all day."

McCarthy gingerly closed the door after following Sara into the corridor.

"Damn," he said to himself.

"Don't beat yourself up," Sara told him.

"I hate when that happens."

"Don't worry, it doesn't happen often. You're usually a stickler for procedure."

"I've had a lot on my mind lately. And that bug sort of knocked me for a loop. Got time for a cup in the break room?"

Sara shook her head. "I want to get home. I'm bushed."

"What did you do all day? Besides hitting on Mafiosi."

"*He* hit on *me*. No, what wore me out was writing that report on Whip. Trying to avoid making it sound ridiculous. Impossible."

"So you didn't succeed?"

"No. Nothing wears me out more than a stint in the Report Writing Room."

"Otherwise known as the Whopper Room."

"That's exactly what Seltzer is going to think."

"That you're lying? That you threw Whip off that balcony? Whip wasn't a big dude . . . I mean, everybody knows you can handle yourself as well as any guy, Sara, but . . . well, you know, you . . . uh . . ."

Jake looked thoughtful. Obviously, something at the back of his mind had been nattering at him as he spoke.

She looked at him clinically. "See? You have your doubts about me, too."

"Hey, wait a minute," Jake was in a hurry to say. He tried to touch her arm as she suddenly turned and stepped away. She was too quick.

"Never mind," she snapped.

"Wait, wait . . . I didn't mean . . ."

"Forget it," Sara said over her shoulder.

CHAPTER EIGHT

After spending the early evening at the public library doing some light research (she found a good book on the new ethnic gangs), Sara ate alone at a fast burger place, perversely ordering salad and a baked potato. Then she went home and watched TV for three solid hours, not realizing how much time was passing.

Finally, she clicked the TV off and got up, looked at the clock. "What a waste."

She sat at her computer, logged onto her ISP, and got her e-mail. She had three news service downloads and six commercial spam messages. No real messages. She deleted everything and logged off.

She sat and stared at the notebook computer's dead screen.

Cops don't have many friends, she realized as she brushed her teeth. Outside the force, that is. You try to mix in, you try to socialize with civilians, but as soon as you let loose what you do for a living, it kind of hangs there in the middle of the conversation like a huge icicle, and the temperature suddenly drops ten degrees. Someone makes a feeble joke. And over the next five minutes, you find that everyone has an excuse to move to the other side of the room. And you find yourself sitting alone with a stale drink, smiling stiffly.

And for her, it was usually worse. Men's pupils became pinpoints; they coughed and look away. Cop? Did she say *cop?* And a detective, yet.

The only thing worse, she'd been told, is for a woman to say she is a deputy district attorney; or worse yet, a judge.

Do all civilians have guilty consciences? Seemed so, at times.

It didn't bother her much. She rarely thought about such things. Only on occasion. By the time she finally crawled into bed, it was out of her mind entirely.

She woke. A weird glow filled the room, a faint spectral light, growing brighter, suffused with a pale greenish tint. Her eyes, adapted to dark, saw it as painfully bright.

Naked, she rose from the bed. The light emanated from her desk. It quickly became apparent that she had left the notebook on, though she could swear that she'd turned it off well before going to bed.

Odd geometrical bands of light played across the screen. The display looked like an elaborate screen saver, forming bright patterns and figures that constantly moved and shifted: concentric circles and squares, moires and zigzags, waves and grids, reticulated fields, all radiating a pale blue-green aura that tinted the walls.

She approached it carefully. When had she loaded this program? It must be something that downloaded itself from the Internet, unbeknownst to her.

A virus!

No computer of hers had ever caught a virus before. She was fascinated, in a way. She wanted to find out more about such rarefied phenomena. She wondered what she should do. Turn the machine off? Probably. Bring it to the precinct, let some expert in the white collar crime section take a look at it? Maybe it was a new virus no one had ever seen before.

The patterns on the screen grew busier, more complex. They interlaced and interweaved; they danced and cavorted, then, inexplicably, burst out of the screen and spilled across the desk, the floor, the walls.

She jumped back.

She froze as the pale green lines flowed around her and took her measure, calibrating and quantifying her every dimension. She felt nothing, but there was something strangely palpable about this light. It had a substance of some kind, she was sure. She felt a presence in it. And all at once she somehow knew this manifestation for what it was: lucent nerves in a sensorium cast out like a web by an unimaginable being far removed. She did not know what kind of being. She was not sure she wished to find out.

A cage of light surrounded her, shifting and flowing over her skin, gauging her, evaluating her. It lingered for several seconds, then moved toward her bed, there to coalesce around something on the nightstand.

The Witchblade.

She watched as the lines of light played across the bracelet. It seemed to resist. The stone glowed brightly, its light throwing a warm backdrop for the cold, alien display. The room came alive with weird color.

She made a move toward the nightstand. Something

held her back. An adjunct structure of some sort extended from the green cage surrounding the bracelet and became force as well as light. Ghostly arms of restraint blocked her, held her back.

She struggled but couldn't make any progress. The glow from the bracelet intensified.

She let out a groan and fell to the bare wood floor, strapped by unseen fetters. The lines of light felt like electricity now, crackling across her bare skin. Prickly threads of static pinned her under a net of force.

She managed to crawl a few inches. She could make progress a little at a time. Painfully, she got to her knees. The floor felt like a griddle, frying her kneecaps. She pushed forward toward the nightstand, reaching a hand upward.

There commenced loud crackling and discharge. Blinding flashes and displays leapt up all around her. It was as if a hundred loose high-tension power lines were whipping around the room, arcing and throwing sparks.

A whirlwind of fire surged from the Witchblade, engaged the pale green grid in a struggle of tension, and a contest between bright displays of color and energy began. Sara kept reaching, trying to touch the bracelet. She could not quite make it.

The battle continued for a full minute. Then, abruptly, the green forces seemed to lose vitality and began an orderly withdrawal to the screen, fighting a rearguard action. Pale fingers of luminescence dimmed and retreated, backing along walls, ceiling, and floor.

Sara finally made contact with the bracelet, grabbed it, and put it on her right wrist. She sat up and looked at the computer.

The green lines were back on the screen. Gradually, they faded; but the screen continued to glow eerily.

She saw faces in it. She thought she saw faces. Strange, inhuman faces.

No, not inhuman. She looked again. They were . . . non-human. Humanoid. Humanish. No, human-like. Simulacra, artifacts, constructs. They weren't really alive. Those . . . things, there, could not have life in the normal sense. They were parodies of that which was human.

The eyes. She could not bear to look into their eyes.

Did she see them or was she imagining? She passed a palm across her face and looked again.

The screen was faintly glowing now. Fading.

Screeeeeeeee.

She did not know where the hell-bird's cry had come from, the sky or the screen. She looked out a window but saw nothing but blankness over the city.

By the time she had put on a robe and walked to the desk, the screen was completely dark, and the computer was not operating. She suppressed a motion to turn it on. Perhaps she should let it rest. She carefully lowered the screen and clicked it shut.

She didn't bother looking at the clock. She knew it would be a long, long wait until morning, and that she would be up the whole time.

"Mr. Kontra, this is amazing."

"What?"

The doctor leafed through a sheaf of reports. Behind him stood about two dozen interns, all with baby faces. To Kontra, they looked like a kindergarten class. "Your progress is phenomenal. Only three days later, and . . ."

"I heal fast."

"I've never seen this kind of . . . these test reports."

"I feel lots better today."

The doctor turned to his charges. "I've heard of cases like this, but you people have been privileged actually to see one. Any questions?"

"How old are these kids?" Kontra wanted to know.

The doctor smiled. "They're all through medical school. We just had a conference on you. Needless to say we're very, very pleased with your progress. We should have you out of here in three days."

"I want out tomorrow." Kontra said.

"Well, that might be premature . . ."

"Tomorrow."

The doctor gave up leafing through the charts. "I'm going to order an other set of X-rays first. Then I'll let the floor nurse know. Okay?"

"Sure."

"Do you have any complaints, any symptoms?"

Kontra smiled and shook his head.

"It's like magic," the doctor said.

CHAPTER NINE

Sara yawned, then said, "I'm sorry."

The array of gray-faced men before her seemed affronted. Gray morning light filtered through dirty windows. It was a gray world out there, and it was pretty grim in here.

"Are you having trouble sleeping, Detective?" Seltzer wanted to know.

Sara began, "As a matter of fact . . ."

"We'll try to be brief, so that you can get your beauty rest."

Flanagan, the man to Seltzer's right coughed. "I don't think we have to get into personalities," he said.

"Who's doing that?" Seltzer wanted to know.

"Let's get back to business," Flanagan said. "Ms. Pezzini . . ."

"That remark could be construed as prejudicial," Sara commented.

"What remark?"

"The one about beauty rest. Lawsuits have been brought on lesser grounds."

Flanagan fussed with his papers. "Detective Pezzini, are you threatening this board with litigation on the basis of a casual remark?"

"Blackmail's not going to get you anywhere," Seltzer told her.

"Does the term 'hostile work environment' mean anything to you?"

Seltzer scowled. "Oh my God, a locker room lawyer."

"Please, Sergeant Seltzer," Flanagan said.

"Sorry. Do go on. By the way, Detective, you might want to be diagnosed for sleep apnea. It's a condition in which–"

"Sergeant . . ." Flanagan said with a warning tone.

"Excuse me."

Flanagan cleared his throat. "Detective Pezzini."

"Yes, sir?"

"Do you have anything else by way of amplification or comment, in addition to the report you filed?"

"No, sir."

"Are you quite sure?"

"I'm quite sure."

"Anything you might have left out, however seemingly slight or inconsequential?"

"I included everything."

"I see. Well, although it looks like a pure case of death by misadventure . . ."

"That is what the coroner's inquest found," Sara reminded him.

"Uh, yes. Yes, that is indeed what the coroner's inquest–"

"Which doesn't have any bearing on the findings of this board," Seltzer said sharply. "We are here to investigate any untoward event that happens in the course of standard department procedure and to look for possible culpability on the part of any department personnel who—"

"I think," Flanagan interposed, "we all know the purpose of this board. As I was saying, although it looks as if this case can be adjudicated in your favor, Detective Pezzini, the file still has to go to the committee for final disposition. At that time you'll be informed of the committee's findings and any action that might or might not be taken. Meanwhile, this hearing is adjourned. Thank you for your cooperation."

Oddly enough, the day was brightening. Sunlight began to leak through heavy cloud cover.

Sara said, "You're welcome."

The concert hall was filled to about three-quarters capacity, for all that this concert was officially sold out. The empty seats were easy to explain: season tickets holders, high-rollers failing to show up and not deigning to let anyone else make good use of their ticket.

Sara and Kontra sat together. Two bodyguards, Anton and Sergei, sat directly behind them.

Good seats, Sara thought. Orchestra Circle, keyboard side. She would be able to see the piano soloist's hands.

The guest conductor, a diminutive Asian man whose name had beat a hasty exit from Sara's mind, walked out from the wings to enthusiastic applause. He stood at the podium and waited. There seemed to be something amiss backstage. He turned to the audience and smiled a little nervously, raising a hand as if to say, patience, please.

Presently, a tall, solidly-built man walked out and took his seat at the piano.

"Damn it," Kontra said. "This isn't new kid. Who is this?"

Sara's mouth was hanging open. Could it be?

Ian Nottingham?

It couldn't. See was seeing things again.

She listened as the pianist struck spooky, mordant chords and sounded the same deep base note after each. After the chords rose to a crescendo, piano and orchestra launched like a great, black ship into a deeply moving, quintessentially Russian melody that took the Romantic to dimensions hitherto unknown. It conjured many things: earth-curving sweeps of land, the soil, the sky, endless weeping, romance, loss and remembrance—the spirit of a vast, tragic, solemn country, distilled in a heady musical draught.

She really didn't know why, but tears instantly welled in her eyes, and she fought to keep them from spilling out.

"He was good, whoever he was," Kontra allowed afterwards, over tea and cakes. "Did you like it?"

"It was so . . . Russian," Sara said.

"Yes, Rachmaninoff. He was old Russia. A life for the Czar, big estates, complacent peasants, old money. He left after revolution and never came back. But he was true *artiste*. You said you think you know the pianist?"

"Yes. I think so. But . . ."

Kontra set his tea cup down. "But?"

"I thought he was dead."

Kontra looked at her for a moment. Then he said, "You are strange woman. Beautiful, but strange."

"Thanks," Sara said. "I think."

"I'm told you . . ." He stopped, seeming dubious about proceeding. "Well, I will say it. You are involved with some kind of magic."

Sara's distrusting frown elicited an expansive gesture of apology from him. She asked, "Where did you hear that?"

"I know a witch woman."

"What?"

"Gypsy woman. Well, she isn't gypsy. Actually, I think she has the blood. But she knows."

"Who is she, if you don't mind my asking?"

"My grandmother. *Baba* is what you call her in old country. Old woman."

"And what does she do, look into a crystal ball?"

He shrugged. "I don't know. I don't believe in such things. But she has the power to see where people can't see."

"The future? Other places?"

Kontra waved a hand vaguely. "She . . . sees things."

"Okay. And she sees me."

"Yes. She says you are witch woman, too. Are you?"

"No. I do wear this bracelet, though."

"I was noticing. I saw it when you come to hospital. I tell my grandmother. She saw it. She says it is demon thing."

"Demon thing." Sara looked at her plate. "Well . . ."

"That make it powerful. But you aren't interested in power."

"I'm not interested in power. It comes in handy, though, I will admit."

"What does bracelet do?"

"Not a lot. Oh, I meant to ask you. What happened to Anton and Sergei? When the concert ended, they weren't around." She also remembered that just before the pianist left the stage after his last bow, he seemed to look straight out at her. "When did they leave?" she asked.

"They hate classical. They like to go out to club. That's probably where they went. Meet women."

"Aren't they your . . . protection?"

Kontra shrugged. "You can't have bodyguard all the time. It's ridiculous. I'm not John Gotti. I'm not big shot. You think I am, but I'm not."

"Funny I didn't see them get up and leave. Or hear them."

"The third movement is loud."

Sara reached for her purse.

"You going?" Kontra asked.

"I have to make an early night of it."

"Really. So sad. You let me take you home?"

"No, I'll get a cab. There's someone I have to see."

"This late?"

"Thanks for the concert. I really enjoyed it."

Kontra sat back and grinned. "No more than me. Good night, Sara."

"Good night, Lazlo."

The graveyard probably dated from New York's Knickerbocker era. All old graveyards look alike: weathered headstones, faded lettering, grass grown to neglect, weeds. Foot markers covered with moss. Forlorn trees.

Her father's grave did not look bad. She had kept after it over the years, but it had been a while since her last visit. She bent to pluck a withered dandelion, threw it away. Then she stood and thought about the past.

"Hi, Dad. It's Peeps," she said to the quiet air.

Her father's pet name for her when she'd been a kid. Kontra's remark about her being a strange woman was probably true. No, it was absolutely true. When most girls tell their daddy what they want to be when they grow up, it's usually a ballerina, a princess, a nurse, a teacher—whatever. But for little Sara it was . . . a policeman. A policeman. There isn't even a good word for a policeman who isn't a man. Policewoman isn't great, and *policeperson*? Ugh.

The job never did him any good. The pay was lousy, and then you died.

She bent her head. She hadn't gotten over it yet, had she?

No. Not yet. She hadn't been there, hadn't seen it, but she had never been able to rid her mind of the image of her father lying on the street, shot by an assassin.

She had no idea how long she had stood there, contemplating her father's grave, when she heard someone call her name.

She turned. The man who had played the concerto was approaching her, his athletic figure limned in streetlight.

"Ian Nottingham," she said. "It *was* you."

"Sara. Somehow I knew you'd be here."

"You always seem to know."

He was still dressed in white tie and tails. A cape fluttered in a sudden gust of wind, along with his impressive mane of hair. She wondered how he had arranged that touch. He had always had a flair for the melodramatic.

"It's getting to be our meeting place," she said. "How have you been?"

"Fine, keeping busy. Something's up. Again."

"Again. Do you have any clues?"

"I always have clues," said Nottingham.

"You pick them up out of the air," she said. "I've always wondered if it were an innate ability, or one you acquired."

"In a way, I've always been clairvoyant. But my various

bouts of training have sharpened what paranormal skills I was born with."

"What's your reading on the current situation?"

"It is something very, very strange."

She walked to a nearby stone bench and sat down. "What do computers have to do with it?"

"Computers?" Ian Nottingham said.

"Something attacked me out of a computer."

"Whoa," Nottingham said.

"And then there's this big bird."

"Big bird," Nottingham repeated dully.

"Not the one from . . . oh, never mind. Maybe we aren't talking about the same thing."

Nottingham seated himself on the extreme opposite end of the bench. "I was only referring to a general sense of impending evil. This is what I've received. An intrusion into our world of something very alien and extremely exotic."

"Well, that sounds something like it. Whatever it is, it's very interested in the Witchblade."

"Precisely. I've sensed a struggle for control."

"Control of what?"

"Perhaps this world. Then again . . ." Nottingham looked off abstractedly.

"Go on," Sara said.

"Have you ever thought about the world in which the Witchblade originated?"

"Nothing specific about it ever comes to mind."

"But you have realized the artifact couldn't come from our world. You do realize that The Wtichblade is an entity itself, and there are no entities like it on this earth."

"One of these days," Sara said, "someone will tell me

what the Witchblade really is, definitively, once and for all, no going back. But I'm not going to hold my breath."

"Have you ever wondered if there are other entities in that world?"

"Sure."

"Furthermore, did you ever wonder if there were factions in this other world who vie for its possession?"

"You're damn right I've wondered."

"Of course. All this goes without saying. But perhaps the struggle is interworld as well as intraworld. There could be competing factions in other worlds who want the Blade."

"It's one popular little item," she said sardonically.

"Okay, that's occurred to you, too. But tunneling through from world to world is a fairly difficult proposition. It happens neither often nor easily. With me so far?"

"So far."

"Somebody's making it easy for somebody. Now, you say you were attacked out of a computer. Are you sure it was an attack, or simply a probe of some kind?"

"Could have been either or both."

"I've never heard of magic being done via a computer. But then again, there are prayer wheels."

"Prayer wheels?"

"Well, same idea. A mechanical device that facilitates a supernatural end."

"I think I see what you mean. But why do you think magic has anything to do with the current situation?"

"As far as I know, there are no technologies that can bridge the gap between the various realms of existence. Only magic can do it. Magic is merely the means of channeling energy from one realm to another."

"I think I see what you're driving at," Sara said.

"What's going on in your world now?" Nottingham wanted to know.

Sara shrugged. "Not a lot. Weird thing happened the other day . . ."

Nottingham waited.

After a moment, Sara said, "Forget it. The thing I'm doing now is nosing around a Russian Mafia gang."

"Any magical element involved?"

"Now that you mention it, yes, sort of."

"Then there's a connection."

"Yeah, if you believe an old Romanian gypsy woman."

"Romanian?"

Sara sat up stiffly. "Oh, no."

Nottingham laughed. "Romania."

"Transylvania," Sara said. "But . . . but wait a minute. All *that* stuff doesn't jibe with what's been happening. I've seen no fangs, no bats, no coffins with soil in them. Birds, Ian. Birds. Or more accurately, one huge, honking bird. How does that tally up?"

"I don't know."

"Birds, computers . . . crime. Russians." Sara let out a sigh.

"Why won't you tell me what happened the other day?"

Sara shifted on the bench. "It was an impaling. Accident, a suspect."

"Impaling?" Nottingham said with some amazement.

"Freak accident."

"Vlad."

"Huh?"

"Vlad the Impaler."

"Wait a minute," Sara said with some alarm. "Wait just a minute, now."

"He was not a vampire."

Sara's eyebrows lifted in genuine surprise. "He wasn't?"

"No. That was Bram Stoker using an historical figure to create fiction. Vlad was possibly demonic, but he didn't suck anybody's blood. However, you wanted a Romanian connection . . ."

"Wasn't he Hungarian?"

"Transylvania was then part of the Magyar empire. Vlad defended it against the Turks."

"I see. That helps, a little. Not much."

Nottingham stood. "You're on your own with this one, Sara."

Sara stood up as he walked away. "I usually am. By the way . . ."

"Yes?" Nottingham turned at the foot of the concrete path.

"Nice playing tonight."

"Evgeny took ill," he said. "I sat in."

"It was wonderful. You play marvelously."

"I'm rusty. Don't get a chance to practice."

"You're too modest."

"Thanks for the compliment. And remember something."

"Sure."

"Remember that the Witchblade is a manifestation in this world of something that we may not be able to understand in its world of origin. That goes for any appearance of the paranormal in this world. What you're seeing on this side may not be what's on the other. Good bye, Sara."

He turned and walked away into the night, cape fluttering theatrically.

CHAPTER TEN

Merlin advanced through the beat-up neighborhood cautiously. He knew a lot of people who lived here, but that was not necessarily a good thing. Not always.

He turned a corner. All clear, so he upped his pace. The sky was blue-white, almost as bright as the sun itself. The Asian-owned convenience stores were open, and kids played on the street. The neighborhood was the worse for wear, but wasn't a particularly bad one. Just poor.

Merlin was feeling reasonably good until a blue Mercedes pulled up sharply to the curb and two familiar Russian torpedoes spilled out.

"Yo, Merlin," Anton yelled, running.

Merlin ducked into the bar that presented itself as soon as he ran around the corner. He knew the bartender, who was bending over the sink. The rest of the place was lightly clienteled: two bar flies and three men at a table sharing a pitcher of beer. The place was dark and stank of spilled beer and splashed urine.

"My man," the bartender said to him.

"Gotta go right out the back. You mind?"

"Cops?"

"No."

"White guys?"

"Yeah."

"They ain't comin' in here."

Merlin hesitated. Might be better to stay put. The Russians didn't like to hang out in this neighborhood. They usually wouldn't follow anybody into a bar like this. But you never knew. And he didn't like to be trapped in a place.

"Thanks," Merlin said, and walked through a door in the back wall into a storage room filled with stacked beer cases. The exit door was slightly open, leaking daylight. Merlin poked his nose out. Nothing happening.

The alley was clear. Soon he got the notion that Anton and Sergei thought he was still in the bar and were probably watching the front. They weren't altogether the brightest guys on the face of the planet.

His cell phone burbled and he took it out of his pocket. He had e-mail, but judging from the address of the sender, he didn't bother to open it now. It was just chat.

There she was again. A woman he'd been seeing around the neighborhood. She filled out her jeans very well, and Merlin extrapolated the curve in his mind. She walked past the end of the alley, and he exited and followed.

His phone beeped again. He ignored it. She heard it, and turned, gave him a smile. He liked her face. *Now, who are you, girl?*

The phone wouldn't quit, so he took it out and flipped it open. " 'Lo?"

"Merlin."

"Yeah?" The voice was unpleasantly familiar.

"Turn around."

Before he did, he knew it was Anton, driving the

Mercedes, creeping along close to the curb. Anton waved and smiled.

Merlin ran past the tight-jeaned woman and got about a quarter-block before Sergei stepped out from the next alley and grabbed him.

The door of the apartment flew open and Merlin lurched in. Blood covered the front of his suede jacket and his face was puffed up and discolored. His left eye had swollen shut. Blood ran from his mouth.

He stumbled into the bathroom and splashed water on his face. He stared at himself in the mirror. Then he ripped off his ruined clothes and stepped into the shower.

He let hot water steam him for twenty minutes. He stepped out and covered himself with a white terrycloth robe. He took a look in the mirror. The swelling had gone down. He looked and felt one hundred percent better, but his face and ribs still hurt.

He sat at his computer and typed. He liked to sit at his computer and type. He'd been doing it since his early teens, which was not all that far in the past. He hit the keys savagely. Colors began to dance on the screen.

The bully boys had always had it in for him. Always. They were all alike, white or black. He would have felt guilty about letting white guys beat him up if so many black ones hadn't done the same thing. He could never defend himself very well, but that didn't mean he was . . . well, what they always called him. He *liked* women. The bastards. The bastards.

He kept jabbing keys.

Sara finally found the place, a small oil distribution company in south Brooklyn. It looked more like a junkyard with some of the junk cleared away. There wasn't much to the non-junk part: a few large elevated tanks covered with rust spots, one or two sheds, a trailer, and three delivery tankers parked in a small lot. The outfit sold home heating oil. If the Organized Crime Task Force report was correct, it bought product in states with low fuel taxes and sold it in New York, which had whopping fuel taxes. The margin of saving was pure profit. Which was purely illegal of course. A common enough dodge, but an extremely lucrative one.

Sara parked the division car and walked through the gate, showing her badge to the uniformed officers who had set up a crime scene perimeter.

As she walked toward the trailer, where a clot of crime scene techs and a few plainclothes had gathered, she saw someone from the Task Force she recognized, Dave Lambert.

"Sara."

"Dave. Got your report. Thanks."

"Sorry to take another case off your hands, but we're mighty interested in this one. So's the FBI."

"Are they here?"

"No, they trust us on some things."

Sara looked at all the techs roving around the yard. "Looks like you're doing a thorough job. Believe me, I have a big enough workload. I have to make a report, though. Who's the victim?"

"Guy by the name of Ashkenazi. He was running a pretty big fuel tax evasion operation here. Somebody whacked him."

"Know who?" Sara said casually.

"Yeah. I think so. I think it was payback for an attempted hit last week. The one on Lazlo Kontra."

"You have a time of death yet?"

"Tennish, last night. Uh, you look thoughtful."

"Hm? Oh, nothing. Go ahead."

"Well, looks like he was here alone, working late. He was a hands-on kind of guy. Didn't like bodyguards much. He was a tough old nut, veteran of Soviet prisons."

"What did he have against Kontra?"

"Near as I can find out, it goes back to the old country. They were enemies of long standing. What I got from informants was that Kontra strangled Ashkenazi's brother, long time ago."

"Strangled?"

"Yeah. Never did find out the details. It was pure vendetta, this one. Well, they're all vendettas in a way. Way of life with these people."

"Know who did the whack?"

"Well, if it wasn't one of Kontra's soldiers, I don't know who it was. Small-caliber pistol left at the scene. Serial number will probably lead nowhere."

"You seem pretty sure about all the facts. Think you can pick up anybody?"

"Possible we might get some forensic links. Let's say have enough to get a warrant to haul in both his top henchmen. Before you know it, they'll produce witnesses who'll perjure themselves to provide an ironclad alibi. You find a whole bar full of people in Brighton Beach who'll submit affidavits. Say they bought the suspects drinks all night and that they never left the table."

And of course their boss will have a different alibi, Sara thought.

"We've been down this road before," she said. "You'd think Kontra wouldn't use two of his closest associates."

"Sara, this isn't the big time. No fifty-thousand-dollar

contract killers flown in. Everything's pretty much done in-house with this crowd."

She didn't spend long inside the trailer. Ashkenazi did not look to have suffered before he died. Nevertheless, she couldn't help interpreting the expression on the corpse's face as relief that it was all over. No more struggling, no more jail time, no more time, for all time.

And now to look up Kontra and have a chat.

She had a bone to pick with him.

CHAPTER ELEVEN

Have another?" asked the bartender.

"Sure," Sara said.

"Same?"

"Gee and tee with lime. No piano player tonight?"

"Coming up. No, he's off Tuesdays."

The place was packed, anyway. Maybe he wasn't such a good piano player. Or played stuff nobody wanted to hear. She tried to imagine Nottingham playing a Billy Joel tune, or maybe doing an Elton John riff. She couldn't. But she really did not know enough about the man's musical tastes to hazard a guess. She did know that he was the only other person of her acquaintance who could wear the Witchblade and live.

"Haven't seen you around before," the bartender overtured.

She'd been wondering when he would get around to it. He seemed a little wary of her. Why, she didn't know, but as this was a bar which Russian wiseguys were known to frequent, he might have figured she belonged to one.

She tried to imagine herself a gangster's moll. She could not.

Actually, she had always been more inclined to imagine herself a gangster. Ma Barker, maybe. Bonnie, of Clyde fame. That was more like it, if she were to indulge in that sort of thing. But cop fantasies had always taken precedence. She could no more fancy herself a minion of the forces of evil than a mongoose could daydream about being a cobra.

"Never get to Brooklyn much," she told the bartender.

"Oh? What's the occasion tonight?" A little on the young side of thirty, he was smiling. He wasn't bad-looking.

"Looking for a friend."

"Yeah? Who? I might know him."

"Actually two guys. Two Russian guys, with accents."

The bartender laughed. "Around here . . ."

"Yeah," she said. "I know. One of them is named Sergei."

The smile vanished. The guy shrugged. "Yell that name here, six guys are going to answer."

"And the other is Anton."

"Oh, yeah." The bartender frowned almost imperceptibly. "I know them. They haven't been in tonight. Not yet, anyway."

"They usually stop in?"

"Late, usually. They friends of yours?"

"Not exactly. Acquaintances."

"Uh-huh."

He was mentally backing off now, sensing something he didn't trust or like.

"Look," she said. "No way you're not going to tip them off now, so I'll tell you that I'm NYPD Homicide."

"Yeah?"

"I've tried to contact their boss, but he's disappeared. Now I'm looking for them. If you see them, tell them I'm going to pick them up eventually. Meanwhile, I want their address."

The bartender threw his arms wide. "From me?"

"Just tell me where they live."

"I don't know them from Adam. Not really. They just come in every once in a while."

"Not what I heard. I heard they practically live here."

"Oh?"

"In here every night, without fail. Now, where the hell are they? I'm tired of waiting."

"They didn't come in."

Sara leaned across the bar. "We've established that, dude. Now, where do they live? They must have mentioned it sometime."

He didn't dare cast eyes on her cleavage, but was having a hard time resisting. "Look, I don't want any trouble."

"Then just tell me where Anton and Sergei live."

"Upstairs."

"How convenient. Is there a back way?"

"Yeah. Just go past the rest rooms. Take these keys. I sometimes go up there and take care of things for them."

"You always so kind to people you don't know from Adam?"

She got up from her bar seat.

"Hey, don't you need a search warrant?"

"You offered me the keys."

"Uh, I didn't . . . I didn't mean—"

"Thanks."

The bracelet had been throbbing faintly all evening. As she climbed the stairs it began to thump like a bass drum.

The stairs showed use. No footprints in dust. They were clean and free of junk and must have been used by the thugs regularly, if not by their houseboy downstairs.

She tried the first key on the ring she'd been given. It didn't fit. The second didn't either, but the smallest one threw aside a deadbolt inside the jamb. It was louder than she wanted it. She waited for some reaction inside.

Silence.

She pushed the door open and stared into a dark apartment. Spilling streetlight outlined a small living room.

"Anyone home?" she called out.

The darkness did not answer. She took a step in and called again and got the same response. She closed the door and felt the wall for a switch. She didn't find one, and had to inch her way across the carpeted floor. As she did, she wished for her jacket and jeans and their many pockets instead of this cocktail dress and silly pocketbook that could barely hold her keychain, which, by the way, had a tiny penlight . . .

She crunched something underfoot.

The Witchblade came alive and began to babble.

She moved forward and kicked something, sending it skittering across the floor. She could now see some kind of upset in the room. The place was a shambles, and as her eyes adapted to the dark, she could see the vast extent of it. The furniture was all overturned, debris littered the floor. She walked on broken glass and scattered paper.

Fumbling in her pocketbook, she wondered where the damned light switches were. There, across the room, by that alcove that went into another area or room. Finally reaching the other side, she still failed to find a switch but got the penlight to work. It cast a feeble beam over the room.

She gasped.

The place looked like a tornado had gone through it. The beam revealed things she was sure she didn't want to see in detail. Things that looked like blood, pools of blood. Through a daze of a shock that reached through her tough hide for such things, she saw heaps of entrails . . .

The Witchblade yammered at her.

Her foot slipped in something. She didn't want to look at what it is. She scuffed her shoe into the nap of the carpet.

She found a cordless phone and hit the talk button. The instrument was dead, and she didn't have her cell phone. She'd have to go back downstairs to call this in . . . whatever it was. A double mutilation murder. She pushed from her mind a pile of messy questions, not the least of which was about how two strapping street thugs could have been . . .

Then, suddenly, weird things began to happen.

It must have come out of one of the bedrooms. Unseen, its odor hit her first. It was the worst wet-dog smell imaginable, an evil musk of dirt and sweat and unnamable exudations.

She turned and saw two red eyes advancing toward her. It was little more than a huge dark shape, a flash of something white and sharp, and slits of molten eyes, all revealed in a second's sweep of the weak penlight beam

There was some discontinuity of time. The thing attacked as a molasses-like goo enveloped everything, a slowness, a dreamlike slow-motion falling, a nightmare environment of some kind took over and she was fighting to move, fighting an inelastic medium that held her back; but not everything was affected. Her right hand, utterly within its own frame of reference, instantly grew a mailed gauntlet to cover it and metal feathers like wings along the side of her hand and wrist to embellish it. The Witchblade had reacted faster than she possibly could have.

The gauntlet lashed out, its metallic talons ripping and tearing.

The thing howled and staggered back.

The rest of her body caught up to the Blade's time frame. She moved back in strategic retreat, back-kicking debris out of the way. She leapt over a cocktail table and kicked in the monster's direction.

The thing howled again and swiped at the Blade as it passed. Flinders flew in all directions. The thing then circled to the right, slowly, cautiously. It had cause now to take the measure of the adversary it faced, to calculate the nature of the threat. It slunk, it crouched. It growled.

She watched it, tensed to spring into action. Her eyes now saw in the dark like an infrared camera.

It stopped. The beast's fiery eyes never wavered, never blinked.

She eased to the right, sidestepping gingerly.

It sprang forward in a rush, wickedly fast. She leapt away and kicked.

The thing grunted as it tripped over an immense

overstuffed armchair deftly slid into its path. It fell over the thing and ended up a heap on the floor behind it. It remained out of sight a few seconds. She moved off and took a stance on the opposite side of the room.

It was annoyed now. She noted that its bestial growling carried an intelligent undertone. It was as if the creature could speak but chose not to, or was contemptuous of communicating with a creature as low as the one it faced. Nevertheless its guttural sounds carried meaning. Now it was thoroughly peeved, as if a simple task had proved surprisingly troublesome. There came a sense that this female creature had been underestimated, and some blame was to be assigned for this failure of foresight. Nevertheless, the job of destroying her had to be done. And this task the creature would accomplish, without further delay. It sprang over the overturned chair and rushed again.

This time it met the full force of the Witchblade, a steely haymaker that sent it crashing against the wall.

The thing was stunned, but only momentarily. It howled out pain and immense anger as it got to its feet.

To Sara, the thing was still just a black shape in the dark. There was a suggestion of the lupine–pointed ears, long muzzle, canine incisors–but there was more to the creature. It was humanoid, it was bipedal, and it had fully prehensile forelimbs tipped with wicked claws. That much detail was visible. But its shape seemed to shift and reconfigure at times, as if it were still deciding what it wanted to be, or perhaps the best shape to assume for the task at hand.

But it was wary now. It almost sauntered to its left, moving away from the wall, side-stepping upset furniture, and from it came a sound faintly like a chuckle, a false note of nonchalance, which was instantly belied. The thing swiped at a shelf, came away with some knickknack that had miraculously survived, and threw it viciously across the room.

She dodged it easily.

It chortled and kept ambling.

She tried to keep the jumble of wreckage between her and it, watching, trying to guess its next avenue of attack, for it was only a matter of time before it came at her again. She moved off to one side, stopped, recomputed the angles, moved once more. She could see enough detail in the apartment to do this. The creature, however, was still amorphous, mostly a black-on-black enigma. It seemed to bleed into the shadows, metamorphosing and flowing, and the shadows writhed themselves in coils and swirls.

They danced this way from room to room and back again to the living area. The thing feinted, swiped at the air, shadow-boxed and threatened, but made no move to carry through an attack. It had been stung, and it was chary of launching into another foray before gaining some overwhelming advantage.

The delaying tactics were getting to Sara. When this horrific *pas de deux* had gone on for over a minute, she took a step forward, tiring of the game.

"Bring it on, puppy dog," she said.

It almost laughed. You could have called it a laugh, a deeply malevolent chuckle that carried an edge of vicious glee.

You could almost hear it say, *Worry not, hellbitch, I shall accommodate you.*

But apparently she wasn't close enough.

"Let's get it on, dude."

You are a vexing creature. What exactly is your nature?

"Guess."

The thing did not answer. It stooped, picked up a magazine stand, and threw.

She ducked. "That all you can do? It seems so petty."

It threw a trivet table in answer.

She zigged, then zagged as a big glass ashtray went sailing past. It shattered in the darkness.

The thing roared as it lifted the huge couch.

"Careful, don't get a hernia. That is, if you have any balls."

But the move was a feint. The critter simply dropped the thing and bounded over it like a gazelle, and in so doing finally caught her by surprise.

In a flash, the enigma was on top of her, slashing and tearing, and it was all she could do to fend off its blows. One miss, and she was steak tartar. But she had no options other than to keep back. Move inside, and come in range of those oversize teeth, those impossibly long and gleaming white spikes of dentition that looked more appropriate on an alligator. Viewed at close quarters, the creature was a polyglot of animal configurations–there a touch of wild bore, here a hint of *Tyrannosaurus rex*. The wolfish composite was simply an overall style.

The thing got hold of her and she had to grab its muzzle with the gauntlet, which crushed the beast's mouth together like a garlic press. The thing howled in pain, and she squeezed tighter.

They rolled across the floor, debris flying everywhere. She kicked and punched, squeezed and wrestled. The smell of it was unbearable.

The rolling and straining and howling and everything else went on for an interminable period. Plaster fell from the walls, windows shattered.

At some point, her memory of specific actions trailed off . . . another discontinuity. Then time resumed and she was on her feet and hitting the thing. She struck it again and again with all her might, summoning all the strength of the Witchblade. She took a step back, hauled off, swung and landed a horrendous blow.

The thing lurched back.

She advanced and struck again. And again, and once more. The creature keened, shrinking under a rain of blows that could have reduced an elephant to hamburger. The beast backed off and hit a wall, fell to a sitting position.

She stood looking at it, arm raised for another smash. She froze.

The thing looked at her.

"Well?" she thundered.

The creature got up, shook itself, and stalked off in a huff, grumbling.

Okay, if you're going to be nasty about it . . .

She couldn't believe it as she watched the critter shamble back into the bedroom, presumably whence it had come.

Bitch.

The door slammed.

Sara bounded over to the door and threw it open. She wasn't surprised to find that the creature was gone.

Some semblance of mundane reality resumed. She finally found a light switch and flicked it on. Her Witchblade accoutrements had withdrawn back into the bracelet, leaving her in tattered clothing.

The place was . . . indescribable. Splinters of wood, scraps of paper, potsherds, blood, body parts–almost nothing in the room was in one piece save the sofa. She didn't want to inventory body bits. Not her job. She knew what had happened to Anton and Sergei. If indeed the parts added up to Anton and Sergei. She saw a severed head in a far corner. She did not want to identify it. Leave it to the forensic examiner.

The door flew open and two uniformed officers rushed in. They stopped in their tracks and gaped. She turned and regarded them, feeling rather odd.

One of them said, "What in the name of all that's holy . . . ?"

She tried to smile. "Uh, I can explain. . . ."

CHAPTER TWELVE

The study of Kenneth Irons was a study in itself, lavish with *objets d'art* and all manner of fine things. Busts of the legendary crowned the bookcases, deistic statues posed in corners. Egyptian antiquities occupied prominent places, the plunder of ransacked tombs lending an ancient resplendence. The room boasted many Oriental pieces as well.

Two Asian gentlemen were ushered in and seated.

"Good evening," said Irons as he seated himself across the lacquered table.

The two men nodded.

"Mr. Fong," he said to the one on his right. "Mr. Kitisawa," to the other. "The Triad and the Yakusa, together at last."

The two Asian men looked at each other and grunted.

"We do business all the time," said Kitisawa.

"Though at times we do compete," Fong said.

"No doubt," Irons said. "I will leave it to you to coordinate your activities with Asian organizations of other ethnic flavors: Viet, Thai, Indonesian, etcetera.

There really is quite an assortment these days. Mr. Fong, your operations center in Hong Kong and extend to San Francisco?"

"Yes."

"Mr. Kitisawa. Tokyo and Los Angeles, is it?"

"Quite so."

"And you both have networks here in the States, of course. I could have called a general conference, but this is more economical. Between the two of you, you control the vast, vast Pacific Rim."

"There is no problem about coordination," Mr. Fong said. "I should not worry, Mr. Irons."

"I rarely do. Gentlemen, by reputation, I know you to be modern-minded, forward-looking leaders. You know what the new spheres of activity encompass, what they entail. And, of course, the key is the computer and the infinite worldwide web it spins."

"Like a steel spider," Kitisawa said.

"One of silicon?" Fong ventured.

Kitisawa smiled.

"They say," Irons went on, "that no one can control the web. I think they are wrong."

Both his guests grinned broadly.

"I need you gentlemen to help me tame it. You need my . . . considerable resources."

"Yes, indeed," Fong replied.

"Quite so," Kitisawa agreed.

"Together I think we can impose some order on the chaos. I don't like wild, anarchic things. I like to control them. For instance, stock markets are wild, anarchic things."

Both men nodded.

"We are entering an entirely new era of world finance.

I can infuse your organizations with seed money that will reap not billions, but *trillions,* in return. You will cut yourself a piece of that. A large piece. I can afford to be generous. I'm interested more in control than in money. In fact, I have other interests entirely. But they are my private concern."

"We won't inquire," Kitisawa said.

"Thank you, gentlemen. My subordinates will contact you with details."

The two men across from Irons sat back, ready perhaps for a nice chat. Tea?

"That is all," Irons said.

The two sat up abruptly. They rose and bowed, then left the room.

Irons leaned back and irreverently put his feet up on the immaculately polished table.

He laughed.

"Okay, let's go over this again," Seltzer was saying. "You were conducting an undercover operation on your own . . ."

"Not exactly," Sara told him.

The room was crowded. At least a dozen crime scene investigators swarmed through the place, swabbing and gathering, scooping and bagging.

"Not exactly. Now, you know these guys. You went to a concert with them last night."

"With their boss, really."

"With their boss, a known organized crime figure."

"Yes."

"And you went out with this criminal for what reason, again?"

"To gather intelligence on his operations."

"On your own hook."

"On my own hook," Sara informed him.

"And you came up here, broke in . . ."

"Had the keys."

"Which you confiscated from the bartender, who, by the way . . ."

"He was there all night. He served me three drinks."

"And now no one's ever heard of him."

"Right. There's a different bartender down there now. He must have reported on duty when I came upstairs."

"But the new guy never heard of this other bartender. The baby-faced kid."

"That's what he says."

"So you have nothing and no one to back up your story."

"It's not a story," Sara told him. "It's a preliminary oral report."

"Yeah. Yeah."

"Seltzer!"

Sara and Seltzer turned toward the door as Joe Siry stormed in. He was about to say something when he caught sight of the carnage.

"Jesus Christ!" Appalled, he scanned the room with disgust. "What in God's green earth went on here?"

"We don't know," Seltzer said. "Detective Pezzini might, but she's not saying."

"Why do you assume she knows anything? Didn't she phone this in?"

"No," Seltzer said. "Patrons downstairs heard a ruckus upstairs and called 911. The local precinct answered the call. The officers who responded found your detective here, dressed like this." He gestured at her torn clothing.

"You off-duty?" Siry asked her.

"Yes," Sara said.

Siry turned back to Seltzer. "Then what's the problem?"

"The problem," Seltzer began, "is that no one else was in the apartment. No one saw anyone go down the back stairs to the bar, and the front entrance, which you get to via stairs on the other side of that door, is deadbolted from the inside. She sat in the bar all evening and even *she* says no one came down those back stairs. She was the only one seen in this apartment all night. No other way in or out."

Siry had wandered over to a shattered window and looked down. "That so?"

"There's reason to believe," Seltzer went on, "that the window was broken just before the officers arrived. They got here fast. They were cruising the neighborhood."

"Yeah? Okay, so you think my detective did all this?"

"I don't have any opinion. She says she found the place this way."

Siry whirled and roared, "*Then why the hell don't you believe her?*"

"I think I've outlined why there are some questions," Seltzer said mildly.

"The ruckus they heard," Sara put in, "happened after I went up."

"What happened when you went up?"

"I was attacked."

"Who did it?"

"Don't know, Cap. The apartment was dark."

"You fought this guy?"

"Uh . . . yeah."

"And what happened?"

"He got away. Ran into a bedroom and I guess went

out a window." She inclined her head toward Seltzer. "So much for the 'no other way out' theory."

"You didn't pursue?"

"As I said, Cap, it was dark. His eyes must have adapted. I was blind."

Siry nodded. "Uh-huh, uh-huh. Okay. Well, that explains that. I guess."

"We'll have to check the neighborhood for any sightings of somebody coming out that window," Seltzer said. "As I mentioned, there are questions, that's all. Plenty of them, including the question of how the guy could have jumped two stories onto concrete."

"Lots of second-story men can jump two stories," Siry said. "What's so hard to understand?"

Seltzer smiled unctuously. "I like a commanding officer who backs his men to the hilt. Loyalty is a two-way street. Admirable. Well, listen. I have to run, and the techs have to do their job. I'd like to see the report as soon as you can get it to me, Detective Pezzini."

"You'll get it," Siry said.

Seltzer shrugged amiably. "Fine." He turned and exited via the back stairs.

Siry walked slowly toward Sara. He crunched something underfoot, stopped, looked down, and kicked. A shard of china went skittering.

"Disturbing evidence?" Sara asked.

"This isn't evidence. This is a goddamn disaster."

"Sorry for another screw-up. Sorry I let him get away."

"What could you do? It was dark. You said."

"Yeah, I said that."

"Is it true?"

"It's true it was dark. It's also true that I don't know what the hell it was I tussled with. It was something weird, and yet another thing I can't really explain. Nor do I have an explanation for this mess. Except to say that the strange thing I encountered must have done it. Beyond that, I'll be novelizing my report again."

Siry laughed mirthlessly.

"Jesus H. Christ!"

They both turned to see Jake McCarthy standing at the back door. His jaw was hanging.

"Excuse the mess," Sara said. "We didn't have time to clean today."

"My God," Jake breathed. He extended his arms helplessly. "What . . . ?"

"Don't ask," Sara said. "What's even worse," she added to Siry, "is that I don't have an explanation for why no one heard anything before I went up. Because if the perp was hanging around, that sort of implies he'd just done it, and I walked in just after. But how did he do this butcher job without making a sound?"

"I see what you mean," Siry said. "That is a problem. You have any solutions?"

"Not at the moment." Sara sighed, shaking her head.

"Got any idea about a motive?" Siry asked.

"Nope. I *do* know that these two guys did the hit on Ashkenazi."

"How? I mean, how do you know?"

"Because I was out with them, and they disappeared at just the right time."

"You were out with their boss. Kontra."

"Yeah, and they were his bodyguards, his muscle. They left the concert about forty-five minutes before the hit went down. The victim was probably the guy who put out the contract on Kontra—the hit that failed."

"So Kontra's good for the hit," Siry said.

"Sure."

"So we can go to a judge and get a warrant. Easy."

Sara frowned and looked at the floor.

"Easy," Siry repeated. "Right?"

Sara started moving toward the door. "See you, Cap."

"Yeah, good night, Sara. Thanks. Oh, by the way . . ."

She stopped.

"You're to stay away from organized crime cases. I don't want you near anything resembling a mob-related incident. Leave it to the Task Force and the feds. And that's an order."

"Sure," she said in a small voice.

CHAPTER THIRTEEN

Mrs. Kontra?"

A dried husk of a face appeared in the crack between door and jamb.

"Who are you?

Sara held up her badge. "New York Police Department, ma'am. Some questions?"

"Who are you?"

As if the question had never been answered. Sara tried again. "NYPD? Police? We have some questions for Mr. Kontra."

"Who?"

"Mr. Lazlo Kontra. He lives here." That was not a question.

"No one lives here but me."

"We've talked to the super. We know who pays rent here."

"Go away, devil woman."

"Mrs. Kontra . . . if that's who you are."

"I'm his grandmother."

"Okay. Your grandson's name isn't on the lease, but he

lives here, full time. At least that's what the landlord will admit. Your grandson pays the rent. Do you live here, too?"

The old woman widened the door and looked at Sara for a long moment. "Come in. I want to see you."

"Uh . . . sure." *And what Bela Lugosi movie did* you *walk out of, Madame Ouspenskaya?*

Sara's idle thought got pushed aside as she entered what was a perfectly conventional apartment. The only thing Slavic about it (were Romanians Slavs?) was a faint odor of cabbage.

"Sit."

Sara sat in an easy chair with a flower-print slipcover. Very Wal-Mart. She watched the old woman disappear into the kitchen.

The babushka-headed woman returned shortly with a glass and a bottle. She sat the glass on the coffee table and poured out about two fingers of an amber liquid.

"Tuica," she said. "Plum brandy."

Ah, a traditional Romanian drink? It sounded good. Should she throw it down or mutter the usual dodge about being on duty? Well, she wasn't officially on duty, was she?

To hell with it. She lifted the glass and took the shot in one gulp. It was thick, sweet, and damn good. "Very nice. Thank you."

The woman sat on the matching sofa. She was smiling oddly.

"Where is Lazlo?" Sara asked.

The old woman shrugged. "He does not tell me where he go."

"My files say he has a farm upstate. Someone else owns it, but like this apartment, he has complete use of the place. But he makes the mortgage payments on the farm. Is that where he is?"

"I never go there."

"Are you saying it's true? That he does visit this farm now and then?"

"We were all farmers in the old country. Nothing else to do."

"I see. How often does he go there?"

"He doesn't tell me his business."

"And he has a lot of businesses. Right?"

The old woman shrugged.

Sara sat back. "You wanted to see me, you said."

"You are beautiful girl."

"Thank you, Mrs. . . . Madame Kontra?"

"I am Lazlo's father's mother. He calls me Baba. You can call me Baba, too."

"Baba, I need to talk to your grandson. He did a nasty thing to me."

The old woman raised her eyebrows. "He touched you?"

"I'm not talking about anything . . ." Sara sat up and unconsciously arranged her blue-jeaned legs more primly. More ladylike? Boy, this was going to be a hard interview. "He wasn't completely honest with me, Baba. He compromised me. Uh, I don't mean . . ."

"You are a strange one. That bracelet on your wrist."

Sara glanced at the Witchblade. "This? What about it?"

"It is old, very old."

"Yes, that's true. How did you know?"

"I don't know much. I am stupid old woman. But I can

see things. I see fire around this bracelet. Ghost fire. It is from a far place, somewhere men cannot reach. It is from hell, but it is not the devil's hell. It . . ."

Sara waited.

The old woman looked off. "I don't know," she said simply.

"Do you do magic?" Sara asked.

"I know some magic. I protect my grandson. He is in danger. He has enemies. He always has enemies. He needs protection by the spirits."

"Which spirits?"

"The good spirits. Not like the colored boy's."

Sara did a take. "What colored boy?"

"The colored boy, works for Lazlo. I see him here once. He is one of Lazlo's men, but not like the two big ones. He is like an owl. Very, very smart."

"And he does magic?"

"As black as his skin." Baba thought about it for a moment. "His skin is not so dark, actually. But you know what I mean."

"Have you talked with him about doing magic?"

"No. I never talk with him."

"I see. But you know he does magic."

"I see the light around him. Like you."

"Oh, I understand. You simply . . . intuited . . . uh, you saw the light."

"Yes. The magic light. He does evil magic. Sometimes. I don't think he is evil. He is just a boy, really. But he does dangerous things."

"There's some danger in using this evil magic?"

"Oh, my God, yes. Danger. The things, they come from Hell, and they do what you want, but then . . . ah, but then . . ." Baba chuckled.

"So this black person . . . what's his name?"

"I don't know."

"It would help if I had his name."

"People don't tell me their names. I mind my own business."

"I see. Baba, do you know what kind of business your grandson is in?"

"Oil. He has men drive oil truck."

"Yes. Did you know . . ." Sara turned and looked out the window. This was useless. She rose and smiled at Baba. "Thank you, Madame Kontra. Baba."

"Beautiful girl. Why do you dress like farm worker?"

"I've always been a tomboy."

"What is that? Why don't you wear a dress? You would look so pretty in nice dress."

"Sometimes I do."

"All the time, in Romania, they make women dress like men. The Communists liked that. I told them, I will work like dog, but I won't dress like man. That is wrong."

"Sure. Listen, thank you very much for talking to me. I'll let myself out."

The old woman got to her feet. She seemed to have life in her, for all that her skin looked like the Dead Sea Scrolls. "You are wanted by many spirits."

Sara looked over her shoulder as she advanced toward the door. "That so? By whom, exactly?"

"Strange spirits. I do not know them."

"Good or evil?" Sara asked as she opened the door.

"I don't know. I would tell you if I knew. I like you. You would make my grandson good wife if this one dies. Good wife."

"Uh . . . thank you. I think."

She went out and eased the door shut.

• • •

Sara stood at her desk, which was a mess. As usual. It was piled with printouts, reports, memos, bulletins, and endless other species of paperwork.

"Why *can't* you tell me?" she demanded.

She pressed the phone tighter to her ear, trying to block out the sound of the radio that someone insisted on playing full blast in his office. "What do you mean, 'need-to-know basis'? What's that supposed to mean? Are we talking about classified secrets, here?"

Jake McCarthy walked into the squad room with two civilians in tow, a middle-aged couple. Both were well-dressed and looked well-to-do. He saw that Sara was on the phone. "This is Detective Pezzini. She might be able to help you. She was the arresting officer."

The man said, "Thank you."

Jake exited. Sara was looking at the visitors out of the corner of one eye. "Okay. Yeah. Yeah. If that's how it is." She hung up and turned to face them. "Can I help you?"

"Yes," the man said. "You were the officer who was present when my son died?"

"Your son?"

"I'm Ross Bromley. Charles Bromley was my son. Charles Morton Bromley, the Second? He was named after his grandfather."

Sara started. "Oh. Oh, yes. I knew him by another name."

"Yes. 'Kool Whip,' I believe." Bromley sighed. "He . . . Charles lived on the street, didn't he? At least, he ended up there. He graduated from college, did you know that?"

"I wasn't aware."

"He studied art. He was quite a good sculptor, so they tell me."

"I see."

"Yes, he studied it in school. He started with painting but he decided it was—what was his phrase?—an 'effete art form.' He liked to work in metal. He had a show. Oh, this was quite a while ago."

"A show," Sara said. "Sculpture."

"Quite a while ago. Ten years. He was very young. And then he . . ."

"He got into drugs," the mother said.

"And he sort of fell apart. What we wanted to ask—"

"I'm very sorry," Sara blurted. "It was a tragic thing, your son's death."

"Thank you," Bromley said. "We wanted to know if he said anything before he threw himself off the balcony."

"Threw himself?"

"Well, that's what the letter from the police department said. It made it sound like suicide. That he threw himself off and killed himself."

"Oh. It wasn't quite like that. He fell. It was an accident."

"Well, the letter was really very unclear about that. It used the word accident, but the way it described what happened . . ."

"We just couldn't believe it," the mother said. "Not our Charlie. He was so full of life. When he was a boy . . ."

"We're not going to sue," the father said sternly. "We wanted to tell you that. Our society is being torn apart by litigation. Entirely too much legalistic folderol. We realize that Charles was in part culpable. We support the police."

"But we wanted to know if he said anything before he died," the mother said. "And he died so horribly. We want to know if he suffered."

"I don't think he did," Sara said evenly. "It was over

very quickly. He didn't have time to say anything. The whole thing was an unfortunate accident. I'm truly very sorry, Mr. and Mrs. Bromley."

"Thank you," the father said. "Uh, your name again? I'm sorry."

"Sara Pezzini."

"Thank you, Officer Pezzini," the mom said. "Can I ask exactly how you came to know our son?"

"He . . . worked with us. He helped us out on occasion. With tips, information."

"Oh, so he helped the police?" Mrs. Bromley asked.

"Yes, he did."

She smiled. "We didn't know that. He actually helped the police department?"

"He did a good job. I also saw his sculpture. He was very talented."

"He was," the mother said, glowing inside. A single tear had welled up, and it hung at the corner of her eye like a tiny diamond. "He was so talented."

When they left, Sara felt as if she had shrunk a few inches during the conversation.

She got back on the phone.

"One bam!"

"Two crack!"

These Chinese played Mah Jongg with a vengeance. Fast, and tiles face down, announced once and then hidden for the rest of the hand. Not American style, where they lie face up. You had to have a good memory and keep your ears open. And lots of money to get a seat at the table. At a buck a point, this was no game for amateurs.

Merlin looked at his tiles. He was waiting for one tile, a white dragon. He had a red and green. A white would give him a rare hand, one worth many points. Dragons were not often discarded, but sometimes a player had no choice but to discard, if he had only one and no match.

Chen was smiling at him. "You haven't put up any tiles? You must be working on something, or trying for a completely hidden hand."

"I like to play it close to the vest," Merlin said.

"I like the way you play," Chen said, picking up a tile. "You play fast. Not like most Americans."

"I'm having trouble keeping up with you guys. Thanks for sticking to English most of the time."

"Least we can do. This is a friendly game. As I said, I think you'll enjoy working with us. You're very talented and knowledgeable. We can make a lot of money in the east. Hong Kong is still a wide-open city."

"I'm sure. What wind are we on?"

"North. This is the last hand, Merlin."

"Ah. Okay, thanks. Is it my turn?"

"Yes."

Merlin took a tile from the Wall, looked at it, and set it down. "Six bamboo."

"Got it," the player to Merlin's right announced. He took the tile and matched it up with two more of its like on his rack. The triplet was worth only two points, but it was good towards Mah Jongg.

"I hear," Merlin said, "that the mainland government is being very cooperative with business. They don't want to kill the goose, so to speak."

"That is completely right. We have many contacts in Peking. Most people don't think that would be the case."

"Seems natural to me," Merlin said.

"You have no problem with that, then?" Chen asked.

"Not in the least. I like the sound of your money."

"You'll find us much more generous than our Russian colleagues."

"They're pretty tight with a ruble. Or a dollar, I should say."

"Then we have a deal?" Chen asked.

"White dragon," said the player in the East position, and put down a tile. Merlin grabbed it. There was no dragon on the white tile; just a black border. A white dragon is invisible in snow.

"Mah Jongg!" Merlin peeled.

"Very good!" Chen said amiably.

Merlin put up his tiles.

Chen's jaw dropped. "Oh, my God."

Merlin laid out one of each dragon, one of each wind, one each of suit in terminals.

"Fourteen Noble Scholars!" Chen exclaimed in genuine amazement. "I've seen that hand only one other time in my life!"

"I was dealt most of it," Merlin said with pride. "I had to draw only three tiles, but had to wait forever for that last dragon."

"Amazing," Chen said. "Well, that's a limit hand. And limit for this club is a thousand points. You've just won three thousand dollars. Thank Confucius you weren't East. You would have cleaned us out."

CHAPTER FOURTEEN

As she drove farther out into the countryside, Sara couldn't get some thoughts out of her mind. The general way the department handled informants sometimes bothered her. How many times had her division used the squeeze, threatening an informant with an indictment unless he or she cooperated? Sometimes the informant had to place his life on the line, risk retaliation, retribution. A few times such an informant had paid with his life. The squeeze was an oft-used tool of the district attorney's office, with the police implementing.

She had always hated it. For all that informants were usually low-life scum, they had rights, too. She felt a general, all-purpose guilt over Charlie Bromley's death. The specifics didn't apply. She hadn't squeezed him, but she could not get shed of doubts about the ethics of standard police tactics.

It was a cold day, the first really cold day of fall. Clouds drifted like smoke across a white sky broken only by bare trees. She urged the little subcompact along a two-lane road, hayfields at either shoulder. She was far into Connecticut, and if she drove half an hour more, she'd be in Massachusetts.

Obeying directions given at a convenience store a few miles back, she bore left at the next intersection and took a narrow oil-and-gravel road. She was looking for a small farm owned by a family named Paunescu. That was the name on the list of Kontra's "Known Associates (Possible Non-Combatants)." People he did business with but were not soldiers in the Organizatiya. The Paunescu family lived on the farm, but did not own it. They lived rent free; nevertheless, they were virtual tenants. They did whatever Kontra needed of them. Kontra's name was not to be found on the deed or any legal title to the land, but he was lord of every acre. The Paunescus were, in effect, his serfs.

At least that was her theory. And it was a pretty good theory. These absentee-owner farms, the fiefdoms of an ethnic rainbow of gangs, lay all over the tri-state area. They served various purposes: hideouts, storage facilities, and potter's fields for the dead bodies of people who would never be seen again by kith or kin.

Thank God she knew someone in the district attorney's office. Guy who'd been wanting to date her for years. She hoped she didn't have to return the favor someday. He was nice, but hardly her type. Another reason to feel guilty.

The Paunescus' farm had been on that list, and its location. She was taking an awful chance.

Siry would kill her if he found out. She knew he would eventually. She wondered if she subconsciously liked it when she ran afoul of him, if she relished the attention that got her. The daddy's-little-girl syndrome again?

She pushed it from her mind.

Besides, she'd missed the dirt road she was looking for. She hit the brakes and turned around. As she did, a few lone snowflakes drifted past the windshield. This early? Then she glanced at the date on her watch and realized how much of the month had melted away. Winter was almost here.

She saw now that she'd driven past a narrow dirt road that debouched onto the pavement behind some tall weeds. The lone sentinel of a mailbox stood beside it. The lettering read PAUNESCU. She turned in.

The road was rutty but passable. Gravel bounced off the undercarriage. The road wound through tall trees interspersed with brambles of brown underbrush. Tufts of green appeared here and there, last remnants of summer making a stand, and here and there branches hung festooned with colorful fall foliage.

A single red leaf fluttered to the hood and blew off.

Fog began to gather. Fast, as if on cue, it coalesced and transformed crisp air to thick, heavy soup. She slowed the car. A farmhouse appeared ahead, something behind it. Another house, or a barn? It was bigger than the main house. Or the rear house was the main house.

She pulled up to the end of the driveway and parked beside an aging foreign pickup. She got out. The place, of dirty white siding with faded blue shutters, was a little run down, but looked comfortable in a squalid kind of way. This was no prosperous farm, if farm it really was. Junk littered a side yard. She looked it over. The obligatory rusting pickup with attendant old refrigerators.

She mounted the rickety porch and knocked on the door. After some activity inside, it opened, and a man in his forties poked his head out.

"Yes?"

"Mr. Paunescu?"

"You probably want my father. He owns the place. He's not well. Can I help you?"

"Is Mr. Kontra here?"

The man, rather sallow-faced and thin, acquired a blank look. "Who?"

"Is that his house in the back?"

"Place has been empty for years," he said.

"Does your father own it?"

"Yes."

"Really? And you live in this place?"

"It's mainly for hunters. Weekenders, that sort of thing. My dad rents it out. Who may I ask are you?"

"I'm a New York City police officer, looking for Mr. Lazlo Kontra. Do you know him?"

"I've heard of him."

"Is he a friend of your father's?"

"Not sure."

"Could he be currently renting the back place?"

"I don't think anyone's rented the back place for a while. I haven't seen a car parked there. My father doesn't tell me his business. Sorry."

"You live here and don't know if anyone's renting the place?"

"Haven't been back there for a while."

"You do live here?" Sara asked.

"Yes, with my parents. They're getting old, and I take care of the place, more or less. Look, what's this all about, if I can ask?"

"I'm simply looking for him. Had trouble getting in touch with him lately."

His eyebrows drew together suspiciously. "Do you have a search warrant?"

"This isn't an official visit. I'm a friend of his."

"Really? Oh. Well, you're asking a lot of questions. Only my father can answer, and he's sleeping. He shouldn't be disturbed. As I said, he's sick. His heart."

"Is your mother here?"

"No. She's visiting relatives. Sorry. I'll tell my father you dropped by."

"Mind if I look the place over?"

"Uh . . ."

"I was thinking about renting a place in the country. For weekends."

The man was reluctant, but didn't want to appear evasive. "I guess you can look around."

"Thanks."

He poked his head out the door. "Weather's turning bad. Looks like snow."

"Yeah, it's starting to come down. I'll just look the place over and leave. Sorry to bother you."

"Okay."

She walked around the back of the place. More junk, but it had an ordered look to it. A large vegetable garden lay on the outskirts of a neglected lawn. A few hardy plants still grew in it, onions and such.

The house in back was farther away than she'd first thought. It stood on a rise that sloped away rapidly to deep woods. She stuck to the trees as she walked around the right side. There was a vehicle parked behind the house, a black late-model SUV.

The house was one of those modern log constructions, but was hardly a cabin. It looked to have at least ten rooms, all on one floor. A huge fieldstone chimney dominated the rear. A big deck patio ran off sliding glass doors and massive windows at the other end of the house.

She sneaked up on a small back window and looked in. The lights were on inside a bedroom that looked to have been converted to an office. A young black man sat at a compact workstation typing on a desktop computer. She'd never seen the young man before, but could guess who he was. Another man, a husky type with the look of a street hood, sat in an easy chair on the other side of the room reading a slick men's magazine. He had the centerfold out and was studying it intently.

She peeked in. Almost instantly, the black man turned and saw her. He made no reaction other than to shift his eyes to the zine-reading gunsel. Then he looked at her again, at first quizzical, then pleading, his eyebrows communicating something. What was he trying to say? To Sara it looked as though he were warning, *Watch out.*

Sara flattened herself against the log exterior.

Wait. This was no good. She wasn't going to break into the place. This wasn't a raid. Couldn't be. She didn't have authorization to be here, let alone a warrant. This was another jurisdiction entirely. Hell, this was another state.

When in doubt, launch an all-out frontal assault.

She walked around the building, mounted the spacious porch, and knocked at the front door. As she did, snow began to fall in earnest.

The door stayed shut. She gave it at least a minute, then knocked again.

The door opened. And there stood the man who'd been reading the girly zine. "Come in, Detective."

"I don't believe I've had the pleasure," Sara said as she stepped into a big foyer. She never seen a log cabin with a foyer before.

"Vladimir," he said.

"You work for Mr. Kontra?"

"Yes. He will see you. Come this way, please."

Vladimir led the way out of the foyer and straight into a huge room with an imposing fireplace, to the right of which began a sweeping panorama of windows.

Kontra stood in the corner, smiling at her.

"What a surprise," he said.

"Was in the neighborhood, thought I'd drop in," Sara said.

"I'm glad you did. I suppose you want to talk to me."

"I'm really pissed off at you."

Kontra nodded understandingly. "I see. I see. Well, I don't blame you. It was unfortunate, the way it looked."

"That way what looked?"

"That I used you as alibi."

"Ah, that occurred to you," Sara said brightly.

"Yes. Yes, it looked that way, but it isn't true. Ashkenazi . . . well, I heard about him. He was my enemy. He hates me from way back. In Moscow. He thinks I killed his brother. He was thief, and his brother, too. His brother was killed in prison, and he blames me."

"You didn't strangle him?"

Kontra's right eyebrow lifted slightly. "How did you hear this accusation?"

"These things get around."

"But this happened in Russia long time ago. Please sit."

Sara took a seat on one of the plaid couches. "So it happened?"

"I misspoke. It *didn't* happen in Russia, long time ago, my killing him. But he died in prison. That happened."

"Ashkenazi was your enemy, but you didn't have him killed?"

"No."

"You didn't send Anton and Sergei to shoot him with a .22 caliber pistol?"

"No."

"But now Anton and Sergei are dead."

"Yes. And you were there."

Sara crossed her long legs. "You have ways of getting information, too."

"Absolutely," Kontra said. "You were there. Not only that, you might have killed them."

"Really. You think that."

"Baba thinks that, too."

"So we each suspect the other of murder."

"Looks that way. I'm wondering why you come here."

"I'm wondering, too," Sara said. "Maybe it's because I have no other way of solving this case."

"What case are you solving. Ashkenazi?"

"Maybe. You wiseguy cases are all the same. It's not so much solving the case as getting court evidence that won't disappear or end up dead. And killing Anton and Sergei is a good way of getting rid of evidence."

Kontra said, "You want a drink?"

"No thanks."

"Why did you come here? What do you think you will find?"

"I don't know. But I wonder what we'd find if we dug around."

Kontra shrugged. "Dirt. This is farm, you know."

"You never know what you might find in the dirt."

Kontra looked off. "There are roads, they run near the property. Anybody can stop, dig, bury something."

"You know where all the bodies are buried."

Kontra laughed. "Where do you think you will start? There are four hundred acres."

"Be interesting to see what we can dig up."

"Have a good time."

Vladimir came in and said something in Russian to Kontra. Kontra expressed annoyance and gave an order. Vladimir nodded and left in a hurry.

"What was that all about?" Sara asked.

"Nothing."

"Did your guest take a hike?"

"Guest?"

"The black kid. Your hacker."

"Hacker?" Kontra echoed.

"Computer whiz. Techno-nerd."

"You know, American slang is still mystery to me sometimes. There is so much of it. Russian slang has lots, too. But I think I hear new American slang every day."

"Romanian have slang?"

"Not so much. More dialect, you call it."

"He seems to be here against his will," Sara told him. "He been giving you trouble?"

"No trouble."

"Are you going to sic the werewolf on him?"

"What nonsense do you speak now? Werewolf. What do you think, you are in movie?"

"I think that's what did in Anton and Sergei."

Kontra frowned dyspeptically. "Now you are making me sick. You accuse some werewolf, but you did it."

"What in the world makes you think that? Did Baba give you that idea?"

"She says nothing about werewolf. She says you are devil woman."

"I don't know, Lazlo. Romania, werewolves. Kind of go together."

"Do you think we are magicians? Witches, sorcerers? Romanians are just people. You shouldn't believe Hollywood."

"I don't. But I know I didn't tear Anton and Sergei apart. I have no motive. I'm a police . . . person." Sara cringed inwardly.

Kontra guffawed. "You think that makes you holy? I made inquiries into your department. You are far from holy person. You are soon to be indicted."

Sara looked at him calmly. But her stomach twisted. "Your sources aren't very accurate."

"We'll see. It is funny. You come here, you charge me with killing stupid thief Ashkenazi. Mob hit, you say. But you are charged with being mob hit man."

"Hit person. The silly things some people say."

"Yes. Like you will dig for bodies here. You won't find anything. And who will listen when district attorney indicts you? No one."

"I'm still going to come here and dig."

"Not today?" Kontra leaned forward. "You don't have warrant?"

"Not today. But I'll be back."

"You don't have warrant? You just come up here to talk?"

"Pretty much. Just to let you know that I'm on to you."

It sounded lame even to Sara. But she wasn't about to let her face show it.

"Oh," Kontra said quietly, nodding. "That's nice."

Sara rose. "I'm taking the kid."

"What?"

"The hacker kid. I believe he's here under duress. I'm taking him back to New York, if he wants to go."

Kontra rose and shrugged expansively. "He's not here."

"I saw him through the window."

"He left. He's not prisoner. You are making a mistake."

"He ran off, probably. Didn't you send Vladimir after him?"

"I sent Vladimir on errand."

"I'll bet."

Sara drew her pistol. Kontra laughed at it.

"You are silly thing. What do you think you will do?"

"Just in case Vladimir gives me trouble."

"You are not in New York. This is state of Connecticut. You have no business up here."

"Connecticut is New York's bedroom. So long, Laz."

Sara walked to the sliding glass door and yanked it open. It slid with alarming ease and thumped violently against the opposite jamb.

"Careful!" Kontra yelled.

"Sorry."

"Crazy woman."

Snow already covered the yard. It was a thick, wet, early snow, the kind that slops down in late October and tries to get a head start on Christmas. But it never works. It melts almost instantly and makes a fool of itself.

Just like Sara now. She struck out into the yard and got to the woods in about fifty quick paces.

The woods were snowy, dark, and deep, but Sara had no promises to keep, and she hoped the kid hadn't run miles into the forest. She found Vladimir's tracks easy enough. She was no woodsman, but the guy had big feet and the snow had just fallen minutes before. A blind man could have seen where he'd lit off after the kid.

The kid. Actually, he could have been in his late thirties. "Baby-faced kid," though, was the part he looked. Maybe it was his nerdly quality. Nerdish?

A shot, followed by three more in rapid succession. An eight-millimeter semiautomatic, for sure. The sound was a muffled popping that somehow hurt the ears.

Sara cut to her left. She wanted to see what Vladimir was shooting at without getting in the line of fire. She loped on into the woods, hearing some commotion off to her right and up ahead.

The snowfall was thinner here because of the trees, but the fog was gathering. It was getting harder to see. She heard something, though. Something moving through the trees. Branches were snapping like toothpicks. It was big.

Very big. And strong. She had no idea what it was or exactly where it was.

More pops. Same gun, it sounded like. Vladimir was shooting at the thing, whatever it was, and he was retreating.

Something in the woods suddenly flashed and burned. The sound was like a huge blowtorch.

Sara thought that was strange. A huge blowtorch in the woods. One that moved. Something was moving up ahead, sliding through the trees and snapping branches. She couldn't see anything definite, though. All she saw was a moving white-on-white blur.

She heard a man scream. Sara stopped momentarily, then jumped to her right. She had found a deer trail, a narrow path, and ran along it toward the commotion.

Before long something very strange came along the trail the other way, running spastically. A burning man. A man on fire, his head and entire body wreathed in flames, his hair a torch.

He was screaming in pain and fear. Sara stopped and let him come at her.

He was screaming in Russian. It was Vladimir, and he

was burning to death. Sara kicked at his ankle as he passed and he went sprawling into the snow. She used her foot again to flip him over.

"Roll roll, roll!" she yelled.

He did his best, flopping over in the snow. The flames wouldn't go out so she grabbed him and rolled him, again and again until his clothes were smoking but no longer on fire.

His face was mostly carbonized, his hair burned away. He groaned and his eyes rolled up white.

"Vladimir?" she said.

He rallied to consciousness briefly, then slipped away again.

CHAPTER FIFTEEN

She tried to do what she could, but Vladimir was never going to get up again. She knelt there by him, a little stunned and mystified.

She got up. Vladimir was charred almost beyond recognition, but still had some life in him. She could only call for paramedics. Surely they had paramedics in this county. She got out her cell phone and hit the call button.

No service. She'd have to go back to the house. She didn't want to, but however Vladimir had conducted his life, whatever he had done in the service of some crime lord, he was still deserving of help, and she would not let him die without a call for medical aid. It was her duty as a police officer. But she had to get back first.

Which way? Simple, follow her own tracks. But the fog grew soupier as she walked and somehow she lost her own tracks. She walked on in the only direction the house could have been, or so she thought. She tramped down a shallow depression and up again.

The big log house wasn't where it should have been.

She was lost, and the fog was congealing into gaspacho;

tree trunks looked like utility poles on a London street. She could see almost nothing else. Again, though, she could hear something. It sounded familiar: slavering and gibbering, with undertones of both menace and glee.

The werewolf was now stalking her.

The fire for Vladimir; for her, getting torn apart in a rustic setting. How quaint, how positively quaint. She began to run. The snow was not yet deep, and she managed a good pace.

She ran for a good five minutes, crossing tracks at right angles twice. At least she was staying in the same general area. She ran through a patch of still-smoking woods where all the snow had melted. Tree trunks smoldered. That had been one powerful blast. More than enough to toast Vladimir.

She took a hard right, the lupine gibbering and slavering still at her heels. The thing could move fast, at least as fast as she could run. And she was now running with all her might.

The thing was gaining. Its insane chortling came closer and closer. She strained to get some distance between her and it.

The inevitable trip and fall.

She had seen it in countless movies. A female runs from the monster; she trips and falls, automatically. A movie trope if there ever was one. The chick can't get three steps before–whoopsy daisy.

And neither could she. Her right foot hit an especially slippery patch of snow, whipped out sideways, and sent her tumbling. She rolled three times and ended up sitting. The werebeast ran full tilt right at her.

She raised her arms to block a lunge for the throat.

Out of the way, bitchface.

The shaggy creature leapt over her and continued running.

Astounded, she got to her feet and followed it. Very soon she came out of the woods, into the yard, and she saw the critter lope across the garden, mindless of the onions and cauliflower, cross the lawn, bound across the deck, and throw the glass door open. The furry thing moved like nothing she had ever seen.

She heard Kontra scream.

Breaking into a dead run, she heard him begin to scream again, a horrible truncated exclamation of terror that terminated in a gurgle.

When she found him on the other side of the couch, there was less to do for him than for Vladimir. His throat was missing and a river of blood was flowing across the beige carpet. The beast was nowhere in sight. As if it had evaporated.

"Lazlo?" she said feebly. He could not answer. She fumbled with the cell phone, then remembered it was useless.

The Paunescu son barged in as she was dialing the house phone. He caught sight of Kontra's body and froze. Then he fixed Sara in a horrified stare. He turned and ran out of the house like a horse from a burning barn.

She hung up the phone, deciding she did not want to deal with Connecticut authorities. She hadn't identified herself to Paunescu. Who's to say she'd been here at all?

She did not want to be put into the position of explaining the unexplainable again, and especially not for strangers. Siry and Jake and even Seltzer were one thing; hick cops or state troopers were quite another.

Speaking of explanations, where was that little twerp?

Well, he wasn't little, not actually. But he was twerp-like, for sure. What the hell was his story?

There was yet another mystery to put with all the others. The Witchblade had been strangely silent throughout all this. She had felt a dull throb or two, but that was all. As if the Blade had seen it all before and was not impressed. Even when the Werewolf was almost on her, it fairly yawned, as if it knew the Werewolf had no intention of attacking it, knew the creature had been charged with a more pressing assignment and was not about to bother with an adversary it could not best.

A flicker of a shadow. She turned, and there on the deck stood the twerp, looking in. He smiled sheepishly as he slid the door aside and stepped in.

"This your handiwork?" she asked him.

The kid inched closer, mesmerized by the sight of the mangled body, the blood. He seemed ambiguous about his feelings. Something like shock and a morbid glee vied for registration on his face. "No, man. Jesus, all that blood."

"The human body has quite a lot. You should have seen Anton and Sergei's apartment."

"Oh, man. Oh, man. That's really disgusting," the kid said, not able to shift his eyes away. "Almost took his head right off."

"Was this any of your doing?" she asked.

He shook his head. "No, no. I didn't do it."

"But did you conjure something that did?"

He looked at her. "Are you serious?"

"I'm totally serious. You do magic, don't you?"

"I dabble. It's long been an interest."

"But you can do real magic."

"I can do some things. But stuff like *that*? I can't do that."

She tried to gauge his sincerity. As far as she could tell, he was truthful. "Well, something did it. And that something wasn't normal. It was paranormal."

He asked, "What was it?"

"You didn't see it?"

"No. I heard some kind of animal noises. But I didn't see anything. Was it some kind of bear or something?"

"Bear? Hardly. It looked to me . . ." Sara scratched her head. It sounded so goofy. "You think you might possibly have conjured a werewolf?"

"Jesus Christ! Nothing I've been doing would conjure a freaking werewolf. Where did that crap come from? You sayin' a werewolf did this?"

"Same one I tangled with in the Russians' apartment. I think."

"You tangled . . ." He stepped back a few paces. Brooding, he walked slowly toward the windows. "Jesus. I don't know what the hell is going on. I gotta think about all of this."

"What went on in the woods?" Sara asked.

"That I have no idea. Some kind of big fire. I took off out the window, and that big dude was chasing me. Then I heard some kind of explosion, and I could see the woods burning."

"The big dude burned, too," Sara told him.

"I know. I saw him layin' out there. He's dead, too."

"What could have done it?"

"Have no idea."

She looked at him levelly. "We need to talk."

"You're a cop, aren't you?"

"Yeah."

"I thought so. Look, these guys were making me do the stuff. Extortion. I had no choice."

"Stuff?"

"Computer scams. I did some stuff for them. They liked it, and wanted more. Lots more. They wouldn't leave me alone. No one seems to be able to leave me alone, ever."

"I have a suggestion," Sara said. "Let's get the hell out of here."

"I second the motion."

"By the way, what's your name? I like to know who my partners in crime are."

"Merlin Jones."

As they headed south, the snow turned to rain and the road became a wet mirror.

It was not long before they were back in the more affluent areas of Connecticut. Huge mansions rolled past, some of the highest-priced real estate in the country.

"You don't think the guy in the house will talk?" Jones asked.

"Don't know. He's spent his life not talking to the police. Runs in the family. He might tell about me, might not. If they think he did it, and start to squeeze, he might blab. But I can't see why they'd think he did it. They'd go for the bear theory. If there are any bears in Connecticut, which I somehow doubt."

"I think there are."

"Whatever. Of course, I don't know what they'll make of Vladimir. Spontaneous combustion? A dragon loose?"

Merlin looked sharply at her. Then his gaze drifted out the window.

"Does that mean something to you?" Sara asked.

He shrugged. "I play Mah Jongg occasionally."

"Mah Jongg?"

"Yeah. Dragons. Red, green, white. You can't see white dragons in snow."

"I know nothing about the game. Never played it."

"Yeah, well in the States it's usually played by ladies of the club, that sort. But in China it's a man's game. Fast and furious and for lots of money."

"They play it in Chinatown?"

"Sure."

"And do you have any Chinatown connections?"

"That's how I ran afoul of Kontra. I refused to work for him, and the Triad courted me. I let them. All Kontra wanted to run were scams that the cyberpolice have been onto for years. He was going to get me busted, for sure. All he was about was money. He didn't appreciate the finer points. He didn't see it as the art it is."

"Hacking?"

"Yeah, hacking. He didn't appreciate the man-machine interface, you know? The cybernetic future dream. He didn't appreciate anything. And he didn't want to pay me what I was worth."

"It wasn't like the novels, was it?"

"Not really. It's just stealing. I know that. But . . . these guys, they just want to take."

"That's what they're into, Merlin. You didn't realize that?"

"I copped to it pretty early. I don't really need them, except . . . well, I had trouble paying the rent on time. I mean, in New York City, they bust your bank account for a pad the size of a closet. Kontra got me this big apartment, he made it easy. But he didn't pay me anything. Or anything substantial."

"You say you don't need them. Why don't you just rake in millions on your own?"

"It's not that easy. Most hackers aren't rich. Quite the opposite. We don't need that much money, really. But to make big money you need connections. You need money laundering. You need guys in Europe and Malaysia, overseas banks, all that stuff. Kontra had guys who could take the stuff I gave them and turn it into lots of cash. But the Triad will pay me what I'm worth."

"I don't know, Merlin. Seems to me some company could pay you one hell of a good salary for your skills. Ever consider going legit?"

"I do some work for legitimate companies, on a consultant basis. Sometimes."

"Like for who?"

"Irons International. I've done some work for Mr. Irons himself."

Sara was silent for a mile or two.

"Let's see if we can sum it up," she finally said. "Werewolves, dragons, Gypsy women . . ."

"Huh?"

"Kontra's grandmother."

"Oh, God, her. Like something out of a cult movie."

"Romanians, Russians. Werewolves. Dragons. Put it all together . . . . wait. And another thing."

She fell silent again. The rain-slick road rolled by as Merlin regarded her.

"Yeah?"

"Know anything about a big bird?"

Merlin chuckled. "Right. *The Horror That Came to Sesame Street.*"

"Big bird in the sky. Coming out of a computer."

"Weird. What's *that* shit about?"

"You tell me. You're the magician."

"I do Kabbala. I mean, I study Kabbala. Numerology, mystical stuff. I do mandalas in Photo Shop. There's some really neat stuff . . ."

"I've heard of it. I mean, Kabbalistic magic. Know practically nothing about it. And mandalas . . ."

"From Sanskrit mysticism. I like to mix different ancient hermetic traditions. That's the kind of stuff I'm interested in. Ancient magic rituals, gods, spirits, demiurges. Fascinating stuff. I've been into it for years."

"Ever run into bird spirits?"

"Oh, of course. Many bird images in the ancient lore. The ibis-headed god of Egypt. That sort of thing."

"So what does it all mean? And what does Irons have to do with it?"

"He's interested in magic. Ancient lore."

"Oh, yeah," Sara said, nodding.

"You know him?" Merlin wanted to know.

Sara nodded. "I do."

"Then you know he appreciates the finer things. He appreciates me."

"That's nice. You like the finer things. Like what, for instance?"

"Art. I do art. Computer art, now. I started in oils long time ago. Studied it in school. But the computer's the greatest artist's brush to come along in years. Hasn't caught on in the academy yet."

"You're an artist?" Sara said. "Techno-nerd and artist. Not a common combo."

"Watch that 'nerd' stuff. I'm no nerd. I'm an artist of the Two Cultures that C. P. Snow talked about. Science and Art. Double-threat guy. That's me. I have things in mind, projects. Things never dreamed before. Works of art that . . . you have no idea."

"I'd be interested in hearing about them. Were you afraid that Kontra would kill you?"

"He knew he needed me. That was my hold over him. There are lots of hackers, but none of 'em can do what I do. I'm good, if I do say so myself."

"Just what kind of stuff were you doing in the magical area? Spells?"

"My stuff is New Age. It's modern, hip. No potions, no gypsy voodoo. It's just good luck-bad luck stuff. You increase your numerological odds, you stack the metaphysical deck in your favor."

"What's the bad luck part?"

"That's a weapon, sort of."

"Weapon?"

"Yeah. For your enemies. It's basic magic. You stack the deck in your favor and against your enemies' best interests. The effects can range from mild to lethal."

"Lethal?"

"Yeah, but I never do that. That involves invoking dark forces. I never do that. I just put a . . . well, you could call it a curse. You could call it bad karma. Or non-optimal feng shui."

"A curse isn't so modern," Sara said. "And who's say you didn't inadvertently invoke something you ought not to have invoked?"

"That's where the computer comes in. Precision. It's the modern magician's tool. I've pioneered this stuff. It's my technology. I'm the George Washington Carver of computer magic."

"So you put curses on people who get in your way."

"*Who mean to do me harm,*" Jones said hotly. "Are you kidding? Of course I do. No law against it."

"Nope. No law. Except the moral one."

" 'Do what thou wilt shall be the whole of the law.' "

"Who said that?" Sara asked.

"Alistair Crowley."

"*He* was a wholesome guy," she muttered sarcastically.

"He penetrated to the mystical heart of the noumena."

"And he was great in the sack?"

Merlin grinned. "Matter of fact, he was reputed to be."

"Merlin, you have to face something. Whatever you've been doing, it may have led to what happened back there. And maybe what happened to Anton and Sergei."

"Can't be."

"Yes."

"No," Merlin insisted. "Take that dragon. Dragons are good luck signs in Chinese lore. That was a white dragon, the luckiest because they can't be seen to be hunted. At least in winter."

Sara nodded. "They don't kill people?"

"Not saying that. But dragons aren't evil in Chinese culture. Not like in the West."

"Okay."

Merlin gave an expansive shrug.

"Whatever that's worth."

She let him off on Seventh Avenue, around Seventh Avenue and West 34th Street.

"I guess you're not arresting me," Merlin said, holding the door open.

"I guess not. Nothing to arrest you for. Nothing anyone

would believe. As for the computer mischief, I'll leave you to the feds."

"Right. Well, take it easy."

"You, too. Don't let any non-optimal feng shui spoil your day."

"Yeah, don't take any wooden werewolves."

She thought about nothing much on her way to the station. After handing in the car at the motor pool, she walked to the squad room wanting nothing more than a cup of coffee. She had an hour to kill before starting her watch, and she wanted simply to relax.

"Pezzini."

She turned. "Hi, Jake."

Jake looked grim. "Sara, uh, this is hard."

"What is it?" She studied his face. "Something wrong?"

"Uh . . ."

She poured a cup of coffee and looked around for artificial sweetener. None here. All out. She made a mental note to order some. She turned and took notice that Jake wouldn't get out of her way. "Jake, what the hell is it?"

"Sara, the District Attorney wants to see you."

CHAPTER SIXTEEN

"Racketeering?" Sara practically shouted. "Are you insane?"

The newly-appointed interim District Attorney looked embarrassed. After all, he hadn't cooked this up. His deputies had.

One of them, Morrison, sat to the right of his boss's big desk. He was thin-faced and balding. "That's right. We may be able to proceed against you under the Racketeering Influenced and Corrupt Organizations Act. RICO. And we have at least five possible counts, possibly six, though the death of Charles Bromley is still officially an accident. We believe . . . that is, we have reason to believe that you are a hired assassin for the mob. A hit man. Uh, woman."

"Any particular mob?" Sara said. She was calm now, and resolved not to raise her voice again. The craziness of the charge had blindsided her.

"You are a known associate," Morrison went on, "of Lazlo Kontra . . . uh, the late Lazlo Kontra . . . who headed up a crime family out of south Brooklyn. You have been possibly linked to several murders that could have been mob executions. You were seen at one of Kontra's hideouts up in Connecticut. The State of Connecticut authorities want to talk to you about two deaths. We suspect your activities are interstate and possibly international."

"Crazier and crazier," Sara said.

"Detective Pezzini," said the District Attorney in a tone kindlier than his subordinate's, "don't you really think you should have counsel present?"

"I haven't heard anything yet to justify my retaining an attorney. I haven't heard you say you have any proof that I'm a hired assassin."

"The RICO law allows the prosecutor a lot of latitude," Morrison informed her. "It doesn't involve the usual 'beyond reasonable doubt' criterion. It's more like a civil case. Preponderance of evidence."

"Even if the evidence is as flimsy as what you have?" Sara asked pointedly. "Besides, RICO is a federal charge."

"We could easily refer the case to federal authorities."

"Why don't you?" Sara said.

Morrison started to say, "We will–"

The District Attorney cut him off. "It's a local matter for now. In fact, it's still really only an internal matter of the police department. Actually, we are really acting on information mainly supplied to us by Mr. Seltzer here."

Seltzer was sitting well back and away. But he was definitely present, as if auditing a course. "Yes, that's quite true. We've been watching Ms. Pezzini for a while. We've tracked her movements. For instance, she was observed heading for the Connecticut state line."

"But your operatives broke off surveillance," Sara said.

Seltzer's perpetual grin faded. "Internal Affairs has no authorization to cross state lines. We don't have jurisdiction.

But that didn't stop you." This last caused his lips to turn up at the corners again.

"Who says I crossed the line?"

"It's reasonable to assume . . ."

"Can you say honestly that they observed me crossing into Connecticut? That going to be your operatives' testimony?"

Seltzer didn't answer.

"I didn't think so."

"You were seen in Connecticut," Seltzer said.

"By whom?"

"By a known associate, albeit a so-called non-combatant, of a known crime syndicate boss. On the property of said boss."

"You going to rely on this witness's testimony?" Sara asked the DA.

"Uh . . . well, could be."

"A witness who's spent his lifetime lying for this crime boss?"

"Two men ended up dead," Morrison said, "under very mysterious circumstances."

"Very interesting," Sara said. "But you have no reliable evidence. At least I've heard none so far."

"Your footprints were found in the snow by the state police."

"Snow?" Sara looked over at Seltzer innocently. "I didn't know it had snowed. Where?"

"Up in Connecticut."

"And you have these footprints?"

"Uh . . . the snow melted."

"Ohhhh," Sara said, as if a great epiphany had dawned.

Seltzer bristled. "Your footprints were found all over that apartment over the bar! In blood!"

"I was investigating a crime scene. I discovered the crime scene. Ask the bartender."

"Your supposed bartender never saw you, never heard of you. Can't identify you. And that other bartender you reported doesn't exist. No one's ever seen him."

"I don't make up bartenders, Mr. Seltzer."

"There must have two dozen people in that bar. We couldn't find one who'd corroborate your story."

"It's a mob night spot, owned and operated," Sara said.

Seltzer made a face. "The barbarity of that crime. The utter brutality! Those men were literally torn apart limb from limb."

"And I did it?"

"We haven't really said . . ." the DA tried to interpose.

"We don't know all the details," Morrison said.

"Any theories as to how I did it? Two big strapping guys?"

"There have been similar incidents in your past," Seltzer said. "Deaths of crime figures. I have your complete file. It makes for exciting reading. Sort of like a pulp novel."

"Who do you think I am? The Shadow? The Scarlet Pimpernel?"

"I think you're a mercenary," Seltzer said, "hiring yourself out to the highest bidder. I think you may be one of the best contract killers in the business."

Sara groaned and rolled her eyes. "I whacked Ashkenazie for Kontra. Then I whacked Kontra's gunsels. Then I whack Kontra along with another gunsel. Makes sense."

"As the Deputy District Attorney said, we don't know all the details, yet. But we will."

"I think she's a rogue cop," Morrison said. "A vigilante cop. Pulp novel? Oh, it's an old story. Organized crime figures are notoriously hard to nail. The temptation to do it extra-legally is just too much for some cops. Especially for a woman whose father was gunned down in a mob hit."

"I wonder what the judge will feel about introducing that kind of prejudicial evidence," Sara said. "They don't even let you bring up prior convictions, let alone prior victimizations."

Maybe it was the use of a variant of the word 'victim' that made Morrison look suddenly uneasy.

"Is he your best trial man?" Sara asked the DA in a chummy tone.

"Actually, Phil only does–"

"That's beside the point," Morrison quickly said. "We have more than enough for a prima facie case for . . ."

Here the DA's gimlet stare cut the ground out from under him.

". . . further investigation," Morrison finished.

Seltzer sat back and crossed his legs, looking disgusted.

"Now, that's exactly what I was thinking," the DA said magnanimously. "This is only a discussion, and we have to investigate this matter a little further. Detective Pezzini, we only wanted to let you know that some questions have been raised and they're serious questions, questions about professional conduct, and . . . and, uh . . . departmental procedure . . ."

The door opened and Joe Siry walked in.

"Albert!" he said with a huge grin. "Sorry I'm late."

"Joe!" The DA rose from his chair and came around the desk. He almost knocked Morrison over. "Joe, damn it, it's good to see you! How long has it been?"

"Too long. How's Edna? Is Tiffany in college yet?"

"Graduate school," Albert said, beaming.

"No! I'll be damned. Has it been that many years?"

"More years than I'll admit to."

"Listen," said Siry, "congratulations on the appointment. It must be hell stepping into someone's shoes. I mean, your predecessor suddenly taking ill like that."

"It hasn't been easy, Joe. It hasn't been easy."

"Albert, I want to talk to you about my girl, here. Pezzini. She's a fine officer, Albert. One of my best. Now, she's a little what you call unorthodox. You know how these kids are today . . ."

Seltzer and Morrison looked at each other, and in unison heaved a silent internal groan.

The room hummed. It was a quiet sound, a soft electronic purr. The room was underground, and the location was secret.

Mr. Irons's car had picked Merlin up. Merlin had been blindfolded, as usual.

He sat typing at a console that looked no different from a dozen similar in the room. Only the technician was extraordinary. He knew exactly what he was doing.

The Macro-Economic Modeling and Simulation Array sat behind him, occupying the central space of the polyhedral room. MEMSA was a thing of polyhedrons itself, composed of wedding-cake tiers surmounted by a topmost hexagon. A few tiny lights shone on its surface here and there. It was a real, as opposed to a movie, supercomputer. No patterns of dancing lights, no odd screens showing flashy nonsense. Its color was black, and it loomed darkly efficient over its various workstations. It seemed demanding, unforgiving. Mercilessly precise.

Merlin typed away. He understood the machine as did

no other technician in the facility. Machines had individual personalities, he believed, just like people. You had to get to know a machine. It had to get to know you. That went double for this particular machine and its highly sophisticated architecture. It bestrode the demarcation between smart machine and true Artificial Intelligence. No one really knew where it stood exactly with respect to that line.

It was of Japanese make, something so new that few engineers in the States had had a chance to take a look at it. Applications for the machine were largely nonexistent. It was in fact so new and so sophisticated that funds for the project that had produced it had gone dry, victim of recent Japanese economic doldrums. The programming for it had been relatively basic until Merlin had been given a chance to work with it.

He was proud of his accomplishments. The screen was showing some very interesting stock data from European exchanges, of great potential interest to day traders, data that shouldn't be available in real time. Or at all, really; not according to law.

The entrance door slid open and Kenneth Irons walked into the room. There was a look of quiet satisfaction on his face. On his way over, he passed his left hand lovingly over a smooth surface or two. "Merlin. Good evening."

"Mr. Irons. You should see this."

Irons came up to the workstation and bent over slightly. "Interesting. Wherever did you get that Ultra-High Level day trading screen?"

Merlin shrugged. "Cracked it, brought it in."

Irons chuckled. "Excellent. But we're not going into the day trading business, are we? I assume you're just flexing your muscles."

Merlin hit some keys, and the esoteric stock-trading tool disappeared. "Yeah, that's all."

Irons straightened up. "Playing the market is fine and there's money to be made. But we're going to make money the old-fashioned way. We're going to take it."

Merlin's turn to chuckle.

Irons stood and took in MEMSA. "Now, the machine's modality is still purely passive at this point?"

"It's still lurking. No one knows it's here. No one will ever know."

"No way for anyone to access, I take it?"

"No chance. No way to log on."

"It's complete isolated, yet infinitely sensitive to all the data conduits to which it is connected. Right?"

"It's a big sponge, soaking up the world's economic data."

"And once we perfect its active functions, this great bird will be able to dip its beak into every single transaction in the economic universe."

Merlin laughed openly. "You have a way of slinging the . . . inflated rhetoric."

Irons turned his head slightly. He was not irked. He smiled. "I admit it. I'm excited by this project. There's only one other lifetime ambition that could get my endorphins flowing this freely."

Merlin said, "I don't know about every single transaction. The main ones, sure. We'll be slicing baloney so fine . . . well, hell, Mr. Irons. There wouldn't be more than a penny missing in any one account after a trillion transactions. That's cutting it *thin*."

"Splendid. Very, very good. I'll be able to drop all the middle-men, such as your former employer, Mr. Kontra."

"But for the moment you'll still be dealing with the Organizatiya, along with all the other wiseguy groups?"

"I'm negotiating with Kontra's successor now," Irons said. "No problems. He's being very cooperative."

"You be the man, Mr. Irons, after we go on-line with this baby."

"When, Merlin? Can you give me a timetable when MEMSA can go completely operational?"

"Oh, give me a few months more to sandpaper some stuff, get out some of the bugs. You know this is a thoroughbred computer. I love the way it interfaces easily with just about every platform known to man and Gates. Speaks every language, knows every protocol, and what it doesn't know, it *learns*."

Walking around the big thing, Irons continued admiring it. "You think it's sentient."

"I think it's learning. It's a baby. Well, a kid. An adolescent."

"Interesting. I wonder . . . isn't there something called a Turing Test? Some rubric by which to ascertain true intelligence?"

"Yeah, theoretical as hell. I don't believe anything definite would come by such a test. You gauge intelligence as you would judge a work of art. I think intelligence is art, and vice versa."

"Interesting notion. Off the subject . . ."

Merlin looked up. "Yes, sir?"

"You mentioned meeting Sara Pezzini. The detective."

"Oh, was that her name? I don't think she told me."

"From your description, there's no one else it could have been. That was an extremely captivating story. From it we can assume that something paranormal has entered the picture."

"Definitely."

"Do you have any idea how it could have been introduced?"

"I'm not sure, sir. I dabble in magic myself, but I don't do dangerous stuff."

"You don't strike me as the dangerous type. Nevertheless, your former boss is dead of something that crossed the barrier between the mundane and the phantasmagoric."

"It wasn't me. I just put a mild curse on him. And his goons. They roughed me up one too many times. They think you can force a mind to think."

"They're thugs," Irons said. "And thugs run true to form. You were right to leave them without notice. They treated you abominably, judging by your reports."

"I appreciate your treatment of me, Mr. Irons. I'll be forever grateful."

"It's nothing. But let's get back to this paranormal element. What sorts of magic do you dabble in?"

"I'm about as eclectic as you can get. I have a CD of 5000 books on magic, the occult, mysticism, and hermetic tradition. It's a lot of stuff. I'm a student, really, not an adept. At least not yet."

"We're all still learning," said Irons. "But you say you put a 'mild curse' on Kontra. On his henchmen as well?"

"Well, yes, the ones who beat me up. But it wasn't black magic. It wasn't a death sentence. I messed with their karma. Their energy patterns, their material world lines."

"Well, it's still all very strange, what you told me. The B-movie aspects, the improbability of it all. I'll have to give it a great deal of thought."

"What does this detective have to do with anything?"

Merlin said. When Irons's hesitation became apparent, he added, "If you don't mind my asking."

"A complicated subject. Actually, her involvement piques my interest more than does the monster rally. All in the fullness of time, Merlin. All in the fullness of time."

Merlin went back to typing.

The big machine hummed quietly as Irons walked out.

"Now where did I put those directories?" Merlin said to the empty room as the door slid shut. He kept hitting keys, becoming increasingly frustrated.

"Hey," he suddenly said. "Where the hell did *that* come from? How did it get–?" He leaned back and gave the situation some thought.

Presently, he said, "Uh-oh."

CHAPTER SEVENTEEN

The library's catalogue computer was simple to operate, but that also meant it was next to useless. Sara had put in MAGIC as the subject key word, and the machine had spewed out hundreds of titles. Better to narrow the search. What had Merlin talked about? Kabbala? Spelled with a K or a Q? The latter yielded little, so she tried K, and got about two dozen titles. The public library system had a lot of books.

She checked back to the call desk and found two titles she had previously requested. She picked them up, found an empty table, and sat down to read.

She read the introduction to one book. It made no sense whatsoever. She looked at the diagrams displayed. Groupings of little circles enclosing Hebrew script, all interconnected by lines. Clear as mud. She flipped through the other book. No help there. She read through a few pages of text and tried to divine the meaning. She was not sure there was any meaning to divine.

No, no. This stuff was extremely interesting and imaginative, but was of no use to anyone interested in the merely rational. Her situation was curiously ironic. There she was, sitting around with a magic talisman (for lack of a better term) on her wrist, and she couldn't make head or tail of any of this magic stuff.

She tried other books purporting to treat of the subject of the occult. They were all of a piece. They seemed to assume the reader understood the terms used in the text; however, there were few if any definitions or explanations of what the terms could mean, and those few offered tended to be conveniently obscure.

The historical books were interesting. She read through sections on magic in ancient Egypt, Mesopotamia, Persia, Israel, Greece, and Rome. She surveyed books on Gnosticism, alchemy, and divination. After going though the Arab philosophers and other medieval figures such as Albertus Magnus and Roger Bacon, she leafed through tomes on witchcraft and black magic. Also interesting were Nostradamus, Paracelcus, and the Christian Kabbalists. But none of this yielded any understanding of what was going on in her life.

A flicker of green hit her eye and she jerked her head up quickly. The computer screen at a nearby table glowed strangely. She watched it for a moment. It did nothing, but she could swear that it had flashed a green pattern. A familiar one, at that.

She shifted her eyes back to a discussion of the Rosicrucians.

Another flash of pale lime green. She didn't like being flashed.

She moved to another table, but after reading for a while, she became aware that a laptop was sitting directly behind her at the next table. It was open and whoever it belonged to had left it unattended, not a good idea in this city of petty pilferers. The owner was naïve or just carelessly absent-minded. Whatever the case, the damned thing was flashing green patterns at her, behind her back. At least she thought so. Maybe she was just getting paranoid. Yes, that was it. She was definitely getting paranoid.

She moved anyway.

By the time she had to go back to the catalogue computer, she had forgotten about it. She did another subject search on OCCULT, got mostly the same listings, and then tried PARANORMAL.

ESP, UFOs, Bigfoot, and the Loch Ness Monster. The strange thing was that most of the books seemed to assume, more or less as a starting point, some reality to the phenomena they presented. There existed a skeptical literature, but it was skimpy by comparison to the true believer corpus. She noticed that Atlantis figured into a lot of this stuff. She dumped out of the catalog and went on the Internet to get what was available on Atlantis, the lost continent.

Faces.

She hit the ESCAPE button repeatedly, but that action did not get rid of the faces, the bland, faceless faces she had seen that night her laptop had suffered a fit of the heebee-jeebies, faces that sat atop robed bodies, all standing in groups staring out from cyberspace at her. She wasn't paranoid; there was no doubt it was her they were staring at her with those vacant eyes, jaws slack and loose. Rounded, moonlike pale faces that did not move, did not register emotion. They had an artificial cast. Perhaps they were not faces, but masks.

"What do you want?" she asked of them, the beings on the screen. "What do you want of me?"

She slammed the mouse until she got a conventional

screen. Ye gods, could these creepy guys have their own web page? Why not? Everyone else in creation did.

Maybe she should get her own web page, so anyone interested could log on and ogle the pictures she'd put up. Nude, maybe. She could charge by the download.

Internal Affairs would love that. They'd get her for international soliciting.

She took off for the open stacks to search the shelves for more books. The stacks seemed to go on forever. From the main aisle, she could not see their end in the shadows. Row upon row, shelf after shelf of dusty hardbacks. More books than anyone could read in ten lifetimes, perhaps more. Sometimes she got the idea that not only was there more knowledge than any one person could absorb, but that no one really knew how much knowledge actually existed. Not only are we ignorant, we are ignorant of how ignorant we are.

Flicker.

First flashes, now flickers. Well, she'd heard of hot flashes. Now these were hot flickers.

Whoa, steady girl.

She forced herself to focus and analyze what she was experiencing. It was as if someone were switching between two TV monitors, each with a shot of the same thing but in two different locations. One, the stacks as she saw them now. The other, stacks in a library somewhere else, some eldritch and unheard-of depository where books were huge, dusty ancient tomes with intricately tooled leather covers.

Flicker. Flicker.

She walked on despite her uneasiness, watching somebody riffle the deck of reality. The alternate tableaux began to acquire some duration. The musty books flickered, disappeared, and flickered back. She reached to touch one. It disappeared, replaced by a conventional book. Again, a flickering. She reached once more and ran her hand over . . . it was not leather but the skin of some infinitely soft, infinitely alien thing. She shuddered and rubbed her fingers.

Masks appeared in the shadowed aisles. Groups of masks. The faces, the mask/faces, staring vacantly. They moved like ghosts, drifting over the quartz floor slabs.

She was no longer in New York. She was in another city, and this city's library had stacks as high as skyscrapers. They towered above, packed with artifacts all the way: scrolls, ledgers, tablets, steles, notebooks, parchments, stones, and boards, all bearing writing of some kind. And books, endless volumes in intricately crafted bindings.

She moved through the stacks, avoiding the advancing forms that confronted her. She turned corners and ran, stopped, cast a look behind. Ran again. She found an aisle and scurried down it, expecting hands to reach out from the shelves and drag her into their depths.

The flickering had stopped. She was in the alternate reality, and the reality of her experience was only an occasional flashback.

She saw an end to the stacks, an open area, and sprinted for it, and when she ran out into its vastness was shocked that the ceiling was lost in mists above. The place must have been seventy stories high, a vast atrium. Her footsteps echoed in droves, endless reverberations that bounced off lofty groined vaults and flying buttresses. She felt like an ant skittering through a medieval cathedral.

Sara Pezzini.

She did not know where the voice originated and did not want to look.

Sara Pezzini.

It was a voice that could not be human, its quality alien and remote and improbable. It could have been a synthesized voice; if so, was a synthesis of something that should not have existed in the first place. But there were human contours to it, and an underlying sense of something resembling emotion. The emotion was . . . urgency? Desperation?

Sara . . .

They knew her name, these specters, these eidolons, and she wished mightily that they did not. She didn't want them in possession of something so vital a part of her. Her name was something sacred. Their very knowledge of it was a violation of some kind.

She was overcome with a revulsion at these creatures, a gut-felt repugnance. She did not have a sense of evil so much as a sense of the complete absence of all that was human and natural. If any being could be unnatural, these creatures were.

Demons?

Why not? It was as good a word as any to describe them. But she thought it very strange that she got no impression of malevolence. Not like the Bird.

Screeeeeeeee . . .

Had she summoned the bird merely by thinking of it? She stopped and looked up. Something was flying in the place's upper reaches, lost in gray fog of distance, a dark something flapping and fluttering, a vague shape, a blur of motion, a click of talons, and what emanated from this was a longing to swoop, to snare, to clutch, to rend.

"Hi, there," Sara said to it.

Flicker.

She was running through the lobby of the public library. She skidded to a stop. A few people were looking at her. She felt like an idiot.

"You okay?" asked a tall black guy in passing.

She nodded. Sheepish and not wanting to be taken for a schizophrenic on the loose, she walked as calmly as she could through the revolving doors and out onto the street.

Sanity, always an issue with her. Perhaps the Witchblade was a huge bloc of symptoms, plain and simple, symptoms of a pathology that existed only in her mind.

Why, why had she been picked to bear the Witchblade? Maybe she could discover the reason if she knew what the Witchblade itself was all about. Down through the ages, it had chosen its champions, and they had all been women.

But perhaps that was all in her mind. Perhaps these transformations only existed in her perception, and everything that happened during them could be explained rationally. Maybe Kontra had been killed by a marauding bear instead of a werewolf.

Ah, but what was a marauding bear doing in a Brooklyn apartment? Explain that.

Nevertheless, doubts about her sanity recurred on occasion, and this was one. Even if the damned thing were real, it would drive anybody crazy.

Flicker.

"Damn it," she said, determined to keep walking no matter what.

Flicker flicker flicker flicker flicker flicker flicker . . .

That city again, the city of impossible buildings, the New York of alternate reality, a city of spires and perches, with doorways half a mile in the air, a metropolis of avian beings, a place that did not, could not exist, flickering in and out of existence, flickering like some old silent film grinding through a hand-cranked projector. She remembered her father taking her to Coney Island . . . in the old Penny Arcade there were still nickelodeons consisting of cards with a single frame of film printed on them. You cranked the machine and the cards came up one by one. The faster you cranked, the faster the action went and the faster the flickering became. This was as if someone had shuffled two stacks of cards with different scenes. A frame of one was followed by a frame of the other, and so on.

The shifting of realities took on the action of a stroboscope; the flickering speeded up and became almost blinding. She had to shield her eyes in order to walk. Even the pavement changed beneath her feet, from ordinary concrete to some shiny obsidian substance. But she walked, more determined than ever. She was going home, and that was all there was to it. Damn Greek choruses, damn strange birds, damn shifting realities. Damn all.

Yes, but where did she live in *this* city?

And where did that Greek temple come from, speaking of choruses?

Well, it looked something like a Greek temple. Sort of. It had columns, very high ones; it also had friezes, bas-reliefs, and all the rest of the architecture, all distorted somehow, bent through a geometry that was not even non-Euclidean. It was just damned weird.

She walked across a street of paving stones like black mirrors and mounted the steps in front, steps that went up at least two stories. She climbed steadily until her legs began to ache, but kept climbing, her footsteps echoing.

At least she reached the floor of the temple and walked

through a forest of columns before coming under the distant roof. The columns, long, fluted, and slightly oval, continued for a stretch, then gave onto an open area. She stopped and took in the huge statue standing in the central area.

It was a statue of herself in full Witchblade regalia.

She stared at it for an interminable period, not comprehending, not able to process the data her eyes were feeding her. Gradually she became aware that she was not alone in the temple.

The Chorus stood arrayed at the foot of the statue. Slowly they all turned to face her, and she regarded them questioningly.

"What do you want?"

To worship you . . .

It was an answer she did not want to hear. She looked up at her own image. The statue was of heroic proportions, a massive figure of silver and gold with glints of other precious substances, perhaps but not limited to onyx, amethyst, and amber. The statue had wings sprouting from a riot of swirls and other metallic flourishes. Jewels sparkled everywhere. The base was inlaid with semiprecious stone in eye-catching arabesques. There was an alien nature to the thing, imparted not by the subject of the work but by the artist. This was not the work of a human artist; this was the work of a being not human at all.

"I'm flattered," she said to the Chorus. "But no, thanks."

She turned and walked out of the temple. No one tried to stop her.

She did not have to descend the two-story stairway. Once out from under the roof of the temple, New York flickered back into existence, and she was on the sidewalk.

She knew where she had to go and it was a long walk, so she hailed the first cab that came by.

Maybe her luck was changing, she thought. The damned cab actually stopped.

CHAPTER

EIGHTEEN

Sophia pushed buttons on the telephone while Baba sat by the window, looking out. Sophia looked back at her.

"It's the only thing we can do. The only justice."

Baba didn't move her eyes from the setting sun. "How much will it cost?"

"A lot of money. Can you think of money now? He was your grandson."

"You never cared for him. Only his money, his position, his power."

"I loved him. He was my husband."

"He had other women."

"That means he wasn't my husband?"

"So," said Baba, "you will take up his business."

"Why not? A woman can't run a business?"

"It's man's work, this business."

"You're old-fashioned," Sophia told her. "Mind your own business."

"I do, I do. Everyone thinks I want to meddle. I don't."

"Then shut up. Hello? Mr. Strauss? Oh, I wish to speak to him. Yes. Yes. Very well. Please tell him that an old friend, Sophia Kontra, wishes to speak with him. I'm calling long distance. Yes, an old friend. He knew my husband." Sophia turned again. "They're getting him."

"How much are you paying the telephone company for this call?"

"Who knows?" Sophia said testily. "Who cares?" She waited patiently. Then: "Hello? Mr. Strauss? This is Sophie. Yes, it is. How nice to hear your voice. Thank you, thank you . . ."

"It's not a good thing, this," Baba said. "It's an evil thing we do."

Sophia went on talking.

The view from a Central Park West apartment is spectacular. The park spreads out like your own personal enchanted forest, and from penthouse height the derelicts, addicts, and gangbangers could be munchkins for all you are concerned.

At night, the park seems the dark domain of dragons and demons. Living in New York is made easier by a rich imagination. It also helps if you're just plain rich.

Kenneth Irons walked away from the window. For all that his imagination—as well as his stock portfolio—was one of the richest on earth, his mind was not on enchanted forests this night. His man had announced a visitor, one he knew well. He was ready to receive her any time of the day or night. He had directed his man to admit her forthwith and send her up.

He sat down in a chair in the picture gallery and waited among oil paintings of heroic women, former wielders of the Witchblade. Amongst his favorites was a portrait of Jeanne d'Arc. Joan astride a horse in full battle regalia. The best known of all the sentient gauntlet's bearers and wearers.

The tall door to the study opened and Sara Pezzini stepped in. She was dressed, as usual, in what he regarded as rags. But on her even rags looked good. Her jeans were usually particularly tight and the T-shirt under her jacket was always undersize, allowing her feminine lineaments to come through nicely. She was tall, thin, well-proportioned, and had a face that could launch several navies. Legs up to the neck. Oh, those legs. And there were other parts of her that shaped up just as well.

He sometimes permitted himself the luxury of simple lust.

"Sara," he said warmly.

"Hello, Ken. What have you been up to?"

"I'm always up to something. How has it been with you?"

"Up to my butt in alligators, as usual."

"I envy those alligators," Irons said with a grin. "Do sit down."

Sara took a seat on a luxurious chaise. "My question wasn't an idle one. Have you been up to anything supernatural lately?"

Irons looked surprised. "Why, what a question. What would bring you to ask it?"

"Strange things have been happening around the Witchblade lately."

Irons had avoided looking at the bracelet since she had come into the room. Now he slowly shifted his eyes and took it in. It was in its quiescent state, taking the form of a simple bracelet. He had seen it in many configurations since he had unearthed the artifact in Egypt years ago.

"What sorts of strange things?" Irons asked.

"Apparitions that do murder in fairly grisly ways. And another phenomenon. The intrusion of a very weird world on ours. This involves a few more apparitions."

"What sort of world?"

"Like nothing I've seen before. I haven't had a lot of time to think it through, but it may have something to do with the apparitions, and it might not."

"That's . . . helpful."

"Okay, it's not. They've got to be related, though."

"All right. What forms do these apparitions take?"

"At least three kinds. One is for all intents and purposes a werewolf, or something like it. Another is a dragon. Another, related to the strange world thing, is a bird of some kind, and associated with it are humanoid forms."

"Werewolf," Irons mused. "Interesting."

"Know anything that can connect up with that?"

"What's the Witchblade's interest been?"

"It's interested," Sara said. "But it's not telling me what it thinks."

"It wouldn't," Irons said. "It's always been rather closed-mouthed."

Sara laughed. "I guess you could put it that way."

"I was being ironic. Let me think."

"I have a connection. Lazlo Kontra was taken out by the werewolf. Lazlo Kontra was Romanian by birth. He has a Romanian grandmother who walked out of a Lon Chaney, Jr. picture."

Irons brooded a moment. "So that's why my sources were so confused on the method."

"I'll bet it didn't sound like a mob hit."

"No. Jobs of that kind are usually done with minimum

mess, except on occasion. So Kontra was done in by this supernatural factor, whatever it is."

"No doubt," Sara said. "And I don't have any ready explanation for it. Except for a crazy one."

"What's that?"

"A crazy nerd kid. Computer hacker. Brilliant kid, but a little odd. Messes with magic. But how he could be summoning monsters . . . what's wrong, Ken?"

Irons had grown a subdued expression of concern. By the time Sara had spoken, it was gone.

"You know this kid," Sara said.

"You really took me by surprise," Irons said. "I shouldn't be surprised by this time. You have a way about you."

"Don't try to snow me, Irons. The kid's name is Merlin. Know him?"

"You've already guessed it. He's been doing some work for me. Consulting."

"On what?"

"That's my business, Sara. Let's say it's a special project."

"Anything to do with magic?"

"Not in the least. But now you tell me Merlin is living up to his name."

"He admitted to a possible motive. He told me without a thought that he could be admitting to a murder. He claimed he didn't intend for his victims to die."

"Interesting, interesting," Irons said, rather too abstractedly.

"I think you know the motive, too. I think you might have hired him away from Kontra."

"I considered Merlin a free lance. Didn't really give it a thought. Actually, he's been working for me for a while."

"I see," Sara said, sitting back.

"If I gave him a motive . . ."

"I don't think you did. I think it was between Kontra and Merlin, and magic was used to settle the dispute, however inadvertent the outcome was."

"Glad to hear you don't suspect me of contributing to this grisly business."

"I've known you long enough to suspect that you had a hand in somewhere."

Irons tried to look pained. "I'm hurt."

"I also know that this whole business has something to do with computers."

This also hit Irons from an unexpected direction. "Indeed," was all he would allow.

"Yeah. Funny thing, the bird and the humanoid creatures came at me from out of my laptop."

"They came at you?"

"Reaching for me, and I think reaching for the Witchblade. Odd. It wasn't particularly threatening, that time. On other occasions, the bird was a little different. It seems to have a grudge against me."

"Curiouser and curiouser," Irons commented. "How about the other creatures? The werewolf, for instance."

"I beat it up pretty good."

"Congratulations."

"The dragon didn't give me any trouble at all. But it killed Kontra's gunsel. Burnt him to a crisp."

"Ah, as dragons are wont to do, no doubt. All very, very interesting."

Sara let out a breath. "Yeah. Like a massive traffic accident."

"Right. You have to look, don't you?" Irons said.

"Any ideas, Ken?"

"A few. I'll let you know if any of them become coherent. They aren't right at the moment."

"Neither are mine. I can't understand the bird thing. It seems unrelated. Whereas the werewolf and the dragons are definitely something some goofy kid would dream up. Or pick up from his environment."

"His environment?"

"He was working for a Romanian. I mentioned the guy's grandma. That also explain the Vlad connection . . ."

"Eh?"

"Another thing entirely. It doesn't fit, not quite."

"You have a puzzle here with rather disparate pieces," Irons said.

"Sure do. And I think you do, too, Ken. Though you're not admitting anything."

"I don't know what to admit. I'm as confused as you."

She leaned forward and looked him straight in the eye. "You may be telling the truth. It's hard for me to tell, most of the time."

"Sara, that's a roundabout way of calling me a liar."

"Really," Sara said, getting up. She began a casual tour of the picture gallery. It was not her first, but the depictions of her predecessors were an endless source of fascination.

Irons got up and followed her. "You know, I still claim the Blade as mine."

"Never said it wasn't," Sara told him.

"Yet you'll be walking out of here with it. You could call that theft, in a way."

"You could. You won't. We both know why I have to wear it. You can't, and neither can anyone else. With the possible exception of Ian Nottingham. But he's a special case."

"True," Irons said gravely. "Undeniably true. So I suppose our little agreement will continue."

"Until we get to the bottom of the Witchblade's mystery. By the way, I saw him recently."

"Oh, you did?" Irons said brightly. "And how is old Nottingham?"

"Doing pretty good for a dead guy."

"He always was resourceful."

"That doesn't surprise you?"

"What, that he's keeping up appearances? Stout fellow, and all that."

"Maybe I saw his ghost," Sara said.

"Perhaps you did. I don't know, and really don't care to follow the careers of former employees. Once they go off the payroll, my interest in them ceases."

"Yes, once you threw him out the window, you pretty much didn't care where he landed."

"As the old song says, 'That's not my department, said Warner von Braun.' "

"Tom Lehrer," Sara said.

"You remember Tom Lehrer?" Iron said, mildly surprised. "You're not old enough."

"I have him on CD."

"You're a culturally literate heroine-goddess."

"That's exactly what the strange guys in the bird world think of me. They say they want to recruit me as their goddess."

"They speak to you?"

"In a sense. That particular statement was extremely clear."

"Extraordinary. You should be flattered. I was just thinking. Instead of headhunters, these people have godhunters?"

"I wonder if there's a signing bonus," Sara mused.

"Well, good luck in your new career."

"Not interested in the job. I have a job investigating homicides in the City of New York."

Irons said, "Do you think that in any universe you could conceive of, let alone the City of New York, you could connect me with the death of Lazlo Kontra, or anyone else?"

"Sure. I could get the DA to believe that one of your employees did it."

"By magic?"

"I don't have to bring magic into the picture. No one would believe it anyway. All I have to supply is a motive, and you start to look like the gray eminence behind all the killing that's been going on. Oh, your lawyers will protect you. You'll get off, but your reputation . . . ?"

"I see what you mean. Nasty stuff, Sara. Why?"

"Let's say I have a few scores to settle with you."

"I'm crushed that you think me an enemy."

"Ken, I think you're up to something. I don't know what it is, but I'd like to find out. I'm going to find out."

"I see."

"Good night, Mr. Irons."

"Good night, Sara. Do drop in anytime."

When she had gone and Irons had been left alone to contemplate, yet again, the pictures in his gallery, his manservant opened the door to tell him he had a phone call.

He walked to his desk. "Irons here."

"Erwin Strauss," came a familiar voice. "Forgive the late call."

"Yes, what is it?"

"I have been offered a very challenging contract. It's on the girl. Your girl."

"Interesting."

"I know your association with her. I have never quite understood the nature of it, but as you are the most powerful man in your city–you are, in a sense, the boss of bosses–I am notifying you of my intention to take the contract."

"I suppose you don't want to tell me who your clients are."

"They are amateurs who don't know what they are asking. They phoned me. Imagine that. Fortunately, I forestalled any mention of business and got in touch with them via a secure line."

"I suppose I can't change your mind," Irons said.

"With money? Yes. One billion dollars."

Irons laughed derisively. "In small bills, I suppose?"

"You will wire it to my account."

"That's rather steep," Irons said flatly.

"True. But the girl means quite a lot to you."

"I can't deny it. But a billion? Even if I would permit myself to be blackmailed . . ."

"You can't prevent it. I am doing it, Mr. Irons. One billion, or the girl dies, and that she is some kind of sorceress will not make a difference."

"Oh. And just how do you propose to take her down?"

"That is my business."

"Nevertheless . . ." Irons could only say.

"Very well. I have given you fair warning. Good bye."

Irons began, "Mr. Strauss, I think you fail to–"

But Strauss had hung up.

CHAPTER NINETEEN

It's one of the bad ones," a patrolman said in passing to Jake and Sara as they entered the crime scene. "Bloody as hell."

"As if murder can be anything but," Jake commented to Sara as they walked into a spacious apartment on the upper West Side.

"Looks like murder by cable guy," another patrolman greeted them. He was standing in front of a wall that looked like a Jackson Pollock painting in blood. At the base of the wall lay a body with about as many bullets in it as a body could contain without being classified as an alloy of lead.

"What led to that conclusion, officer?" Sara asked.

"We have at least two people saw the cable truck double parked outside, saw the cable guy enter. Residents then heard lots of what they called 'popcorn popping.' A silenced Mac 10, we're thinking."

Jake said, "Are you bucking for a promotion, Patrolman . . . ?"

"Linaweaver. Matter of fact, I'm taking the sergeant exam next week."

"Very good work, all that deduction."

"Thank you, sir. Uh . . . actually, I'm just reporting the facts as we got them."

"So we have witnesses to the cable guy," Sara said, "to the shots, and what else?"

"Uh, I called up the cable company. The victim was scheduled to get a digital box installed today. Real cable guy is working on the other side of town. Ergo, this was obviously a fake cable guy."

"Aren't they always?" Jake said.

Sara asked, "No one saw the cable guy leaving?"

"No one's come forward. But the truck's gone."

"Okay," Sara said. "Thanks, Linaweaver."

"So we have a cable guy who's a homicidal maniac?" Jake said.

"No, we have an assassination with the hit man posing as a cable TV company employee."

"You think the victim's mobbed?"

"Sounds like a pro job," Sara said. "Who would suspect the cable guy of being a hit man?"

"No one. Right, you let him right in."

"Has all the earmarks of a hit."

Jake nodded toward the wall. "What do you think of those marks?"

"Don't make jokes."

"I'm not," Jake said. "I was about to make the comment that there have been some pretty spectacular hits lately. And this one looks like another."

"Linaweaver?" Sara called.

"Yes, sir. Ma'am?"

"Didn't you leave something out of your report?"

"Uh, I don't think so, ma'am."

"No?"

Linaweaver frowned and thought.

Sara prodded, "The name of the victim? Whose apartment is this?"

"Oh! Sorry, sorry. Uh, name's Bubnov." Linaweaver fished out his notepad and thumbed through it. "Ivan . . . uh . . . Ilyich Bubnov."

"Need I say more?" Jake asked.

"Right," Sara said, taking a stance a few feet from the wall. "Close range. Perp was standing about here. Opened up and emptied the magazine."

"Wonder why," Jake said. "Wanted to do a thorough job, or he liked to see the blood spatter?"

"Little of both?" Sara said. "Linaweaver, is the victim the tenant here?"

"Uh, yes. Super ID'd him. Sorry, I should have said that."

"Yes, you should have, right straight off. Hope they don't have that question on the sergeant's exam."

"Sorry."

Linaweaver slinked away.

"Well, another mob-related death."

Sara still stood looking at the wall. Jake watched her for a moment.

"Sara?"

She glanced at the bracelet on her wrist. Then she said, "No."

"No?"

"Right," Sara said.

"No, what?"

"It's not related. Not related at all. For all that spatter, looks like it could be hanging in the MOMA."

"Huh?"

"Never mind. Let's do our job and get all we can out of the place. But I can tell you now it's not going to connect up with anything."

Jake and Sara were the last ones out of the apartment. The paramedics, techs, uniformed officers, and all related personnel had cleared out a least a half-hour before the detective partners came out the front door of the building.

"So he was nominally in real estate, but head of an extortion ring," Jake commented as they walked down the avenue. "Nice things people are up to behind the façade of respectability. You ready for lunch?"

"Yeah, I'm starved," Sara said. "Façades are what it's all about. Your modern mobster wants a low profile. The lower the better. The smart ones do, anyway."

"Street gang types aren't among the smart ones, I guess."

"There's always plenty of that type. I'm talking about the upper echelons."

"Yeah, they always have a way of protecting themselves. Except sometimes they don't. Like our Comrade Bubnov. Oh wait, do they use 'comrade' as a title anymore? In Russia, what do they call–?"

The shot sounded like the explosion of a fairly good-sized firecracker. The sound came from high up, a roof or a window.

Jake's mouth was still open and in the middle of his last sentence. He closed it and hit the pavement behind a parked car. "Sara!"

She was still standing in the middle of the sidewalk, her right arm raised.

Covering his head, Jake peered between his fingers. He

saw something he had seen before. A strange gauntlet, a mailed glove of some kind, busy with swirls and arabesques of metal filigree, covered Sara's right hand and forearm.

Jake knew what had happened, but didn't want to believe it. Besides, he didn't have time to think about it just now.

Another shot came, and with it the whining ping of a ricochet. She had deflected another bullet off her gauntlet. Jake got to his knees and searched for the source of the fire.

"Jake, stay down!"

He obeyed. Another shot, and another, both whanging off the gauntlet. Sara's arm was a blur of motion.

How? How? Jake screamed in his mind.

Sara was looking up, searching the high vantage-points. She lifted her left arm. "There! Jake, I'm the target. Get across the street and cover the back of the place. This creep's not going to slip away if we can help it. Call backup now!"

"Right!" Jake yelled, getting up and dashing out from cover. He ran across the street as fast as he could make it. The building was a typical apartment for this neighborhood, a lobby locked to nonresidents, a security man sitting at a desk in the lobby. Jake had to pound on the door and wave his badge before the security-doorman would let him into the lobby, where he phoned for backup and a SWAT team to back up the backup.

Sara looked up and down the street. Jake did the same. Arrayed all around them were SWAT team members, regular police, and county cops. Around the corner lurked fireman, paramedics, news reporters, and the general public, all milling about. They had the building covered from all angles. Jake had gotten to the back door immediately after phoning in.

Sara was ticked at him for that. But he had felt bad about leaving Sara all alone out there. He'd run to the back fire doors as soon as he got off the phone. They had been closed, and opening them would have tripped alarms. He was fairly sure that no one could have left the building.

Sara turned around and sat on the concrete with her back against a squad car. "He's gone."

"How?" Jake asked. "Most of the residents are still in the building. Maybe he's hiding out in an apartment, holding the tenants hostage."

"We'll screen everybody inside. We won't find him. I just have a feeling."

"Could the shots have come from another place?"

"I saw the barrel. High-powered rifle, big scope, up on the roof."

"Okay, I believe you. On the roof."

"Of that building," Sara said.

"So he has to be still in there," Jake said without feeling.

"No, he does not."

"How'd he get out? And so quick?"

"I don't know. But obviously we are dealing with an accomplished pro."

"Know why he's out to get you? Because I think you're right, you were the target. He didn't even try a shot at me."

"I don't know why. I don't know who. But the rest is obvious."

"Obvious? Why do you say that?" Jake asked.

"This thing is telling me," Sara said with a glance at her bracelet.

Jake was again reminded that she seldom referred to the thing on her wrist, and when she did it was usually in an indirect manner. "Okay, but what is it that's obvious?"

"Let's call these guys off and go in and question the residents. We are going to hit every apartment. And I want to look into every apartment that doesn't have somebody answering the door."

"Sara, we're not papered for searches."

"I didn't say search. I said look into."

"Oh. I guess we can do that thing."

They did that thing, and after talking to just about everyone in the building, mostly aged Jewish people of foreign birth and/or recent citizenship, Sara realized that the search was hopeless.

"Still up for lunch?" Jake asked when everyone was readying to go back whence he had come.

The SWATs were packing equipment into cases, the police were gathering up barricades and yellow police tape. The paramedics had pulled up to the front of the building in case any resident had heart trouble caused by the commotion. The firemen, having better things to do, had left.

"You're incorrigible," Sara said.

"I'm human. I have to eat at least once a day."

"Listen, you go grab a dog or something, I'll run into that Starbucks across the street. We have an interview at one, remember?"

"Yeah, okay. Thought I saw a street dog vendor when we arrived. Wonder where he got to?"

"I'll meet you at the coffee shop," Sara said, heading for the intersection.

She wasn't dejected. Just frustrated. This was the most frustrating Witchblade snafu to date. Not only did it all make zero sense, it didn't even—

"Miss Pezzini."

"Huh?"

Sara whirled. Out of the proverbial dark alley stepped a man in a utility work uniform. He looked strange. Something about even the shape of his head was sinister. Every line in his forehead and face exuded menace. Yet overall there was something bland, almost bureaucratic about him. The prosaic malevolence of a genocidal civil servant, a true sense of the banality of evil, radiated from him like an aura.

Sara took an instinctive step backward.

"My name is Edwin Strauss. I have been hired to assassinate you. I intend to do just that."

He spoke with a pronounced middle-European accent, but with overtones of culture and refinement. Sara took another step back.

"This was a test, a test of your powers. You passed admirably. You did not even look to where the first shot came from before you blocked it. Truly remarkable, Miss Pezzini. To say that your powers are extraordinary would be an understatement by several factors of magnitude."

Sara said simply, "What do you want?'

"I always try to meet my subjects and introduce myself. It makes the interaction a more human one. I do it whenever possible—*whoops!*"

Sara had made a motion. Strauss had his gun out, as if by magic.

"Hand me your weapon please, and please step back from the street. We are conspicuous here. Come into the alley. I wish to speak with you."

Sara obeyed, handing him her revolver as she stepped by him. In the alley, she turned to face him.

"Your talisman is fast to defend you but not as quick on the offensive. Curious. I suppose I still have much to learn about it. But I am learning very quickly."

"How do you come to know about me?"

"I know many things I should not know. That is how I stay alive in this world, Miss Pezzini. I know about you, about Kenneth Irons, and perhaps a bit more."

"Perhaps," Sara said. "And then again, you could be lying."

"I don't lie," Strauss said.

"How did you get out of that building so quickly?" Sara asked pointedly.

"Ah. But I did not say I would divulge my trade secrets."

"Then say what you have to say. I was on my way to lunch."

"My apologies. But I have said it already. I have introduced myself, and have announced my intentions. That is sufficient."

"Who hired you?"

"Again, a secret that hired assassins guard with their lives. Sorry. I must decline to answer."

"Okay, you said your piece. Here's mine. You won't kill me, and I will catch you and put you away for a long, long time. There's lots to explain lately, and you are the likeliest explanation to come along yet. In fact, you're a welcome sight. You're going to come in mighty handy, mister."

"Oh, my." Strauss was grinning from ear to ear in a ghastly rictus that was not at all a pleasant sight. "You do have spunk. Oh, my. I think you may prove a great deal of fun."

"I'm so glad for you."

"I'm not alone, you know. There is a veritable team out for your demise."

"I hope you and your chums have all the fun you can get. You'll be having none in Sing Sing."

"Ah, Sing Sing! The very name rings with the sound of high crime and misdemeanor. An American institution in every sense of the word. I should be proud to be an inmate. But I must decline the offer. I have never come close to being apprehended. I do not intend to be caught now, or ever."

"Well, I guess it's rah rah, team, then."

"Indeed. However, it also must be admitted you will be a challenging subject. This test tells me that ordinary methods will not be sufficient. Next time, I might be one of a number of . . . shall we say, unnatural adversaries?"

"Got it."

"Yes. You see, I am not unacquainted with the occult. Neither are you, as evidenced by . . . that." Strauss gestured with his gun at the bracelet, which, while he had been talking, had slowly grown and metamorphosed into its gauntlet form, albeit a subdued and compact variation.

"Okay," Sara said simply.

Strauss looked at his gun. "Strange. Standing here like this, part of me is wondering why I couldn't just shoot you now and get it over with. But, as I see, you would simply ward off the bullet in magical fashion, the shot would draw attention, and I would be in a pickle."

"Very interesting," Sara said. "Here's something to think about. If that gun is doing you no good, what's preventing me from clouting you with this mitten I have on and hauling you in right now?"

"I told you I was not alone. I am for the moment protected from you by magical means. You see this?" Strauss reached into a pocket and pulled out a bright orange feather. The color was more than iridescent. It was almost incandescent. "It is a feather of the firebird."

"Eh?"

"The firebird. Its feathers are magical and can ward off any attack. I am thus protected from you. The gun is simply for psychological effect."

"Let's do an experiment," Sara said, stepping forward and reaching for him with the gauntlet hand.

He disappeared.

"You see? Behind you, Miss Pezzini."

She turned. He was indeed standing behind her. She lunged and tried again. Again, he vanished momentarily, only to reappear about twenty feet farther up the alley.

"Sorry," Strauss said. "We are at a stalemate. I can't hurt you, and you can't lay a glove on me. Now is not the time of our final confrontation. So I will simply say good-bye. Good-bye, Miss Pezzini, and good luck to you. I will leave your weapon in a trash receptacle in the back alley. Sorry for the inconvenience."

"Thanks," Sara said cheerily. Then her smile faded as she saw the lettering on the back of his work suit: MANHATTAN CABLE..

She watched him disappear into the shadows.

CHAPTER

TWENTY

When Sara and Jake reported back at the end of their watch, there was a note in Sara's message box. It was from Siry. It read simply: *Sara, see me immediately. Joe.*

She knocked on his door. For some reason the frosted glass panel struck her as quaint. It had never occurred to her before. She didn't know how old the precinct house was; doubtless it was ancient.

Speaking of which, Joe Siry was looking his age today. The lines of his face seemed deeper, darker, and his eyes had receded into their sockets. He looked as though he had done himself up in stage makeup to play an older part. Maybe it was just his somber expression.

"I take it the news isn't good," Sara said, standing at the door.

"You are in some deep do-do," Siry said in a sepulchral tone.

"That isn't good," she replied. "How not good is it?"

"You do a bad impression of Johnny Carson."

"I thought it was Ed McMahon. You're at least trying to crack a joke. That must mean I'm not being indicted."

"You're awfully close to being indicted. Well, let's just say that Morrison wants to convene a grand jury, but I still have Albert convinced you're a good cop who's simply misunderstood. A maverick, you go your own way, get into lots of trouble bucking authority, that sort of thing. He's bought it so far, and he's still buying it. But Morrison's been working on him, and just about has him worn down. Old school ties aren't unbreakable. They only hold up under so much weight. And your indictment is hanging by a thread."

"They still don't have any evidence I'm a hit girl for the mob."

"No, I don't think they do," Siry agreed. "What they have is a lot of gruesome crimes that have only one connecting factor: you. You are very handy and not very well liked in some quarters. Partly because you refuse to toe the line, partly because you're a girl. Uh, I'm sorry, woman."

"Funny, around you I always feel 'girl' is the more appropriate term," Sara said as she came in and took a seat.

Siry grunted. "I'll take that as a compliment. As I was saying, you are prime material for taking the fall."

"Oh, yeah? I play the sap for no one, see. Gosh, Cap. Let's do more 1930s B-movie dialogue. It's fun."

"Goddamn it!"

Sara sobered up and sat up. "What's wrong, Joe?"

"Here I go to bat for you, trying to save your skinny little ass, and you sit there and make silly jokes. Don't you think an indictment is going to reflect badly on me? Or do you always think just of yourself?"

"Sorry, Joe. I didn't mean to hurt you. I was just trying to cheer you up. You look tired. I've been worried."

"I look tired? I *am* tired. Sick and tired of this job, this endless battle with the brass. They expect me to run this department on a shoestring, and instead of backing me up, instead of giving me all the moral support I need, they sit up there on their salaried butts and think of ways to cut the ground out from under me on a daily basis. And I'm damned sick of it, Sara. I'm sick to death of it."

Siry suddenly grimaced and clutched his left shoulder. "Damn it," he muttered.

"What is it?"

"Pain. Right here at the tip of the shoulder."

"How long have you been having it?"

"Christ, I dunno. Couple of months."

"How bad and how often?"

"Never mind. It's bursitis."

"Whenever you have pain there, at your age, it's cause to see a doctor."

"To hell with doctors. Overpaid quacks."

"You ought to get it checked out."

"Don't nag. We were talking about *you*. I'd like to see you change your attitude. You think you're invulnerable. You're just laughing this business off. But it could happen. They not only could boot you off the force, they could drop a conspiracy charge on you like a bag of hammers."

"Nice image."

"There you go again!"

"Sorry, Cap. It's just that it's hard to take Morrison seriously, let alone Seltzer. They are both so totally clueless. They haven't the slightest idea of what's really going on."

"And you know what's really going on?"

"No, but I have my own fall guy."

Siry's expression softened. "You do?" he asked with genuine interest.

"Yup."

"This guy have a name?"

"Yup. Erwin Strauss. Austrian by birth, former STASI officer. East German secret police and intel. I had some Eurocops fax me his file."

"What's he do?"

"He's been a general utility hit man for the Organizatsiya for over ten years. He's very good. Skilled, intelligent, crafty, and has never been arrested in his life."

"Sounds good. And he's here in New York?"

"For the moment. He did the Bubnov hit, and I think we can make all these weird murder cases stick to him."

"Wonderful," Siry said. "But that doesn't sound like you. Anybody else, I would say, how can we set him up? But you're not usually so cynical. What happened?"

"He's so slimy, he deserves anything he gets. I read his file. He supervised torture. It was his specialty. He's cesspool slime."

"I can show you a hundred guys in Attica who are worse just on paper. I guess you're not really turning cynical after all. Okay, I like him for all this stuff. When can we pick him up?"

"I'm working on it, Cap. I'll let you know."

"Okay, okay." Siry was nodding and looking better. "Yeah. Good." He sat back and continued nodding.

Sara decided this was a good moment to get up and get out. He was still nodding, heaven knew to whom, as she closed the door.

"Good night, Joe."

"Huh? Yeah, good night."

• • •

New York was quiet that evening. A hush pervaded the million-footed city. Baba sat at a small table, laying Tarot in patterns on its top.

Sophia sat in a comfortable chair off to one side. "What do you see, old woman?"

"Death."

"I hate that card. Whose death do you see?"

"A woman's. She is powerful, but she will die."

"That is a good sign for us."

"I see no good at all," Baba said.

"We will avenge Lazlo."

"Is that so important?"

"It is to me. Besides, we cannot run his business with such a potent adversary about."

"Why do you think you can take a man's role?"

"I was the only thing giving him substance. He would never have risen in the ranks if I hadn't pushed him. I grew weary of being the woman behind the man. Now he is gone. I grieve for him, but now I am free. I will stand where he fell and carry on."

"You dream," Baba said, laying another card. "Ah," she added, nodding.

"Oh, play your cards, do your magic. Mr. Strauss is doing the actual work."

"He works with what I give. He has nothing himself."

"Except strength and brains and skill." Sophia snorted. "Nothing, my eye."

"My eye sees the future. It is not good to summon demons to do one's bidding. They will turn. They always do. They are smarter than we. They are dangerous."

"I don't know if I entirely believe in that nonsense. Like Lazlo, I tend to be skeptical."

"It is working beyond my wildest dreams," Baba said. "If I had known, I could have been queen of Romania, and Hungary, and perhaps all the Russias. Had I known. Had I the courage. But I am only a poor old woman. I do not really think it is my magic. It is the witch woman's."

"Oh, hush. How can that be? The witch woman casts an evil spell on herself?"

"I do not understand the nature of her familiar. But he is wily, and perhaps treacherous. Succubi are that way."

"And this succubus is really doing the magic. Against her?"

"That is the way I see it. As I say, I do not completely understand, but I see."

"Ridiculous. Mr. Strauss is a skilled magician himself."

"Oh, he knows more than he can actually do. He is evil incarnate himself, but he has limitations."

Sophia looked at her grandmother-in-law suspiciously. "Sometimes you surprise me. Most of the time you play the idiot. But you are shrewd in your way."

"That is the way I choose to play my cards," the old woman said.

Sara got home late and didn't know what to do. She wanted to worry about her predicament, feeling somehow obliged. It was serious enough. A man had been assigned the task of killing her, and his past history tended to speak highly of his qualifications for that job. He was a professional and had a track record of fulfilling his contracts.

For some reason, though, she could not muster an overall sense of urgency, the sense of danger and alarm most people would feel with a price on their head. She was more worried about not being worried than she was . . . well, whatever.

There was a sense of improvisation hanging over this entire affair, and she had to get to the bottom of it. Someone was behind it. She could not take werewolves seriously. Or Mah Jongg dragons. The werewolf had not taken himself seriously, at times.

The city of the temple, though, for some strange reason, she took as real. Which was all the more strange, because it struck her as the most improbable of the recent apparitions. Nevertheless, those surpassingly strange beings seemed in deadly earnest.

Why on earth would they want her as a goddess? They weren't human. Wouldn't they require an anthropomorphic god from their perspective? Judging from the design of their cities, they were avian. Birds. And their resident (if you could use the term) god was definitely of the same genus. Why would they want an alien creature, which she certainly was, for a goddess? Not a lot of sense there.

Then again, humans have had human gods and nonhuman gods. Maybe the bird worshipers wanted to trade theirs in on a new model. She wondered about the consequences of such blasphemy. Would not the resident god be.... miffed?

Rather miffed, one should think. Then again, who says this god is a jealous god? Don't model your theology after the earthly kind.

The Witchblade began to pulsate.

Ah-hah. And why would that be? Suddenly her hearing became more acute. The door seemed to vibrate with echoes from the hallway, echoes of heavy footsteps. The sounds came from the stairwell, growing louder and nearer.

She got out her .38 special and looked it over, pondering. She had a suspicion, and if it proved accurate, the gun would do her no good. Joe had warned an indictment was imminent. What she needed was a good lawyer, not a representative of the firm of Smith & Wesson. She put the gun back in the drawer of the nightstand.

A bothersome thought occurred. Hell, she'd spend the night at the Tombs, and they'd take the bracelet. She had never thought of that. Damn it, that could not happen. And in jail, without the Blade she would become a fish in a barrel. Through his mob connections, Strauss could reach his tentacles into the Tombs like a giant squid probing a sunken cathedral.

How many disgruntled former informants would there be in the Tombs, more than ready to act out their revenge fantasies by whacking a supposed dirty cop? Plenty. Sure, she'd be segregated, in the women's wing, and probably in special custody reserved for dirty cops. But who knew what guards were on the Organizatsiya payroll?

What could she do? Nothing. Her taking a powder would not only reflect badly on Joe Siry; it could cost him his job and retirement.

An authoritative rap sounded on the door. Sara opened it.

"Detective Pezzini?"

"Yes?"

A strange-looking man flashed a badge at her. He was flanked by four equally odd-looking ducks.

"Who the hell are you?" She didn't see any reason to be civil. "Never seen you before. What precinct do you work out of?"

"We have a warrant for your arrest."

"That so? What charge, exactly?"

"Criminal conspiracy." He fluttered a blue-slipped paper at her.

"So they didn't go for the RICO rap? Okay, come in."

They followed her into the apartment.

"We also have a search warrant," the leader said.

Sara narrowed her eyes. "What's your name and rank? I'd like to know who's commanding this detail."

"Detective Smith," the man said.

"Okay . . . Smith."

"You have the right to remain silent," Smith recited. "Anything you say can and will be used against you. You have the right to an attorney. If you cannot afford an attorney, one will be provided to you free of charge. Do you understand these rights?"

"I don't understand why you're telling me you have a search warrant, when you don't need one on a bust. You can trash this apartment if you want to. You're telling me the DA doesn't know this?"

Smith's eyes suddenly grew . . . strange. Everything was simply wrong. All these jamooks had an odd look.

The Witchblade's pulsing was verging on the painful. Sara took a few steps back from "Smith."

"Sara Pezzini . . ." the creature named Smith began.

"You're not from New York, are you?"

Smith shook his head. "No, Sara Pezzini. We want you to come with us."

"Come where?"

"To our world. Please accompany us. We will escort you."

She turned and took them all in. They were simply standing around as if not knowing what to do. Perhaps the others could not even talk.

"Please do come. We invite you."

"Who are you?"

"We are the Order of the Raven," Smith said simply.

"And what is that?"

"It is hard to explain."

"Okay, Order of the Raven. What the hell do you want?"

"We need you to reign over us, as our deity. You and the symbiotic entity." He pointed to her wrist.

"The symbiotic entity?" Sara held out her right wrist. "This bracelet?"

"Yes. You are one thing, it is another. Together, you are yet a third. A godhead."

"And you want me as your . . . deity?"

"Yes. We desire it with every fiber of our collective being. Will you come?"

"No. You come from a funny kind of place."

"Funny?"

"Yeah. Most places, you go to them. Your world is the kind of place that comes to you. I've been there. It's not my kind of town. No offense."

"Ah," Smith said with deep regret. Somehow he looked crestfallen, for all that his mask-face had not changed one iota.

Sara did not understand how that could be, but set the issue aside for the moment. "What I want to know is, why? Why do you want me as a goddess?"

"Relations with our present god have become strained beyond all possibility of repair."

"I see. I don't understand, though."

"Again, it is not easy to cast into terms which you could understand in your present state of consciousness."

"No doubt. How can I get a change of consciousness?"

"We believe you will come to understand through the altered states afforded you by virtue of your symbiosis."

"I don't think of it as a symbiosis," Sara told him. "I

am an independent, self-contained individual. I do feel a kind of obligation to this thing on my wrist. It's chosen me for a role in a drama that's been going on for a long time. Exactly what that drama is all about, I really don't know. I'm still struggling to understand. But that is the extent of my relationship with it."

"We are not entirely knowledgeable of some things. We do not completely understand the entity you wear on your person, and your own nature is mostly a mystery to us. Forgive our presumption in posing some hypotheses."

"I forgive you. I'm going to confess that I haven't the foggiest notion of what you people are all about. And frankly, again no offense, I wish you'd leave me the hell alone."

"If that is your wish, we cannot refuse. However, we cannot let the issue rest. Not yet. Our humblest apologies."

"Smith" bowed deeply, turned and walked out of the apartment. Single file, his buddies followed.

The door closed softly.

"Sheesh," Sara said, shaking her head.

After microwaving a frozen dinner and eating it while watching TV, she went to bed and dreamed about dark skies full of birds, and creepy guys with masks all running about below, getting crapped on and liking it.

Next morning, she stopped into her favorite coffee shop and bought a hot mocha latte with whipped cream. A square of cinnamon crumb cake took her fancy, and she got that, too. Then, sitting at a table eating it, she remembered that a contract was out on her life, and that she should get her butt out of public view, pronto. So she gathered up the cake on a paper napkin and, coffee in the other hand, walked to the station. Some patrolman was kind enough to open the door, but he let it go prematurely. She got bumped in the rear and got her hand scalded. She dribbled coffee and crumbs all the way to her desk.

"Sara, I've got something to tell you," Jake said behind her back.

"What . . . oh, damn. Jake, did you know you had a way of sneaking up on people?"

Jake looked down at the crumb cake, now on the dirty station floor. "Oops. Sorry."

"Rats, that was good, too. Okay, what is it now?"

"Uh . . . Jeez, Sara, I don't know how to tell you this . . ."

"Tell me. It was a bad night and it's been a bad morning so far. Nothing you could say could put me in a worse mood."

"Wanna bet?"

"No. What is it?"

"You're under arrest."

CHAPTER TWENTY-ONE

The worst thing about a stay in the Tombs is the smell, a multi-layered phenomenon. On top of everything sits the fumes of a strong disinfectant, capstone to a wall of odor that permeates the place. The stink of all manner of body effluent, from armpits to excrement, lives in the mid-levels. And bottoming all of it, on the floors and along the walls and baseboards, in drains and pipes, amongst the dust bunnies beneath the bunks and in the musty stuffing of mattresses, dwells the dank smell of mold, mildew, and fungus of every variety, a century in the growing.

The women's wing was a little better than the men's, but not much. Sara had spent all day here. It was evening now, and there was nothing to do but lie in the bunk. At least the sheets were clean. Well, as clean as they could get. The fabric looked to have been woven sometime in the 1950s. It was threadbare and rife with holes. At least the blanket didn't smell. Not much, anyway.

She hadn't been alone. Joe Siry had come and gone, promising to pull every string he could to get her special treatment. She did not tell him not to. No way. She needed every break she could get. One good thing, she had no cell mates. If there had been another cop in jail at the time, maybe. She was alone in the cell, though there were two other cots.

One toilet, the usual stainless steel affair, open to public view.

Charming.

Jake McCarthy had come and gone. He was upset and worried, but tried to cover up with smarmy cheer. She'd beat the rap. No problem. They'd get a good lawyer. He knew a woman who was a great trial performer. She'd get Sara off, if she didn't get the case dismissed at the pretrial hearing.

Sure, Jake. Sara had gone along, surfing on Jake's wave of Pollyanna optimism. But as she had told Joe, she needed a fall guy. And the guy she had in mind was rather difficult to pin a conspiracy charge on. And just how does one go about making a measly state charge stick to a genuine international man of mystery?

The lights went out. It must be ten o'clock. Ten o'clock. That means up at six. Ye gods.

No, don't say "gods," please.

She lay still until her eyes got used to the dark. When forms appeared in the shadows, she rolled over on her left side, plumped the thin pillow, and tried to get some rest.

She was just about to doze off when she caught movement in her field of vision. Something skittered through the cell door and disappeared under her cot.

She jumped up. She hadn't got a good look at it. Spider, roach, mouse, rat, something like that. One of those critters. Well, jails had 'em in abundance. She got on her knees and peered under the bunk. She couldn't see a thing. No matter. If it had been a spider, it probably wasn't poisonous. A mouse she could live with. A rat? It hadn't looked big enough. Likely it had been an oversized roach. So what.

She got back on the cot and stretched out.

Drifting out of sleep, she became aware of something nibbling at her right hand. She rolled out of the cot, hit the floor, rolled again, and brought her hand up to catch the light that had just come on out in the corridor.

The Witchblade was hugging her wrist, throbbing urgently. *This* was what she had seen scurrying under her cot?

"Sometimes you really blow my mind, kiddo," she told it as she picked herself up and got back on the cot. "Glad to see you, though."

A guard appeared at the cell door and fumbled with keys. Sara sat up and looked at him.

"What's up?" she asked, squinting at the light.

"You're being transferred," he replied. He was a big man with a short haircut. He looked like a typical turnkey.

"Funny, nobody told me," she said, wondering what the Blade was warning about. And then the obvious answer occurred to her.

"There's probably a good reason," the guard said pleasantly. "Let's go. Your new cell is in another cell block. Guess they want to keep moving you around for safety's sake."

"Do we need the cuffs?" Sara asked, wanting to avoid his seeing the bracelet. She shouldn't have it.

"Don't see why," he said amiably. "I don't think you're going to try anything, Detective Pezzini. You probably want to get this thing cleared up real fast. Have a good lawyer?"

"Haven't met her yet. Will tomorrow at the arraignment."

"Well, good luck. Hey, I'm on your side. We cops have to stick together."

"Yeah, sure."

"Let me get that," the guard said, applying a key to the cell block door.

"You kinda have to," Sara said. "Don't have my key on me."

The guard laughed and let her through the door.

It was a long way, though door after door. Eventually Sara found herself walking through empty corridors that didn't look like cell blocks at all.

"Where the hell are we going?" Sara asked, turning her head.

The so-called guard was aiming a silenced pistol at her.

In the quiet of the night, the shot made a lot of noise, a sharp whack that echoed off cold concrete.

The Witchblade jumped up to ward off the slug, which went whizzing off at an angle and thunked into the wall a few feet down the hallway.

"What the hell?" the bogus guard said in shock. His eyes widened at the sight of Sara's curlicue gauntlet shapeshifting on her arm. He aimed and fired again.

Same result.

Sara grabbed the gun off him and pocketed it. "Tell Strauss he'll have to come up with better stuff," she told him.

The guy was backing off, eyes as round as manhole covers. "What the hell is that? What the hell *are* you?"

"Oh, Strauss didn't say? Good. You'll never know. Give you something to think about in your old age. If you reach it. By the way, what's your name?"

Nonplused, the phony guard could only answer, "Sam."

"Say good night, Sam."

"Good night."

She sent a simple bolt of kinetic energy at his jaw. Just a tap. He flew about six feet and ended up a sprawl on the blue-painted floor.

She found an emergency box, broke the glass, pulled the cord, and waited for the real guards to show up.

After Sara's arraignment, at which she pleaded not guilty to a charge of criminal conspiracy to commit murder, Joe Siry bailed her out, putting his own house up as security for the bond. Sara emptied her meager savings account and paid Joe what she could, and signed a promissory note for the rest. She had to borrow from the police credit union for legal expenses.

Her lawyer, Cathy Greenwood, was a small woman with an attractive, elfin face. She looked young, very young, but said she was 35 years old. She just had that kind of face. Sara was not reassured.

Siry was forced to suspend her without pay. He had no choice, of course. She could not continue to work while under indictment for a felony. Full back pay would be awarded if she beat the rap. To Sara, though, pay wasn't an issue. It meant she could not do any further investigating on her own. Her badge would be temporarily inactive. She instructed Cathy to ask if she could be kept on active status with the police department.

"We can't have her investigating her own crimes," Morrison, the assistant DA, said.

"Alleged crimes," Cathy Greenwood corrected.

"Of course, alleged crimes."

"Nevertheless, you'd better plead your client. We have more than enough to bind her over for trial."

"We'll see," Cathy said. "Frankly, I don't think you even have a case. I just might mount a defense at the hearing."

"Be a mistake," Morrison said. "If you have a defense, you'll want to save it for the trial. Don't want to tip your hand."

"I'm always suspicious," Cathy said, "when the prosecutor starts giving me courtroom advice. Usually means he doesn't have anything to back up his case."

"We have forensic evidence, we have witnesses, we have the defendant's own statements and official reports."

The DA was leaning forward in his chair, looking uncomfortable. "We wouldn't go to trial if we didn't think we had a case," he said, more to Morrison than anyone else. "Would we?"

"No way, Cap," Morrison said.

"I think what you have are surmises, assumptions, and just plain guesses. My client is a police officer. She's investigating the very crimes you accuse her of committing. Of course you're going to find evidence of her presence at the crime scene. The whole thing is ridiculous. An outrage."

"It's not outrageous to prosecute crime," the interim DA said. "That's our job."

"Absolutely," Morrison agreed, not at all thrilled by the DA's insipidity.

"My client has been attacked in custody. Clearly an assassination attempt. Doesn't that throw doubt on the case?"

"Who knows what mob rules she broke or what toes she stepped on?" Morrison said, his hands out. "I think it tends to bolster our case rather than the reverse. It's clear she has mob affiliations."

"It's also logical to assume that she's a mob target because of her zeal in pursuing organized crime figures."

"That's your interpretation," Morrison countered.

"It will be the jury's interpretation as well," Cathy said.

"We'll see at the trial."

"We won't even get to the hearing. I'm filing a motion for dismissal."

"On what grounds?" the DA asked.

"Lack of evidence. Let's face it, you didn't investigate any other suspects. I wonder what tale the jail hit man has to tell. Who was bribed? How did he get in there? You haven't even offered him immunity."

Morrison said, "We're not obliged to. That's another case entirely. Simply because your client was the intended victim has no bearing on this case."

"I should say it does," Cathy said hotly. "Ridiculous to say it doesn't!"

"Not at all. I think you're making a mistake taking that tack."

"Why so?"

"Well, if you're claiming that the real conspirators are trying to bump off your client, it could be a bid to hush her up in a plea bargain."

Cathy sat back. "Oh," she said quietly. "I see."

"Kind of blindsided you," Morrison said with some satisfaction. "That's exactly what we'll be countering if you bring up the hit attempt."

"But the whole thing rests on appearances," Cathy said lamely.

"Where there's smoke, there's fire," the DA said in hopes of being relevant to the issue at hand.

"True," Morrison acknowledged diplomatically.

Sara was sitting with her long legs crossed, following the exchange with interest.

"You have the semblance of a case," Cathy went on. "But you have no case. It's all appearances."

"Appearances can be deceiving," the DA blurted, then realized he had said the wrong thing. Morrison gave him a sidelong look of irritation.

"Exactly my point," Cathy went on. "My client looks guilty, and lacking any other line of investigation, you target her. She was strictly a target of opportunity, and that's what the jury will think."

"Oh, we're back to the trial again?" Morrison grinned impishly. "Counselor, you'd better plead your client."

Cathy looked at Sara before saying, "What are you offering?"

The DA started to say something, but was preempted by Morrison.

"Murder Two," he said. "Twenty-five to life."

"For which murder?"

"Any of them."

"That's absurd. Sir, weren't you about to say something?'

"Yes, I was," the DA said indignantly. "I was about to offer immunity in exchange for information about the new ethnic mobs." The DA was suddenly all business. "I'm on a crusade," he added, wanting to be helpful.

Morrison was dismayed. "Uh, well, wait a minute . . ."

"I'm the District Attorney."

"Hold it," Cathy said. "Are there two offers on the table? One from the DA and one from the assistant DA?"

"No, there's one offer," the DA said, satisfied to have put his foot down.

"Immunity. Uh, in exchange for reliable information which could lead to a prosecution, which . . . well, which could lead to a conviction."

Cathy was incredulous. "Is the plea bargain going to be contingent on a desired verdict?"

"No, no, not at all," the DA said. "We can offer witness protection, too."

"But that's a federal program," Cathy said.

"We are starting up our own program, funded by . . ."

"It doesn't matter. My client is innocent of any conspiracy charge."

"She's the mistress of a Russian mobster!" Morrison exploded.

"Okay, that's it," Sara said suddenly, getting to her feet. She towered over the DA.

"Uh . . . yes?"

"No plea bargain, no deal, no nothing," Sara said. "There's only so much nonsense I'm going to put up with."

"Counselor," Morrison said, "tell your client she's not helping her case with that attitude."

"Sara, sit down, please. I'm not going to do anything you don't want me to do. Trust me."

"Cathy, I trust you. File your motions, make a defense at the hearing, do anything you have to do, but don't ever consider the possibility that I'll cop a plea to something I didn't do."

"If I had a nickel for every time I've heard that in this

office," Morrison said, shaking his head. "Next day, they bargain."

"There won't be any bargains, not today, not any day," Sara said. "And you won't get a nickel from me, Mr. Morrison."

She executed an about-face and walked out of the office.

Albert the DA was impressed. "Your client has spunk, that I'll say."

"Please," Morrison said.

CHAPTER TWENTY-TWO

To say that Joe Siry's day had been rough would have been an understatement. Sara was out of jail, but had blown the interview with the DA, and Joe had gone to considerable lengths to soften Albert up for some kind of deal. Hell, she could have promised him anything. Information. She had information to trade. Didn't she date that Russian mobster? Well, okay, once, but she could have given them details about him, stuff for their files. Stuff they wanted. Mostly trivial, but Albert would have gone for it.

Promise them anything. That's what he always did. Promise them anything and deliver what you got. Bupkis. Nada. The old bait and switch.

But, no, she had to go and blow it, walk out in a huff. She didn't know you saved that tactic for when they're desperate to make a deal. That's a last-resort ploy. It was a tricky maneuver. He'd pulled it off any number of times in his career.

Sara was young and inexperienced. Hot-headed, impulsive. Most young cops were. She was dedicated, for sure. But she had a wild streak. And that . . . weird business she was always into. He still didn't know what to make of all that.

He left the office and walked to his favorite bar, Grogan's, on West 34th Street. It was a nice little place. He knew the owner, Shamus Grogan, an old reprobate who had long lived on the peripheries of what was left of the ancient Irish mobs of New York. He was long in the tooth, Shamus was. In and out of the hospital for the last ten years. He must be in his nineties by now, but he still showed up at his own joint once in a while to have a glass of Guiness.

There now. He, Joe Siry, was an old acquaintance of Shamus Grogan. Did that mean he had "organized crime affliations," for pete's sake? Don't make him laugh. Same thing with Sara. So she took a fancy to some Albanian. Whatever. So what? Didn't mean she was his mistress. Did it?

Well, Joe didn't really know everything about Sara's love life. That was her business. Right? Right.

He walked in the door. The place was empty, but it wasn't even four-thirty yet. He'd knocked off early. Some days, you gotta knock off early.

A man was standing behind the bar, washing glasses. Joe had never seen him before. "You the new bartender?"

He was a thin and wiry guy with long hair. "Yeah, just got hired."

"What happened to Frank?"

"He needed some time off. Family."

"Oh," Joe said. "This your first day, huh?"

"Yes, sir. What can I get you?"

"The usual. Oh, yeah, you don't know my usual. Half and half."

"Yes, sir, coming right up."

"And some peanuts. Shamus always likes peanuts on the bar."

The new man looked at the clock. "I guess I should get them out. Happy hour coming up."

"Happy hour," Joe said to himself. "I'm happy."

"Yeah?" the guy said, not getting the irony.

"As a lark. When I'm here. When I'm drinking with my buddies. Then I'm happy. If only I didn't have to go to work."

"Oh? What do you do?"

"Police."

"Oh, you're Joe Siry?"

"Yeah. My reputation precedes me, I bet."

"Sure. I've heard of you. Just wanted to make sure."

"Wanted to make sure. What do you mean?"

Suddenly, the front door slammed shut.

Joe jerked his head around. Another guy had slammed it. Big guy. With a gun. "Hey, what the hell is going . . . ?"

"Captain Siry?"

Joe whirled on his barstool to find the voice. A slim, well-dressed man had come out from the back. His face was extraordinarily ugly. The man was a well-groomed toad.

Joe scowled. "Who the hell are you?"

The toad bowed. "Permit me. My name is Erwin Strauss."

Merlin was writing a program on one of his many laptop computers when he heard the cops knock. He always knew when cops knocked: a certain sharp, authoritarian rap, as unmistakable as Morse code.

Muttering mild profanities, he went to the door and

peered through the peephole. He saw a pretty face, a familiar one, distorted by the extreme wide-angle lens. It was pretty even with the distortion.

Well, he couldn't very well pretend he wasn't home. That never worked. He opened the door. It was Pezzini and another guy, likely her partner. He looked like someone out of an old beach movie.

"Merlin," Pezzini said. "You are one elusive dude."

"I like it that way. Do come in."

Merlin led them into the living room.

"This a bust?" he asked casually, knowing they would have said so immediately but wanting to set the tone of the visit.

"Did you know you have about two dozen cell phone accounts?" Sara said. "All inactive?"

"Oh, yeah. Never seem to get those cleaned up."

"And none with a real address. How did you manage that?"

Merlin shrugged. "Talent?"

"Wonder how many cloned cell phones we could find if we searched this sty?" the surfer dude said.

"Plenty, but I get the feeling you guys want to know about something else."

"Yes, we do," Sara said. "Your connection with Irons International Investments and Holdings."

"I've worked for them."

"Or for Kenneth Irons personally?"

"Same thing, no?"

"Not quite, but you have been working for him?"

"Right."

"On what?"

"Big computer."

"What kind?"

"Supercomputer. Powerful one. New type."

"What's it for, Merlin?"

"Controlling the economic world."

"You're being quite forthcoming, aren't you?" Sara said, absently kicking debris.

"Got nothing to hide. It models the world economy, taps into data bases, and comes up with strategies for making money. Big project, but pretty simple concept."

"Got anything to do with computer crime?"

"At Irons's level, there's no such thing. If there is, they call it arbitrage."

"I'd be willing to bet that an investigation would determine the crime angle pretty quickly," the beach blanket dude said.

"I'm just a technician," Merlin said hastily.

"Sure," Sara said. "You only work here. There. Where is 'there,' by the way?"

"You mean the computer."

"I don't mean Hoboken."

"They blindfold me."

Sara and the blond guy exchanged looks. The guy said, "That so?"

"Yup."

"So you don't know where this computer is," Sara said.

Merlin looked out the window. "I might."

"What do you mean?"

"Depends on what chips you put on the table, vis-à-vis Yours Truly."

Sara looked at her partner. "Sounds like he wants a deal, Jake."

"Sure does," Jake agreed.

"Let me ask you this," Sara said. "Did you send the e-mail about Joe Siry?"

"Who?" Merlin said.

"My boss."

Merlin did a take. "Your boss? I don't get it."

"The e-mail sent to my on-line address, informing me he'd been kidnapped. Did you send it?"

"No! I don't know your e-mail address. Anyway, I didn't send any e-mail about any kidnapping. Never. Not ever. No way, man."

"Jake, what do you think?"

"I was watching his reactions. I'm willing to buy them as genuine."

Sara said to Merlin, "Does the name Erwin Strauss mean anything to you?"

"Not a damned thing. Hey, I had nothing to do with it. Your boss, for God's sake. We *are* talking about a policeman, here, right?"

"Right. Strauss claimed credit. You see, there's a contract out on my life, and Strauss took it. This a good way to get me in range, at least. The e-mail suggested a sort of exchange. He'll release Siry if I'll meet him on the field of honor, as he put it, for a personal duel. I want to find out where Lieutenant Siry is being held. I've connected Irons with you, and now, if I can connect Irons with Strauss, I can probably find my boss and free him."

"And you think the computer installation is a good place to look?" Merlin asked.

"It's a start," Sara said. "It's secret. That sounds promising."

"Yeah, I can see where you're going," Merlin said. "What's in it for me? Wait, let me put it this way. What's not in it for me?"

"What's not in it?" Jake said airily. "Mucho jail time for whatever we find in this room. This looks like Evidence City for the computer crime squad."

"Ah-hah," Merlin said, with a profound nod. "I think I see where you're going. Uh . . . okay."

"Okay what?"

"I'll take you to the installation."

"I thought you said . . ."

"Ain't no one can keep me from knowing where I'm going in Manhattan. By ear alone, I know exactly where the place is. And I have other ways."

"Yeah?" Sara said.

"I got my mojo working, baby."

"That is so retro," Jake said.

Sara looked out the windshield. This neighborhood was beginning to look familiar.

Driving, Jake was saying, "Merlin your real name?"

"Middle name," Merlin said. "Lloyd Merlin Jones. My mother always wanted a kid named Merlin, but my dad insisted on naming me after my grandfather. I've always preferred Merlin. Suits my nature."

"How long have you been into magic?"

"Since I was a whelp."

"There's been a lot of magic about lately," Sara said. "And you seem to be behind a lot of it."

"Me? But you the witch lady," Merlin said.

Sara looked at him sharply. "What makes you say that?"

"I didn't know who you were up in Connecticut, but when Irons mentioned you, I put two and two together. You're the witch chick I've been hearing about. Witch cop."

"Where have you been hearing it?"

"On the street. You have no idea how much has been out about you. Some wild witch policewoman who kills guys, messes them up."

"My name's out there?"

"No, no. No names. They don't know who you are. But I do, now. It's got to be you. Man, you're scary."

Sara shoved her hands deeper into her jacket pockets. "I've encountered some weird stuff in my career," she said, trying to sound as noncommittal as possible.

"Like that weird stuff up in Connecticut? Oh, by the way, I finally figured out why Yuri got fried."

"Why?"

"His shots scared the thing."

"He saw it? I thought white dragons are invisible in snow."

"You can see white on white, sort of," Merlin said. "Yuri saw something big moving toward him. He shot at it. The dragon freaked out and vomited fire. A nervous reaction, that's all. Like I said, dragons aren't evil in Chinese mythology."

"I don't believe what I'm hearing," Jake said. "You guys saw dragons in Connecticut?"

"We think," Sara said. I didn't see anything at all. I did see the werewolf. Or someone dressed like one. You're sure it wasn't you, Merlin?"

"Are you kidding me?"

"Didn't think so," Sara said. "Okay, it sounds good. We'll put that one down to 'accidental death by dragon.' As if."

"As if?" Merlin said.

"As if you can put that in an official police report," Jake supplied.

"I get the feeling *all* of this is kinda off the record and unofficial," Merlin said. "I mean, you can't write any of this crap in a report. And not get carted off to the nut nursery."

"Remember all the crap in your room, Merlin," Jake said. "Hardly the stuff that dreams are made of. Get my drift?"

"Got it," Merlin said. "Never mind. Turn into this alley here."

"Is this the place?" Sara asked.

"Near. You should park here. It's walkable."

Merlin sprang the door and jumped out of the car. Sara and Jake were half expecting him to make a run for it. He moved off a few feet, but didn't bolt. He wasn't the type.

"Hope he doesn't get an inkling just how unofficial this is," Jake said.

"Maybe illegal, too. Jake, you don't have to do this. You could get into trouble."

"We get Joe back quick, we don't have a problem," Jake said.

"Let's do it."

They got out of the car and followed Merlin. Sara realized that she was heading east into a neighborhood that she usually entered by a westerly route.

The ramshackle machine shop that was Kool Whip's studio took shape in the gathering fall evening darkness.

Sara said, "You knew Kool Whip."

Merlin stopped in his tracks. He turned slowly. "Uh . . . Charlie Bromley? I knew him. Why?"

"Did you tell Charlie Bromley about any of this witch woman stuff?"

"Yeah. We were talking just recently. Look . . . I had

nothing to do with his death. In fact . . . wasn't it you who tried to arrest him?"

"Tried to *question* him, about the murder of Smokey Drexel."

"Uh-huh," Merlin said, his voice small. He took a deep breath. "Anyway, that's where Whip had his studio. But that's not where the computer installation is. It's under that building."

"The one across?"

"Yeah. That's how I knew this place. I suggested it to Mr. Irons. He bought the whole block. By the way, how were you planning to get in? There's security."

"We have a search warrant," Sara lied.

"Nobody to serve it on. No guards. But there's pretty good electronic security."

"Why no live guards?"

"Security risk themselves, I guess," Merlin said. "Irons wants as few people as possible to know this facility exists. Why he hid it here."

"Then there's no way we can get in?"

"Didn't say that. Follow me."

CHAPTER TWENTY-THREE

Merlin led the way through a battered door and down a stairwell. At its bottom was a steel door.

"The first layer of security. Keeps the riffraff out. This one's easy."

Merlin took a small tool kit out of his back pocket, extracted a screw driver from it, went to one knee, and spent only a few seconds picking the conventional-looking lock before standing up and opening the door.

Merlin directed his guests through to a short corridor, at the end of which stood another, more formidable door. It had a lock with a security code keyboard.

Merlin punched a four-digit number, then grasped the door's handle and pulled. Once through, the trio walked another corridor to an imposing vault door that rivaled the best of some big banks.

"Now we have to use high tech," Merlin said. He took out another screwdriver and went to work on some screws in a small panel.

"You seem to have done this before," Sara commented.

"Yeah. Once I figured out the location, I came here

on my own to play with the computer. It's the biggest toy a boy ever had. And I had loads of fun defeating the security."

"Have your fun."

Merlin attached leads from computer to panel and watched patterns dance on the tiny screen. "Won't be a sec," he said cheerily.

"No alarms?" Jake asked.

"I am disarming them as we speak, Detective, sir," Merlin said. "However, there's a camera in the room, and it's always on. We can knock it out, of course. But the video goes to a private security company, and you know how efficient and dedicated the average private security employee is. Armed guards could come storming through the door within ten minutes. Or they could be out to lunch."

"Any way of knowing if there's anybody in there?" Sara asked.

"Not really," Merlin said. "Be prepared to storm in with guns drawn, or do whatever cop thing you guys do."

"Ready to do the cop thing?" Jake asked his partner.

Sara drew her revolver. "Let's do it."

"Uh, I didn't mean right this minute," Merlin said. "Sorry."

With a sharp hiss, the door slid to the left and disappeared into the concrete wall. The portal gave onto yet another corridor and yet another door, this one more massive than all previous.

"What was Irons thinking, nuclear attack?" Jake asked in amazement.

It took a good fifteen minutes for Merlin to open what proved to be the final door to the facility. It opened onto the multi-sided computer control room.

It was deserted. The computer contentedly hummed and flashed in solitude.

"Manny!" Merlin greeted his toy.

"Why do you call it that?" Sara asked.

"It has a dumb name: Macro-Economic Modeling and Simulation Array. MEMSA. That's junk, so I call it Manny. Let me show you how it works."

"We don't have time," Sara said, who had been immensely disappointed at the sight of a deserted facility. Perhaps Strauss and Irons were not connected. That meant a dead end and no further leads.

"We can use the computer's remote viewing function."

Sara stopped her pacing and turned. So did Jake.

"What did you say?"

"Remote viewing. Manny is psychic. I just discovered it recently. One of the reasons I've been visiting on the sly."

"A psychic computer."

Merlin had taken his place at the workstation. "Yeah. It's very cool. It's magic, guys. Manny's not only sentient, he's an adept. He got hold of my magic CD, and I don't really know what happened, but he absorbed it some way. I don't understand how he got it. It may have been when I brought my laptop in for an upload. Must have left the CD on the drive, 'cause Manny got hold of it and copied it. When I saw it on a weird directory, I knew what had happened. This is the world's first magic computer, dudes. You would not believe what it can do."

"Or what it's been doing all along, maybe," Sara said. "This is becoming clearer and clearer."

"Yeah? You mean the dragons and stuff? Maybe, maybe. I've been thinking about that. It's maybe been doing some conjuring."

"No maybe about it," Sara said.

"I guess you're right. All the weird stuff. The monsters."

"You summoned them, Merlin."

Merlin turned on his seat and searched Sara's face for some clue that she had meant it only as a possibility. But his expression betrayed the guilt he felt.

"Shit," Merlin said, turning back to the screen. "I'm a murderer."

"I don't really think so," Sara said. "You said you only meant to cause bad luck."

"I meant for people to stop bothering me. People have always bothered me. I don't want to get into the 'I was beat up as a kid' nerd story, but it's true. I just wanted to get back at people. I didn't mean to kill them. It just happened."

"What did you have against Charlie Bromley?"

"Huh? Same thing I had against Smokey Drexel. I put them up when they got evicted, and they stole my favorite canvas, an original, and sold it to get crack money. Both of 'em. They said they'd pay me back, but of course that was bullshit. I put a curse on both of 'em. And they deserved it. But they didn't deserve to die."

Jake said to Sara, "So Smokey was mugged. Did he have anything to get mugged for?"

"Yeah, all the cash I had in the apartment," Merlin said. "They took that, too. That I would have given them. The painting, no."

"When did Manny get hold of the CD?" Sara asked.

"Couple of months ago, maybe. No telling, though. I've been working for Irons off and on for over a year."

"Okay," Sara said. "It's all coming together. But I have pieces that don't even look like part of a puzzle, much less look like they fit. What was this remote viewing thing you mentioned?"

"Manny can get TV pictures from places where's there's no TV camera. I've been doing . . . well, you can imagine the possibilities."

"Can Manny find my boss?"

"You have a picture of him?"

"Huh? No. Jeez, would I be carrying–?"

"No problem. The NYPD computer would."

"You can log onto it?"

"Sure. No prob. Manny can crack any computer, anywhere. I developed programs to deal with almost any situation."

Merlin typed something at lightning speed, grabbed the mouse and clicked. He then alternated between keyboard and mouse, working swiftly, expertly.

Very soon, an image of Joe Siry appeared on the screen, along with vital statistics from his personnel file.

"Amazing," Sara said.

"Now I'll activate the remote viewing program."

"How's that work?"

"I've no idea how it works or why it works. It just works."

"I'll bet Manny knows."

"Yeah. Okay, here he is."

The CRT showed the face of Joe Siry, and this time it was not a photo. This was a live image. Joe was tied to a chair in a bare room. There was no window in the room, and no real clue as to the room's location.

"Utterly amazing," Sara said. "But not really helpful."

"Yeah, I know," Merlin admitted. "But . . . well, it's a crazy idea, but . . ."

"But what?" Jake prodded.

"There's a summoning spell."

"Which is . . . ?"

"A spell to bring something from a remote location to this location. I've never tried it. Kind of afraid to."

Jake looked at Sara. "What do you think?"

"It's worth a try. It would certainly end the hostage crisis. Merlin?"

"Uh, yeah?"

"Do it."

"Right." Merlin went back to typing and mousing. "I gotta put you in as the summoner, since he's connected to you."

"Do anything you have to. Just get him here."

"I will. Just don't be surprised by unexpected side effects."

"I'll try not to be."

Presently, the huge black wedding cake of a computer began to glow with a faint blue aura.

"Whoa," Merlin said, glancing up.

"Something wrong?" Jake asked.

"Never seen that before. Cherenkov radiation!"

"What the hell is that?"

"It's science creeping into magic. Or the other way around. Hold on."

The aura increased in intensity until it became a flaming aurora borealis effect, a diaphanous fabric of multicolored plasma filling the room. The intensity became enough to blind. Jake and Sara took cover behind some control consoles, but the effect filled every nook and cranny of the installation and every cubic foot of air.

A blinding blue-white flash exploded in the room, accompanied by a loud pop and a numbing concussion.

When the glow had dissipated and the air was clear

again, Sara stumbled out from cover, trying to make her eyes focus. First she saw Jake and Merlin lying atop each other. They were knocked cold. Then she saw something astonishing.

Joe Siry sat in his chair a few feet in front of the main stack of the computer. He was still tied. He looked around, then looked at Sara. "What in the bloody blue blazes?"

Sara was on him immediately. She cut the ropes with a pocket knife.

"Judas H. Priest," Siry said. "Where did you come from?" He got up, stretched, and looked around. "Where the hell did this place come from?"

"Hard to explain," Sara said. "Never mind. You're back, you're safe. Where was Strauss?"

"I dunno. He might have been in the other room."

"Have any idea where they were holding you?"

"Isn't it here?"

"No. Joe, I said it's hard to explain."

"Well, if it's not here, I don't know. They stuffed me into a trunk."

"The important thing is that we got you back."

"Yeah," Siry said, grabbing his back. "Ouch, damn it. Yeah, thanks."

"What's wrong, Joe?"

"My friggin' arm. Hurts like a bastard."

"Any chest pain?"

"Yeah, some. I'm okay."

"Sit back down. Sit down, Joe."

"Damn," Siry said, clutching his left shoulder. "Going right down my arm. Hurts."

"I'll call 911." Sara took out her cell.

"Damn. Damn. God, that smarts. Never thought it would hurt this much."

"Joe, keep calm. Hello? Heart attack, abandoned warehouse . . ." She gave the address.

"Jesus."

"Keep calm. I'm here."

"And so am I," came a voice from behind the stack.

CHAPTER
TWENTY-FOUR

Sara turned as a figure came out from behind Manny the computer. It was a large, bearded man in the dress of a past century, somewhere in the Middle Ages. He wore a fur cap and cape, red tunic, black tights, and boots. His eyes were dull black, like soot on a crematorium.

"And who might you be?" Sara asked as the Witchblade began to transform.

"Vlad Tepys," the man answered. He pronounced the surname *Tepish.*

"So, we finally meet," Sara said. "I've been observing your handiwork for some time."

"I don't know what you mean," Vlad said. "I have been summoned for a killing. You, I think, are the one intended. You can submit now, and I will be merciful. Resist, and I will create a death for you that will linger for an eternity."

"I'll just bet your women can't get enough of you, Vlad," Sara said.

Vald continued walking forward. "You are a beautiful

woman. I've never seen your like. And you have... something... what is that thing? Ah." He took another step. "Ah. I know of that."

"Then you ought to know I will resist," Sara said, "and that I can provide you with a death that will make one of your impalings seem like fondling."

Vlad's smile spread across his face like a stain. "You are tigress. This will be sport for me."

"Let's play," Sara said.

A huge sword with a two-handed haft appeared in Vlad's left hand, and he advanced swinging it. It made a swishing sound like an immense scythe.

The Witchblade grew into its blade configuration, a double-edged shaft of steel that gleamed like a mirror. It took Vlad's first cut, issuing sparks from where the blades clashed.

Vlad swung again, and again Sara blocked with her blade. His cuts were wickedly fast, viciously forceful. She blocked again and again, and had no time for a riposte.

But that was not the worst of it. The worst of it was that the swipes became ever more forceful, the momentum packing more and more punch, until she came within a hair's breadth of losing her footing.

Vlad's blade came round and hit hers like a runaway freight train. She staggered and lurched across the room, hit the wall and sprawled.

Vlad laughed. "A woman warrior. What a silly thing. How can you hope to stand up to a man?"

Sara picked herself up and looked around. The wall seemed to have receded. The room seemed bigger now. Lots bigger, but she had little time to notice.

Vlad came at her. She backed off, having the space now.

Vlad swung. She blocked the blow and a stinging sensation went up her arm like a bolt of electricity.

"Ah, you hurt," Vlad said with satisfaction. "It feels like fire in the arm, eh? Like your hand is on fire. It will hurt more. I will defeat you, little woman, and I will make you feel pain. I will gut you from gills to gullet and relish your screams. Then I will take your soul to Hell with me."

Sara suddenly dropped to her knees and swiped at his shanks. The move forced him into an awkward position, which Sara capitalized on immediately with a thrust at his midsection. He barely knocked the point of her blade away.

"Ai!" He laughed maniacally. "You make it interesting! Lovely!"

He began swinging again, more forcefully than before. Sara got batted around like a stuffed toy and was beginning to think she did not have a chance when something extraordinary happened.

Vlad's head detached from his body and hit the ground. It bounced twice and came to rest. The eyes were round with incomprehension. And the mouth spoke. "What . . . who . . . ?"

Fire came out from the truncated neck.

The body went to its knees. Behind it stood the figure of Ian Nottingham, hair flowing, dressed in studded leather and black velvet.

"Hello, Sara," he said pleasantly.

"Ian! Where the hell did you come from?"

"I believe you summoned me. No?"

"I guess I did," Sara said.

"Not sure of the circumstances, but here I am. Anything I can help you with?"

As if in answer, Vlad's body rose and charged Ian. The

head shifted its eyes to follow the action as it attacked. Ian backed, off parrying slamming blows that seemed to come from all directions. Even headless, Vlad was as demonic as the flames and smoke issuing from the neck.

Sara rushed to attack from the headless body's rear. She thrust at the spine, wondering whether it would do any good to attack anatomical points. It did not. She buried the Blade squarely in the middle of the back, severing what would have been the spine, if it existed, but the body did not go paraplegic, did not collapse. Flame shot out of the hole she had made in the fur cape.

The mouth on the disembodied face roared, and the body turned around. This stereo-like effect was disconcerting. Sara backed off to take the thing's measure.

Ian took advantage of Vlad's presenting his back and attacked. He had some success backing the apparition toward Sara, who lunged.

Vlad's blade came around fast and blocked, then slashed back at Ian. Sara swung, was blocked, then Ian swung and met the same defense on his side. The sword moved fast enough to snap the air like the end of a whip.

Sara and Ian locked eyes and swung together. Vlad chose to block Ian, letting Sara's sword bite through his right arm, severing it at the elbow. Flame shot from the stump.

The head bellowed its frustration again, but the body did not stop fighting. Left-handed, it hacked and slashed at its two opponents.

The fight ranged across the now-cavernous room, which hardly resembled the computer installation any more. The monstrous, unnatural thing fought furiously until Ian managed to land a solid blow on its left shank. The huge form stumbled and fell.

"Witch woman!"

Sara spun toward the disembodied head.

"Tell me. Do you know what they call me?"

"Other than Vlad? Haven't the slightest."

"I am called Dracula."

"Not without justification," Sara said.

"Do you know what it means?"

"Nope."

"The Dragon."

"Uh . . . okay, if you say so."

The headless body disappeared in a gout of flame.

Something else took shape out of the smoke and fire and fluid electricity of the expanded space. An immense saurian form flapped its wings and roared.

"Ian, thanks awfully much for showing up."

"Ah, I do not think the show is over."

"Not by a long shot. How do you propose we deal with this new thing?"

"I propose we run like hell."

"Good idea. In what direction, might I ask?"

"Around in panicked circles, if nothing else."

"Right."

"By the way, when did this room become a cave? A flaming cave, to boot."

"Don't know. Wasn't paying attention."

The dragon opened its mouth and vomited fire. It hit them like the blast of a tactical nuclear weapon.

When the heat had passed off and the acrid fumes dissipated, Sara and Ian raised their heads and looked. The dragon was advancing toward the lake of fire that occupied the middle of the cavern.

Sara felt her eyebrows, checking to see if they'd been

singed off. He felt her hair. It was still intact, at least not on fire.

"I guess I have to handle this," she said.

"Why don't you go and do that, old girl," Nottingham said.

"I wish we were doing Chinese mythology."

"Say what?"

The dragon glided into the liquid fire like a duck taking to water. Flapping its huge leathery wings, it began swimming across, puking flame in a narrow, directed stream like something out of World War Two combat footage.

Sara used the Witchblade to ward it off. Fire splattered to her left and right, dancing off the black rocks, cascading and spreading, dark smoke rising from it.

When the monster paused to take a breath, Sara sprayed.

Not fire, but foam, thinking she'd continue the scientific motif of the original location. The modern stuff hit the ancient dragon and enveloped it in runny white goo, spewing out with a sound not unlike whipped cream from a can. As it landed on the surface of the lake, a great hissing and bubbling commenced. The fire churned and spat.

Sara continued spewing foam, delivering great quantities of the stuff, mounting in the middle of the lake like a mound of dessert topping. Underneath, the fire reacted violently, sputtering and throwing back huge gouts of the foamy stuff. Splatters hit the shore and doused fires among the rocks.

Ian Nottingham stood on the shore of the lake of fire, astounded beyond words. He thought the sight of the dragon being enveloped a singular sight indeed. He applauded.

Sara finally decided enough was enough. She could see nothing but foam, a mountain of it. All it needed was some nuts and a cherry.

She walked over to where Ian was standing. "See the dragon anywhere?"

"No sign of it from this standpoint."

They watched. The foam was sliding and slopping every which way. Something could have been moving underneath at any number of points. Finally, with a splash of foam and fire, the dragon's head emerged. It swam to shore and lay its long neck along the rocks. It coughed and sputtered and spat white stuff. Then it exhaled, and nothing but blue smoke came out.

"Out of gas," Sara said.

The dragon looked at the two forlornly.

CHAPTER TWENTY-FIVE

Gradually, the lake of foam and fire began to fade. The rocks turned to smooth flagstone. The floor flattened out, and the dragon and his foam coat receded into mist. Perspectives shifted. The subterranean world was gone.

"Sara, I don't know quite how to put this," Nottingham said, his voice growing faint, "but are you by any chance *growing*?"

Sara, already beyond Nottingham's ken and filling another space and a different time entirely, found herself towering over the polished temple floor.

Reality shifted, and the million-stranded warp and woof of existence twisted into a new thread and wove itself into a new fabric.

Screeeeeeeeee . . .

Sara looked up. The Bird approached, consumed with a jealous anger. Its feet were extended, and its talons gleamed with metal. It was not a natural creature. It was a god, and it was angry.

She was ready for it. She looked down at herself. She was a giant. She was the statue she had seen, the Witchblade, standing atop her inlaid pedestal. But there was no roof to her temple. It was open to an infinite sky.

Sara had never taken flight. She did now. She leapt, and the air took her. She climbed on her immense metal wings, wings that rent the air with their beating.

She found it hard work, but felt exhilarated. She rose higher and higher in a widening spiral, into thinner and thinner air, then banked and soared on an updraft.

It was glorious. The wind was in her face and the earth . . . no, not the earth, but the ground . . . spread out beneath her like a blanket. Pastures, meadows, forest and field, mountains in the distance. An idyllic land, yet a strange one. She saw the city below, the whole of it. It was a tower-covered island between two rivers, and but that was all it shared with its counterpart in Sara's world. There were no other cities around it. It was a bustling urban island in the middle of rural expanses.

She folded her wings and dove, leveled out, rose on thermal currents, dove again and glided. She got the idea then that her wings were merely symbols, that she did not need actual wings to fly. She acquired the overwhelming sense that she could do anything she wanted.

The strange world got smaller, its horizon curving slightly. The sky darkened to violet and clouds were now scudding at her feet. Yet she could breathe. Or she did not need to breathe.

She decided to glide to a lower altitude, gathering speed in great widening circles. Wind snapped at her hair, sent it flowing behind her. She felt the low temperature of these altitudes but did not feel the cold. The winds were icy but they did not bite. It seemed as though she were born for flight.

She grew greater and greater wings. They spread out

against the curve of sky and space, ethereal and yet substantial at the same time, and they undulated rather than beat, like a display of northern lights against the fall of night, like veils of energy, sparkling multi-colored plasma.

Something came up below, a huge palace complex sitting atop a high mountain, a glory of alabaster colonnades and marble porticos. She swooped and landed on a capacious terrace.

She looked down. The world of the Chorus spread out beneath her. She looked around and knew this to be her intended home, her Olympus.

Screeeeeee . . .

The Bird approached, beating its wings furiously, seething with righteous anger, resentful of the intruder, wanting confrontation. It flexed its talons in anticipation, extending them forward, ready to swoop, to pierce, to clutch and tear. It needed prey and it would have it. It needed something to attack, for violence was at the heart of its being, its nature, its reason for existence.

Diving from the terrace, she obliged.

She headed straight for the god-creature and as she neared she sensed something of its fierce nature. It was petty and avaricious, demanding horrendous sacrifices. It loved the smell of fresh blood, and relished pain and suffering.

It bulked huge against the clouds. She had never realized just how massive the creature was. And it was getting bigger.

She extended the gauntlet and directed a bolt of energy at it.

A sharp report split the sky, and the bird-god tumbled, its wings gone slack and rubbery. She was shocked to see that it did not have much strength, for all its bulk. It was too used to bullying creatures of lower link on the great chain of being, much too used to having its sadistic and arbitrary way. After all it was a god, and few can oppose the gods.

She had no trouble. She banked to the right and watched the Bird recover and begin to climb. She glided, picked an angle of attack, and dove, coming at the creature out of the low sun.

At the last minute the Bird executed a whirling turn and counterattacked, bringing its razor-sharp talons up to slash at her. Her gauntlet swiped at them and sent the huge bird tumbling again.

She waited for it to rise again. It seemed dazed a bit, somewhat disoriented, and disinclined to continue the conflict. But it mustered the strength and shot out toward the horizon, needing time and space to gather its resources.

She did not intend to let it. Beating her wings furiously, she took off after it, pursuing it into an expanse of rarefied, etheric blue. She overtook it and directed bolts of searing energy at the bird-god, ionizing energy that came from the depths of her own resources.

The god screamed its pain. It was a new sensation. If it had ever felt pain before, it had been eons since the event. Yet it kept up its counterattack, its talons clicking as they flexed and tried to grab, tried to sink into human flesh, a kind of flesh they had never tasted. The creature was intrigued by its smell. It was sweet.

But it would not get a sample.

A flash of red fire came out of the sky and grew into an explosion of light and radiance that enveloped all of space. The concussion shook the world below and was of such power that it knocked the Bird's true nature loose, the form that it had been hiding for ages. Its true form, that of a vast scaly beast, amorphous and shifting, ever-changing. The Bird was simply a guise, had been its cover and stability for millions of years.

She watched the thing fall, but not wanting to see its end, for she knew it already, she turned and headed back to the palace.

As she alighted on the terrace, a concussion of light grew on the horizon, followed by a huge volcanic gout of flame. The earth had swallowed the Bird for good. It was banished from the skies forevermore.

She looked down at her transfigured form. The Witch-blade had transformed and was now a glory of silver filigree, a cloak of scrollwork and arabesque, flowing from her almost naked body and spreading out from her flanks and behind her.

The gauntlet still covered her right arm, and she brought it up to look at it. Its own nature was changing, and hers with it. Together, they were becoming a third entity, something whose dimensions she was just now beginning to grasp. Vistas of new consciousness extended before her, ranges of thought and feeling and sense far beyond those of human ken, intelligence and perception undreamed of. Her sensorium cast its net over her proud new world, from which a great chorale of joy had arisen.

My people, she thought. *My world. A world over which I will reign in glory and in truth, in justice and in mercy.*

Joe . . . what had happened to Joe?

My domain, my dominion. I am a goddess, and I will reign forever and ever . . .

Hallelujah?

Listen to those voices singing praise. I am a god. I am truth and light. I will rule wisely and with compassion . . .

What the hell is going on? The Blade. The Blade . . .

Millions singing my praises. I am a goddess, my dominion is the sky . . .

No!

My worshipers are legion. Millions sing my exploits and will for generations untold . . .

No! What happened to Joe? I want to know. He was sick, he needs me . . .

Forget all your earthly ties. Stay here. This is your home. You belong, you are one with this world.

Shut up! Shut up, damn you . . .

Don't go back to that dreary world. Don't give up all this. Don't give up being a goddess!

I must go back. I must.

No!

Have to. Have to. This is not for me. I am not a goddess. I am a human being.

You're more than that with us.

With us? Who's "us"? Tell me that. Tell me finally who you really are!

You will know. You will have the understanding. You will never understand as long as you stay the creature of clay you were born. You must transform and transfigure, and we can help you. You are great, you are a champion. You must stay here.

No. I must go back. You can't drag me along like this. I am an individual, not some component of a gestalt.

You can be, and you will fulfill your destiny.

No. I must decline the honor. I am going back to the world.

No.

I must.

No, please . . .

• • •

She came out of the skies, down from the cold violet reaches, spiraling, gliding, wings extended to their fullest extent, savoring the last of the sensations of flight, sensations she knew she would never experience again.

She touched a foot on the inlaid pedestal.

The Chorus stood at its base, looking up. If their masks could plead, they would. But the masks were unchanged, as masks always are.

She swept her eyes over them. "Do you really need a goddess? Do you need a god at all?"

They all nodded.

"Well, good luck."

She descended the pedestal's steps. "Farewell, people. It was interesting."

There came a shift in the fabric of reality.

She was climbing down from Manny. At the computer's base stood Ian Nottingham. He gave her a hand to the floor. "Must have been a heady experience."

"You were there?"

"Saw it all on the CRT."

"So you know. You saw."

"I saw. I didn't quite get everything. Don't really know what it was all about. I won't ask where it was. Just how it was."

"It was . . . very interesting," Sara said, looking at her wrist. The Blade was back to its bracelet configuration, and she was in mufti. Suddenly, her memory was jogged. "Joe! Where's Joe?"

"He's conscious. They're working on him."

"Who?"

"The paramedics. You've been gone for quite a while. The cavalry arrived."

"He had a heart attack."

"Looks like, but as I said, he's conscious. They're going to be taking him to the hospital. I really would like to get out of here. Oh, by the way . . ." Nottingham stepped away, reached behind a console, and dragged out a semi-conscious Erwin Strauss. "Know this blighter?"

"Yes. Let me get cuffs on him. Where's Jake?"

"Still out cold. I think he'll be all right. Listen, I'm leaving while the leaving is good. I've discovered a back way out of this place. Emergency exit, it looks like. I'm going to use it, right now."

"Thanks, Ian. See you soon?"

"Are you forgetting the bond between us?"

"No."

"Then what makes you think you've seen the last of me?"

With a Cheshire Cat smile, Nottingham strode away. He stepped behind a wall of instruments, and did not reappear again.

"What in the name of God has been going on here?"

She turned to see Kenneth Irons approaching. He looked completely astounded, and thoroughly irritated to see his installation occupied by intruders.

"We've been playing games on your new computer," Sara said with a wry smile.

EPILOGUE

Siry was still in ICU when Sara had time to visit him. The nurse told her that he was recovering nicely, and outlined what procedures they had done.

"So what did they do when they poked that needle up my thigh?" Joe wanted to know.

"They did an angioplasty on two coronary arteries, and inserted stents."

"What the hell are those?"

"Expandable titanium rings that hold the artery open so that blood can flow through them, you fool." Sara raised an eyebrow. "Didn't they tell you anything?"

"I was so doped up I couldn't understand a thing they were saying. What's it all mean?"

"It means you don't have to have bypass surgery. It means that you can go home in a week and watch your diet, exercise, and live."

"And stop smoking, I guess."

"And stop smoking, you fool."

"Don't talk to your boss like that."

"I will when my boss is a fool."

He sighed. "Okay, I'll stop smoking. Thanks for calling the paramedics."

"You remember anything about the attack?"

"Other than it hurt like hell? No. What the hell did go on? How the hell did you get me away from that Strauss guy?"

Sara glanced at the floor and smiled. "I'll explain it someday. Strauss came in very handy. The DA dropped its case against me and prosecuted him."

A big smile sprang to Siry's face. "So you're in the clear?"

"I'm free as a . . . I'm off the hook," Sara said. "The DA ended up with egg on his face, though."

"What happened?"

"The feds wanted Strauss for questioning, and when they took him off to one of their facilities, he escaped."

"Escaped!"

"He's gone. So the DA ends up with nothing to show for all his trouble."

Joe laughed. When he was done he coughed and gasped, "Poor Albert."

"Poor Morrison," Sara said. She glanced at her watch. "Look, I have to run. Enjoy the flowers."

"Thanks, Sara. You know, there was a lot of weird stuff again."

"Yes, there was."

"Good thing I can't remember any of it. But I want to talk about it someday."

"As I said, someday. See you later, Joe."

On her way out, she thought about what was still bothering her.

What had been the source of the magic? The candidates

were Merlin, Baba, and Manny, and none of them seemed strong enough. Something had spooked Manny, and it was undoubtedly Merlin. But who had spooked Merlin in the first place? Or had he become the magician he wanted to be?

Irons? Was Irons behind it all?

No. Irons was no magician. He was a wannabe.

In the hospital lobby, she stopped and looked at the bracelet on her wrist.

Of course. There was only one source of magic that she knew of. The Witchblade must be unhappy, weary of this mundane world it was stuck in. It wanted something better; it wanted to be a god.

"You sons of bitches," she said. "I hope you had fun."

She left the hospital. As she walked along the streets of the city she loved, she could have sworn she heard a faint, distant giggling.

A TERRIBLE BEAUTY

JOHN J. MILLER

ibooks
new york
www.ibooks.net

DISTRIBUTED BY SIMON & SCHUSTER

PROLOGUE

It was late September. New York City was in the grip of a lingering Indian summer. The cool promise of autumn had barely touched the streets. The temperature was scorching hot during the day and uncomfortably warm at night, but the old man walking down the dark, deserted street had more pressing things on his mind than the unseasonable weather.

Something was following him. Something that wanted to kill him.

The old man paused as he heard the sound of clanking chains being dragged on asphalt. There was almost an element of harsh music to the noise, like a rhythmically lurching techno-industrial dance mix. He thought he'd shaken whatever was following him by suddenly dodging into a dark cross-street, but that sound meant that it was still on his trail.

He realized he shouldn't be standing alone in the night, listening to strange sounds emanating from nearby alleys. It wasn't a prudent thing to do. The streetlight on the corner, forty yards away, cast what little light there was on the pavement. He suddenly felt as if the dim illumination thrown by the flickering lamp could protect him from the unknown thing following him in the darkness.

He took a faltering step, then another, but suddenly the noise of clanking chains was almost upon him. It had moved faster than anything human. He only had time to turn his head, time to see the thing looming above him like an avalanche of death with one long arm raised above its head.

The figure was huge in the night, bigger by far than the old man. It was dressed in tattered rags and, yes, dragging several lengths of chain behind it on the sidewalk. A portion of its face gleamed like ivory in the darkness, and the old man saw that the thing wasn't a man–it had only half a face. The rest was bare skull with flesh stripped away from bone and one empty eye-socket a deeper darkness than the night that surrounded them both.

The old man recognized him now. He knew who he was and who had sent him. Worse, he knew what the creature was going to do to him.

The old man took a deep breath so he could scream his lungs out, but choked instead on the stench emanating from the thing. The creature stank of the grave, of rot and mildew and wet ground. The old man put his hand out helplessly, and the thing's upraised arm swept down with terrific speed and the old man caught a glint of light off a machete blade and then felt a terrible blow to the side of his neck.

His head slipped sideways and hung downward, connected to his body by only a shred of flesh and skin. For a long, horrible moment, the old man still could see. He blinked rapidly at the gleam of white finger bones in the hand that wielded the machete, and, as his blood gushed out of his body in a pulsing column, his eyes closed and his legs failed and he slipped bonelessly to the sidewalk.

The last thing he knew was the high, cruel laughter of the creature that had killed him, as he slid into welcome oblivion.

CHAPTER ONE

Brooklyn was not Sara Pezzini's regular turf.

She was a detective working out of Manhattan. She was young to be a detective, and, many thought, too beautiful. Being a young, beautiful woman made for constant battles in the cop world, but to Sara her age and looks were at most a minor distraction. Usually she had more important things to worry about.

Currently her worries centered about what the press had already dubbed the Machete Murderer. Twenty-four hours earlier a headless and handless body had turned up in a Manhattan Dumpster. It was still unidentified. Twelve hours later two more corpses had washed up on the Manhattan side of the East River, also headless and handless. Although they'd been discovered after the first, the coroner had established that actually they'd been killed and dumped in the river twelve hours earlier than the Dumpster John Doe. The East River was just a lot bigger than a Dumpster, and it took longer for them to be found.

Precinct Captain Joe Siry gave the case to Sara and her partner, Jake McCarthy. There was a reason for that.

Though both were young, they were tough, smart, and dedicated if not entirely orthodox in their approach to police work. They got results. They'd already developed a reputation for solving the tough cases, the oddball killings, and to Siry these beheadings and behandings already looked more than a little kinky.

Jake concentrated on the Dumpster corpse and Sara the floaters. After twenty-fours of fruitless labor, they'd decided to call it a night, head for their respective apartments and grab some sleep. But, once home, Sara couldn't sleep. Something was pricking at her consciousness, some little bit of information she should have looked at further, some avenue of investigation she should have explored.

Besides, it was also a bad night for the voices. They nagged at her, not letting her sleep. She got up with a sigh, turned on her computer, and checked into a database she'd previously overlooked.

And found the connection that led her to Brooklyn.

Normally this meant, at the least, polite queries of the appropriate Brooklyn precinct, but Sara had no time for polite queries that often led to not so polite runarounds. She also didn't like second-hand information. Second-hand information was often inaccurate information. She didn't care to deal with other peoples' mistakes. If mistakes had to be made she preferred to make them on her own. Nor did she want Jake involved, at least not yet. She didn't want him to pay for her mistakes. Besides, the boy needed his rest.

She found herself wandering around Cypress Hills, a quiet Brooklyn community with narrow, tree-lined streets and rows of mostly semi-attached two story houses. She liked it. It was mostly clean, mostly neat. There was a sense of age about the neighborhood, though a tide of recent immigrants from Haiti and India sprinkled among the older residents of eastern European origin also gave it a certain color and vivacity.

Sara found Fulton Street, which seemed to be the heart of the community, the main street, and business district. It was fairly early on a warm September evening, and the street was still crowded. The pedestrians were a mixture of black Haitian, brown Asian, and white eastern European, though the European population seemed to consist mostly of older people with only a few youngsters here and there. The stores that lined the streets were mostly mom and pop types, and though it was nearly ten o'clock at night, most of them were still open. Although Sara passed three curry joints and a couple of Caribbean-style coffee shops, there was nary a golden arch in sight. For some reason, maybe because it gave the community a stamp of individuality and independence, Sara liked that.

She found what she was looking for at the entrance to an arcade already crowded with young people. Three young black men, in their late teens or early twenties, were heading into the dark cave to slay virtual dragons, steal virtual cars, and blow away virtual citizens by the score. The one wearing a black Batman T-shirt had a cross tattooed on his left cheek, reaching from his eye-socket to his jaw line. Another had a cross tattooed on the back of each hand.

She followed them surreptitiously. The arcade was incredibly noisy with computer-generated *beep-bop-boops*, the sounds of racing engines, and continual muffled blasts of artificial gunfire. The third member of the group, she saw, had the tattoo on his neck, under his jaw and running down to his shoulder.

As she'd discovered on the 'net, the cross tattoos were the recognition sign of the gang called The Saturday Night Specials. They would have other, probably more elaborate, cross tats on their bodies hidden by their clothes, but they all had to have at least one visible at all times as a recognition sign both to those members of the public who were aware of the gang and, of course, other gang members.

They stopped before "Blast Billy the Kid," a quick-draw shooting game, and Sara went up to them before they had a chance to feed their quarters into it.

"I'm looking for a friend of yours," she said.

The oldest of the three Specials, the one in the Batman T-shirt with the cross on his cheek, looked her slowly up and down.

"You found me, momma. Can I do?"

"Probably not," Sara said.

She took out a photo and held it up so all three could see it. It was a Polaroid taken by the coroner, showing a thin torso that had three crosses tattooed on it, one large one between the flat male breasts, flanked by smaller ones under each nipple.

"Achille–" one of the Specials blurted, and the one with the cross on his cheek threw up his hand against his chest, silencing him.

"What makes you think we'd recognize some skinny guy's tats?"

Sara smiled. "They're gang symbols. Specifically, for The Saturday Night Specials. Each gang member has a unique, identifying tattoo. You should know that, considering you all have the recognition cross on your face or hands or neck."

"It's not a gang," the spokesman said. "It's a social club."

Sara shrugged. "Whatever."

"What you want him for?" he asked Sara.

"I don't want him," she replied. "I've got him. His body, anyway. He's dead."

She pulled out another photo, this one a full body shot, showing–or not–the missing heads and hands. The bangers glanced at each other. The one who'd blurted the name looked a little queasy.

He's the one, Sara thought, *I can break.*

"You a cop?" their spokesman asked.

"Do I have to show you my badge?"

The three again exchanged quick glances.

"No. I guess not." He pursed his lips and seemed to come to a decision. "Look here, momma–"

"That would be 'Detective Momma' to you."

He smiled, without humor. "Sure. Whatever you say. Listen, uh, Detective, this ain't no place to talk. Meet us in the churchyard. Say, about an hour?"

"Churchyard?" Sara asked.

"Yeah–St. Casimir's. Right down the street. You're a cop. You should be able to find it."

The voices roiled in Sara's brain like an angry medusa.

"Insolent brat–"

"–teach him a lesson–"

"–teach him to mock us."

Later, Sara said silently. Aloud, she said. "I'll manage. In an hour, then."

She left the arcade, suppressing a smile.

* * *

A little way down the street, on a cross-street running roughly north and south, Sara saw an old, dark, stony mass of a building poised on the crest of a sloping hillside south of Fulton. The church looked as if it had been built sometime around the turn of the century, give or take a couple of decades, and hadn't seen prosperous times recently. It was constructed of dark stone that hadn't been sandblasted in a couple of generations. The sloping churchyard was almost entirely taken up by a cemetery whose monuments ranged in age from the last century to last month. As Sara climbed the worn concrete stairs leading up the hillside, she could see that the churchyard was neatly maintained, but many of the older tombstones were in need of straightening or more serious repair. Like a schoolteacher with a dusty eraser, the toxic city air had rubbed out many names and dates with its acidic breath, leaving behind sad, blank slates that had once commemorated generations of New Yorkers.

It was dark and quiet. A nice place for a secret meeting. Or, of course, an ambush. She settled down in the darkness behind a concealing tombstone. She didn't have long to wait.

The three gangbangers showed up fifteen minutes later. Cheek Cross, as Sara thought of him, evidently had high ambitions, and had seen this as an opportunity to begin his long and probably bloody climb to the top.

"I just got off the phone with the man," he was telling his associates, "and he said this was our chance."

"Our chance?" asked Neck Cross, who had blurted out the name "Achille" when Sara had first showed them the photo.

"Our chance to go big, dog. He said I got to handle this

cop. I got to get her off the case. Then, I move up, and I bring my bros with me."

"We got to *kill* her?" Neck asked, clearly uncomfortable.

"We got to do the job," Cheek said. "You just back me. That's all."

He took a snub-nosed pistol out of his pocket and caressed it lovingly.

The voices took exception to his apparent plan.

"Impudent fool—" they told Sara.

"—let us punish him—"

"—punish him severely."

Sara almost laughed.

I don't need your help with these morons, she said to herself. She drew her .45 from its snug hiding place in the small of her back, and stepped out into the open from behind the tombstone.

"School's out, boys," she said, the barrel of the .45 centered on the middle of Cheek's chest, not more than seven feet away. "Welcome to the real world."

Their eyes got round, their jaws dropped. Cheek made an abortive move to raise his pistol, but Sara only shook her head. "Freeze or die."

He froze.

"I need only one of you bozos to give me the info I need, and you're not my favorite banger right now."

She approached him, smiling.

"Hey," Cheek said, trying to laugh. "You're here early."

"Early bird gets the scumbag," Sara said, and slapped him on the side of the head with the barrel of her automatic. He went down like a bag of cream of wheat. She turned to Neck Cross. "You."

"Me?" He swallowed hard. His eyes were soft and scared. Sara could almost smell the fear coming off him in waves. *He's the one*, she thought again. She tossed him a pair of handcuffs.

"Cuff yourself to that bush." It was more a sapling than a bush, with a main trunk that was almost too big for the cuffs. He fumbled in his haste to comply with her orders, but finally succeeded in chaining himself to the tree.

He'll be an easy nut to crack, Sara thought.

She waved her pistol at the last Special.

"Come with me."

"Where?" he asked suspiciously.

"Where we can have a little chat. Privately."

"I don't–"

She jammed her gun barrel into his solar plexus, hard enough to hurt but not to stun. He made no more protests as they went off into the depths of the graveyard.

"Far enough," Sara said. "Now, call for help. Not too loudly."

"Help," he said tentatively.

She pushed the barrel of her gun up one of his nostrils.

"Like you mean it," she suggested.

He called out in a low voice, but with some desperation, like he meant it.

"Now groan a little. Moan, too."

He did. Sara reached out and grabbed the flesh between the thumb and index finger of his left hand. She squeezed and twisted and he went down to his knees with an authentic yelp of pain, cut short as she released him. He kneeled in the dark, looking up at her with fear in her eyes.

"You're crazy, man," he said.

Sara nodded. "And don't you forget it. Now get out of here."

He looked at her as if he couldn't believe what he'd just heard.

"You got it right," she said. "Scat."

She didn't have to repeat herself. He took off between the tombstones as if the wolves of hell were on his track. Smiling, she went back to the banger she'd left cuffed in the other part of the churchyard.

He was practically shaking with fear as she walked up to him, stopping a moment to check on Cheek Cross, who was still dreaming on the ground.

"What'd you do to Henri?" he asked, eyes wide.

Sara shook her head.

"You don't want to know. But I'll tell you—he wasn't smart. He wouldn't answer my questions." She fell silent, looking at him. He started as she touched his forehead with the barrel of her automatic, and ran it down his nose, around his mouth to the tip of his chin. He was trying not to shake, but failing. "On the other hand, you strike me as a smart guy. You let me know what I want, I let you go. Simple as that. If you don't tell me what I want to know . . ." Sara let her voice trail off, and shrugged.

"What you want to know?" Neck asked. "I'll tell you what I can."

"Of course you will," Sara said. "You're the smart one."

She showed him the photo again. "You know who this is." It was a statement, not a question.

"Yes, yes. That is Achille de Petion. I've know him a long time—"

"He was a member of The Saturday Night Specials?"

"Yes, of course," Neck said, eagerly.

"What happened to him?"

"I don't know—"

Sara shook her head. "Not what I wanted to hear."

She lifted her automatic.

"I swear, I don't know. I know he was in trouble. He and the doc."

"Doc?"

"Doctor Caradeuc. Dr. Cladius Caradeuc. He has a clinic farther down on Fulton. They was involved in something, together. I don't know what. They—something went wrong. We heard whispers, is all. Something went wrong."

"Caradeuc." She took out another photo, showed it to him.

He squinted at it in the uncertain light.

"I don't know if that's him. Could be. He's got no head, man. Like Achille."

"Observant," Sara said. "Ever think of going into police work?"

He cringed as she took him by the wrist, but she only unlocked the cuffs from his arm and the tree.

"Get out of here," she said, "and take your friend."

Neck scuttled back, and after a couple of tries managed to heave Cheek up from the ground, and, hugging him to his chest, started to drag him out of the churchyard.

"One last thing," Sara said.

He stopped and looked at her.

"Take my advice. Find another social club to join. You're not cut out for this one."

He looked at her as if seriously considering what she said, finally nodded, and disappeared into the night.

CHAPTER TWO

At least, Sara thought, she had someplace to start. At least the vics now had names.

She should either call Jake and let him know what she'd discovered, or better yet, go home, get some sleep, and call Jake first thing in the morning.

Instead, she did neither. She stood at the edge of the quiet churchyard and looked at the church.

It had been many years since Sara had seen the inside of a church.

She'd been raised Catholic in a conservative Italian Queens parish. Her mother had been devout. Her father, a cop, less so. He'd gone to Mass sometimes to please Sara's mother, but he'd died in the line of duty when Sara was very young, and she didn't have many memories of him. She cherished those few she had, but none of them were of him and church.

Something inside her made her pause in front of the church, some inner need unconnected with the case. Something deeper than the voices in her head told her to go in, just for a moment. There was something or someone who could help her. The urge was irresistible. She went up the rotten concrete stairs and the voices, started again to whisper in her head.

"What are you doing–"

"–do you want with this place–"

"–nothing for you here–"

"–nothing to help you–"

"–only we can help you."

"I've had enough of your help lately," Sara replied aloud. She strode up the pathway to the double-doored entrance. One of the doors had a worn sign whose weathered words welcomed her to St. Casimir's. She flung open one of the double-doors and entered the vestibule.

The voices shrieked as her hand touched the door, and rose to a cacophonous maelstrom as she crossed the small vestibule and opened the door leading to the nave. Her knees weakened as the shouts and shrieks buffeted her brain, but the part of her that was the fighter, the part of her that refused to give in to the voices' suggestions and sly offers, knew that if the voices didn't want her to enter the church, she should.

With the great force of will that had driven her to the rank of detective before she'd reached the age of thirty, Sara bulled her way into the nave, and suddenly the voices were gone. Finally, there was blessed peace in her troubled, tired mind.

She'd almost forgotten what internal peace felt like. It was such a relief that she had to grab the back of the pew in the last row to keep from collapsing. The tranquility, the utter isolation that she felt, alone at last in her own brain, almost bought tears to her eyes. She wouldn't, however, allow herself that last bit of release. She held onto the back of the pew and surveyed the church's interior.

It looked like what it was: a small, unpretentious church that served a small, poor parish. It was dark inside, lit only by infrequent, dim electric candelabras, and by banks of votive candles alongside the old-fashioned confessional box and before the low, white railing that separated the altar from the rest of the nave.

To the right of the altar, opposite the confessional, was a baptismal font–currently dry–and behind the font something Sara had never seen in a Catholic church before. It was an exhibition of crosses. Crosses, hundreds of crosses, some metal, some wood, some plain and severe, some intricate and fanciful, were crowded together in a jumbled mass against the wall behind the font. It was a chaotic, but somehow beautiful display that suggested a mountain, or at least a hill, of crucifixes.

A handful of people were sitting or kneeling in the pews, praying silently. They were mostly women, mostly elderly. None were as young as Sara or as well dressed. A group of them sat together, saying the rosary in a European language that Sara didn't recognize. Others were scattered about the nave, some at the banks of votive candles lighting tapers, dropping change into the money boxes and lighting their own offeratories with the long white wicks supplied for that purpose. An old man leaning on a cane, hobbled by his many years, came out of the penitent side of the confessional box and made his way slowly to a nearby pew where he knelt rustily, and started to say his penance.

It had been years, Sara realized, since she'd made confession. Not since she'd joined the force, certainly not since she'd taken on the burden of the Witchblade.

If the voices that were the spirits of the Witchblade didn't like her being in the church, how would they react to confession, penance, and a cleansed soul fit for holy communion?

She hadn't thought of that before. Maybe the voices had purposely blotted that notion out of her mind, until something, some slight lapse of attention on their part, some deepening of Sara's need to get a respite from them, culminated in this visit.

Without thinking about it any further, Sara scurried to the confession box along the side wall, entered the penitent side and pulled the curtain shut behind her. She kneeled on the uncushioned wooden rail.

Sara realized that this parish must be at least as conservative as the one she'd grown up in. When she'd been a little girl, twenty years before, many Catholic parishes had initiated a somewhat more informal method of communion. Penitent and priest met privately, but in the open, face to face. However, some parishes with deep roots to their old countries and their old traditions, still maintained the ancient form of the rite, the anonymous confessional.

The Catholics of Cypress Hills must be more conservative than most, Sara thought. *Inside the confessional, you couldn't tell if it was the twenty-first century or the twelfth.*

It was dark inside the box, but cozy rather than claustrophobic. Sara felt like a little girl tucked safely in her bed. The penitent's side was separate from the priest's side by a blank wall with a small, wire-screened window.

All she could see in the priest's side was a vague shadow waiting silently.

"Bless me, Father," she murmured. The words of the ancient ritual came back to her easily across the intervening years. "For I have sinned. It has been . . . too long . . . since my last confession."

She halted for a moment, then a voice said quietly from the darkness, "Go on, my daughter."

She took strength from the voice's quiet strength. It sounded young, deep and resonant, but soft. Almost, Sara thought, like the trained voice of an actor or singer. It was the voice of a man you could believe in. You could trust.

"I accuse myself of the following sins . . ."

She stopped again. The voices hadn't come back, but memories of them did, like echoes recounting her past transgressions, of the men she had killed, the deeds she had done while under the influence of the Witchblade.

The Witchblade . . . the source of her all her problems and, paradoxically, a great portion of her strength. She still didn't know exactly what it was, though it had been in her possession for some time now. It was a mystic artifact that had a horrible life–or maybe lives–of its own. It spoke to her constantly in the form of murmuring voices, tempting her, trying to seduce her to abandon herself to its use. She had used it, God knows, used it repeatedly, often to good effect. She had saved lives with it, but she had also killed with it, too often and too easily. And it was hungry for blood. It feasted on the blood of the evil, the blood of the guilty, but it took innocent blood just as eagerly. And it always wanted more.

But this was the twenty-first century. How could she confess sins such as these, and have anyone believe her?

Worse, she whispered to herself, what if the priest *did* believe her? The transgressions she'd committed under the influence of the Witchblade ran too deep and too cold in her soul. Could she ever do sufficient penance to be forgiven of them?

She stood suddenly and swept the curtain aside and bolted from the confessional. The voices thrilled somewhere deep in her brain, as if exultant at her weakness as she fled from the box, her shoes clacking on the bare flagstone floor. She glanced back at the confessional as she ran, and saw the priest look curiously out from behind the curtain that shielded his side of the box. He was young and handsome, with a broad brow and the pale complexion and dark compassionate eyes of a saint. He was clearly puzzled as he watched Sara. She felt a stab of longing as the handsome priest watched her, but was unable to overcome her sudden shame and fear, unable to respond to the offer of understanding and forgiveness on the priest's face.

As she stepped outside the church the voices came back, briefly and exultantly, in a quick babble of derision. But they cut themselves off quickly, as if afraid of pushing Sara too hard too soon, and steeling her resolve while she was still close to St. Casimir's.

The thought swept through Sara that all she had to do was open the door, go back in, and unburden herself to the priest. After all, he was in the business of healing hurts of the soul and dispensing forgiveness. She stopped, half turned to the door, and then her cell phone rang.

"Yeah," she said, half-thankful for the interruption, half-angry.

"Yeah, yourself."

It was Jake McCarthy, her partner. He was a blond, handsome young surfer dude who had somehow found his way from the left coast to New York City, and traded in his surfboard for a badge and a gun. As a cop he was as tenacious as a bulldog and as honest as Abe Lincoln. He not only watched Sara's back when they were in action, he guarded her from official inquiry as well. He didn't know about the Witchblade, exactly, but he knew something spooky was happening with Sara. He was fiercely protective of her, whether from scum in the street or higher-ups in the department.

"I wake you?"

"No," she said. "I've been checking out some things."

Jake grunted. "Too bad Siry didn't call you, then. I was sensibly getting some shuteye when he phoned me."

"What you got, Jake?" she asked.

"Another body," he replied laconically. "Brooklyn, this time. Cypress Hills."

Sara paused. "That's not our turf," was all she said.

"Yeah, but you'll want to see this body. It looks familiar."

"Familiar?" Sara said. "You mean, familiar like you know him?"

"Yes and no. The deceased is one Philip Pierre-Pierre, according to the I.D. in his wallet. When I say 'familiar' I mean he resembles certain other *corpus dilecti* we've come across recently."

Sara felt a cold finger poking her heart. The voices twittered loudly, excitedly, in her brain. She could feel her nerves twinge, like the hot flashes that raced across her muscles when the Witchblade took over.

"You mean—"

"Yep," Jake interrupted. "Dude's missing his head."

CHAPTER THREE

Two uniforms stopped Sara at the crime scene tape. It was a big city; she'd never run into either before.

"Nothing here for you to see. Better move on, miss," the taller one said.

They were both taller than Sara, though she was five-ten, and wore their facade of authority as easily as they wore their blue uniforms. Sara suppressed a tinge of anger. She knew she was beautiful. Her looks were an advantage in many social situations. In the cop world they meant that she had to prove herself over and over again. It was tiresome. At times it was infuriating.

"They are arrogant," one of the voices whispered.

"They are weak and puny," a second took up.

"Teach them a lesson," pleaded a third.

"Show them our might," ordered a fourth.

It'd be easier, Sara said to herself, *if I just showed them this.*

She took out her wallet and flipped it open, showing them her detective badge.

"Well, Detective Pezzini," one of them said after a moment, "come right in."

He lifted the length of sagging tape so Sara wouldn't have to duck under it.

"Yeah," the second said with more than a trace of false solicitousness in his voice, "but be careful. It's pretty gruesome over there."

Sara, already past the checkpoint, turned and looked at the two cops. "I've seen worse than headless bodies, boys—a lot worse."

She smiled. From the look on their faces, they seemed to believe her.

Sara was the last to arrive on the scene. The Emergency Medical Technicians were waiting to take the body away in their ambulance, the Crime Scene Unit was crawling all over the street, taking photos, measuring, scouring the vicinity for clues under the glare of their too-bright flashlights. Later, they would come back in the daytime, just to make sure they hadn't missed anything.

Jake McCarthy was standing with a heavy-set black guy in plain clothes, watching as representatives from the coroner's department put a loose-limbed corpse in a body bag, and zipped it out of sight.

Sara didn't recognize the other cop with Jake, but she recognized the man leading the coroner's team. It was Coroner's Assistant Kilby, well-known to Sara from past cases. His presence on the scene was both good and bad news. Good, in that he really, really liked her and would answer totally and truthfully any question she asked. Bad, in that he really, really liked her and was basically a pain in the ass who didn't hesitate to make inappropriate suggestions and offers in the mistaken belief that he was being romantic.

"Sara," Jake said, as she approached. "Meet Lt. Carl Dickey. He was first detective on the scene. Carl, Detective Sara Pezzini, my partner."

Dickey was a middle-aged black man with a round, sad face. Sara thought he was either a poor dresser or had recently lost a lot of weight. Though Dickey was more beefy than lean, his unfashionable brown suit hung on him like it belonged to his fatter brother. If Sara's weight-loss theory was correct, he still had a few more pounds to go.

"Pleasure," Dickey said. "Sorry for the circumstances."

Sara shrugged. "I'm used to it."

Dickey shook his head. "I'm not. Never will be."

Kilby came over to join them like an eager puppy, leaving the body bag to carried away by the waiting EMT's.

"And you know Kilby, of course," Jake said sardonically.

"Hi, Sara," Kilby said eagerly. "Fancy meeting you in a place like this."

"Yeah," Sara said, glancing over the crime scene, her disinterest in him evident. "Fancy, all right."

"What you got for us, Kilby?" Jake asked.

"Strange case, all right. Probably not the place of death." He gestured at the ground. "There'd be blood all over if he'd been decapitated here. Only blood was on his clothes and body. Those were soaked, but maybe not as much as you'd expect in a beheading."

"So," Sara said, "he was killed elsewhere, then dumped here after his heart stopped pumping."

"*Exactly*," Kilby said brightly, beaming at Sara as if she were his prize student. "But, dumped not too long after he was killed. Minutes, at most. Hell, the body was still warm when we got to it. Kind of surprised that there wasn't a trail, or anything. No blood, no footprints, nothing being dragged here. It's almost like he dropped here out of the sky or something."

Sara and Jake exchanged glances, but said nothing.

"Who found the body?" Sara asked.

"The classic anonymous informant," Dickey said. "Uniforms were on the scene in three minutes. As it happened, I was close by and arrived two minutes after the uniforms."

"Could the anonymous informant be the one who killed, moved, and dumped the body?" Sara asked.

Dickey shrugged. "Why not?"

"Interesting. Why the call reporting the body, then?"

"Killer wants the body found," Jake theorized. "He wants the world to know about this killing."

"He does?" Sara said. "That's a change. Why hide the identities of the first three vics and not this one?"

Jake shrugged. "He's getting careless."

"Or cocky. What was the vic's name again?"

"Philip Pierre-Pierre. How can you forget a name like that?" Jake checked his pocket notebook. "Apparently he owned a restaurant on Fulton Street."

"Cypress Hills? I just came from there," Sara said.

"You did?" Jake asked.

"Yeah. Met an informant. He's the one who gave me the names of the other vics."

"Other vics?" Dickey interrupted, finally able to get a word in. "What other vics?"

"A couple of possible victims of this so-called Machete

Murderer turned up earlier in Manhattan," Sara said. "Three to be exact. Two, at least, seem to have ties with Cypress Hills."

"That's news to me," Dickey said.

"Don't you ever watch TV?" Jake asked.

"Only sports," Dickey said morosely. "The news is too depressing."

"Can't argue with that."

"But I shouldn't have to get information like this through the TV," Dickey said doggedly.

"I just identified the first couple of victims," Sara said smoothly. She wasn't above spreading a little fudge to smooth things over. "I was just on my way to the precinct to let you guys know when I got the call from Jake about this new killing."

"Uh-huh," Dickey said, but Sara could tell from his eyes that he didn't believe her. She shrugged, to tell him she didn't particularly care.

Sara turned to Kilby. "This Pierre-Pierre was killed with a machete?"

"Well . . ." though clearly happy with Sara's attention, Kilby was too good a coroner to jump to conclusions. "Officially, all indications are yes. No broken bones. No stab marks from a smaller blade. No bullet wounds. Could conceivably been strangled, poisoned, bludgeoned, and then beheaded to confuse things. The autopsy will tell for sure. But, just for now, for something to go on, I'd say death was probably caused by decapitation by a heavy blade."

"Single blow?" Sara asked. The voices within were getting excited at Kilby's news. She had to concentrate to block them out.

Kilby nodded. "Yeah, but it wasn't clean. The blow cut

through most of the neck, leaving the head attached to the body by a flap of skin and flesh. Then, it looks like the perp just ripped it away." He stopped. From the expression on his face Sara knew that he had more to say, but was uncertain if he should reveal anything further.

"What else?" she asked.

"Well, I . . . I shouldn't say. Not really certain." Kilby brightened, and smiled at Sara. "But, for you, sweetcheeks . . . There were marks around the stump of the vic's neck. Teeth marks."

Jake frowned. "You mean, like the killer was biting the vic's neck?"

Kilby shook his head. "No. More like he was sucking. Sucking at the stump."

Sara and Jake looked at each other. Dickey made a noise somewhere between sadness and disgust.

"My God," the detective said. "My God."

"Maybe that's what happened to the missing blood," Sara said. "Maybe he was killed right here after all."

"And someone slurped down a couple of gallons of blood?" Kilby asked.

Sara shrugged."It's a possibility."

Kilby looked thoughtful.

"It's disgusting," he said. He smiled at Sara. "I like it."

"Here we are," Jake said. "Fulton Street, Cypress Hills."

"I was just here," Sara said, as they parked Jake's car in an open spot next to a fire hydrant.

"Canvassing the neighborhood for info on the other murders?" Jake asked.

"Something like that."

Jake looked at her suspiciously.

"Look," he said, "I know you've got your methods, and I know that sometimes they even work. But let's not forget we're partners. You're not holding out on me, are you?"

Sara forced a smile. She couldn't tell him about her trip to St. Casimir's. Even if the voices would have let her, and she didn't think they would. "Holding out on you? My partner? Nahhh.

"When I left the station house I couldn't sleep. Thought I'd do some checking on the 'net, and on a site devoted to New York City gang symbols. Found a reference to a gang called The Saturday Night Specials that used cross tattoos as a recognition sign and initiation symbol. Remember those crosses on the one floater's body?"

"Yeah," Jake said.

"Well, I was able to find someone who could identify the corpse from the tattoos. He was one Achille de Petion. Haven't been able to run a check on him yet, but I expect he'll be in the computer. My informant told me that an associate of his, Dr. Claudius Caradere, is also missing."

"And how'd you get this informant to be so talkative?" Jake asked.

Sara smiled. "You know what a winning personality I have. Oh, look." She changed the subject, gesturing at the restaurant before them. "This must be the place."

The sign over the door said PIERRE-PIERRE'S. Engraved in the glass window was the same name in an elegant flowing script with FINE FRENCH CUISINE below it. There was also a CLOSED sign in the window, and, indeed, the restaurant was dark and empty though most of the other businesses on the street were still open.

Jake put his nose up to the glass and looked in.

"Seems like no one's about," he said. "Weird."

"Maybe Mr. Pierre-Pierre was having some financial difficulties," Sara said.

Jake shrugged. "Maybe the people next door might know something."

"Maybe they might."

The shop to the right of the restaurant was a bookstore called THE SERPENT AND THE RAINBOW. The store to the left was somewhat more mysterious. It seemed to be a souvenir or gift shop of some kind, called MAMBO MARIE'S NOTIONS, POTIONS, AND LOTIONS. Like many of the Fulton Street stores, both were still open though it was getting late.

Jake and Sara looked through the shop's front window. It was dimly lit inside by a mixture of low-wattage fluorescent, some pastel neon signs, and electric faux candles. Despite the less than brilliant lighting, both cops could see the tall, voluptuous black woman behind the counter with tight, low-riding jeans that exposed her pierced navel and svelte waist, and a form-fitting, low-cut T-shirt that was two sizes too small.

"I have a notion," Jake said. "Let's check this place out."

Sara looked at him. "Bookstore. Bimbo store. Not hard to figure which one you want to investigate."

Jake shrugged. "We'll get to the bookstore. This one looks like it has more possibilities."

Sara gave a wordless grunt as she followed her partner into the dimly lit shop that was also ripe with dozens of heavy, clashing scents, and cluttered to the point of claustrophobia. The aisles were narrow, the tables and shelves were piled with all sorts of strange and tacky merchandise, from fake plastic glow-in-the-dark skulls to sprays of chicken feathers dyed bright flourescent colors, to bank upon bank of glass-enclosed candles to arrays of perfume and incense, to bundles of what looked like suspiciously real chicken feet.

Jake went up to the counter where the girl was watching them closely. He flashed his badge. "You'd be Mambo Marie?"

"I'd be Juliette," the girl said. "This place is a franchise."

Her skin was a golden honey-brown, her eyes were dark and almond-shaped. She wore her hair in a retro Afro. Close-up, Sara, could see that she didn't wear a bra under her T-shirt, and, despite the size of her breasts, didn't need one. Jake seemed to realize that, too.

"Detective McCarthy," Jake said, smiling. Juliette smiled back.

After a moment Sara said, "I'm Detective Pezzini."

Juliette continued to smile at Jake, who eventually remembered to put his badge away.

"Can I help you, Detective?" Juliette asked. Somehow she managed to make her innocent question sound like an indecent offer.

"I hope so," Jake said. Sara realized that if they were going to get any information relevant to the case they were working, she'd have to take the lead.

"Do you know why Pierre-Pierre's is closed?" she asked.

"The restaurant next door?" Juliette spoke to Sara but continued to look at Jake. She leaned forward, putting her hands on the glass countertop in front of her, creating a deep valley between her large, round breasts. Jake looked at them as if he were gazing at the clue that would wrap up the case. "I hear the owner is having problems. I hear he's sick."

"He's more than sick," Sara said. "He's dead."

Juliette looked at her for the first time. "That's too bad. He was a nice man."

"What can you tell us about him?"

Juliette leaned back languorously. She seemed as supple as a big, black cat, a fact obviously not lost on Jake. "He was a nice man. That's all I know."

"What kind of store is this?" Jake asked, finally managing to get a word in.

Juliette looked at him. It was as if, Sara thought, she herself wasn't even in the room.

"This is a voodoo store, honey. We sell candles to call the spirits, charms to soothe the savage breast." Juliette crossed her arms under her own, lifting and emphasizing. "Even Sir John the Conqueror root." She gestured down at the glass case in front of her. Among the rows of cheap silver-plated ear and toe rings were some small, shriveled brown things that looked like dolls parodying the shape of men. "Make you strong for love," she said, half-closing eyes that were glued on Jake. "But you don't look like you need Sir John, do you?"

"Not usually," Jake said.

Sara looked disgustedly at her partner. The bell on the front door chimed as someone else entered the store. The newcomer was a tall woman with a lean, boyish figure, pale skin, and fine, narrow, fox-like features. Her blonde hair, so light as to be almost white, was cut short and slicked back like a silent film star's. She moved with a sinuous litheness that spoke of a highly-conditioned athlete or martial artist. Her eyes had almost a physical impact when they met Sara's. Sara couldn't tell their color in the dim light, but there was strength in her gaze and a promise, if they'd been man's eyes, of an extraordinary erotic appetite. Sara caught herself catching her breath as she swept past.

The newcomer looked at Juliette, and nodded almost imperceptibly. She went into a back room off the main body of the store. Jake didn't notice.

"I think we're done here," Sara said after a moment. "I'm going to check out the bookstore."

"Okay." Jake said, smiling at Juliette.

"You coming?"

"I'll catch up."

Men, Sara thought. She strode out of the shoppe and had almost reached the bookstore when Jake hurried up to her side. She glanced at him.

"That was useful," she said.

"I got her phone number," Jake said. "Just in case."

"In case?"

"In case we need to investigate her, uh, more closely."

Sara just looked at him and reached for the door handle. A bell jangled musically as Sara pushed the glass door open, Jake at her heels. They stepped inside and looked around what seemed to be the classic small-time independent bookstore. The lighting was pleasant. The bookshelves were from floor to ceiling and stuffed with books both new and used. A comfortable old rug cushioned the floor and comfortable old chairs were scattered about. Some of the chairs were occupied by customers thumbing through books and magazines, other customers were browsing the shelves.

"Hey, take a look at this," Jake said. Sara joined him where he stood before a bookcase and gestured at the shelf that was on eye-level.

"*Spirits of the Night*," Sara read. "*Strange Altars, The*

Serpent and the Rainbow, Divine Horsemen, Written in Blood, Voodoo Fire in Haiti, Mythologie Vodou, Go Tell My Horse, Magic Island."

"What's with all this voodoo stuff?" Jake said. "Pretty freaky, huh?"

"Can I help you?" a voice asked in French-accented English.

They turned to see a young black man standing behind them. He was Sara's height, and slim, with short hair curled tight against his skull and large, dark eyes. His hands, Sara noticed, were large and well-kept with short, neat nails. He seemed to be regarding them with bland suspicion, as if they were tourists who'd been caught remarking on the quaintness of the local customs. Which, of course, they had been.

Sara pulled out her wallet, and flashed her equalizer, the badge, which gave them the upper hand in almost every social confrontation.

"I'm Detective Pezzini," she said. She nodded at Jake. "This is my partner, Detective McCarthy."

The man before them seemed unaffected by her revelation.

"Yes," he said coolly.

"You are?" Sara pressed.

"Paul Narcisse. This is my shop. Is there a problem?"

"Do you know Philip Pierre-Pierre, who owned the restaurant next door?" Jake asked.

Instantly, Paul Narcisse's eyes became hooded. "Owned?"

The voices in Sara's brain started to chitter. It seemed they didn't like Paul Narcisse. It seemed they were wary of him. Grateful for the warning, Sara nevertheless wished they would shut up so that she could concentrate.

She also wished that Jake wouldn't blunder through conversations like a bull in a china shop. She put her hand on Jake's forearm, stopping him from answering the question. "We're sorry, Mr. Narcisse. Did you know him? Was he a friend?"

Paul Narcisse nodded. "Yes. He is."

"He was killed earlier this evening. Murdered," Jake said baldly.

If Jake expected Paul Narcisse to gasp aloud, run away screaming, or make any other kind of incriminating gesture, he was disappointed. Paul Narcisse's gaze narrowed further and his expression hardened.

"Killed with a machete?" he asked.

"How'd you know that?" Jake asked quickly.

Paul Narcisse shrugged his shoulders impatiently. "He would not be the first from this street to die that way, would he?"

"No," Jake admitted.

"Mr. Narcisse–" Sara began.

"Call me Paul," he said. "Most do."

"Paul, then. Is there somewhere we can talk?"

He gestured toward the rear of the store. "I have an office in the back. Please–"

Paul Naricisse waited for the two policemen to precede him, and stopped to have a few words with a young woman who had been behind the counter, working the cash register.

"This way." He led them through a curtained doorway and down a short hallway, opened the door to his office and gestured to them to enter.

It was a small, comfortable room with an old wooden desk heaped high with paperwork, a recent model PC, near-shapeless old chairs, and an old, over-stuffed sofa along one wall. The Serpent and the Rainbow, Sara could see, was not exactly making money hand over fist.

Along another wall an amazing collection of artifacts rested on a wooden table that was set up like an altar. In the middle of the table a tree branch was braced against the wall. Carved, cleverly jointed and brightly painted wooden snakes climbed around it. Set up beside the limb were empty wine and rum bottles, some with white candles stuck in their open mouths. Dozens of earthenware pots and jugs jostled for space. A small bowl with a cluster of chicken eggs occupied a central place of honor, and the wall behind the altar was covered with framed religious lithographic portraits: a whole cast of Catholic saints.

Paul Narcisse took the seat behind the desk, watching as Sara and Jake took in the altar.

"Yes," he told them, "I am an adherent of voodoun, the religion of my native country. That is my shrine to Damballah, my personal *loa*."

"There a lot of that in this neighborhood?" Jake asked.

"A lot of voodoun?" Paul Narcisse asked. "Of course. Cypress Hills is home to many thousand Haitians, more than anywhere in the United States, except Florida. More Haitians live here than in most cities in Haiti."

"This Damballah dude," Jake pursued. "What's he all about?"

Paul Narcisse smiled. "You mean, does he encourage his worshipers to go around chopping off peoples' heads with a machete?"

Jake was unembarrassed. "For starters."

"Hardly," Paul Narcisse said. "Damballah is the cosmic

snake. The world was hatched from his egg. He is a *loa* of life, regeneration, and rebirth. Together with his wife Aida-Wedo, who is the rainbow, he rules the sky."

"*Loa*," Sara said, "what's that?"

"*Loa* are sacred spirits. Those on the right hand, like Damballah, Papa Legba, and Erzulie Freda, are the good spirits who help mankind. Those on the left are the *malfacteur*, the dark *loa*. Erzulie je Rouge, Baron Samedi and his brothers, are those whom the *bokor*—the evil sorcerers—call upon."

"Yeah," Jake said. "Any of them have machetes?"

"Some," Paul Narcisse said with a smile. "Some don't need weapons. Their teeth and claws are potent enough."

There was a brief knock at the door, and it swung open.

"Hello, Paul," said the newcomer. "Clarisse told me you had visitors."

Paul Narcisse nodded. "Indeed. Come in, Father Baltazar. I'd like you to meet Detectives McCarthy and Pezzini."

"I've already had the pleasure of meeting one of your visitors," he said, nodding at Sara.

She looked at the newcomer with surprise. It was the handsome young priest from St. Casimir's. Seeing him in good light gave Sara an even more favorable impression. He was every bit as handsome as she'd thought he was. His hair was thick and black. He wore it combed back and long enough to fall to his shoulders like a thick mane. His face was pale, not with the pallor of ill health, but rather the purity of fresh ivory. His forehead was broad and unlined, his cheekbones high and prominent, his jaw strong and charmingly dimpled. His eyes were dark, almost black, and Sara could discern both compassion and wisdom in them, for all his comparative youth. He looked like a model portraying a saint. As Sara looked at him her pulse raced, but that might have been caused by the voices which had begun to stir in her brain when he'd first appeared.

"We should continue our little talk," Father Baltazar said to Sara, "whenever it would be convenient for you."

"Sure . . ." Sara said. Desperate to change the subject, she blurted, "Baltazar. That's an odd name."

The young priest smiled, showing a set of straight, white teeth. "Not where my family came from."

Sara flushed. "Of course."

McCarthy, not fearing to rush in, said, "Where's that?"

Father Baltazar turned his smile to Sara's partner. "Poland by way of Lithuania. It means 'Baal protect the king.' Somewhat ironic for the name of a Catholic priest, no?"

McCarthy shrugged. "I guess. So, Cypress Hills is a mixture of–what?–Haitian, Jamaican, Indian, and Lithuanian?"

Paul Narcisse nodded. "That's right. The Lithuanians came mostly at the turn of the century, the Indians after World War II. The Jamaicans in the 1960s, the Haitians last of all."

McCarthy smiled, as though he found this all very interesting. "And how do you folks all get along?"

Paul Narcisse and Father Baltazar looked at each other. It was Narcisse who answered the detective's question. "We get along fine."

McCarthy smiled again. "Yeah. Until bodies started showing up without heads."

"That is not a question of race or ethnicity," Father Baltazar said firmly. "That is a question of good against evil."

As he spoke Sara almost staggered. The voices in her head had turned up the volume from a gentle background murmuring to a full-fledged roar. They were agreeing, it seemed, with the priest. He was telling the truth. This wasn't a simple gang-inspired conflict. Some aspect of it existed on a cosmic scale, which made it the provenience of the Witchblade.

McCarthy didn't say anything, but Father Baltazar obviously read the skeptical look on his face. "You don't believe me, Officer?"

"Well, this is the twenty-first century. I believe more in gangs and guns than I do in evil spirits."

Father Baltazar turned to Sara. "How about you?"

She couldn't look away from his eyes. They seemed to captivate her, draw her inside his own. The voices were yammering at her. She couldn't quite understand what they were saying. There was warning and approval mixed in their fragmentary messages. *Screw the voices*, she finally told herself. She couldn't let them make all her decisions for her.

"I–I have an open mind," she finally told the priest.

Priest and bookseller looked at each other, and seemed to come to some kind of silent decision.

"All right," Paul Narcisse said. "We shall take you at your word. We've been reluctant to take this matter to the police because we've felt, first, the police wouldn't believe us, and, second, couldn't help us if they did." He looked at Jake McCarthy. "There are some things the police are ill-equipped for, possibly precisely because this is the twenty-first century. But not all knowledge was born in this century, nor was all evil."

McCarthy frowned. "What do you mean by that?"

Father Baltazar smiled. "You can see tonight, if you want."

Paul Narcisse smiled, too, and it made Sara uncomfortable. "You shall look upon the face of evil. And your guns will do you no good."

In Sara's mind the voices finally all spoke as one. And what they said was, "But we will. *We will!*"

CHAPTER FOUR

"I don't know," Jake McCarthy said. "This isn't exactly my thing, but I wouldn't call it *evil.*"

The detectives stood in a tight knot with Paul Narcisse and Father Baltazar at the rear of Club Carrefour. It was packed with an audience that was going wild to the heavy, yet eerily melodious sounds of the Goth Rock band on the small raised stage at the end of the hall. The music was so loud that everyone had to lean towards Jake to hear his words, despite the fact that they were well in the club's rear.

Narcisse shook his head. "Not the band. Listen, and wait."

Sara had to agree with Jake. This music was not really her thing either. But there was something to it, some vital, original beat that she could feel in her heart which was throbbing almost in time to the music. And the voices in her head really dug it. They went silent as the band played. She could feel them absorbing the sound like it was energy, absorbing it and pulsing wordlessly in time. Odd that, but she couldn't see exactly how this was forwarding the investigation. She was tired. She didn't feel like clubbing, and she was regretting the impulse that had caused her and Jake to accept the priest's offer.

Still, the voices seemed to approve of their presence at the club, and while she was more than a little wary of them, she also knew that frequently it was worthwhile to follow their often-cryptic advice. Besides, she was more than willing to give Father Baltazar some slack and let him prove himself. Or, maybe, disprove himself.

She leaned forward and got Father Baltazar's attention by tugging on the sleeve of his cassock. She took her hand away quickly, not wanting to let it linger on his arm. "Who are they?" she asked.

"What?"

"The band. What's their name?"

"Oh. Mountains of Madness. A local group that's just made the national scene."

She nodded, and turned her attention fully to the group, as the male lead singer said, "I think you might all know this one—our first charting hit, 'Dreams in the Witch House.' "

Sara wasn't familiar with it, but almost everyone else in Club Carrefour roared ecstatically.

There were five musicians in the band. The lead singer was tall, broad shouldered, and long-legged. His black hair fell in a torrent around his shoulders. Sara was too far away to discern his facial features, but he was dressed all in black with leather boots and a long black duster that was probably way too hot for a crowded club on an evening that was as warm as mid-summer. His voice was strong and deep, and sang lyrics too complicated for Sara to follow, even if she'd been interested enough to try to understand them. Which she wasn't. She was more interested in gathering an overall impression of the band to see where they might fit in with the recent odd occurrences in Cypress Hills.

A pale-faced girl who also was wearing layers of black clothing played the keyboards and supplied counterpoint vocals. She, too, had long black hair, heavy dark eye make-up, and red, red lips. Her voice was light and soaring, perfectly complementing the lead singer's bass tones as they wove a complex set of lyrics around the eerie melody supplied by harpsichord and guitars.

The guitar and bass player couldn't have contrasted more with the other band members. Their pale hair was short and they were dressed simply in jeans and T-shirts, one bright orange and the other a vibrant yellow. They dashed frenetically around the stage, making faces at each other and the audience, cavorting where the singer and keyboarder were serious. They were underdressed by rock star standards and colorful by Goth standards. Sara couldn't be sure from a distance, but they looked like twins. They certainly resembled each other so closely that they had to be brothers.

The drummer, the final member of the band, was so far in the rear of the stage that Sara couldn't really see him. He was black, and lost in the darkness among his drumset. It seemed as if he was someone who didn't seek out the limelight.

Sara could catch only the barest essence of "Dreams in the Witch House." It was evocative of lost dreams and forgotten hope, of spirituality in a mechanistic age. When it was over the lead singer raised his hands, bowed deeply, and left the stage. The rest of the band followed him as the crowd went nuts.

"Let's go," Paul Narcisse said.

Though Sara and Jake stood within a couple feet of him, they could barely hear him for the delirious crowd noise. They followed him and Father Baltazar as they made their way toward the stage. When they reached the curtained door heading to the wings, a big bald black dude with biceps the size of baby heads blocked them for a moment, then obviously recognized either Paul Narcisse or Father Baltazar, or both, and let them pass.

"You're better than a backstage pass," Jake said as they went past the curtain.

Father Baltazar smiled. "We're not unknown in the community."

As they went backstage the band was retaking the stage for an encore. A short, balding man in a gray rumpled suit was standing among the light and sound crew. Paul Narcisse went to him.

"Kristoforas—good to see you again, my brother."

The man turned a harried face to them, and relaxed somewhat as he recognized Paul Narcisse and Father Baltazar. He was young, not much—if any—older than Sara, but was prematurely balding, prematurely chubby, and his face had what seemed to be a perpetually worried expression. But he did seem genuinely glad to see Paul Narcisse and Father Baltazar, though he cast a momentary suspicious glance in the direction of Sara and Jake.

Paul Narcisse turned to the cops and gestured at the man he'd just greeted. "Detectives Pezzini and McCarthy, this is Kristoforas Gervelis. He manages The Mountains of Madness. His brother, Aleksandras, is the lead singer."

The worry was suddenly back in Kristoforas' eyes. "Detectives? They're police?"

Jake looked at Sara, his eyebrow quirked significantly, but Father Baltazar laughed. "Relax, old friend. Don't worry so much. We were just showing the detectives around the neighborhood, and what better place to take them than the triumphant return of Mountains of Madness to Cypress Hills?"

Meanwhile, on stage, the band had settled back behind their instruments, and Aleksandras was shouting, "Thank you! Thank you, my friends! We're so happy to come home for tonight's benefit, hosted by our first and greatest patron, Mister Guillaume Sam!"

Aleksandras pointed to the opposite stage wing and a large black man wearing a silk Armani suit strolled out onto the stage to take a bow. He was huge, with great shoulders, a wide, deep chest and an expansive gut. He wore dark sunglasses that hid his eyes. A three-inch-long gold crucifix dangled from his left ear. He waved at the crowd, and they responded vociferously, as if most knew him. Then he turned, bowed politely to the band, and made his way back into the darkness of the wings.

As Aleksandras gestured and the band swung into their encore, Sara suddenly froze, her gaze on Guillaume Sam. She almost didn't need the confirmation of the twittering voices in her head. She could tell from his arrogant posture, from the self-satisfied set of his mouth. He was the one. He was the evil that Paul Narcisse and Father Baltazar had brought them to see.

As the band began to play their signature song, "Rats in the Walls," he looked up across the back of the stage and caught Sara in his gaze. The voices in her head bleated with sudden urgent warning, and, almost unheard of from them, fear.

"—power, awful power—"

"—the one to watch—"

"—the blade, call upon the blade!"

For a moment Sara was almost unable to fight them down. For a moment her gaze darkened, her will weakened, and she could feel the constricting bands of cold metal began to appear upon her flesh, shredding the fabric of her jeans on her upper right thigh. But she clenched her teeth and drove the Witchblade back, telling herself, telling the voices, "No! Now is not the time!"

For once they obeyed, and the Witchblade flickered and subsided. She could only hope that no one would notice her ruined jeans, or if they did, just think them fashionable.

But as her eyes came back into focus, she found herself still staring across the back of the stage. As The Mountains of Madness rocked into "Rats in the Wall" she saw Guillaume Sam looking at her with unconcealed interest. And there was something, some dark thing sitting crouched on his shoulder, unseeable in the dim light, save for two glaring red eyes.

She broke Sam's gaze with a conscious effort, and turned her head to see Father Baltazar looking steadily at her with concern, wonder, and, yes, even a little suspicion in his eyes.

It took only a simple request from Paul Narcisse to get them all invited to the post concert party on the second floor of the club, which consisted of Guillaume Sam's office and, as Kristoforas imprecisely put it, "private function space." Club Carrefour's second floor was a bit more intimate and furnished a lot fancier. The bar was almost as big as in the club downstairs, but was much more ornate, with a marble top over a teak and mahogany base, a huge mirror dating to a previous century or two, and bottles of liquor, wine, and brandy that were also aged and rather more exotic than those found downstairs.

To Sara's eyes there seemed an inordinate amount of religious iconography about the place. Crosses, saintly icons, and the like festooned the bar, the walls, and even the metal candleholders on the tables adjacent to the dance floor. Music rumbled on a stereo system that sounded almost as good as the real thing. One end wall was dominated by a large throne-like chair that was set atop a three-step dais.

As Sara and the others entered the hall the throne was empty, though there were already several dozen people dancing, collecting drinks at the bar, or attacking the buffet laid out on a series of long tables set against one of the long walls of the rectangular room.

McCarthy spotted the spread, said a hasty "Excuse me," and headed for the food at a run. Clearly, he hadn't been to the donut shop lately.

"Can I get you a drink, Ms. Pezzini?" Kristoforas asked with genuine solicitude.

"A soft drink," Sara replied. "On duty and all that. And please, call me Sara."

Kristoforas smiled briefly, a smile that was extinguished as the Mountains of Madness guitar and bass players approached.

"Hey," one of them said.

Close up, Sara could see that they were indeed twins. They were about Sara's height and probably not much more than Sara's weight. Skinny would be an accurate description of their build, and not quite endearingly ugly an accurate description of their features. Their eye color was as non-committal as their hair, gray-green and brown-blond. Their front teeth protruded, their chins were almost non-existent.

"Hey," the other one said.

"We're in the band," the first said.

"We're brothers," the second said.

"I'm Roger Stern."

"I'm Jerry Stern."

They got on either side of Sara and each put an arm around her waist.

"Want to be the filling in a Stern sandwich?" they asked in unison.

"Jesus, Jerry, and you, too, Roger," Kristoforas said, "behave for once. This is Sara Pezzini. *Detective* Sara Pezzini, N.Y.C. Police Department."

"Wow," Roger said.

"Cool," Jerry said.

They looked at each other.

"I don't think I've ever done a cop before," Roger said.

"I *know* I haven't," Jerry said.

"Rog–Jer–" Kristoforas said in warning tones.

Sara began to understand why he had a perpetually harried look. She stepped back out of their grasp.

"Don't worry," she said. "I can take care of myself. I'm armed, after all."

"Wow," Jerry said.

"Cool," Roger said. "Can we see your gun?"

"Later." Sara looked at Paul Narcisse and Father Baltazar, who had been bemusedly watching the exchange. "Right now I'd like to meet the rest of the band."

"Sounds like a good idea," Paul Narcisse said. He took Sara's arm and guided her away. "Come along."

Sara glanced at the brothers as they ambled off to the bar with Kristoforas.

"Are they for real?" she asked.

"Oh yes," Paul Narcisse said. "Pretty much harmless though. Shameless hedonists, but they can play. Alek is the only one who's ever been able to keep them in line for more than a couple days at a time. I'm not sure how he does it, but he does have a somewhat dominating personality." They stopped at the buffet table, where the lead singer of Mountains of Madness was helping himself to some chopped liver from the statue shaped into the Angel of Death. "Right, Alek?"

Alek turned around slowly, smiling. He was a tall man, perhaps six-two, and the wild hair and dark clothes and leather boots made him loom even larger. His pale face was untouched by the usual Gothic make-up. His eyes were dark like Father Baltazar's, but they had a different quality to them that made him seem harder, tougher than the priest's. He was as handsome and impressive as a man could be. When he spoke, his deep, rich voice only added to his aura of power and dominance.

"Paul," he said, smiling. "Great to see you. I'm glad you made it to the benefit."

He turned toward Sara and their eyes met. His smile widened. It was difficult to say which was more attractive, his eyes or his smile. She felt herself smile back automatically, and caught herself, angry at her unthinking response. Sure, he was a handsome, charismatic guy with great eyes, a great smile, and a great voice, but she had to watch herself. This was developing into the weirdest case she'd run across in a very weird career. She had to maintain her distance from all those involved, as well as her hard-edged perspective.

"Hello." His voice oozed charm, but it was a natural, almost unconscious ooze. He wasn't trying to charm her. He just did. "I'm Aleksandras Gervelis. Please, call me Alek."

"I'm Detective Sara Pezzini," she said, her voice harder, more formal than she intended it to be. "You can call me Detective Pezzini."

Damn! Sara said to herself. She sounded like she had a stick up her butt. But something was making her keep her distance from Gervelis. Were the voices, though quiet, perhaps exerting a more subtle control over her mind?

"Certainly, Detective Pezzini," another voice said, interrupting her thought. "Can I ask why the New York City Police Department sees fit to make its presence felt at my little get-together?"

Sara turned toward the new speaker, and caught her breath. The voices in her head suddenly chittered like mad mice, offering a mixture of challenge tinged with fear, which was most unusual for them. Normally they feared nothing.

It was Guillaume Sam. He loomed taller than Alek Gervelis, and bulked much larger. His face was bland and expressionless, though Sara could well believe that his eyes could burn with fire and emotion if he'd let them. His suit was impeccable, his large, powerful hands faultlessly manicured. The beady-eyed creature still sat on his shoulder, its long, naked tail looped around his neck, great bucked teeth gleaming in its pointed muzzle.

"Excuse me," Sara said, "but is that a rat?"

Guillaume Sam laughed. It was deeply musical and seemed genuine.

"You are not much of a naturalist, Detective. This is Baka, my pet possum."

"That's . . . unusual . . ." Sara said.

"Much about Guillaume Sam is out of the ordinary," Paul Narcisse said.

Guillaume Sam turned his eyes upon the bookstore owner and for a moment he let the power in his gaze shine through. "Ah, Paul, always good to see you. I trust you're enjoying yourself."

Paul Narcisse bowed. "As you say, monsieur."

A palpable tension was in the air, broken when Kris Gervelis hustled up to the group with the drink he had promised Sara. He bumbled forward and there was a moment's confusion as if he realized he was breaking up something, but not sure what, then Guillaume Sam excused himself, saying he had other guests to attend to. The female member of Mountains joined them an instant later. Kristoforas introduced her as Magdalena Konsavage. Like the Gervelis brothers, she was a member of the Cypress Hills Lithuanian community. She and Sara chatted amiably for a few minutes. Alek asked if she wanted to dance, but Sara made her excuses to go hunt down her partner.

She was wary of Alek, whether it was the voices subtly warning her or whether she was subtly warning herself she couldn't say. She also felt that it'd be more useful if she drifted and mingled. So she did.

The results were interesting if not conclusive. She wandered through the crowd, collecting impressions and what information she could. Guillaume Sam was now ensconced on his throne-like chair, drinking rum like it was water, Baka sitting on his shoulder and observing everything far too intently. She passed Paul Narcisse and Father Baltazar, who seemed to be keeping their eyes out for her, and also her partner, who seemed more interested in the food and the females present than police business.

She ducked the Stern brothers, who were drinking up a storm and eating and chatting up everything in a dress.

At one point she noticed they were with someone who seemed familiar, so she let the eddies and swirls of the crowd's tidal flow deposit her close behind them where she could watch and listen unobserved.

"Hey," Rog—or maybe it was Jer—was saying, "how'd you like to be the filling in a Stern sandwich?"

They were standing with their arms around a woman's waist, each looking a little worse for wear from the ever-present drinks in their hands. This woman was as tall as Sara, though slimmer. Her short, blonde hair was slicked back and she was wearing masculine evening dress, an elegant black tuxedo and tails, as if she'd escaped from a Fred Astaire movie. It took a moment, but Sara recognized her as the woman who'd come into the notions and lotions store earlier that evening. She was elegantly seductive, and, as Sara watched, left the ballroom arm in arm in arm with the twins.

It was, Sara thought, all a mystery. Unfortunately, she wasn't Sherlock Holmes. Jake wasn't even Dr. Watson. But she'd figure it all out in the end, somehow. In the meantime, she realized that she'd been awake for over thirty-six hours, and was running on empty.

She looked around the room to track down Jake. Finally she spotted him and Magdalena Konsavage engaged in what seemed to be earnest conversation. When she made her way over to them she heard them arguing the merits of the Beach Boys versus Nick Cave and the Bad Seed. Jake wasn't winning, but was obviously willing to give the discussion the good old college try. He paid Sara minimal attention as she said her goodnights.

Before she left the ballroom she hunted down Paul Narcisse and Father Baltazar.

"Thanks for an interesting evening," she told the pair.

"Is your mind still open?" Father Baltazar asked.

Sara shrugged. "Yeah, but I don't want it so open that my brain will fall out. Still . . ."

"Think about what you've seen tonight. We'll talk later."

"That's a promise," Sara said. "Right now, though, I need some sleep."

Father Baltazar nodded.

"Pleasant dreams, Detective," he wished, or perhaps predicted, for her.

But, unfortunately, he was wrong.

CHAPTER FIVE

Sara fell into the bed as if it were the welcoming arms of a long-sought, sorely-missed lover. Her head hit the pillow, her eyes closed. For once it seemed that the voices were as tired as she was. At any rate they didn't bother her with unnecessary chatter as she reviewed the day's events like she always did when she was on a case. Sometimes as she approached the walls of sleep her subconscious gave her insights that her wide-awake mind missed. Sometimes, she even remembered those insights upon awakening.

Four bodies were now laid at the hands of the Machete Murderer. One, found in a Manhattan Dumpster minus hands and head, was still unidentified. Two had washed up on the Manhattan side of the East River, also minus heads and hands. Also with no I.D., but tentatively identified as Haitians living in Cypress Hills. One had been a doctor, perhaps a respected citizen, the other a not-so-respected gang member. Both probably had been killed if not together, then at about the same time. Finally, one found in an alley, in the Cypress Hills neighborhood itself. No head, but identified by cards found in his wallet.

The differences in the last killing bothered Sara. It seemed as if the killer really wanted to hide the identities of the first three victims, but could care less about the fourth. Assuming, of course, that the murderer took Pierre-Pierre's head for some arcane purpose of his own. Perhaps there was a reason for the decreasing attempts at secrecy. Or perhaps the killer was getting a little more out of control with each slaying. Maybe the Machete Murderer was feeling more invincible after each murder, more contemptuous of the police.

If that was the case, he would get caught sooner than later. The killer would get sloppier and sloppier and make a critical mistake. At least, Sara fervently hoped that it would be sooner than later.

In the meantime . . . meantime . . . her mind conjured up a pair of eyes, brown and soulful. Father Baltazar looked at her with kindness and understanding. She realized that she was attracted to him . . . but he was a priest. Untouchable. Vowed to celibacy. Not like Alek Gervelis. His eyes held understanding, too, understanding of what she wanted, what she needed. They were dark, too, brown . . . no . . . red . . . Red glaring pinpricks that burned with a feverish heat.

Sara sat up, startled. She was sitting on a thick grassy sward, a clearing in a luxuriant jungle lit only by the light of the full moon. She was wearing the short silken chemise she'd worn to bed, and could feel warm breezes whisper about her face, her bare shoulders, and long, lean legs. Vines entwined about the trees surrounding the clearing and night-blooming flowers were everywhere. They perfumed the warm, caressing breezes with their heady musk.

"Welcome to Guinee, *blanc*," a voice said.

Sara stood slowly. The voice was soft and pleasingly

feminine. Sara couldn't fear it. In fact, she felt more at peace than she had for months. It took a moment before she realized the voices in her head were utterly silent. It was as if they'd vanished. She searched for them among the corridors of her mind, but if they were still present they were hiding. That seemed good enough for now.

Sara turned to see a beautiful black woman who had thick, wavy hair that fell to her waist. She wore heavy eye make-up: mascara and eye-shadow, and probably false eyelashes as well because no natural lashes could be so luxuriantly long. She had large hooped earrings and a shiny necklace of silver and gold, as well as three bands on the ring-finger of her left hand. A crimson and gold orchid was enmeshed in her hair behind her right ear. Her dress was long and flowing with rather more flounces and of a costlier fabric than an ordinary peasant's shift. She looked like a goddess.

"Guinee?" Sara repeated. "Where is that?"

The woman gestured around herself.

"Guinee is here, where you are. More importantly," she said, "you should ask *what* is Guinee?"

Sara smiled. "All right. What is Guinee?"

The woman smiled a smile that was the definition of charming. "It is the dream-home of the voodoun *loa*, the spirits of voudon."

"Are you a *loa*?"

"I am Erzulie Freda Dahomey, patroness of love and lost dreams. Someone has asked that I watch over you. Come, *blanc*, walk with me, and we shall talk."

Erzulie gestured and Sara fell in step with her as they went down a path Sara hadn't noticed before, leading out of the clearing.

"Who set you to watch over me?" Sara asked.

"Ahhh," Erzulie said. "That is the mystery, is it not? Who are your friends, who are your enemies?"

"Can't you tell me?" Sara asked.

On a branch above them there was a sudden stirring where moments before there had been only silent darkness. A black shadow leapt down to the ground, and Sara started as she realized that a leopard had landed right next to them. She drew back in fear and surprise, but Erzulie didn't seem to notice her reaction. She simply put her hand out and the leopard slunk down low, as if bowing, then licked her hand with his long, raspy tongue.

"Your enemy," Erzulie said, scratching the leopard on top of its sleek head, "is Guillaume Sam. You know that, even if you don't quite believe it. He is a *malfacteur*, a person of the worst sort. He never sacrifices to me, but to my sister Erzulie je Rouge–someone, believe me, you never want to meet. Baron Samedi is his patron."

The leopard joined them as they walked down the trail, pacing along calmly by Erzulie's side.

"Samedi?" Sara asked. "Who's he?"

"He is the head of the Guede Family," Erzulie told her. "Baron Saturday. The *loa* of Death, Guardian of the Cemetery, and Protector of Sorcerers. He is very powerful. Though you seem to have your own odd . . . abilities . . . you would never be able to defeat him."

"Defeat him?" Sara said. "I don't want to have anything to do with him. I just want to catch a murderer. I just want to be–"

Sara abruptly shut up. She was about to say: *I just want to be normal again. I'm sick of these voices whispering in my head. I just want to be a cop, go to work, catch the bad guys. Maybe meet somebody someday and fall in love . . .*

Erzulie laughed. "Yes, *ma petit*, you do not want much, do you? Still—" She shrugged. "People have asked for more than you do. You are not unreasonable."

A white dove fluttered down from the branches of one of the trees over-arcing the trail and landed on Erzulie's shoulder. Erzulie put a soft hand on the bird's back, caressing it.

"I must be going. Be sure to thank the *houngan* for his sacrifice to me, in your name. Think of me sometime. I cannot fight your battles. It is not our way to contend against each other. But I will give you what information I can. For now, a final gift: I am not the only *loa* who knows you walk in Guinee tonight. Beware Bakula-baka."

Sara looked at her, confused. "*Houngan*? Sacrifice? What are you talking about?"

But Erzulie and her leopard were only broken spirals of mist, shimmering on the hot night breeze.

"What's a Bakula-baka?"

"Not what, foolish *blanc*! Who!"

Sara whirled at the unexpected voice coming from behind her to face something out of a madman's nightmare. It was a huge dark figure, taller than Sara, broader by far. It was human-shaped, but could hardly have been alive. One of his eyes was missing. The empty socket was dark as the mouth to hell. Half of his face was exposed skull, skin and flesh stripped away to the white bone underneath. He was clothed in torn, filthy rags, and Sara could see that other parts of his body were missing flesh as well. White bone gleamed here and there as he moved toward her. He dragged several lengths of thick chain, as if he had been tied down but had burst his bonds. As he approached Sara smelled him on the night breeze. She gagged at the waves of noxious corruption that came off him in waves. He smelled like a recently opened grave. He smelled of death and corruption and black hatred, and in his right hand, half flesh, half naked bone, he carried a machete.

"I am the least of Samedi's brothers," Bakula-baka snarled. "If you dare to oppose him, you must face me first."

The part of Sara's mind that wasn't cringing in fear wondered how he could speak so clearly with a mouth that was half naked teeth and bone, but she quickly realized this wasn't the time to worry about such petty things. Bakula-baka was bearing down on her like a riptide. She could see dried blood caked on his machete blade. She thought she knew where the blood had come from.

The Machete Murderer had taken the lives of four men, but now, she thought, he faced the wielder of the Witchblade. She held her right hand out pointing at the creature, and called silently, imperiously, for the mystic artifact to appear, to sheath her in its invincible armor, to put the razor sharp blade in her hand or blast the charging *loa* with its sphere of deadly fire.

She called upon it, but it did not come. The voices remained silent in her head.

She stood there a moment, stunned, her mind blank. She gestured again, but nothing happened.

"Jesus!" the word sprung from her lips, prayer or curse she didn't know, and the thing was upon her.

Sara took a deep breath, choking on the creature's charnal house stench as he loomed above her, machete starting the downward sweep of a death blow, when her subconscious, or perhaps her instinct to live, made her move her feet, twist, and duck away. Bakula-baka's machete just missed her. She felt the wind of its passing, heard the creature grunt as the force of the blow buried the blade of the machete in the dark jungle soil at their feet.

The voices are gone, Sara thought, *and so is the Witchblade.*

It had refused to come to her before, she thought, but this was not the time for it to be sulky. She knew full well that wherever this place was, she could die here. Permanently. And without help, having to face Bakula-baka bare-handed, her death seemed pretty likely.

She sprinted down the path, trying to put some distance between herself and the horrid creature, looking for a weapon, a way out, anything she could turn to her advantage. The *loa* followed with thundering footsteps. Once she risked a glance backward and to her horror saw that despite his size and awful bulk, he was fast on his feet. He was catching up to her. She was losing the distance she'd put between them when he paused to wrench his blade from the ground.

He was charging like a deadly tsunami. She could smell his awful stench get stronger and stronger. The flesh between her shoulder blades crawled as she imagined the terrible pain of the machete biting into her back, perhaps cutting through her neck. Bakula-baka growled an inarticulate cry of hate and bloodlust and Sara, heart bursting, tried to put on more speed.

But she couldn't.

Crying out in frustration, she decided to turn and throw herself upon her foe and hope for a miracle, and suddenly there was an imperious ringing sound and she sat up in her bed, drenched in sweat, the Witchblade blossoming around her body as she became a flower enshrouded in thorns.

Her chemise ripped to shreds. The metallic armor of

the Witchblade cupped her soft flesh in its hard, cold grasp as she gasped for breath. The imperious ringing continued to shrill in her ear. She took two, long shuddering breaths, and reached for the phone that sat on the night table by the side of her bed.

"Hello?" she gasped.

There was a momentary silence, then a familiar voice came over the line.

"Sara?"

It was Jake.

"Yeah, what?" she shuddered out.

"I, uh, you, uh, alone?"

"Of course," she said sharply. And she was. The Witchblade vanished, leaving the shreds of her chemise hanging on her like it had suffered the death of a thousand cuts. "What do you mean?"

"Well, uh," Jake said, "you sound all out of breath and all. Like you've been running a marathon. Or something."

Sara lay backward. Her pillow was soaked with sweat.

"You woke me out of a dream," she said. She took a long breath, calming her shuddering lungs. "It was a nightmare." It was, Sara thought, more than that. It was her death. "Thanks."

"Sure. No problem."

Sara closed her eyes. She didn't want to think about what had just happened. She wanted to put it away, and, maybe examine it more closely when the sun was shining, when the stench of Bakula-baka was gone from her nostrils. It still lingered there, more than a mere memory. Meaning, perhaps, that she'd just experienced more than a mere dream . . .

"So what's up?" she asked her partner.

"Thought you'd want to know first thing," Jake said. "The first vic's been ID'ed."

"And?" Sara prompted.

"His name was Tom Jackson. He was an agent for the Immigration and Naturalization Service–"

"Working out of Cypress Hills," Sara interrupted.

She could almost see Jake nod his blond surfer-boy head.

"That's right," he said. "His office was in Manhattan, but the region he was in charge of included Cypress Hills."

It was a nice late September day, warm, slightly breezy. The Mets were in first place. The city was in a good mood, but Sara wasn't. There was too much on her mind. The case of the Machete Murderer was too hard to fathom, just too damn weird. And now she had to visit the morgue.

That place always put her in a bad mood, and when she was in a bad mood to begin with it was really a downer. It was never warm enough down there in the basement and the air was always dank. Kilby assured her this wasn't so. They had to keep the humidity low because of–as he put it–their clients. But it always felt clammy on Sara's skin. The smell didn't help any, either. It was always antiseptic but not *fresh*. There were undertones to the morgue's odor that Sara didn't like. No matter how hard they scrubbed, they couldn't rid the place of its aura of loss, sadness, and incipient decay.

Plus, Kilby was always so damned cheerful. He grinned like a demented cherub. Today was no different as Sara came in, still rather shook up by her experience of the night before.

"Hello, Detective," Kilby said, bustling up to her, white lab coat rustling, clipboard clasped to his chest like a shield.

"Jake said you had some info on the vic from the dumpster."

"Right-o. Come this way."

On the best of days, the morgue was a downer. This wasn't even close to the best of days.

"I don't want the tour," Sara said. "Just the information."

"Right-o," Kilby said in the same happy tone, incapable of taking offense. He looked at Sara with the eyes of a devoted puppydog, and Sara sighed. "Here we go."

He handed Sara the clipboard. She scanned the form on top.

Thomas Clayton Jackson. 38. Caucasian. Divorced. Two children in the custody of his ex-wife, Mildred Jackson, Forrest City, Queens. Death by physical trauma (decapitation). Employed by Immigration and Nationalization Services, Manhattan branch.

"I picked his name out of missing persons," Kilby said proudly, "and ID'ed him from an old football injury. Compound fracture of the left tibia."

Sara glanced at him.

"Good work," she said, and he practically wagged his tail.

"Everything else seemed to fit, so we had the wife come down and ID the, uh, body. It's him, all right. No doubt about it."

"Donuts, anyone?" Jake appeared with a grease-stained paper bag and a couple of cups of coffee.

"Any cream-filled?" Kilby asked.

Sara sighed. "Try not to so stereotypical, Jake. Donuts. Would it hurt to eat healthy for a change? How can I maintain my figure on a diet of sugar and grease?"

"It looks great to me!" Kilby said gallantly.

"Hmmm," she said, non-commitally, but she did take one of the plastic cups of coffee as Jake and Kilby fought over the cream-filled donuts.

"The problem," she said, sipping the cold brew, "is that we have almost too much to look at, but no leads leading anywhere in particular."

"Let's split 'em up," Jake said around a mouthful of his second donut, "and run 'em down. I'll take the restaurant guy–"

"Uh-uh. I know why you want to take the restaurant guy. Juliette lurks nearby. *I'll* take the restaurant guy, the doctor, and the gangbangers. They're clearly all connected. Maybe. You check out the details on this I.N.S. guy."

Jake sniffed. "And I know why you want to go back to Cypress Hills. I saw the way you looked at that priest."

"What?" Sara and Kilby said simultaneously.

Kilby looked at her with hurt in his eyes.

"A priest?" he said.

He sounded disappointed as well as hurt.

Sara made a sound of annoyance. "God, it's nothing like that."

Jake and Kilby looked at each other and nodded.

"Sure," Jake said.

"Is that all you guys think about? Yes, there are some questions I'd like to ask him–questions about the case."

Jake and Kilby exchanged looks again.

"Of course," Kilby said. "Whatever you say."

Men, Sara thought, as she stormed out of the morgue. Outside, it was warm and sunny. Inside, she was cold and shivering. The voices chuckled quietly in the back of her mind.

CHAPTER SIX

St. Casimir's rectory was located behind the church, nestled in a small pocket-like depression. It was cottage-sized, from the outside appearing to be no more than a couple of small rooms, and of the same general age and dilapidation as the church.

A looping gravel path ran from the front of the church to the rectory. As Sara went along the walkway she passed a figure going the opposite way, as if from the rectory itself, which Sara could just see around the bulk of the old church. She kept walking after only the barest glance at the pedestrian who in turn looked at her disinterestedly and kept going in his own direction.

Sara took a few further steps around a loop in the path and stopped. She'd recognized the figure. Or thought she had. It was the woman she'd seen first in the potions shop and later at Club Carrefour. The same facial features, the same lean build, the same slicked-down hair. Except this person was a man. Or at least he'd had a distinct pencil-thin mustache on his upper lip. Maybe she was mistaken. When their eyes had met briefly there'd been no recognition in his, as if he'd never seen Sara before. And she'd gotten only a glimpse of his face as they passed on the path. But she was a trained observer with a quick mind and she was pretty sure of what she'd seen. Indecision usually wasn't one of her problems.

She stood in the curve of the pathway for a moment, hidden from his view in case he happened to glance back. Her cop instincts were vibrating like a struck gong. His look-alike was connected somehow to Guillaume Sam. He probably was as well. He'd had a furtive air about him, an aura difficult for a civilian to pick up, but quite readable for a cop who dealt with dissembling on a daily basis. He was possibly, if not probably, up to no good.

As Sara saw it, she had two choices. Check where he'd been. Follow him to where he was going. She hesitated, torn. If Father Baltazar was involved in a struggle against Guillaume Sam, he could be lying hurt—or worse—in his rectory even as she stood there, desperately thinking. On the other hand, the blond guy hadn't been carrying a blood-soaked machete, and had looked perfectly cool and composed as they'd passed on the path. There were people in the world capable of whacking somebody's head off and then sitting down next to you a couple minutes later at McDonalds and calmly eating a double cheeseburger. But the Machete Murderer seemed to be more of a maniac gore-splattering and blood-sucking type. You'd expect him to be at least a little disheveled after lopping somebody's head off. Besides, he hadn't looked anything like Bakula-baka. Of course, the creature might not have same physical manifestation on Earth as he had on Guinee.

Damn, Sara thought. *There were too many if's to con-*

sider in this case. There were too many things out of the realm of ordinary experience. Give me a plain old murder for hire any day.

Sara made up her mind, but realized she didn't have to leave Father Baltazar hanging, either. She got out her cell phone and punched Jake's number on the speed-dial. He answered immediately with his laconic, " 'Ello."

"Jake–Sara."

"Sara, hey, wait until you hear what I found about this Jackson guy–"

"No time," she said tersely when she could break into his excited exclamation. "I'm on to something–but I need you to check on something else for me."

"Sure." Jake could be terse if he had to.

"Come on down to St. Casimir's. Immediately. Make sure Father Baltazar's okay."

"Why wouldn't he be?"

"Someone's been lurking around the rectory. Looks like a double of that blonde chick with the slicked-back hair we saw at Carrefour's. You remember?"

"Sure. She went off with those Stern dudes. Man, what–"

"Yeah, well, never mind. This one looks like her brother. I suppose. Just hustle on down and check on the Father."

"Okay." Jake was silent for a moment. "You be careful."

"I will." Sara peeked around the corner. Her quarry had reached Fulton Street. He was, in fact, crossing the street and heading deeper into the residential part of Cypress Hills. "The suspect is crossing Fulton Street, heading north. I'm after him."

"Check in early and often."

"Will do."

Sara pocketed her phone and started off down the path at a brisk walk.

Tailing a quarry in the city is fairly easy as long as you're observant and there're plenty of pedestrians between you and the target. Sara was and there were. He moved at a good clip himself, as if he had places to go and things to do, but wasn't a fanatic about it. Sara stayed within forty feet of him, slipping between the knots of pedestrians like an angelfish in a school of mullet. It helped that he didn't look around, didn't window shop, didn't glance at birds, or flowers, or pretty girls as he went down the street.

For the first couple of blocks north of Fulton the pedestrian traffic was fairly thick, but it began to thin out as they got away from the commercial thoroughfare and deeper into the residential part of the community.

Even among the rows of town homes, though, there were plenty of people hanging out on the sidewalks. The neighborhood seemed to be predominantly Lithuanian. It had the look of an old settlement, not rich but moderately comfortable, relatively well taken care of. Kids played on the streets, old people hung out on the stoops or ambled up and down the sidewalks, gossiping with friends and long-time neighbors. Sara sauntered on, trying to look as much as possible as if she belonged there. It wasn't too difficult.

She followed her target for a good twenty minutes as he made his way north on the meandering streets. This was an old part of the city, constructed when growth had been more organic and followed the natural patterns of local geography. The streets twisted like cowpaths. Trees that were more than a century old grew in sidewalk cutouts. As they went further north, the aspect of the community changed from urban to village-like. The houses were set on bigger plots of land, with wooden, single-family dwellings predominating.

The landscape changed again, taking on a relatively rural aspect as Sara's quarry made a sharp turn into what seemed to be a fenced-in park, going through an open arched metal gateway.

Sara followed him at a distance, even more carefully, as there were no other pedestrians around the park entrance.

Only it wasn't a park, she quickly discovered. It was a cemetery.

A bronze historical plaque on the wrought-iron barred gate provided the snippet of information that the Cypress Hills National Cemetery was the only national cemetery located in New York City. Sara wasn't sure of what exactly a national cemetery was, but apparently it had something to do with (as the plaque said) the burial of Union soldiers from a nearby military hospital. The cemetery had been opened in 1848 and was used extensively during the Civil War, but there hadn't been any burials there for almost fifty years. From Sara's observation, it was clear that the abandoned grounds had gone wild.

Though it was peaceful and quiet, Sara's cop mind couldn't help but notice that the cemetery's overgrown state offered numerous places of concealment and almost unlimited opportunities for ambush. She watched as her quarry slipped between two wildly overgrown rhododendrons that towered fifteen feet in the sky, choking what apparently was a path that had once gone between them.

She hesitated.

This isn't too smart, she told herself.

"What are you afraid of?" a voice asked.

"You bear the Witchblade–"

"–you carry the mystic weapon–"

"–you should fear no puny mortal–"

"Maybe," Sara said to herself. "But I'm not stupid, either."

She went cautiously into the park, taking her cell phone from its belt pouch. "Jake."

"Right here," he answered after the first tone.

"Father Baltazar–"

"He's fine."

"Then I was just being paranoid about the blond guy?"

There was a slight pause. "Maybe not. Seems that he delivered a message to Father Baltazar."

"A message? What kind of message? From who?"

"It was an *ouanga.*"

"What?"

"*Ouanga.* A, a kind of talisman, an evil charm. Father Baltazar says it's a warning from the *bokor* to back off. He says be careful. It seems you're following one of the *bokor's* right-hand men. His name is Gene. The Father doesn't know his last name, or even if he has one. The sorcerer's other right hand man is Gene's twin sister. Her name is Jean–J - E - A – N–if you can believe it."

Why not? Sara thought. *I've come to believe a lot stranger things.*

"Where are you?" Jake broke into her reverie.

"I've followed him to Cypress Hills National Cemetery. That's why I'm calling. It's a hell of a place for an ambush."

"Wait," Jake said. "I'll be right there."

Sara was approaching the bank of humongous rhododendrons, so she spoke quietly. "Can't," she said. "I'm going to lose him."

So what–"

Sara didn't have time to articulate an answer, and wasn't even sure herself why she was following him into such a dangerous place. She couldn't tell if it was her cop intuition that something important was about to happen, or if it was the voices whispering insidiously in her head, promising her that such risky activity was worth pursuing. Unfortunately, it'd been her experience that sometimes the voices' promises were lies.

"Come quick," she told her partner. "Be careful."

And she flipped her phone shut and put it back in its holster.

She stood before the rhododendrons, listening, and hearing nothing.

Here's the first test, she thought, *as to how good a job I did shadowing this Gene guy.*

If he knew she was on her trail, this was the perfect ambush point. She took a depth breath, and pushed into the leafy, enfolding arms of the feral bushes. Thin, pointy branches grabbed and poked her as she tried to slither by them without making a sound. She didn't quite succeed, but she was fairly quiet. She made her way through about six feet of rhododendron jungle before bursting out into the open, blinking at the sudden sun and the figure looming right in front of her.

The Witchblade surged to life, but before it could encase her in its sharp metallic shell she pushed it back to wherever it went when she wasn't wearing it, as she realized suddenly that she was confronting a stone angel.

It was an old angel. Its marble body was pitted with age and acid rain, eaten into by almost one hundred and forty years of corrosive city air. It was also crippled. One marble hand, reaching upwards to heaven, had broken away from its arm, one marble wing had cracked off its shoulder. Oddly, the angel's face was relatively untouched and still smiled a tender stone smile at all passersby.

It stood on a stone pedestal. The words once chiseled into the face of the pedestal had been obliterated by age. What few marks that still remained were hidden by a tangle of wild rose growing from the grave over which the angel stood guard, twining around the pedestal and up the angel's legs to its waist. The rose was thorny, its buds small but numerous, and fiery as a sunset in various shades of orange and red.

For a moment Sara stood contemplating the aged monument and felt oddly at peace. It seemed a gentle, somehow appropriate guardian for the apparently forgotten old soldier buried beneath its upraised arms and beatific smile.

Then a sound came from further inside the cemetery turned to jungle, the sound of a pick or shovel striking stone, and Sara's head snapped up. The noise came from behind another screen of greenery. She crept closer, sunk low, and got down behind an unidentified bush with lots of foliage, and, feeling like a character out of *The Last of the Mohicans*, slowly and carefully parted the branches in front of her.

Her sensibilities lurched from *Mohicans* to a Boris Karloff flick about bodysnatching, because that was happening twenty feet in front of her. Three men were taking turns digging up a grave while Gene supervised, leaning back casually upon the canted tombstone and smoking a cigarette.

"I don't have all day," Gene said in a slightly irritated drawl.

The man leaning on his shovel looked at him respectfully. From her vantage point behind the wall of greenery, Sara could see fear in the man's eyes. Gene, she thought, must be a lot tougher than he looked. The resemblance to his sister, now that Sara could study his face at leisure, was indeed remarkable. They had the same high, delicate cheekbones, the sharp chin, the lofty, unlined brow. In fact, the only discernible difference between the two was the pencil-thin mustache that Gene affected. Even their physical build was quite similar. They were the same height, had the same breadth of shoulder, and slim hips. Sara had never seen male-female twins that so resembled each other.

Could it all be, Sara wondered, some kind of elaborate charade? Were they really only one person, pretending to be two? But . . . to what purpose?

Whatever the reality of their supposed identities, it was clear that the graverobbers were wary of Gene.

"But you don't have to be–" the voice insinuated softly in Sara's brain.

"You have the Witchblade–"

"Use it–"

"Use it–"

"Use it–"

Sara snarled to herself, to the voices murmuring in her brain. She shook her head as if to clear it and rattled a nearby branch.

"What was that?"

The man leaning on his shovel looked up, in Sara's direction. Gene flicked his cigarette aside. Down deep in the grave, one of the digger's shovels grated on wood.

"We hit it," he announced.

Gene looked back down at him as the idle digger shouldered his shovel like a rifle and started to meander in Sara's direction.

"The coffin?" Gene asked.

The man in the grave who had spoken grunted. "Must be."

There were more scraping sounds as the other stopped digging, and watched his colleague drop down to hands and knees and scrabble among the well-rotted boards.

"Yep," he said with satisfaction. "Here we go."

He reached down into the partially uncovered and broken coffin, and stood up holding a round, brownish ball. Only it wasn't a ball. It was a skull.

Gene grunted. "Good. We need two more for the ceremony," he said, to the apparent disappointment of the diggers. They complained but not for too long, or too audibly.

Meanwhile, the man with the shovel over his shoulder wandered casually, perhaps a bit too casually, Sara thought, in her general direction. He whistled, looking everywhere but at her. When he pounced, she was ready.

He came right at her with a shout, holding his shovel near the end of its handle, ready to swing it like a club. But Sara was partially shielded by the bushes she was hiding behind, so his swing was ineffectual. She stood and drew her .45 from the holster snugged down against the small of her back.

Sara was furious, and ready to take it out on her assailant. She didn't know if she angrier at herself for her carelessness, or at the voices that again seemed to have goaded her into an unthinking action that had given away her hiding place.

To hell with them, she thought as she sprang to her feet. *I'll handle this on my own.*

The man screamed again as he swung the shovel clumsily. Sara slipped through the shrubs that separated them and floated inside his striking range. She could have shot him half a dozen times, but instead slapped him against the side of his head with the barrel of her automatic. He went down like a pig in the slaughterhouse. As he fell Sara noticed the cross tattooed on his forehead.

"Hold it!" she shouted, gripping her gun with both hands and taking a wide-legged shooter's stance.

One of the bodysnatchers had jumped out of the excavated grave and was advancing towards her in a crouch, shovel gripped low and high as if it were a fighting staff. The other looked on stupidly, mouth agape. Gene, meanwhile, had also taken a few steps forward, casually, silently, his eyes narrow slits.

Sara shifted her pistol back and forth between the two who seemed the most dangerous. "I said freeze! I'm a—"

Something glittering spun through the air, hooked, and caught around the barrel of her gun. Astonished, she realized that Gene had trapped her weapon with one end of a weighted chain. He yanked and the gun's muzzle snapped upward. Her finger tightened on the trigger and it fired once, harmlessly, in the air. Gene shifted his grip on the chain, twisting so that Sara lost her hold on the automatic. He jerked the chain and it went flying back to him, taking her gun along. It fell to the ground halfway between them. She tried to keep an eye on it to see exactly where it landed, but the graverobber rushed her, demanding her attention.

"Use the Witchblade," the voices screamed shrilly, but Sara had closed her mind to their urges.

"No!" she screamed aloud, and leapt forward to meet her assailant.

This man was smarter than the first. He wielded his shovel like a fighting staff, hands far apart on the handle, ready to strike with either the wooden handle or pointed metal blade. Small crosses were tattooed on the first joint of all his fingers. He was another Saturday Night Special.

The Special took a short, vicious swing with the shovel's blade end, aiming at Sara's midriff. She twisted in mid-stride and the gleaming blade missed her stomach by a fraction of an inch. His follow-up with the other end struck her across the ribcage. She rolled with the blow, trying to absorb as much of its force as she could. It hurt like hell. Pain flashed across the left side of her body. She was relieved when it slackened and she discovered that she could still breathe easily.

But her assailant didn't give her much time to catch her breath.

He came at her again, this time swinging the shovel more wildly in a two-handed, over-the-head fashion, trying to finish her off all at once. Sara rolled, and the shovel's blade thudded into the ground, sinking deeply into the fine soil covered by the cemetery's green sward.

Her assailant jerked the shovel head free. Sara kept rolling, hoping that her memory was accurate. He ran after her, winding up for another deathblow.

Fortunately for Sara, her memory *was* accurate.

She rolled over the implement dropped by her first assailant, and came up in a half crouch, the shovel's handle planted firmly against the ground, the shovel head pointed outward like a spear braced against oncoming calvary.

The graverobber ran into it, gut high, and gave himself an unexpected appendectomy.

The voices in Sara's head roared with delight.

He screamed in agony, clutching his punctured abdomen, and fell writhing to the ground. Sara looked up. Gene was smiling, and pointing his pistol at her.

"Police!" a familiar voice roared behind her. "Drop it! Drop it *NOW!*"

She risked a glance over her shoulder and saw Jake standing braced in the approved shooter's stance, gun aimed unwaveringly at Gene. Behind him stood Father Baltazar, consternation on his face.

Her eyes went back to Gene, who made a small moue of disappointment as he slowly bent over and carefully placed his gun on the ground. The last of the graverobbers had already flopped down in the open grave in an ultimately futile attempt to escape notice.

"What the hell is going on here, Sara?" Jake asked.

She stood, flinching a little as her ribcage twinged.

"Arrest these mooks," she said.

"On what charge?"

"Attempted murder of a police officer, assault with a deadly weapon, resisting arrest, graverobbing. Oh yeah, and corpse abuse," Sara said. "I'm sure we'll think of a few other counts when we get them down to the precinct."

Father Baltazar hurried up to her. "Are you all right?" he asked.

"Sure. Perfectly fine."

His dark eyes caught hers and held. "No, you're not.

Something troubles you. Something beyond–" he gestured vaguely, implying the recent actions "–all this."

The voices snickered in her head.

"No," Sara said. "Really–"

He laid a gentle hand on her arm. "We'll talk later. Maybe we'll finish the discussion we'd started when we first met."

He went past her, to minister to the man who'd impaled himself on the shovel, as Jake called for transport and an ambulance. Sara took a deep breath, winced, and started to fight off the shakes as they descended upon her.

CHAPTER SEVEN

Captain Joe Siry was a big man with a gray-dusted mustache and severe male pattern baldness. He still had most of the hair around the side of his head, but it was mostly gone from the top, save for a strip across the very crest of his skull running from front to back like a thin and tired Mohawk. He had a florid face that got even redder when he was angry.

Now it was very red indeed.

"So." Sara knew he was mad because his voice was so soft and low. "You *didn't* identify yourself as a cop when you drew down on them?"

Sara had her faults, she knew, but lying to her boss wasn't among them, even if it came down to saving her butt. "There wasn't time—"

"Wasn't time!" Siry's voice exploded. Jake, along for the little chat in Siry's office, gazed up at the ceiling, pretending to be somewhere else. Siry, sitting behind his disheveled desk in an uncomfortable chair that was old during the Lindsey administration, slammed his big hand down on the only slightly more recently acquired blotter, making stacks of paper shift and slide as if they'd caught the edge of an extremely localized earthquake.

Siry looked down at the open manila folder in front of him, again scanning Sara's report. Sara stood at stiff attention, holding back her anger as the voices twitted at her in her brain.

"Corpse abuse!" Siry said. "Corpse abuse! Jesus Tap-dancing Christ!" He looked up at Sara. "It's a damn good thing the thugs you pistol-whipped and carved on with a shovel didn't die. If that'd happened, we'd *all* be up to our asses in lawsuits. As it is . . ."

His voice slipped into inaudible grumbling, and Jake cleared his throat.

"Sir?" he said.

Siry fixed him with a stare. "Yes?"

A lesser man might have wilted, but Jake plunged ahead. "There's no doubt those perps are involved with the Machete Murderer. Somehow. Sara could have been killed–"

Siry waved a beefy hand. "I know, I know." He fixed them both his hard-edged stare. "That's why Pezzini's career is still hanging by a thread. And you're both still on the case." Siry waved his hand again, indicating a dark form silhouetted on the shades that were drawn down upon the glass walls of his office. "I've spoken to the Padre. God knows why, but he seems to think highly of you two. He seems to think you're making good progress on the case and are going to eventually get this Machete Murderer–hopefully before more bodies end up in either the East River or random Dumpsters."

"He–" Sara began.

Siry pointed a blunt forefinger at her and she stopped.

"But this is my last warning. No more cowboy stuff. No more lone wolfing around abandoned graveyards. And for Christ's sake, try to let the Brooklyn people know what you're doing. Every now and then, at least." Siry glanced down at the report. "Lieutenant Dickey is being assigned to the case as a liaison. *Do* keep him informed."

Sara and Jake exchanged wary glaces.

"Yes, sir," they said in unison.

"One last thing," Siry said in a hard voice, stopping them as they turned to go. As they looked back his face softened, took on a worried expression. They could also hear concern in his words. "This isn't a normal serial killer run amok. This case smells funny. Really funny. Just–be careful."

"Yes, sir," they said again, and turned and left the office, Jake closing the door behind them, letting out his breath in a deep sigh as he did so. He turned to Sara.

"What the hell do you think you're up to?" he said in a low, insistent voice, so quietly that even people working at the nearby desks couldn't hear him.

"What?" Sara asked, confused.

"Siry's right. Partly, at least. I'm your partner, dammit. You seem to conveniently forget that when you want to go haring off on one of your lone wolf adventures–"

"I didn't forget," Sara said. "I thought of you immediately. I called you because I knew you'd be there, at my back."

"Oh." Jake frowned, as if he only half-believed her.

He should, Sara thought, *since I'm telling only half the truth.*

She knew that Siry and Jake were both right. She was too much of a loner, taking risks that were too great, rushing in where any other fool would dread to go. Part of it was her fault. She *was* reckless. She did sometimes act before thinking through the consequences of her actions.

But part of it was the fault of the voices and the temptation of the Witchblade. They encouraged her recklessness. Their whispered promises played to her deepest desires, but as she well knew, their promises were sometimes lies. The Witchblade sometimes had an agenda of its own, one that didn't always coincide with Sara's interests or well-being.

She knew that she'd be well-advised to keep that in mind, for she was certain that if she always gave in to the voices, one day they'd lead her to her death. Or worse, perhaps her damnation.

She looked up and met the eyes of Father Baltazar, who was standing alone in the precinct room, watching her with compassion in his eyes.

Did she see something else, she wondered, besides compassion? Was there a promise of release as well, release from what had become the curse of the Witchblade?

"Well," Sara said, sitting back gingerly, all too aware of the pain in her ribs—which, thankfully, had been bruised but not broken, "that was a wasted day."

Sara, Jake, and Father Baltazar sat in a dark booth in a quiet bar on a placid street, far from the maddening crowds of Manhattan or even Cypress Hills. It was a time to regroup, for thought and quiet discussion, and, Sara hoped, for the sharing of secret knowledge on the Father's part. It was evident that he knew more about what was happening in Cypress Hills than he'd told them. So far he'd tossed out some hints for them to investigate.

Sara hoped that now he trusted them enough to open up and tell the story behind those hints.

"I wouldn't say that," Jake said in reply to Sara's complaint, smiling as he took a long pull from his beer glass.

"Why not?" Sara asked.

"While you were playing tiptoe through the tulips with our graverobbing friends," Jake said, "I was getting some real information on our vic, Thomas T. Jackson."

Sara toyed with her own beer glass. She was too upset to drink, contenting herself with pushing the glass back and forth on the tabletop, spilling a little bit every now and then.

"Like what?" she asked.

Jake made a dramatic flourish out of consulting his pocket notebook. "Let's see. He lived alone in a middle-class four-room apartment in Forrest Hills. No surprise there. He was always on time with his alimony and child support. Maybe a surprise. Maybe he was just a good father. But here's the fun stuff: he also owned a beach home in the Hamptons. Small, but pricey. His car was a mid-priced Porsche." McCarthy looked at Father Baltazar. "I don't know what they pay priests nowadays, but mid-priced Porsches are usually out of the price range of cops."

Father Baltazar took a small, precise sip of his beer and smiled. "Priests, too, I fear."

"Also, Jackson had a 'cabin' in the Adirondacks that was bigger than his Forrest Hills apartment. He also took three vacations this year. A luxury cruise to the Carribean, a long weekend in Paris via the Concorde, and ten days on some island in Micronesia for skindiving. First-class airline tickets, of course. I forgot to mention that he took a different honey to each exotic location."

Sara whistled. "Man, we should go to work for the I.N.S."

"Yeah," Jake said seriously. "They seem to be a lot more generous with their vacation time than N.Y.P.D."

"And their salary," Sara pointed out.

McCarthy shook his head. "Nope. According to Jackson's tax returns he made a little over sixty thou last year."

Father Baltazar took another precise sip of beer. "That's more than I get."

Sara smiled. "Maybe. But is it enough for an apartment in Forest Hills, child support, a beach house, car payments, a mountain cabin, plane tickets, scuba diving, and three demanding girlfriends?"

"What makes you think his girlfriends were demanding?" Jake asked.

Sara's smile widened. "Just a guess."

Jake downed most of his beer. "Anyway, you're right. Where did this guy come up with all the extra jack?"

"What does Immigration and Naturalization have that's all that valuable?" Sara asked.

"Green cards, of course," Father Baltazar said into the sudden silence. "One of the most valuable commodities in a community of recent immigrants. A green card can make all the difference in their lives. Without one you're subject to what can be little more than the whims of elected, or even non-elected, officials. With one, you're a citizen. There's no one looking over your shoulder. You can breathe easy and live a real life in your new country."

"You knew this?" Sara asked.

Father Baltazar shook his head. "Knew that someone was selling green cards? No. Suspected . . ."

"For how long?" Jake asked.

"Not long," the priest said. "And we had no proof of it. We still have no proof. We had suspicions, and when the bodies started showing up our suspicions were somewhat confirmed."

"Who's we?" Sara asked.

"Paul Narcisse and I," Father Baltazar said.

"The bookstore owner?" Jake asked.

Father Baltazar smiled at him. "He's more than that. Paul Narcisse and I are also brothers of the cloth. Unofficially, of course."

"He's a priest, too?"

"Of course. He is a *houngan*. A priest of *voudon*."

"Dude," Jake said, "you mean, he's a voodoo priest? Like with the dolls and pins and zombies and stuff like that."

"You watch too many Hollywood movies," the priest said with mild reproof in his voice. "And that is not the best source to get your knowledge of historical or cultural matters."

Sara suppressed a smile. "Better than comic books."

"Perhaps," Father Baltazar said. "In any event, *voudon* is an ancient, authentic religion. Now is not the time to give you a lesson in its history and theology, but I assure you that the business about the dolls and pins was grafted onto it by Hollywood to thrill credulous audiences."

"And the zombies, too, huh?" Jake said, quaffing the dregs of his beer.

The priest looked at him. "Oh, no. Zombies are quite real."

Only the low level of beer in his glass prevented Jake from performing a classic spit-take. As it was, the remnants of brew swam up his sinus passages and trickled out of his nose and down his chin as he snorted first in disbelief, then in sudden, burning pain.

"Gee–" Jake coughed as his eyes watered. He waved his hand under his nose. "Holy crap, Padre–"

Father Baltazar held up his hand. "Let's not get distracted from the matter at hand by a theological discussion. If you want to learn about *loa* and zombies and *zobops* and such, I'll tell you all I know later."

"And Guinee?" Sara asked.

"Yes," the priest said, "and Guinee."

Sara nodded, and something of a promise passed between them.

"What–" Jake began, but Sara cut him off.

"The Father's right. Voodoo later. Now, let's try to figure out how all these murders fit together."

"It seems fairly clear," the priest said, "although, of course, this is all theoretical."

"You seem to know the situation better than we do," Sara said. "Theorize away."

"All right." Father Baltazar took a deep breath. "One: Thomas Jackson. He had access to official documents. Two: Cladius Caradeuc. A doctor. Through his clinic he had access to the people who needed the green cards." The priest paused to sigh. "His death, though, was a surprise. And a hurt. We always thought he was one of us."

"Us?" Jake inquired.

Father Baltazar nodded. "An informal group of Cypress Hills citizens. Those in opposition to the *bokor* who is the source of most of the evil in the community."

"Paul Narcisse spoke of a '*bokor*,' " Sara said, half-questioningly.

"Yes. An evil sorcerer who walks the left-hand path.

Who serves the dark *loa* for his own personal gain. Who preys on his own people like a *loup-garou*."

"I don't even want to ask what that is," Jake said.

Sara remembered some of her high school French. "That would be werewolf," she said.

"God," Jake groaned. He looked at his empty glass. "I need another beer."

"Just a minute," Father Baltazar said. "Two more people need to be tied into the web of killings."

"Achille de Petion," Sara said. "He was just a thug, just a street criminal, wasn't he?"

"Not entirely," the priest replied. "He was also a *zobop*."

Sara shook her head. "That, I don't know the meaning of."

Father Baltazar smiled. "A *zobop* is a low-level *soldat*, that is, initiate in the *bokor*'s secret society. I suspect he was the go-between between the I.N.S. man and the doctor."

"So what happened to cause the bloodbath?"

The priest shrugged. "I don't know. Perhaps someone got greedy and wanted a larger cut. Perhaps someone got scared, or got a conscience, and threatened to go to the authorities. The precise reason for the killings still needs to be uncovered, and in fact may never be known."

"How big a business are we talking about, to make it worth all these murders?"

"A green card can go for three to five thousand dollars apiece on the street. If you sell a thousand a year—certainly a conservative figure—that's three to five million dollars. Tax free, of course, with little cost to the seller. And these cards were *real*. Not counterfeit. Impeccable and unquestionable."

"But we're forgetting one thing," Sara said. "The fourth victim. Jean Pierre-Pierre, the restauranteur."

Father Baltazar shrugged. "No. I'm not forgetting him. But I don't understand how he fits into this scenario."

"Was he one of your allies?" Sara asked.

The priest nodded. "Yes. He was one of us." He was silent for a moment. "The best I can figure is that his death was a warning from the *bokor*, to all of us. Despite our best efforts, we've been little more than a thorn in his side. But we've been getting stronger. We've been unifying the community against him. Perhaps this was a warning to us to cease our activities, or suffer the same fate as poor Pierre-Pierre." The priest took a drink from his glass, and put it back down on the table. "Of course, there is another explanation."

"What's that?" Sara asked.

"The *bokor* is playing with great forces. He has called something powerful and evil into the world."

"Bakula-baka," Sara said in a low voice.

Father Baltazar was startled. "Yes. That is what all the signs point to. How do you know?" he asked in a worried voice.

"Apparently," Sara said, twisting her beer glass as if trying to screw it down into the surface of the table, "I've met him. I've been to Guinee. Maybe in a dream."

"My child," the priest said, placing his hands on hers.

Sara flinched, as the voices roared in her head at the touch of the priest's hands. Father Baltazar took them away, as if he sensed he caused her pain, and the voices went back to a background rumbling.

"Just what is going on here?" Jake asked.

Sara shook her head. She couldn't even begin to explain about the Witchblade, about the mystic forces swirling about her, imprisoning her with the promise of great power. Not now. Perhaps not ever.

"This Bakula-baka," she urged the priest.

"A dark *loa,*" he said. "One of the worst. Not as powerful as his brothers, but vile and vicious and difficult for any human to control. Often the human thinks he's riding Bakula-baka, and then discovers to his surprise that the opposite is true."

Sara felt a shiver run down her spine. The exact same thing could be said of herself and the Witchblade. If Father Baltazar and his friend Paul Narcisse understood this, perhaps they knew a way to help her deal with her own mystic problem.

"So," Jake said, frowning, "what you're saying is that our serial killer is really some kind of demon or spirit called to earth by this *bokor,* who may be losing control, who may be unable to keep it from going on its own murderous rampage?"

"That could be," the priest agreed, "the situation."

"And if it is," Sara said, "then God help us all."

Father Baltazar nodded.

"And this *bokor,* this evil sorcerer—"

"Is Guillaume Sam, of course," Sara said.

Jake shook his head.

"I need another drink," he said.

CHAPTER EIGHT

Club Carrefour was as crowded as if it were Saturday night, but it was actually only Tuesday.

Sara and Jake made their way across the floor and through the obstacle course of densely packed tables. The air was hot from the press of bodies and the frenetic activity on the adjacent dance floor, redolent from the fumes of perfume and aftershave, beer, wine, and hard liquor. Many of the drinks had been made with fruity bases whose aroma reminded Sara of the odors wafting through the Guinee jungle that she'd visited in her dream.

The music blaring over the sound system was loud and punctuated by a complicated rhythm. It was salsa-like, but spiced with unfamiliar Carribean overtones. It would be fun to dance, Sara thought, if she had someone to dance with. Fun to lose herself if only for a little while in the music and the motion and to forget all about death and murder and evil spirits. And whispering voices in her head.

At that thought they giggled on cue and Sara knew

they were laughing at her. She knew, also, there was nothing she could do about it.

Jake put his mouth close to her ear and spoke just loud enough for her to hear him. "So, how do we go about proving that Guillaume Sam is a *bokor* summoning evil spirits to do his murderous bidding?"

Sara would have smiled, but she didn't find the question all that amusing. It was a serious problem. New York State wasn't about to burn someone at the stake for witchcraft. It was, after all, the twenty-first century. If they accused Guillaume Sam of sorcery it was more likely that they'd lose their jobs than that Guillaume Sam would be bought to justice.

"We'll just have to find evidence proving the green card racket. Or any of the other rackets he's undoubtedly got his dirty hands in. That would probably be enough to burn him."

Jake nodded. "Easier said than done."

Sara looked at him, and did smile this time. "Jake, if it was easy, anybody could do our job."

His retort was silenced as someone came out of the crowd and slipped an arm around his waist. He looked down, surprised, to see Juliette from the voodoo shop smiling at him.

She looked stunning. Her hip-huggers, riding low on her waist, looked painted on. Her T-shirt looked even tighter, clinging to every curve and angle it covered. The shirt's neckline was rather more demure than the one they'd first seen her wearing. But more than making up for that were the numerous horizontal slits in the fabric, running from waist to neck, that gave tantalizing glimpses of the curves her shirt was supposed to cover.

"Well, it's my big policeman," she said in a purring, melting voice. "Why haven't you been back to visit your little Juliette?"

"Been out bringing criminals to justice," Jake said with a smile. "Without my constant vigilance the city just isn't safe."

"How 'bout using some of that vigilance on me, honey?"

Jake shrugged. "I suppose I can entrust the safety of the city to my partner for a few minutes. Let me have a word with her, and I'll be right with you."

"Don't be long," Juliette said with a teasing tone in her voice.

"Uh-huh."

She headed toward the dance floor, looking back with an imploring smile. He leaned over and spoke again in Sara's ear.

"I should really follow this up. I think she may know something."

Sara nodded with skepticism. "I'm sure she does. I'm not sure if what she knows has anything to do with this case."

Jake grinned. "Hey, let me enjoy myself for at least a few minutes. What's it going to hurt?"

He started off after the girl, who was backing onto the dance floor, beckoning him with open arms and hips undulating to the music. Sara caught his forearm.

"Jake," she said, "be careful. Nothing in this case is what it seems."

He shook his head, laughing. "Sure."

"I mean it!" Sara insisted.

Jake paused for a moment, his face serious. "I know, partner, I know." He spoke almost reluctantly. "You know, it wouldn't hurt you to relax for a bit, to loosen up a little. You're wound tighter than a yo-yo string, and some day you're gonna snap."

Sara had nothing to say. Jake nodded gently and stepped onto the dance floor with Juliette. Within seconds they disappeared in the mass of boogying humanity, lost to Sara's sight in a sea of waving arms and gyrating torsos.

He's right, of course, Sara thought, but what could she do? She wasn't in the sixth grade. She couldn't go out on the dance floor by herself and dance the night away with a pretend partner. That would be just too–

Almost as if on cue a voice said, "Well. Detective Pezzini. How nice to see you again," and Sara turned, a smile on her face. A smile she quickly lost when she realized who was standing beside her.

"The last time we saw each other we were pointing guns. I'm glad that this time we're in more congenial surroundings."

It was Gene. There could be no doubt that he was one of twins, because next to him, her arm around his waist and his around hers, was his sister Jean.

They were a stunning pair. Both wore formal evening clothes, Gene, a wonderfully tailored, classic black tuxedo, Jean, a tightly clinging dress that plunged daringly from neck to waist and was cut high up the side of her thighs, exposing plenty of ivory-white flesh in both areas.

It was, Sara thought as she looked from one to the other, fairly mind-boggling. They looked so much alike that without Gene's mustache and without the masculine/feminine clothes they wore, it would be difficult if not impossible to tell them apart. Yet both were beautiful, and, more so, smouldering with a palpable sexuality.

Sara had always been attracted to large, masculine men, but there was something about Gene, his superior smile, his air of utter confidence, the hard edge to his eyes that promised more strength than that found in most. Too bad, Sara thought, he was a thug. Or maybe that overt sense of danger he exuded added something to his potent aura.

She cleared her throat, realizing that some time had gone by without her reply.

"Made bail, then?" she asked.

Gene shrugged elegant shoulders. "It wasn't hard. You didn't have much of a case." He looked her up and down, shaking his head. Rarely had Sara ever felt more scrutinized than when his and his sister's eyes were on her. "You'd think a policewoman of your experience would have remembered to identify yourself. Why, my colleagues and I thought we were being robbed, and only acted in self-defense."

"Thought you were being robbed," Sara said, "while you were robbing a grave?"

"It's a strange world," Gene said blandly.

Jean took a long pull from the cigarette she'd been holding at her side and let the smoke out in a stream through her nostrils. She regarded Sara intently, her head tilted to one side.

"Corpse abuse," she said. Her voice was husky for a woman's, but not unpleasantly so. Not unpleasantly at all. "That was a very imaginative charge. A new one to add to your list, dear brother." She suddenly smiled and her face became that of a charmingly beautiful carnivore who seemed undecided whether to lick you or bite you. "I should thank you, Detective. Rarely does something new like that come into our lives."

This is, Sara thought, *the strangest conversation I've ever had in my life. And that's saying a lot.*

"Would you care to dance, Detective?" Gene asked urbanely.

"With you?" Sara asked, disbelievingly.

"With both of us," Jean said.

"Ummm—" was the best reply Sara could come up with.

"No need to be shy," Gene said. "So you arrested me." He shrugged again. "We both have our jobs to do. That doesn't mean we can't enjoy each other's company when we're off the clock. Besides—" and here again came that wicked grin "—I admire the way your handled yourself in the graveyard this afternoon. Your exhibition of shovel-fu was most entertaining. And the manner in which you used your gun . . ." Gene shook his head like a gourmet remembering a particularly lavish and tasty meal.

"Um —" Sara repeated.

She was saved by a sudden commotion that diverted all their attention.

"Hey, hey! We're here!"

"Let the party start!"

It was Rog and Jer Stern. As far as Sara could tell, they were wearing the same clothes they'd had on the previous day, as well as the same carefree, if more than slightly goofy smiles.

"Hey, momma!" One of them caught sight of Jean—Sara at this point couldn't remember which twin was wearing what and so couldn't tell them apart—and put his arms around her from behind. She gave her brother a knowing smile, and turned her sleek head on her elegant neck and caught Stern's mouth with her own.

Stern said something like, "MmmmmHmmmm," as they kissed deeply.

"Hey," the other Stern said, "save some of that for Pappa Jer." He pushed in from the other side and kissed her at the same time as his brother.

Gene looked knowingly at Sara, his smile sliding into a leer. Sara was suddenly grateful to see Aleksandras Gervelis standing behind the increasingly occupied brothers.

"Alek," she said with a hearty smile. "Nice to see you again."

Gene's smile slipped a little, then became fixed as Alek came forward.

"Thanks," he said to Sara. "I can say the same." He nodded in Gene's direction, and Gene nodded back a precise millimeter. He glanced at Jean, but she and the brothers were already slipping away to the dance floor. He looked back at Gene. "Give my greetings to Jean when she manages to extricate herself from the boys."

"They seem . . . persistent," Sara said.

Alek sighed, watching them flail away with arms and legs as they did their best imitation of dancing. "If only they were so persistent with their music. Well." He looked back to Sara from the trio as they disappeared into the maw of the dance floor. "Can I get you a drink?"

"Yes," she said. "That would be great."

Alek turned to Gene, whose eyes were turning icier by the second. "Gene?"

"No. Thank you. I have some business to attend to."

"All right, then."

"All right."

Gene nodded to Sara. There seemed something of a promise in his gesture, something that said that he wasn't finished with her. Despite her essential toughness, she had a hard time suppressing a shiver as he walked away.

"He doesn't seem to like you very much," Sara said as they both watched him stalk off.

"That's all right," Alec said. "I don't like him very much, either. Although, he seems to like you. A lot."

Sara shook her head. "I arrested him earlier today," she said.

"Really?" Alec seemed surprised and amused. "Let's get those drinks and you can tell me all about it. If it doesn't involve police secrets."

"Secrets?" Sara laughed. "I have no–" She hesitated for a moment, catching herself in an unintentional lie. "–official secrets."

Alek held his hand out and Sara found herself taking it without thinking. It was large, warm, and strong. It felt good in hers. They started toward the crowded bar. "So, what'd you arrest him for?"

"Corpse abuse. Among other things."

Alek looked down at her. "*Corpse abuse*? Man, this should be good."

Sara knew she should be working. She tried to tell herself that maybe, in a sense, she was. Alek Gervelis knew Guillaume Sam, had known him for years. He could be a valuable source of information about Sam's operations. The trouble was their conversation regarding Sam was over pretty quickly. Alek really didn't know much about him.

Sure, he'd helped Mountains of Madness in the beginning of their career, but that was all money stuff. Management. That was Kris's territory. Kris worried about all that stuff–worried too much about it, in fact–and Alek took care of the music end. That was what he lived for, that was what he loved. That was all he cared about.

And yet, Sara discovered that Alek wasn't a man who

talked continually about himself. Most men Sara knew were like that, though Sara had to admit that when she thought about it she didn't know many men. Practically none outside the job. She had no time for a personal life. The job was everything.

But as she sat and talked with Alek about what it was like to be a cop—and she told him a suitably edited version of events of that very afternoon—and he told her stories of his life, of what it was like being a creative person in a field where they wanted you to be precisely as creative as the last successful band—and no more—she felt the pressure of the job flowing away from her.

She forgot momentarily about the Machete Murderer, about her strange visit to Guinee, about the necessity of getting the goods on Guillaume Sam before his henchmen could kill again. She forgot even the voices in her head and the thing called the Witchblade. She began to enjoy herself.

Alek Gervelis wasn't an ego-driven rising rock star. He was an interesting man with an interesting life, who also seemed interested in her life and what it was like to be a cop. It didn't hurt any that he was also crushingly handsome, and that it really didn't seem to matter to him.

Time went by. They had a few drinks, but found themselves talking more than drinking, and taking turns listening more than talking. Sara was surprised at how fast the time went. She checked her watch when Kris Gervelis and Magdalena Konsavage showed up and sat at their table, and was surprised to see that nearly three hours had passed.

Alek went to the bar to get fresh drinks for all as Sara studied his brother. She didn't want to slip back into cop mode, but her conscience was bothering her. She'd been having too much of a good time and she had to get back to work, even if only for a little bit.

"You know Guillaume Sam pretty well?" she asked Kris.

He shrugged. He was smaller than his brother, and not nearly as handsome. Not, in fact, handsome at all. It could have been tough having an older, much more charismatic brother, but Sara was glad to see that they seemed to have a decent relationship. She thought of her own sister and despaired of their relationship. Their different attitudes toward life was only one of the reasons why she thought of her so infrequently, if at all.

"Know him?" Kris frowned thoughtfully. "Not really. We're not friends or anything. We don't hang out together, if that's what you mean."

"No, but you do have a business relationship."

"Sure."

Alek returned with the drinks and managed to set them down on the crowded table without spilling any. He had to step over his brother to get to his own seat, and put his arm around Sara's shoulder to steady himself during the maneuver. Sara did not object.

She took a sip of her drink and leaned toward Kristoforas. "I'd like to get together with you some time, maybe tomorrow, talk about him some."

"Sure," Kris said, "if you want to. I'm got some stuff to do in the morning, some contracts to go over with a couple of different venues in the city, but I'll be free in the afternoon. Call me and set up a time. Here's my cell number."

He handed Sara a card, and she tucked it away.

"Sara gave me an idea for a new song tonight," Alek said.

"What about?" Magdalena asked.

"Corpse abuse."

Kris sighed and shook his head. "I just don't get you artists," he said.

Sara laughed, the case again slipping away from her mind.

The night turned toward midnight and beyond. The four sat laughing and talking. Sara was tired, but it was a pleasant weariness. She couldn't remember the last time she felt so completely relaxed. Jake had been right, she thought. She did have to unwind a little, she did have to take a little time and enjoy herself. For a moment she wondered about Jake. She hadn't seen him in hours. She thought of looking for him, but something told her he was no longer on the dance floor. She figured he had taken Juliette to a more private venue for questioning, probably of a somewhat personal nature.

Sara was with Kris and Magdalena for only a little while before she realized that Kris loved the singer passionately, but she didn't return the feeling. Sara didn't think that Magdalena was playing him–she seemed too nice for that–but there was an almost desperate sadness about Kris when he looked at her. He tried to conceal it, but wasn't very good at dissembling. It was as if he knew that her love was beyond his reach, but he couldn't keep himself from trying to grasp it over and over and over again.

With visions of unattainable love running through her mind, Sara was surprised to suddenly realize that she was also thinking about Father Baltazar, wondering where he was and what he was doing. She brought herself up with a start, glancing at Alek.

He smiled at her. She smiled back. The voices in her

brain, silent almost all evening, suddenly chittered laughingly. Further confused thought was cut short when Jean suddenly appeared before their table.

"Where are the boys?" Alek asked, as if amused to see her unaccompanied by the panting Stern brothers.

"I've left them to their own devices for a while," Jean said. She turned, looked directly at Sara. "Mr. Sam wants to see you."

"Me?" Sara was glad to turn her mind to something immediate, something concrete. She was afraid of where it had been wandering lately. "Why does he want to see me?"

Jean shrugged. It was a lithe, almost lascivious movement. "I was told to bring you. That's all."

Now, if ever, was the time to be cautious, but Sara felt more excited than cautious. Who knew what this meeting portended, but it was likely to lead to something big, perhaps something that could help break the case.

"All right."

She made her excuses to the table, stood, and followed Jean through the press of the crowd, still thronging the bar despite the lateness of the hour. They went around the dance floor, through an unmarked door next to one end of the bar. The short corridor beyond terminated in a dark wood door that had MR. SAM embossed upon it in metallic lettering. Jean gestured at the door with a cryptic smile, half of humor, half of anticipation. Sara raised her fist to knock, but the door swung open silently, as if, Sara thought, they were in a cheap horror movie.

The room beyond was of middling size and expensively if eccentrically furnished. Along the far wall was a wooden desk with two comfortable-looking chairs in front. Guillaume Sam, lit cigar in his mouth, sat behind it in an even larger and more comfortable-looking chair. It was obviously a working desk, not just for show, and littered with papers. Sam, pen in his left hand, was reading through them carefully and making notes. Baka, perched on his shoulder, his naked tail curled around his master's neck, seemed to be giving the papers as much attention as Guilaume Sam was.

It would have been comical, if the possum didn't appear so damn serious. There was also a half-empty rum bottle on the desk accompanied by tumbler-sized glasses, and a human skull that had a strange depression at the top of its cranium.

"Ah, Ms. Pezzini," Sam rumbled in his deep voice. "Come in. He gestured at one of the chairs in front of his desk. "Sit down."

The luxurious carpet muffled her footsteps as she crossed the room, glancing from the desk to the altar that took up a whole corner of the room. It was similar in its chaotic busyness to the one she had seen in the back room of Paul Narcisse's bookstore, but different in its details. There were many empty liquor bottles and the central place of honor was taken up by another human skull, this one wearing a top hat, with crossed human thigh bones set before it. The altar was also adorned with dozens of crosses, much like the display in Father Baltazar's church. The crosses were of wood and metal, stone and glass, plastic and paper. Behind the altar, looming over it, was a large wooden cross, its horizontal arm hung with scores of rosaries.

Sara sat in the chair before the desk while Jean circled around and stood behind the desk next to Guillaume Sam's chair. Baka watched with what Sara would swear was an almost human grin on its pointy little muzzle. The voices in her head were suddenly hushed. Guillaume Sam scared them. Sara knew that that fact should scare her as well, but somehow it made her feel just a little bit cheerier.

Sam put his pen down, leaned forward and placed his smoldering cigar in the cranial depression of the skull that sat on the corner of his desk. Sara suddenly realized that it was an ashtray.

"I don't believe in wasting time, Ms. Pezzini," Sam said, regarding her closely, as both Jean and Baka looked on. "I am a businessman. Time is money to me. I prefer to keep things as simple as possible. So tell me, what do you want?"

"Want?" Sara asked, surprised.

"Yes, Ms. Pezzini. It is a simple question. What do you want? What do you desire? What do you dream about at night when you lie in bed and dream true dreams? Money? Power? Fame? I can give all of that to you. All you want, and the best you've ever had."

"No one's ever tried to bribe me quite like this," Sara said, impressed despite herself.

Guillaume Sam shrugged. "We're all adults here, and as I've said, I don't like to waste time. I'm not subtle. I'm direct."

"Me, too," Sara said, "so I'm sure you'll take it the right way when I tell you to go to hell."

Guillaume Sam grinned, and the sight was enough to make Sara feel suddenly queasy. "I've been, Ms. Pezzini. Oh, I've been there and back again."

He leaned forward and took the still smoldering cigar out of his skull ashtray. He puffed on it until the tip glowed red, then with the barest glance at Jean he stubbed it out against her chest, on the bare skin between her small breasts.

She arched her back, but did not pull away. A small cry slipped between her clenched teeth. Sara couldn't tell if it was a cry of pleasure or pain.

"Jesus!" Sara said, starting up from her chair.

Guillaume Sam continued to look at her with no expression on his face as the stench of burnt flesh soured the aromatic fragrance of his cigar smoke. He took the cigar away from Jean's chest and put it back in the skull ashtray. Jean panted rapidly, but smiled, glancing down at the circular burn mark that marred her ivory flesh.

"You've just seen what I've done to a loyal associate whose work is indispensable to me. Imagine what I'd do to someone who angers me."

"I'd arrest you this minute if I had a charge that would stick," Sara said between clenched teeth.

"But you don't," Guillaume Sam pointed out. "And you won't. Ever."

They looked at one another for a moment, and Sam nodded.

"There's something about you that is unnatural," he finally said. "In that respect we are similar. You may make a fine foe. In the end, though, you will die. I'll have wasted time. You'll have wasted your life, and, perhaps, the lives of those around you."

"First a bribe," Sara said. "Now a threat. Neither's gonna work."

"We shall see, Ms. Pezzini. I'll give you tonight to think it over."

"I don't need any more time. I've already given you my final answer."

"As you will, Ms. Pezzini."

Sara marched out of the room, pausing in the doorway, sickened to see Jean touching the burned spot on her chest, her face screwed up in exquisite agony, while Guillaume Sam gazed at her expressionlessly.

Only Baka watched Sara leave the room, and she could swear that she saw a predatory hunger in the creature's beady eyes.

The voices in her head sounded impressed as they twittered about what they had just witnessed.

CHAPTER NINE

That night, Sara walked again in Guinee.

The air was warm but not hot, humid but not soggy. The sweet-smelling nectar of night-blooming flowers perfumed the refreshing breeze. There were no buzzing, annoying insects, only large, slow-fluttering moths that beat the heavy air with their great painted wings. It would have seemed an idyllic place if Sara didn't know what lurked in its shadows.

The night was lit by a glorious full moon and more stars than Sara knew existed, stars that were mostly drowned out by the hazy city lights of her time and place. The light was softer, revealing more than illuminating, giving everything it touched an almost out-of-focus aura that contrasted strangely with the harsh reality of the waking world.

No one came to greet her as she wandered through the quiet land, neither beast nor *loa*. The fear she felt upon arriving gradually dissipated, turning completely to wonder when she came upon a dirt road, which was the first sign she'd discovered of man's hand upon this land.

She hesitated, then decided to try the road. Presumably, it led to or from somewhere, and taking it seemed preferable to walking randomly through a jungle, no matter how beautiful the jungle was. Also Sara's practical part realized it would be hard for anyone, beast or *loa*, to ambush her on an open road. The shadowy jungle, on the other hand, presented limitless opportunities for an attack.

She walked for a while. She had no idea for how long. The road's surface was soft earth, easy on her bare feet. It was relaxing. It seemed almost as if she were again in Father Baltazar's church. As before, the voices were gone from her head. The universe seemed to consist of only her, the darkness, and the road. She felt free and unencumbered for the first time since taking on the Witchblade.

A crossroads came into view. An old man was standing in one of the corners where the roads met, almost as if he were waiting for her.

He looked harmless, but then at first almost everything seemed harmless in this place. Still, Sara figured there was nothing to be gained by avoiding him, besides the fact that she'd feel pretty foolish if she just turned around and started walking the way she'd already come.

She kept going toward the crossroads. The old man stood waiting patiently. As she approached Sara realized that he was a *really* old man, with white hair, a seamed face, and thin body and limbs. His clothing was ragged and he leaned heavily on a crutch as he watched Sara approach. The benign expression on his ancient face was marred by the fact that the whites of his eyes were red as fresh spilled blood. The color of the irises floating in the scarlet pools was only a shade somewhat less subdued.

"Hello, missy," he said as she approached.

An odd sense of formality made Sara drop a brief curtsey, something she hadn't done since she was a small child. Somehow, here and now it seemed appropriate, and it did seem to please the old man.

"Hello, father," she said, still feeling as formal as a deb on her coming-out night, "can you tell me where I'm headed?"

The old man smiled even wider, revealing strong white teeth, unusual for a peasant of his apparent age.

"It seems you recognize Papa, even if you do not know my name. You are a courteous child, and your courtesy should be repaid."

"Thank you," Sara said, feeling obscurely pleased.

"I am Papa Legba," the old man said. "I guard the crossroad. I let people in. I let people out. Sometimes I help them." He grinned wickedly. "Sometimes, as the mood takes me, I hinder. But since tonight you are so beautiful and also so courteous to an old man, and also since someone has begged me to look out for you, I will give you three boons. I believe that is the customary number."

Sara knew now that she was dreaming. She wondered if momentarily Prince Charming would show up with a pair of expensive Nikes to shod her naked feet, and then they would dance until midnight when she'd be forced to run away, ultimately waking up alone and Nike-less in her little apartment back in Manhattan.

"Further," Papa Legba went on, "I will invoke one of those boons immediately, because I perceive that without my immediate help you'll wander into disaster."

Sara nodded. She felt she could trust the old man. There was no rational basis for this feeling, but it was rock solid and unshakable.

"Don't go further on this road tonight," the old man

said. "Further lies the cemetery and you're not yet ready to confront what lies there. You have no idea of your enemy's strength, and in entering Guinee you've left a portion of your own strength behind. Learn more before you enter the cemetery. I am tempted to say more, but cannot."

"Thank you for what you have said."

The old man smiled. "It's little enough. I wish I could do more, but I am bound by laws just as you are. Though we both ignore them, sometimes, when we want, eh, missy?"

Sara laughed in agreement.

"Remember," Papa Legba said, "you can call upon me two more times. I cannot stop the world from spinning in its tracks, nor bring love to a frozen heart, but, eh, I have my abilities. I can help you when you need it, either in Guinee or in your world. Twice you can call, and I will answer."

Sara nodded. "What can I do to repay you for your kindness?"

Papa Legba looked thoughtful. "Some rum might be nice, when you get the chance. Oh, and double-cheeseburgers. I like those."

"I'll remember," Sara said.

"Now," the old man said, "you'd better get home. A friend needs your help."

Sara frowned. "Who?"

But the old man didn't answer her. He made a loud, horrible ringing noise, and for an instant Sara's mind went dark. She could see nothing, only hear that incessant ringing. When she finally thought of it, she opened her eyes and realized that she was in her apartment, lying on her bed, and it was her phone making that awful noise.

She grabbed it. "Hello?"

"Detective? This is Lieutenant Dickey."

It took her a moment to chase the remnants of her strange dream from her head, but finally she remembered the detective who'd been on the crime scene when they'd discovered Pierre-Pierre's body.

"Yes, what is it, Lieutenant?"

He sighed heavily. "We've found another body. I've been trying to get ahold of Detective McCarthy, but he's not answering his phone."

"That's strange," Sara said. "He's usually pretty conscientious about staying in touch."

"Well, not this time," Dickey said, and something cold and unsettling flashed through Sara's mind.

"The body," she asked, "male or female?"

"Female," he replied. The sudden wave of relief almost made Sara feel guilty. Jake was alive, then. But that meant, of course, somebody else wasn't. "Headless, of course. Young. Probably pretty . . . thanks," he said, off phone. "Somebody just handed me her purse. Either the murderer is getting careless, or he doesn't care if we ID his latest victims immediately. Hold on . . . let me look . . . Yeah, she was pretty, even in her driver's license photo. Her name was Juliette LeMaye . . . Detective?" he asked, after there was a long silence.

"I'm here," Sara said. "I'll be right there."

Dawn arrived, and so did Sara at the murder scene. Three hours' sleep punctuated by strange dreams wasn't near enough, but she had no choice. Even if Lieutenant Dickey had told her to go back to bed, she couldn't have. The first thing she'd done, even before dressing, was try Jake's cell phone number herself. It rang and rang, but he didn't answer. That wasn't normal. Jake never went anywhere without his cell phone. Sometimes she thought he took it into the shower with him so he wouldn't be out of contact even for a few minutes. He was that dedicated.

Given the not-so-veiled threats that Guillaume Sam had made the night before—given the fact that Jake's companion for the evening had been horribly, brutally murdered, it seemed as if Jake himself was in big trouble. Guillaume Sam must have him. Guillaume Sam must be holding him hostage for her good behavior.

Sara had no proof of that, of course. *But screw proof,* she thought. If she knew where Jake was, she'd just go get him. *Screw the law, and screw Guillaume Sam, too.* But she had no more idea where Jake was than she knew where Jimmie Hoffa was buried. Sam *might* be hiding him somewhere in Club Carrefour, but if she went busting in there with guns blazing they'd probably just kill him. There were certainly at least half a dozen places where they could secret Jake's body where no one would ever find it.

Papa Legba! she suddenly thought.

But could she gamble Jake's life on a dream, no matter how real it seemed? It was a risk she might have to take, but first there might be some clues to his current whereabouts at the crime scene, which, as it turned out, was somewhat familiar.

Police crime scene tape sealed off the entrance to the Cypress Hills National Cemetery. Sara recognized the uniforms guarding the tape. They'd been doing the same job at the last Machete Murderer killing.

"Detective Pezzini," one said with mock courtesy. "So nice to see you again."

Sara just looked at him until he lifted the tape for her

to pass under. As she went into the cemetery grounds she heard him say to his partner, "Just who the hell does she think she is?" but she walked on, her anger growing with her fear for Jake's safety.

The body was waiting, covered by a sheet, on a go-to-Jesus cart. The Crime Scene Unit was swarming like locusts, taking photos and measurements and scouring the area seemingly grass blade by grass blade.

Sara stopped by the dolly waiting to be loaded into the ambulance. She didn't really want to check the corpse, but knew she had to. There was always the possibility of wild coincidence. Perhaps this wasn't the girl Jake had been with last night.

But even that forlorn hope was mercilessly dashed by unpleasant reality as Sara lifted the sheet and gazed at the decapitated body. Even though the corpse was missing a head, there was no doubt that it was Juliette from the lotions and potions store. She was wearing the same clothes that Sara had seen on her the night before, and her body was rather unmistakable, even without a head.

Once vibrant and full of life she seemed sadly diminished as she lay on the dolly. The spark that had animated her was gone, blown out, and now she was just so much cold meat without beauty, with hope, without promise.

Sara turned away and saw Lieutenant Dickey watching her with a hangdog expression in his sad eyes. He, too, was much the same as the last time she'd seen him. He was even wearing the same suit, or one remarkably similar, that looked like it belonged to his bigger brother. His expression was the same. Sara wondered if he were habitually lugubrious, or if that was just a mask he wore to conceal his real feelings.

Sara looked around their surroundings, struck by a sudden thought.

"Who found the body here?" she asked, here being the proverbial middle of nowhere.

Lieutenant Dickey approached, gesturing at the emergency med techs to put the body in the ambulance and take it away. He sighed profoundly. "A passerby heard gunshots coming from the cemetery—" he checked his small pocket notebook "—at 3:37 and phoned nine-one-one. Didn't leave a name. It took a while, but the first uniform on the scene found the vic."

"No gunshot wounds on her that I saw. Was it her gun?" Sara asked, knowing already that it wasn't.

Dickey shook his head. "No, and probably no. From footprints in the area it looks like she had a companion. Male. He may have fired the shots. CSU is looking for slugs, but . . ."

Dickey gestured. Sara knew what he meant. The cemetery was wide open. There were no convenient walls to stop a bullet soon after it'd been fired. If they'd missed their intended target they might have hit a nearby tree, they might have plowed into the ground. Or they might have traveled hundreds of yards in any direction. It was an almost impossible trail to follow, but if anyone could do it, CSU could. In the meantime, Sara had something more important to consider.

"This companion," Sara said with a slight catch to her words. "Any trace of him. Or his body?"

"Not yet," Dickey said. "But we've got men out looking." He gazed around the cemetery grounds, not looking very happy. "It's like a damn primeval forest out there. It'll take days to search it properly."

"Yet the killer didn't bother to hide the body," Sara said hopefully.

"This killer," Dickey said with some deliberation, "is nuts. Who knows what's motivating him?"

I do, Sara told herself. *And it's all my fault.*

But she couldn't tell Dickey that Guillaume Sam had had Jake snatched so she'd back off the investigation. He'd think she was as nuts as the Machete Murderer himself. Maybe he'd be right, too. It was only a theory, but it fit the facts as she knew them, it fit the warning Guillaume Sam had given her the night before. It was somewhere to start, but how in the world could she follow up on it with Dickey on her tail?

"We got a place of residence and a place of employment from the vic's ID," Dickey said. "Where do you want to start?"

For once Sara agreed with the voices as they told her to watch out, to move carefully as far as Dickey was concerned. They didn't want other people to know of them and the Witchblade. She didn't want Dickey to know that Jake had been with the girl last night. She couldn't say why with any degree of certainty, except she was coming around to the feeling that the less people who knew the details of this case, the better.

"Let's see the address," she said, and Dickey handed over his notebook. Sara nodded. "Maybe we'd better split up. If her companion's not lying dead somewhere in the cemetery—" *Please, God, no,* Sara thought to herself "—maybe he's been taken hostage, for whatever weird reason. Time may be of the essence."

Dickey nodded agreeably.

"I remember this shop from my last trip to Fulton

Street," Sara said. "I'll check that out. You can go to her home address."

"I don't like to deal with grieving families," Dickey said.

"It's part of the job," Sara replied, trying to sound sympathetic.

"Never said it wasn't," Dickey said, taking his notebook back from Sara and returning it to his jacket pocket.

Fulton Street was just waking up. Coffeeshops and lunch counters were opening for breakfast. Bakeries and some of the small food stores were opening their doors as well. Lotions and Potions was still closed, of course. The sign on the door said it opened at nine. Sara looked into Paul Narcisse's bookstore as she went past, but it, too, was dark.

She stopped at the walk-up window of a hole-in-the-wall coffeeshop and ordered a large black coffee and, not to be stereotypical, a danish. She wasn't hungry at all, but she knew she had to eat something. She needed the calories and caffeine for energy. A long day stretched ahead of her and she felt as if she were already running on empty.

She ate and drank as she walked. The coffee was hot and strong and fragrant. Any other day she would have enjoyed it immensely. Now it just burned a hole in her gut that the danish did little to fill. She had to, she thought, take better care of herself.

The voices agreed sternly, but fell silent again as she reached her destination.

People were walking down the path that led to St. Casimir's, alone and in groups of two or three. The first of the daily masses had ended. Father Baltazar, she thought, was on the job as early as she was.

She went into the church where the priest was talking to a little old man who seemed as ancient as the Papa Legba of her dream. The language they used seemed to consist of mostly consonants, and the conversation ended with the old man hobbling out into the autumn morning on his two wooden canes.

"He reminds me of someone I met last night," Sara said, "I think."

"You think he reminds you of somebody, or you think you met somebody?" Father Baltazar asked with a smile.

"Depends if you count dreams," Sara said, and told him what had happened, and how it had ended with the phonecall waking her up. She completed her story with the discovery of the body in the cemetery and her theory of what had happened to Jake.

The priest justified her trust. She could see that he believed her, immediately and implicitly. "You're probably right about Guillaume Sam kidnapping your partner. He's more than capable of such an act. As we've seen—he's done worse." He looked seriously at Sara. "There's no shame if you back out of this. Though you're brave and clearly seem to have more experience with such . . . odd . . . occurrences than most people, you're out of your depth here. Guillaume Sam is like nothing you've ever faced before."

"Yes, he is," Sara said flatly. "He's a criminal. He's a killer. Maybe not by his own hands, but certainly by his orders. It's my job to put scum like him away so he can't hurt anyone any more. Besides." She frowned, feeding on the anger building up in her mind. "He's made it personal."

"All right," Father Baltazar said gravely. "Just so you

understand. This isn't something you can solve with a pistol. Or even the weight of the law."

"What can we do then?" Sara asked.

"We face the devil with our courage, our knowledge, and our faith," he said quietly. "First, though, we must rescue your friend. With him under Guillaume Sam's control, our hands are tied. We dare not make a move against the *bokor.*"

"Do you have any idea where he might be keeping Jake?"

Father Baltazar shook his head. "There are several possibilities, but we have no room to guess. If we guess wrong, then Guillaume Sam will know you've completely rejected his offer, and . . ." The priest paused, as if gauging his words. "And he will kill your partner. You can depend on that."

"Then we must be certain when we strike," Sara said. She looked at Father Baltazar. "How can I get in touch with Papa Legba?"

The day seemed to go on forever. Sara tried to immerse herself in the routine of police work, but the minute hands on her wristwatch dragged like hours. It didn't much help that she was chained to Carl Dickey. He seemed like a decent man and a good cop. He was thorough in his investigation and respectful of Sara and her capabilities, but she couldn't confide in him. She couldn't trust him with her knowledge and her suspicions, so basically they spent the day spinning their wheels as they tracked down background information on Juliette LeMaye.

Dickey was curious about Jake's continuing absence, but Sara made a plausible excuse for him, saying that he was investigating the death of Agent Jackson of Immigration and Naturalization and trying to define how it related to the case.

It was night before she managed to shake him off, saying that she was going home to get some sleep. Instead she doubled back to Fulton Street and The Serpent and the Rainbow, where Paul Narcisse and Father Baltazar were waiting for her. Both looked solemn. Both were clearly deadly serious.

"This isn't a frivolous step," Paul Narcisse said. "It may have repercussions regarding your career–your entire life."

"I'm prepared for that," Sara said.

"Father Baltazar has told me that you've had . . . unusual . . . dreams of Guinee. That you also seem to have or know something you've chosen so far to keep to yourself that may have a bearing on all this–"

"Believe me," Sara said sincerely, "if it was something I felt I could share . . ." She paused as the angry murmur of the voices swept over her. "I would . . . but I can't. Now. Don't ask me to explain. I simply can't."

"You ask much of us, Detective Pezzini," Paul Narcisse said. "You ask us to reveal our secrets, yet keep yours hidden." He regarded her silently for a moment. "But very well. It seems as if that's the way it has to be. For now." He looked at Father Baltazar, and nodded. "Let's go."

They went out the bookstore's back door, locking it behind them. The priest, Sara noted, was wearing civilian clothes, not his usual clerical garb. Paul Narcisse was dressed in white, white pants, neat and sharply pressed, and a white shirt of soft linen. They went up a dark alley, traveling north from Fulton Street, up a couple of residential blocks to the area less densely settled than the streets around the business district. The houses here were single-family dwellings instead of attached townhouses. They sat on their own plots of land with taller trees, more expansive lawns, and fewer streetlights. It all looked somewhat familiar. She thought she knew where they were headed.

They walked in silence, though right at the start of their journey Paul Narcisse had looked at her and asked, "What's in the bag?" gesturing at the small white paper bag that Sara carried.

More because she felt somewhat foolish than because she felt any need to be mysterious, Sara simply said, "A present for someone."

"I see," Paul Narcisse said, leaving it at that.

Though they were approaching it from a different angle and via a different street, Sara knew that they were headed in the direction of the Cypress Hills National Cemetery. And they weren't the only ones. Single pedestrians, as well as small groups of two or three, were silently walking along with them in the darkness, all headed for a common destination.

She wanted to confirm her feeling with Paul Narcisse or Father Baltazar, but the night through which they moved was permeated by a deep silence that Sara was loathe to break. It was almost unbelievable that they were within the boundaries of New York City. Only occasionally did a city noise, the sound of a car horn, the sudden squeal of brakes, penetrate the quiet night through which they moved. It was almost as if they'd been transported to another place or time where there was no city around them, only the quiet solitude of an empty countryside.

Within minutes they arrived at the cemetery's open gate. They followed those who had arrived before them, acknowledging others with a nod or a glance, but never a murmur, never even a single word passed anyone's lips. If the others thought Sara's presence strange or unusual, they never said so, nor even indicated such a feeling with an expression or gesture. The fact that she was with Paul Narcisse and Father Baltazar seemed to confirm an instant acceptance.

They went deep into the cemetery, deeper than Sara had gone when she'd followed Gene the previous day. At one point they approached what looked like an impenetrable thicket, but to Sara's surprise once they reached the veritable wall of bushes, shrubs, small trees, and entwining vines, she discovered several paths. Reaching the beginnings of the paths involved a lot of stooping and twisting and pushing through the living barrier that protected them, but once past the initial camouflage the foliage opened up so that the going became as easy as a stroll through the park.

They came upon a sheltered hollow surrounded by a dense stand of trees. The trees were thick with scores of pigeons and doves. They cooed quietly and incessantly like a continuous, wordless chorus. Open torches blazed in the night and Sara felt as if she'd stepped back into another century. The voices murmured to her, uncertain. She didn't like that. She didn't want to be bothered by them now. But then, she never wanted to be bothered by them.

An odd structure stood in the center of the sheltered hollow, with perhaps a hundred people standing quietly around it. More were joining the crowd as Sara and her guides approached, but it seemed that they were among a final trickle of newcomers. Most of those attending the night's ceremony were already present.

Paul Narcisse turned to Sara. "I have to leave you here. I have many duties to perform this evening."

"You'll put me in touch with Papa Legba?" Sara asked. "Is that what all of this is about?" Her gestures included the sheltered hollow, the structure, and the assembled crowd.

Paul Narcisse shook his head. "I am but a vessel. It is impossible to predict who will fill me." He glanced at Father Baltazar. "My brother seems to think that you have the favor of at least some of the *loa*. Sometimes they have their own reasons for doing things, and they chose certain people as their champions. We shall just have to see how it all works out."

Paul Narcisse and Father Baltazar exchanged nods and he walked off through the crowd, exchanging murmured greetings with many as he went to the wooden structure beyond.

"What is this place?" Sara asked.

"It is the *hounfort*," Father Baltazar said quietly. "The temple, if you will, of this particular parish."

"Why here, in this graveyard?"

The priest shrugged. "Why not? It's consecrated ground, a holy place already. It's hidden. Few except the believers know of it. Others who might know a little look away and let the people worship as they will."

"Don't you have a problem with any of this?" Sara asked. "You're a priest. A Catholic priest."

"I'm a believer. I have faith in God and his creations. I have seen things here . . ." A sudden faraway look came into Father Baltazar's eyes. For a moment he looked up at the heavens, and when he looked back at Sara there was something of knowledge in his gaze.

"You of all people should know that the universe is a mysterious place. Man has only skimmed away the top-most portion of its secrets."

Sara nodded. He had her there.

"Besides," the priest continued, "over the centuries *voudon* and Catholicism have grown together in many ways. The saints are identified with *loa* and worshiped as such." He shrugged. "Who knows which guise they may prefer? The Father in Rome may say one thing, but he's in Rome and I'm here. I have seen things . . ."

"What exactly is going to happen?" Sara asked as Father Baltazar's voice faded away. He seemed to be watching the reminiscences playing in his mind.

He shrugged. "Paul will call upon the *loa* through music and dance. One can never be certain what will happen or exactly who will answer the summons. If all goes well Papa Legba will come forth first. He's the gatekeeper. He opens the way for the other *loa* to enter the world."

The *hounfort,* Sara saw, had two main parts. In the back of the structure were a series of small rooms built of stone. Father Baltazar called them the *caille mysteres,* or the sanctuary. He explained that they contained altars to various *loa,* along with supplies and equipment needed for the ceremonies that took place in the front of the *hounfort,* which was called the peristyle.

The peristyle consisted of a corrugated tin roof held up by a number of poles painted brilliant shades of red and green and orange and blue. The central pole, called the *poteau-mitan* (or, naturally enough, the center post), was the pivot around which the dances would flow. Also, according to the priest, it was the ladder by which the *loa* descended to the earth. Instead of being a single solid color like the other posts, it was decorated with tightly wound spirals of various bright, complimentary colors, so that it looked like a big, multi-flavored candy stick. A circular pediment ran around the base of the *poteau-mitan*, about four feet high and two feet thick. Sara watched people approach this ledge, put items on it, bow respectfully, and then rejoin the waiting crowd. She couldn't tell exactly what they were leaving behind. Some of the items were bottles, some were bowls, some were so swathed in wrappings they were complete mysteries.

"What's going on there?" she asked Father Baltazar.

"The initiates are leaving offerings for the *loa*," he explained. "Food, drink, perhaps small bottles of perfume, or other items associated with specific *loa*. They hope that the *loa*, if called, will find favor with them because of their gifts."

Sara nodded. "Excuse me for a moment."

She made her way through the crowd. Though she was a stranger, no one spoke to her or tried to hinder her. They watched as she approached the concrete altar around the base of the pillar, and placed the small paper bag she carried among the plates of chicken, bowls of rice and egg, and small bottles of soda or spirits, then rejoined Father Baltazar.

"What was that?" he asked.

"My own little sacrifice," Sara said with a smile. She nudged the priest and pointed. "What's happening now?"

"Ah," Father Baltazar said, "Paul is 'drawing' the *veve* for tonight's ceremony with flour."

He had come out of one of the *caille mysteres*, accompanied by three other men. Taking handfuls of white flour from the burlap sacks they carried, they carefully sifted it onto the dirt floor around the *poteau-mitan*, drawing, as Father Baltazar put it, a complicated pattern.

"Pretend that I know nothing about *voudon*," Sara suggested, "and tell me what's going on."

"All right," he said. "I don't want to come off like a stuffy university lecturer, but if you're interested–"

"I'm interested," Sara said. "I've got to understand this stuff if we're going to find Jake and stop the killer."

And, she added to herself silently, *to see if any of this could help with me own predicament*. At that, the voices roiled quietly, almost amusedly. They had been rather quiet so far, as if they too were observing everything around them. Perhaps they were learning about voudon themselves, and were leery of its power and uncertain of its efficacy.

"Each *loa*," the priest explained, "has its own symbol, called a *veve*. It's like a . . . wave pattern that draws a symbolic picture of the *loa*'s characteristics. For example, that of Erzulie Freda Dahomey, the goddess of love, dreams, and romance is basically, a checkered heart surrounded by lace. However, that of her sister, Erzulie je Rouge, her left-handed incarnation, is that of a heart with a dagger plunged through it. Red Erzulie's love is jealous and angry. Those possessed by her throw tantrums. The muscles of their bodies tighten in uncontrollable spasms, their fists clench in rage."

"Who would call upon such a creature?" Sara asked.

"Those who want to do harm. *Bokors*. But," Father Baltazar added, "sometimes she comes when her sister is called. *Voudon* is not a science. And it is more than an art."

Finally, Paul Narcisse and his helpers seemed satisfied with the design they'd created around the *poteau-mitan*. After a brief, quiet consultation, they retreated back into the rooms at the rear of the *hounfort*.

It looked as if the peristyle was a later addition grafted

onto the *caille mysteres*, which were older structures, built in mossy stone. They were attached like townhouses, arranged in a shallow, semi-circular arc. Sara suddenly realized that they were above-ground crypts, probably once used by a large family or group of related families when the Cypress Hills National Cemetery was still an active concern.

There was a sudden murmur in the crowd as a man emerged from the sanctuary carrying a large drum. He looked familiar. Sara realized that he was the drummer of Mountains of Madness. She also realized that she didn't know his name.

Two other men accompanied him, carrying, respectively, a medium-sized and a small drum. They took up a place together behind the *poteau-mitan*.

The drummer from Mountains of Madness skimmed the surface of his drumhead and a low rumbling came forth.

"It begins," Father Baltazar said quietly.

As the assembled crowd turned their attention to the dancing ground, Paul Narcisse came again out of the *caille mysteres*, his arms spread wide, his expression intent and serious. Following him, a woman dressed in white led a line of a dozen or so dancers out of the sanctuary and they stalked counter-clockwise around the *poteau-mitan*. The men wore white shirts, the women white dresses and colorful kerchiefs tied about their heads.

Paul Narcisse started to speak in a language Sara had never heard before. Somehow, maybe from knowledge leaking from the voices in her head, she knew it was an old language from an antique land. She couldn't understand the words, but from the intonation of Narcisse's voice she could tell that it was a plea, an invocation of strong and strange powers. It was, Father Baltazar whispered to her, *langage*, the mystic tongue *hougans* used to communicate with the *loa* in Guinee.

It seemed as if everything in the world was waiting, silent, expectant. The crowd was quiet, without a whispered murmur or shuffle of feet. The three drummers stood alert by their drums, watching Paul Narcisse who, face shining with sweat, arms thrown wide with gourd rattles in each hand, still prayed in *langage*. His eyes were closed, his teeth clenched. Those who had accompanied him from the *caille mysteres* were also watching him, silent and expectant.

When he finished his impassioned plea the sudden utter silence exploded like a thunderclap on Sara's brain. Even the voices in her head went totally silent. Tension built to an almost sexual peak. Sara could see the dancers' muscles start to twitch.

And then the drums began.

The small one first. It was no more than eighteen inches tall, and the only one played with sticks instead of the drummer's hands. It sounded like a staccato barrage of hail hitting a tin roof.

The medium drum added a steady, rolling surf surging against a dark beach.

Then came the largest drum, played by the drummer from Mountains of Madness, and from it erupted the booming heartbeat of the world.

They each had their own pitch. They each had their own rhythm but they blended together like the braids of a rope. Sara had never heard anything like it before.

Led by the woman in white, the dancers began to weave around the *poteau-mitan*, ignoring the delicately-drawn *veve* at their feet, mixing it with sand as they shuffled through it. They danced singly, not in pairs, almost flat-footed, their shoulders shuddering and arms flapping clumsily.

Sara wasn't sure how long the dancing went on, but suddenly the man on the big drum threw his head back and she saw that his eyes were wild. Before he had played passionately but he'd been in control. Now he played like a man possessed. The big drum broke away from the others, smashing the rhythms that had meshed them together. Its beat hurled a broken counterpoint that struck the dancers like a volley of spears.

Suddenly something seemed to strike Sara in the head, exploding like white darkness in her brain. She grabbed her temples, swaying. Father Baltazar, noticing her distress, caught her. She sagged into his surprisingly strong arms.

"What is it?" he asked, concern on his face.

"The drum," she gasped. "Every beat feels like a nail driven into my brain, down my spine, across every nerve ending . . ."

"We can't stop the ceremony now," Father Baltazar said. "It would be dangerous to all involved!"

Sara grit her teeth. "I can take it."

She was panting like an animal, trying to control her pain.

"Hold on," Father Baltazar said, gripping her closely as if he could confer his strength to her shaking body.

Sara tried to focus on the dancers. Like the drummer, they too, seemed to have lost control, and were wildly shaking and gyrating, no longer in concert, but as if in some chaotic mosh pit where everyone was dancing to a different song.

She blinked rapidly. Paul Narcisse was gone. He'd disappeared from the dancing ground.

The pain in her head mounted, and with it the babbling of the voices. They were almost incoherent as if they too were in pain. Sara felt her grip loosening. Under her garments a metal band popped into existence and she gritted her teeth trying to hold it back. She couldn't allow the Witchblade to materialize in front of all these people. For one thing, its razor-sharp edges would tear Father Baltazar to pieces. She concentrated fiercely, holding it at bay, but she knew she couldn't keep it away for long.

And then Paul Narcisse emerged again from the *caille mysteres*. He must have ducked back into the sanctuary soon after the drummer had gone into his mad beat. It was Paul Narcisse returning to the dance floor, certainly. Yet, as Sara gazed at him, she couldn't be sure.

He had shrunken, somehow. Become smaller and twisted. He walked now with a pronounced limp. He probably couldn't have walked at all if it wasn't for the crutch that he leaned against heavily.

He shuffled slowly like an old man, and, even from where she stood Sara could see that his eyes had changed. They weren't the eyes of Paul Narcisse at all. They were ancient eyes, old with knowledge and experience well beyond a human lifetime. Their whites were shockingly bloodshot.

He went to the concrete altar built around the *poteau-mitan*, walking through the gyrating dancers as if they weren't there. He went straight to the bag that Sara had placed there, took out a double cheeseburger, unwrapped it, and began to eat. He looked directly at Sara, and the pain in her head went away. She hung in

Father Baltazar's arms, more from her desire for warm human contact than from weakness.

"That was good," Papa Legba said, as he slowly came towards Sara with his hobbling gait. "Next time bring a large fries, too."

He stopped before Sara and the priest. The rest of the crowd continued to watch the ongoing ceremony, giving them a bubble of privacy in the controlled chaos that had gripped the old graveyard.

There was no question in Sara's mind that this was Papa Legba, that he'd descended from Guinee and taken over Paul Narcisse's body. The movements, body language, facial expression, even vocal inflections were those of the ancient *loa*. Wherever Paul Narcisse was, he no longer inhabited his own body.

"I need your help, Papa Legba," Sara said.

The spirit inhabiting the body of Paul Narcisse nodded. "You may ask for it, twice more. I'm afraid that is all I may help you, for many are in need of my aid."

"That should be enough," Sara said. "My partner, Jake McCarthy, is missing. We think Guillaume Sam has taken him as a hostage."

"Ah, the great *malfacteur*. He is a dangerous one, with a powerful patron."

"Who, Papa Legba?"

"Baron Samedi, master of the Guede Family, god of death and patron of sorcerers. A most puissant *loa*."

Sara was afraid that Legba would confirm what she had been told. It looked as if rescuing Jake would fall somewhere between the impossible and the miraculous, and she figured that she couldn't do it alone. She would have to call upon the Witchblade.

With that thought, the voices inside her, strangely quiet and respectful in the presence of Papa Legba, quivered with barely suppressed delight.

"How can I find Jake?" she asked with determination.

"I will send you a guide," Papa Legba promised. "His name is Sandro. Meet him at the Club Carrefour. He will show you a place you never thought existed in this city."

Sara looked around herself. "I've already been to such a place tonight."

Papa Legba laughed. "No, you haven't, child." He gestured freely with the hand that did not grip his crutch. "This must all seem very strange to a most modern *blanc* as yourself, but, believe me, much more good than harm ever comes from this *hounfort*. Why, you yourself have sought–and received–help here." He shook his head. "No, Sandro will take you to a place is not like this at all. He will take you to the heart of darkness in the city, where play the *loup-garou* and *zobop*. You must go there if you're to save your partner, but–" and here the old spirit looked concerned "–I despair of your ever coming out."

"She will not go alone," Father Baltazar said, speaking for the first time. "I will accompany her."

The *loa* nodded. "That is good. You are a man of the spirits. A strong man. She will need your aid."

Sara shook her head. "I can't have you coming with me. The danger–"

"That's why," Father Baltazar said with quiet firmness, "I'm going with you."

"Let him come," Papa Legba told her. "You'll need his help." He turned to the priest. "And Father–"

"Yes?"

"You will be better off bringing a gun then a cross. Just so you know."

The priest nodded solemnly. Papa Legba turned back toward the *poteau-mitan,* where the drumming and dancing had continued unabated.

"Now I must return to the ceremony," Papa Legba said. "The night is young. There is much dancing ahead and many *loa* will be called to possess a mount and walk again on this earth."

He hobbled back toward the *poteau-mitan.* They watched him for a moment, then Sara turned to Father Baltazar.

"What kind of dream have I fallen into?" she asked.

"For these people," he said, indicating the dancers and the raptly watching crowd, "it is simply life. For others—for you, for Jake, for those fallen to the Machete Murderer—it is a nightmare."

He took her arm and together they walked swiftly from the forgotten graveyard.

CHAPTER TEN

"How are we going to find this Sandro?" Sara asked. She paused, thinking. "And how will we know him when we see him?"

"Good questions," Father Baltazar said. "Let's just hope he—or she—is better informed than we are."

There were again in the city, a world of cars and noise and electricity, only a few miles removed from the primeval sanctuary where the *hounfort* lay unsuspected, where the drums called down the *loa* to meet their worshipers on quite a personal level.

A crowd had already gathered around Club Carrefour. Many stood outside, smoking and talking, and getting a breath of fresh air. The autumn warmth still lingered, but something else was also in the air, a sense of expectancy. Of hesitancy. Sara could feel it, but she couldn't quite understand it. It was as if the city were waiting for something. There was a sense of change in the air, and Sara felt sure that it was connected to Guillaume Sam and the Machete Murderer and spirits coming down the sky to dance in old, forgotten graveyards.

A familiar figure came out of the club, noticed them standing outside, and headed in their direction. It was Alek Gervalis. He had a worried look on his face.

"Hello, Sara. Father," he said.

"What's the matter?" Sara asked.

"Oh, probably nothing," Alek said. He shrugged, and Sara could see that there was an element of annoyance as well as worry on his face. "It's the boys."

"Rog and Jer?" Father Baltazar asked.

"Who else?" This time the exasperation showed clearly in his voice. "We're trying to work out some new songs before we leave next week for the road, and they've gone off somewhere. You haven't seen them around, have you?"

"Not since last night," Sara said.

Alek sighed. "That's the last time I saw them myself. They were with that chick Jean." He shook his head. "I never cared much for her. She's strange. Beyond strange, actually. Her and her brother."

Sara, remembering the stench of burned human flesh, nodded in agreement.

"This isn't the first time they've gone off, is it?" Father Baltazar asked.

"No," Alek said. "And probably not the last. It's damned annoying, though." He stopped for a moment, frowning slightly. "What are you guys doing here, anyway?" he asked. "If I'm not prying into police department secrets, that is."

Sara and Father Baltazar exchanged glances.

No, Sara said to herself, *you see, we just came from a voudon ceremony where Papa Legba promised us a spirit guide to lead us to the lair of an evil sorcerer who's kidnaped my partner.*

"Um," Sara said, looking at Father Baltazar.

"Um," Father Baltazar replied, looking at Sara.

Alek, who was facing the opposite direction, suddenly started. "Jesus Christ, did you see that?"

They both turned quickly, but the dark alley down which he pointed was quiet and empty.

"No," they said together.

"What was it?" Father Baltazar asked.

"I'm not sure," Alek said slowly. "I just caught a glimpse of it. It was moving fast. Some kind of big animal, I think. It went right down that alley beside the club."

"Well," Sara said, "maybe I'd better check it out. Uh, good luck finding the boys."

Alek made a sudden grimace of annoyance. "Ah, screw the boys. I want to see what that thing is."

Sara and Father Baltazar exchanged glances.

"No, my son," the priest said. "Don't worry about it–"

"I'm not worried," Alek said. "I'm curious."

"You know what they said about curiosity," Sara muttered.

"I'm not a cat," Alek said. "There's something there. Let's find out what it is."

He stalked off toward the alley. Sara opened her mouth, but Father Baltazar laid a hand on her arm.

"He saw it, not us. Maybe he's meant to accompany us. I've often thought there was something about him, an aura of power–or at least the possibility of power."

"I can't let him go into danger unknowingly–"

"What danger?" the priest asked. "What can happen here in the open? Besides, it's probably nothing."

Alek, already at the mouth of the alley, turned towards the others. "Are you coming or not?"

"We're coming," Father Baltazar called out.

They caught up to him, Sara muttering to herself, "Yeah, what could happen?"

The voices, though, seemed to approve of Alek's presence—though whether that was good or bad for Alek, Sara didn't know. But she decided that it would be foolish to fight the voices and the priest both when they finally seemed to agree on something.

The alley ran between the Club Carrefour and an adjacent three-story building. It was longer than Sara would have expected and narrower than she liked. There were no streetlights, no lights at all. It was choked with Dumpsters and old garbage sitting piled up around Dumpsters. The Dumpsters on the Club Carrefour side were overflowing with empty liquor bottles and the combined fumes wafting from the discarded bottles—beer, wine, and every kind of spirit known to partiers at the dawn of the twenty-first century—was enough to turn Sara's stomach. The narrow confines of the alley seemed to trap the odors so that a swamp-like miasma clung to the vicinity.

"Phew," Alek contributed. "This place stinks."

"Thank you, Dr. Watson," Sara said. "What did this thing look like, anyway?"

"I told you," Alek said, "I didn't get much of a look. But it was some kind of animal. Furry. White. Maybe a weird dog of some kind. It was too big to be a cat."

"Was it?" Father Baltazar said in an odd-sounding voice.

"Yeah—" Alek turned to where the priest was looking. "Holy . . ."

It was, after all, a cat, but a cat unlike any Sara had ever seen before.

He was standing by a side door to the club, staring at the three of them with eyes the color of blood. He was white, gleaming white, as if a spotlight was shining on him. His fur was thick and fluffy, his tail was a high plume that he carried arching over his back, his breast was covered by a bushy mane like that of a lion. He was three times the size of an ordinary domestic cat, probably forty pounds of long, lean, and lithely muscular feline.

"I wasn't expecting something like this," Sara said in a soft voice, "but that must be him."

"Him?" Alek asked. "Who?"

She looked at the singer.

"This is something you don't want to be mixed up in," she told him.

"Police business?"

Sara hesitated.

"Yes," she finally said.

"You're looking for a big white cat on police business?"

"Look–"

"Does this involve the boys in any way?"

Sara looked at Father Baltazar. He shrugged, as if telling her that it was her call.

"Possibly," she said, unable to lie to him. "But this could be dangerous."

"Not could be," the priest corrected quietly. "Will be."

Alek looked from Sara to the priest.

"Count me in," he said.

This is not going, Sara thought, *exactly by the book.* But then things she was involved in rarely did.

"All right," she said. "But you do what I tell you. You obey my orders, or I'll send you packing."

"Yes, ma'am," Alek said with an amused grin.

"I mean it."

The tone of Sara's voice wiped the smile from his face.

"I know you do."

"You better."

Alek nodded. Sara took a deep breath. "All right. Let's . . . go see the cat."

"Just who *is* the cat?" Alek asked Father Baltazar in a low voice.

"Possibly a spirit guide sent by Papa Legba. If it is him, his name is Sandro."

"Oh," Alec said.

The cat was sitting, waiting patiently, his great plume of a tail curled around his feet. As the three approached he stood and stretched languidly. He arched his back in greeting and rubbed against Sara's legs, his head nearly reaching her thighs. She hunkered down. He reared up and put his front paws on her knees so that they were almost eye to eye.

"Are you Sandro? Did Papa Legba send you?" she asked, feeling more than a little foolish.

The cat didn't speak or make any other kind of overt response, but there seemed to be understanding in his red eyes.

"We're looking for Jake McCarthy," she continued, only somewhat reassured by the cat's continuing attention. "Can you lead us to him?"

He stalked off, stopped in front of the side door to Club Carrefour, and waited there patiently while the three exchanged glances.

"It seems he wants us to go in," Father Baltazar said.

"Maybe he can give us a sign," Alek suggested. "Like meowing twice, or something."

Sara thought she could detect a sign of growing impatience on Sandro's feline features.

"I think we should just go on in," Sara said.

She pulled open the door, which squeaked alarmingly, exposing a portal into blackness. Sandro slipped past them into the dark, pausing only long enough to toss a backward glance in their direction as he disappeared into the building.

Sara took a deep breath and drew her weapon.

"All right," she said in a low voice. "I'll go in first, then Alek. Father Baltazar, you bring up the rear. And move *quietly.*"

They were in a short corridor. Sara could barely make out Sandro at the other end of the passage, waiting before another closed door. The hallway was unfurnished, and just this side of filthy. Evidently, it was a short service corridor used to ferry garbage to the alley Dumpsters, more than a little of which had ended up on the floor rather than in the alley. Sara figured they'd better move quickly before they met with a busboy carrying another carton of empties.

The door blocking the corridor turned out to be an unlatched swinging door. Sandro waited for them to get closer, then he reared up on his hind legs, put his large paws against the door, and swung it open himself. Thankfully, it opened a lot more quietly than the outer door. As they moved closer to the interior of the club they could hear music throbbing. They could feel the muted vibrations of numerous pairs of feet on the dance floor.

Sandro waited only a moment, as if confirming that they were following, then took off like a flash down the next stretch of corridor, turning left down the first branching hallway.

"I hope he knows where he's going," Alek said in a low voice.

"Shhh," Sara and Father Baltazar admonished simultaneously.

They followed the cat down a set of rickety wooden stairs, moving slowly because they were going into deeper darkness. Sara almost stumbled at the head of the stairs, and Father Baltazar hissed to get her attention.

"Here," he said, passing down a pen flashlight.

"Thanks–" Sara began, and cautiously started downwards, the light focused on Sandro's plumed tail as he pranced along ahead of them.

They got halfway down the stairway when a sudden sound made them all freeze. Sara clicked off the light and they stood on the stairs, holding their breath, looking back behind them toward the source of the noise.

Behind and now above them, in the corridor they'd just quit, someone came through from the club, whistling off-tune and dragging a full garbage bag. They could just barely discern him in the corridor. They waited until he passed, until they heard the sound of the outer door screeching open, a signal he'd reached the alley. Then Sara flicked on the light and they went down the stairs as quickly and quietly as they could, only to find themselves in a dark storeroom.

Sandro was waiting for them patiently at the foot of the stairs before a stack of crates of Importer Vodka.

"We don't dare turn on the light," Sara said after the penflash had swept over a bare bulb hanging down from a wire in the ceiling. "This'll have to do."

Alek looked around.

"They couldn't have stashed Jake here," he observed. "There's no door. He could just walk away."

He was looking at Sara, and it seemed that the same thought hit both of them at the same moment.

Unless, Sara told herself, *they were stashing a body.*

"Uh–" Alek said. "He could be tied and gagged, though."

"Yeah," Sara said in a low voice. Bleakness shot through her at the thought.

"I don't think it's as simple as that," Father Baltazar said. "Papa Legba wouldn't go through the trouble of sending us a spirit guide to lead us down a corridor and a flight of stairs."

The three looked at Sandro. He seemed to be nodding in agreement. He went down an aisle formed by two rows of stacked liquor cartons and stopped about halfway to the far wall. He stood there for a moment, then began scratching at the floor at his feet, barely visible in the light cast by the small penflash.

"There's something there," Sara said.

They followed the tiny spotlight. Sandro looked up at them expectantly, then down to a spot on the floor covered by a rubber carpet runner. Alek kneeled down and flipped the runner aside to expose a wooden trapdoor set into the floor, held in place by a padlocked shaft shot through an eyebolt.

"What have we here?" he asked rhetorically.

The three hunkered down around the trapdoor, glancing at each other.

Sara rattled the padlock. "I don't know about you guys, but my breaking and entering skills are a little weak."

"I'm a musician," Alek said, "not a burglar."

Father Baltazar shook his head, but then glanced at Sandro. "Papa Legba is the opener of the way. The guardian of the door."

Sandro, who was sitting on his haunches in his familiar position with his tail wrapped around his feet, seemed to grin a feline grin. He stood, reached out, and tapped the lock gently with a paw. It sprung open like he'd used a lockpick on it.

The three looked at each other.

"Thank you," Father Baltazar said.

Sandro seemed to nod.

"Carefully and quietly," Sara said, as he reached out to shoot the bolt and open the trapdoor.

The door was well oiled and opened without a squeak. Alek carefully set it down on the floor without making a sound and the three–the four, counting Sandro–kneeled around the opening, looking down at a ladder leading into blackness.

A soft breeze wafted up from the unknown below. It was cool and rather moist, smelling of damp and naked earth. Sara leaned over the opening and cautiously flashed the beam of the penlight into the darkness, but it was too feeble to illuminate whatever lay below.

"Can you see anything?" Father Baltazar asked in a low voice.

Sara shook her head. "We'll have to go down blind." She looked at the men. "I don't think Sandro'll be able to negotiate a ladder. One of you will have to take him."

Alek cleared his throat. "I don't want to, uh, shirk any duty, but I'm, uh, allergic to cats. I'd hate to sneeze at a critical moment."

"No problem," Father Baltazar said. He held out his hands and Sandro leaped lightly into his arms, pressed against his chest, and hooked his front paws over the priest's shoulder.

"All right," Sara said. "Down we go."

It was not a long descent, no more than thirty or forty steps down a ladder made of narrow gauge metal piping. Descending a ladder in utter darkness isn't the easiest thing to do, but at least the rungs were regularly spaced and the ladder was solidly constructed. This must be, Sara thought, a commonly used route to wherever Sandro was taking them. She wondered if it was used frequently enough to be guarded, or if security was lax. Or, better yet, non-existent. She hoped it were the latter.

Sara reached the bottom first, descending to a paved surface of some kind. She stepped aside, giving the others room to drop down from the ladder, and stood listening and looking as hard as she could.

She heard only silence, saw only darkness. They seemed to be in a tunnel of some kind. She waited until all were down from the ladder, then chanced a brief flash of the light. It really wasn't bright enough to illuminate anything, but there was no reaction from hidden guards, so she thumbed it back on after some moments of quiet darkness.

They were standing, she discovered, on a raised concrete platform that dropped off into yet more darkness only a few feet in front of them. She went forward cautiously. Sandro, who had been let down by the priest, stalked at her feet.

Leaning over the edge of the precipitous drop-off, Sara saw that they were overlooking a dirt-floored tunnel some ten feet below their current level. She pointed the penflash upward, but couldn't discern the tunnel's ceiling in the feeble light.

A sluggish rivulet of water was running through the center of the tunnel's floor. Running, though, was the wrong word, Sara thought. It was barely trickling. They could all smell it from where they stood, especially Sandro, who seemed displeased with its strong odor of decay. Also in the center of the tunnel floor were broken iron tracks, clearly long unused.

"A lost subway tunnel?" Father Baltazar speculated as he kneeled next to Sara, looking down with her at the tunnel floor.

"Seemingly so," Sara said. "It could make for a convenient hideout, all right."

Sandro rubbed against her arm, impatient to get on. He did all but announce, "This way," as he led them down the tunnel's platform into the waiting darkness.

They walked for fifteen minutes, though perhaps because of the darkness it seemed much longer.

The concrete platform ended abruptly after twenty yards or so. They had to hang from the lip of the platform and drop down four or five feet to the tunnel floor below. It was an unnerving thing to do in the near darkness, and less than pleasant to walk so close to the stinking rivulet paralleling their path through the subterranean depths. The ground was soft, almost muddy, and seemed to suck at their feet with every step, making Sara feel like they were trekking through an underground swamp. The air was cool, but with that peculiar musty taste common to caves and other sunless, closed-in environments. It was almost impossible to gauge time and distance, but eventually Sara knew they were approaching something when she could see faint light leaking in from around the tunnel curve.

She switched off the penflash. It was light enough so she could discern the white blur of her companions' faces, as well as the even whiter blur that was Sandro, leading them onwards.

She looked at the others, and held a finger across her lips. They nodded, Father Baltazar grimly, Alek with suppressed excitement. They went on, Sara using gliding steps to minimize even the tiny sucking sounds made by their feet oozing through the mud.

Finally they rounded the curve and stopped to stare at what lay before them.

It was a subway station, built in the 1920s and perhaps abandoned and forgotten not too long afterwards. But though it was clearly old, it showed no signs of decay. Someone had lavished time and money on its upkeep, even pirating electricity to flood the station with light.

The platform was clean and neat. There was no garbage, not even any dust on the platform. Its tile walls were a colorful Art Decoish mosaic depicting a desert oasis at night that looked as fresh as the day it was made. Several empty kiosks stood next to the blocked-off stairways that once led upwards. On the tunnel floor, resting next to another platform, was a subway train, an indeterminate number of cars stretching out into the darkness beyond the lighted area.

The cars looked as old, or older, than the station, and were in just as fine condition. They were red with gold trim. Lights glowed dimly inside the first couple of cars, but Sara was at the wrong angle to see into the cars' interiors.

Sandro fastidiously found a dry spot to sit while he regarded Sara and the others with a look that plainly said, "It's your show. What do you want to do now?"

Sara thought about it.

"I'm going on ahead," she finally said in a low voice. "You wait here until I give the signal to advance–" She shook her head, stopping Father Baltazar's objections before he could voice them. "That's the way it's going to be," she said. "Don't worry. I'll yell for help if I need it."

She handed the penflash back to the priest, and again unholstered her sidearm. She and Sandro went together deeper into the subway station.

It was action time. Or soon would be. The voices in her head were whispering excitedly to each other, as if they could already smell that blood that would soon be spilled.

Sandro regarded her suspiciously with a sideways glance, as though he could hear or otherwise sense the voices.

"Don't worry," she told the guide. "They want to help."

He regarded her dubiously, but said nothing.

She moved as silently as the cat by her side. Together they reached the last car in the line, and went up the short stairway to its rear door, Sandro in the lead.

Sara put her hand on the door handle and tested it. It was unlocked.

She'd gone through a lot of doors leading to unknown but probably dangerous situations, sometimes alone, usually with Jake at her side. Never before with a cat.

Always a first time for everything, she told herself. She looked down at Sandro. He seemed to wink at her. She pushed the door open and he darted into the subway car. She followed after him, her gun drawn, arms braced in the shooter's stance, ready to fire.

There was no one to shoot at. Though furnished with luxury appliances, the car was otherwise empty. All the seats had been torn out and replaced by what seemed to be a modern, well-appointed kitchen. A refrigerator emitted a low hum next to a stove and oven combination. What looked like a closet at the far end of the car turned out to be a pantry, well-stocked with canned foods, dry goods, and various bottles of expensive scotch, tequila, gin, rum, and other liquors.

Sara went through the car wonderingly. The kitchen in her apartment had a sink, a can opener, a stove she rarely used, and a microwave. This p ace was a gourmet's delight.

Idly, she stopped at the refrigerator and opened the door to glance inside. Immediately she wished she hadn't. Among the leftovers and condiments, resting on their own shelf, were five heads, glassy-eyed and staring, sheered through cleanly at the base of their necks.

She recognized one of them. Juliette. She could imagine who the other four were. At least Jake's head wasn't among them. That had to be a good sign. She closed the door quickly, anger and nausea fighting for control of her brain.

The anger won.

Sandro, waiting impatiently by the far door, turned to face her. Sara didn't need his warning glance, nor the whispers in her head. The lights in the second car glowed through pulled window shades. They went quietly through the door and stepped over to the platform of the second car. Sara listened for a few moments, but could hear nothing.

Something inside her—not the voices, but something of and by her own self—told her that this was it. She tested the door. It, too, was unlocked.

Please, Jake, she plead silently. *Be inside. Be okay.*

She flung the door open, and was thrown into deep, dark disappointment, as she realized that her prayer had gone unanswered.

The interior of this car had also been gutted and refitted, but as a bedroom, not a kitchen. It was the most luxurious bedroom Sara had ever seen.

The bed itself was enormous, bigger than king-size, with brass head and foot boards. On each side of the bed was a nightstand with a small Tiffany lamp glowing with stained glass, depicting blooming orchards that looked disturbingly sexual. She didn't care to examine the paraphernalia heaped up on the nightstands too closely.

Erotic paintings hung on all the walls. Erotic statues—from bronze miniatures to life-sized marbles—were scattered about, seated on pedestals, small tables, and, in the case of the life-size Hercules and the Three Graces, resting on the deep, ancient, richly colorful handmade rug that covered the car's floor.

Sara had no time to study the paintings and statuary, though a glance showed her that some were playful, some passionate in the extreme. She moved toward the bed and then stopped, staring at what she saw among the rumpled linen.

There were two forms. One, face up, was handcuffed to the brass headboard. One, face down, was handcuffed to the brass footing. One was Roger Stern. The other was Jerry Stern. They didn't look to be in good shape.

Sara went to the side of the Stern—Jerry?—at the head of the bed. His eyes were open, but staring and glassy. An empty vodka bottle lay on the rumpled sheet next to him, a half-empty pizza box rested on top of various implements and impedimenta that lay on the night stand. There were bruises on his face and across his skinny chest.

Sara reached out to feel his pulse, but immediately knew she wouldn't find one. His flesh was already cold.

With a grimace Sara moved to the other Stern. His back was marked with livid welts. Gently she turned and lifted his head to look at his face. One eye was swollen shut by bruising. A trickle of dried blood traced a line from his nose down his chin. He, too, was cooling.

"You just can't find good toys nowadays," said a voice. Sara dropped Rog–or Jer's–head back onto the mattress, and jumped backwards, swinging her gun up.

It was Jean. She stood at the front of the car, legs braced wide, hands on her hips, so that her short black silk robe covered nothing of importance. Her body was as white as the marble statues that adorned the sleeping car, and all lithe muscle. Her breasts were tiny, although the nipples were large and dark. Her hips were narrow, but she exuded an overpowering female sexuality.

Her skin was flawless, and, Sara realized, that was wrong. The spot between her breasts burned only the previous day by Guillaume Sam's cigar was as smooth and white as the rest of her ivory skin. There was no way such a burn could have healed in a single day. No way.

"They break so easily," Jean said with a teasing smile.

"I should blow you away right now," Sara said, scarcely needing the urgent voices clamoring in her brain.

"Really?" Jean stretched like a cat, lifting her arms high over her head and arching her back. Her breasts disappeared, except for their hard, dark nipples. "I don't think Gene would let you do that."

Sara followed the direction of her gaze, glancing behind her to see Gene, drawing down on her and smiling. He was wearing the matching pants to Jean's silk top. He was as slim as his sister, only somewhat harder sculpted, with taut muscles standing out on his arms and chest. There was a burn mark in the center of the muscled ridges of his chest.

Wait a minute, Sara thought.

"Drop it, copper," Gene said out of the side of his mouth. He grinned sardonically. "I've always wanted to say that."

"Detective Pezzini has been so good to us, darling," Jean said. "She's enabled us to indulge all sorts of fantasies."

Sara wavered, uncertainty whirling in her brain. It had been Jean whom Guillaume Sam had burned, she was sure of it. Yet it was Gene who now bore the scar on his chest. How could that be?

"He means it, Detective," Jean said in a hard voice. "Drop the gun or he'll drop you."

Sara started to let her gun droop and Sandro made his move.

He came out of nowhere, striking silently and viciously, leaping like a tiger and fastening his teeth in Gene's gun wrist. The masculine twin screamed in sudden pain as Sandro's forty pounds dragged his gun arm out of line.

Sara brought her arm back up and squeezed the trigger three times as fast as she could. She didn't have time to be fancy so she went for the torso and put three slugs inside a soda-can top sized circle around the burn spot in the middle of Gene's chest. The bullets made small holes going in and blew out big chunks coming out. Gene jerked at their impact like he was being hit by hammer blows. He flew backwards, knocking a small bronze of a passionate Pan off a pedestal. Blood spewed from his mouth to mix with that flowing down his chest and he collapsed in a strangely graceful heap.

Jean screamed in agony, and by the time Sara had turned her weapon toward her, she was gone, the door of the sleeping car slamming behind her. Sara went after her, Sandro at her heels.

They went through the door recklessly, heedless of possible ambush, and stormed the next car without even thinking about what might be waiting for them.

Sara could register only a confused impression of the third car's contents. It was dominated by the same kind of altar that she'd seen in Paul Narcisse's office, though it more closely resembled Guillaume Sam's. But she had no time to take in details.

Jake was kneeling in chains before the altar. He'd been viciously beaten. His face was battered and swollen. His eyes were shut. Jean held his head up by a fist wound in his hair, and was jamming a gun against his temple. Her face was screwed up as though she were crying, and strange dry sobs were wracking her chest.

She crouched over him like a menacing animal, and Sara knew that her partner was a moment away from death.

"Let him go," she said, her voice as calm as she could make it, her pistol centered on Jean's forehead.

"Oh, no," Jean said. "He's going to die. He's going to die right now."

Sandro flashed towards them, wailing like a banshee. Sara could see with great clarity as Jean's finger tightened on the trigger. Her mind seemed to throb with her heart as milliseconds seemingly stretched into minutes. She knew that Sandro wouldn't reach them in time. She knew that if she pulled the trigger of her own weapon, her bullet couldn't save Jake, but only revenge him.

"Nooooo!" she screamed as she watched Jean's finger start to depress the trigger of her gun, and as she screamed she changed.

The Witchblade ripped into existence, drawn from the plane where it slumbered when it wasn't riding Sara. Instantaneously the detective found herself encased in metal so cold that it burned her skin, so sharp it razored her clothes into fragments, so hideously intelligent that it shot a limb forward faster than a human finger could pull a trigger. A thin, needle-sharp tentacle took Jean between the eyes, punching upward through her skull and shattering her brain. Her body went lax, her gun slipped from her dead fingers.

A paean of exultation slashed through Sara's mind as the voices blended together in a great harmony of joy. But they weren't finished yet. They weren't satisfied.

The metallic tendril of the Witchblade withdrew from Jean's skull and, like a striking snake, whipped towards Sandro, who had watched Jean's death with something like suspicious disbelief on his feline features.

Only his more than cat-quickness saved him as the Witchblade shot in his direction. The tendril clanged against the floor as Sandro leaped sideways and up, landing lightly on the altar and scrambling behind the centrally placed wooden cross that had half a hundred other crosses nailed to it. The cat arched his back and hissed his outrage as the questing tendril withdrew and readied itself for another strike.

"*Noooooo!*" Sara cried again, and only her fierce will drew the Witchblade back to her. It clasped her in its cold embrace, shuddering, begging to be released, but Sara's iron control clamped down upon it, holding it tightly to her like a lover cold from his grave. It withdrew sullenly and suddenly disappeared. Only the voices remained, crooning like sated gourmets, whispering about the quality and essence of the kill they'd just made.

Sara ran to Jake. She cradled his head, relieved to feel that his skin was warm against her exposed flesh, relieved to feel his heart thudding strongly under his own ripped shirt.

"Jake!" she called. "Jake! Come on, man, come on!"

After a moment he opened one battered eye, barely able to see for the swelling and bruising.

"Hey," he said in a weak, but almost recognizable voice. "What took you so long?"

Sara hugged him, almost crying.

After a moment he said, "And what the hell happened to your clothes?"

"I'll tell you later," Sara said.

Alek and Father Baltazar burst into the car, their panic barely under control.

"What the hell?" cried Alec, as the priest crossed himself repeatedly.

The musician looked from the altar to Jake to Jean's body to Sara's body, peeking out of the torn remnants of her clothing. "What . . . what happened to your clothes?"

Sara shook her head. She rattled Jake's chains in frustration. "Forget about that. See if you can find the keys to unlock these chains."

"Maybe Sandro can help," Father Baltazar suggested.

The cat remained sitting on the altar, staring at Sara and twitching his tail.

"I think he's mad at me," Sara said.

"What happened?" the priest asked.

Sara shook her head. "Later. Just find the keys."

Wordlessly, the priest shrugged out of his coat and handed it to Sara. She slipped it over her shoulders, still cradling Jake's head, and nodded her thanks.

"How about these?" Alek said. He dangled a set of keys he'd found on a big ring that'd been looped around the horizontal arm of one of the altar crosses. Sara gestured and he tossed them to her.

"Wow," Alek said, disgust and a certain amount of admiration in his voice as he hunkered down over Jean's body. "You killed her. A single shot between the eyes."

Sara, looking through the couple of dozen keys for one that would fit the padlock on Jake's chains, didn't bother to correct him.

"I never exactly liked her, but she wasn't an asshole like her brother,"

Sara grunted. "He's in the next car."

"Dead?" Father Baltazar asked quietly.

Sara nodded. "Got it," she said, finding the right key to unlock Jake's chains.

"Should I make sure?" Alek asked uncertainly. "Maybe he's just wounded."

"No. He's dead," Sara said. "Give me a hand here."

Father Baltazar hurried to her side and helped her lift Jake to his feet. The two had to support the cop's entire weight until his knees stopped shaking.

"I'm okay," he muttered.

"Can you hold him?" she asked the priest, and he nodded.

She went up to Alek, who was examining the altar with a look of fascination on his face. She didn't want to do this, but she had to tell him. "Alek."

He looked at her, surprised by her solemn expression. "What?"

"It's Rog and Jer. They're in the next car."

"Why didn't you say something before?" he asked eagerly. "Are they tied up or something? We'd better go get them."

Sara grabbed his arm as he went by her, heading for the sleeping car. His eager, inquisitive expression turned uncertain as he looked into her face.

"What's the matter?" he asked. Then, seemingly, it struck him. "They're not dead . . . are they?"

"I'm afraid so."

From her hand on his arm Sara could feel the strength run out of Alek's body. He wavered for a moment, and she almost put her arms around him to hold him up. But he stiffened and looked at her wildly.

"I'm so sorry," she said. "They were already gone when I entered the car."

He pushed by her without a word and rushed for the sleeping car. Sara stopped to glance at Father Baltazar and Jake.

"Go on," the priest said. "Go after him."

"Jake?" she asked.

He nodded, almost impatiently. "I'm okay. Make sure he is. And go make sure that asshole Gene *is* dead. He's the one who did most of this to me." Jake touched his face gingerly, wincing as he traced the swollen bruises that blossomed over his features like malignant flowers.

Jake was right. She should have confirmed the kill. Still, even if he wasn't dead, Gene wasn't going to be up to making mischief with three holes punched in the center of his chest.

Alek had gotten to the car ahead of her. He stood in the doorway, blocking her view.

"Where are they?" he asked in a strange soft voice.

"On the bed," Sara said, pushing past him.

Only they weren't.

The bed was still a mess with rumpled, stained sheets, empty booze bottles, and even fragments of food strewn about it, but Roger and Jerry Stern were gone. Startled, Sara looked up at the other end of the car where she'd last seen Gene lying in a crumpled heap, blood running from his mouth and oozing out of the holes her bullets had punched in his chest.

He was missing, too.

"It can't be," she said.

"You're sure they were dead?" Alek asked insistently.

"They weren't breathing. They had no pulse. They were *cold*."

"Something weird is going on here," Alek muttered.

"I know that," Sara said flatly. She looked at the musician. "Some of Guillaume Sam's people must have snuck in and taken the bodies out."

"We would have seen. Or heard," Alek said distractedly, staring at the rumpled bed. Suddenly he snapped his head up and looked at her. "Wait a moment. Did you say Sam? Guillaume Sam?"

Sara sighed. "He seems to be the one behind this, this whole spree."

"Sam?" Alek said again, as if trying to convince himself.

Sara was thinking fast. If Guillaume Sam knew they were here, he wouldn't waste time beating around the bush. He was, as he told her, a direct man. He would send an assault team powerful enough to crush them.

"Come on," she said, grabbing Alec's arm. "We have to get out of here."

"But Roger–Jerry–"

"There's nothing we can do for them now," she said. She shook his arm, trying to break him out of the daze into which he'd fallen. "We've got to get out of here before reinforcements show up."

She suddenly had a vision of Bakula-baka chasing them through the abandoned tunnels, his bloody machete held high. She didn't like it. Neither did the voices in her head. Seemingly finished congratulating themselves on the Witchblade's kill, they agreed with Sara's assessment that the sooner they left the tunnel, the better.

"Come on."

Sara practically dragged Alek back to the altar car. Jake draped an arm around each man's shoulder, and they helped him hobble away.

Once out of the train, Sandro found an unblocked stairway that led to the street above, so they didn't have to trace their steps back to Club Carrefour. He sprang the locked door that led to the open street. Jake insisted that he could walk by himself. Although that proved too optimistic an opinion, Sara could see that his injuries weren't terribly serious. He was already starting to recover.

Sandro refused to come near her. She couldn't blame him. The Witchblade would have taken him just as it had taken Jean. Sandro seemed to know that. She could read it in his eyes. In the end, he simply vanished when they reached the open air. No one saw him disappear, but one moment, when no one was looking, he simply ceased to be with them. They couldn't tell if he'd literally vanished or had just ducked away when no one was paying attention.

"He saved my life," Sara said in a low voice. "Gene had the drop on me, and he wasn't afraid to tackle him."

And then, she added silently, *I tried to kill him. But it really wasn't me. It was the Witchblade.*

"Perhaps you'll see him again," Father Baltazar said.

Sara shook her head.

I hope not, she thought. *For his sake.*

CHAPTER ELEVEN

It was quite late by the time Sara finally stumbled into her apartment, physically exhausted and mentally depleted, as she always was whenever she used the Witchblade. Like the macho idiot that he was, Jake refused to go to the emergency room, so Father Baltazar had volunteered to wash and bandage his cuts, bruises and minor wounds. They hadn't discussed in any detail an official report. One look from Jake had told Sara that he'd defer to her judgment, as he always did when something "out of left field" happened. No way could Sara envision explaining the night's events in the plain black and white of an official report. Some things, she knew, were best left unofficial.

She barely had the strength to strip off her tattered clothes and drop them on the floor beside her unmade bed.

She was so exhausted she couldn't even conceive of taking a shower, despite the fact that she smelled strongly of an unpleasant combination of odors: adrenalin sweat, the stink of the subterranean station, and the metallic stench left on her skin by the Witchblade.

She collapsed naked on the mattress and pulled her rumpled sheet over her dead-tired body and closed her eyes, desperate for sleep.

But it wouldn't come. The voices wouldn't let it. They were angry at her. They had tasted death, but it hadn't been enough. They'd wanted more, and were furious that Sara hadn't let them have Sandro.

"How dare you deny us?"

"We saved your wretched partner."

"And you would not let us have the creature."

"Vile, vile creature."

Stop it, Sara told them. *Stop it! He was on our side. He helped us–*

"It was a thing of the others."

"It was NOT a good thing."

"It was not one of us."

WILL YOU LET ME SLEEP! Sara shouted at them.

They ignored her, but somehow, despite their annoying twitterings, Sara did finally manage to drift off into coal-black slumber so deep she was still asleep when she reached the shores of Guinee.

She felt something moist and rough slather across her face and she awoke, opening her eyes to see that she lay on a beach with gentle waves washing almost to her feet and a big black panther, perhaps the very one that had accompanied Erzulie during Sara's first visit to Guinee, standing by her head, licking her face with his sandpapery tongue.

She was too tired to be afraid.

"Hello," she said, looking the big cat in the eye. "Are you any relation to Sandro?"

He smiled a sly feline smile and sat on his haunches like Sandro with his tail curled around his feet.

"If you are, tell him I'm sorry. Tell him that I never

meant the Witchblade to hurt him. Tell him that sometimes the thing gets out of control–oh, hell." She sat up, unsurprised that she was still naked. Little, or maybe nothing, could surprise her now. "Here I am in a dream, sitting on my bare butt and talking to a cat while there's a perfectly good ocean right at my feet."

She stood in a single lithe movement and ran into the waves until they surged over her waist, lapping against her torso. The water was warm and indescribably soothing. She dove below the surface and swam out deeper, letting the gentle rocking of the surf envelope her entire body. The waves felt like a thousand caressing fingers delivering a soothing massage from head to toe. She flipped over on her back and floated for a few moments, eyes open and staring at the star-spangled night sky, riding the gentle waves like they were a lover.

She felt better by the second. The weariness washed out of her muscles. The voices, perhaps afraid or unable to exist in this place, were out of her mind. There was no sense of time passing. She may have rested in the waves for an instant, she may have rested in them for an eternity. When she finally reached the point of complete contentment, she simply headed back to the shore with strong, hard strokes.

She walked back onto the beach, water running in sensual rivulets from her hair down her back to her buttocks, puckering her skin with fleeting goosebumps as they dried in the cool breeze. She felt rested and richly alive with her skin washed clean of all the awful odors as the perfumed breezes dried her hair.

The panther was still waiting for her on the beach, but he wasn't alone. His master, the *loa* Erzulie, sat next to him, rubbing his head between his ears and eliciting a rumbling purr that sounded like steam escaping from a leaking pipe.

Somehow Sara didn't feel uncomfortable in her nakedness before the *loa*, though she was glad that it was Erzulie and not Papa Legba who sat before her.

Erzulie stood, brushing the grains of sand from her palms with a business-like gesture.

"Papa Legba asked me to come see you," she said grinning, "though, seeing you, I'm sure he would be sorry not to be here himself."

That almost made Sara blush, though she said, "It seems like I don't have a choice when I come here or how I'm dressed."

Erzulie laughed.

"How little people know. You are here because you want to be. You need help. You are vexed by terrible problems that need solutions. You sense that you can find the solutions here, but you are groping about, unsure how to find them. Tonight you found the tranquility that you crave. It has refreshed your body and soul, no?"

Sara nodded. She had been desperately weary. Now she felt ready to take on almost anything. Even Guillaume Sam. Perhaps even the voices and the Witchblade.

"We cannot solve your problems," Erzulie told you. "That, mainly, is up to you. But we can provide a place where you can solve them for yourself. This—" she gestured around them at the beach "—is one such place. You come here searching for peace . . . and find it, ultimately, in your own heart and mind. There is another place where you may be able to solve another problem."

Sara followed where Erzulie was pointing, and saw

past the beach, past a line of trees to iron gates highlighted on the horizon. Iron gates that enclosed a forest of crosses. The cemetery looked ancient and frightening, and alive, not dead. Alive and waiting.

"But when you go there, *blanc*," Erzulie said in gentle warning, "be careful. Be very, very careful. For some problems, you see, are solved simply, by death. And that, I think, would not be a solution to your satisfaction. No, not at all."

Sara awoke before the alarm went off, still feeling more refreshed than she had any right to be. She even smelled clean. The stink of sweat and gunpowder and underground goo was gone from her body, as if they had indeed been washed away by clean water with a salty tang and the residue of tropical breezes.

If it was a dream, she thought as she rummaged through her closet for clean clothes, *it was quite a powerful dream*. She shimmied into underwear and pulled on a new pair of jeans. *If it wasn't a dream . . .*

For some reason her mind refused to complete the thought.

Sara concentrated on getting dressed and down to the precinct. She and Jake and Detective Dickey from Brooklyn had a meeting scheduled that morning with Captain Siry about their progress–or lack thereof–in the Machete Murderer case. She would, Sara knew, have to walk a fine line with Siry this morning.

Siry greeted her in an almost human manner as she knocked and entered his office. Jake was already seated before Siry's desk, looking only a little worse for wear. He was young, almost as young as Sara, and his recuperative powers were enormous. That, and his thirst for justice kept him going when almost everyone else would have quit.

"Come in, sit down, have coffee." Siry made it more of an order than an offer, but Sara shook off the coffee anyway. Her stomach was squishy enough as it was. She didn't think it could survive a cup of precinct-house coffee. She had barely settled in her chair when Lieutenant Dickey from Brooklyn came in. Today, he was wearing his too-large grey suit.

"Come in, sit down, have coffee," Siry repeated.

Dickey moseyed around the captain's desk and helped himself from the pot on the adjacent credenza.

"Donut?" Siry offered.

Dickey declined. "I'm on a diet," he said, emptying a couple of packets of Sweet'N'Low into his little plastic coffee cup.

"Looks like it's working," Siry grunted.

"Thanks." Dickey sat down carefully, looked carefully at Jake's face. "That's something new since I last saw you," he observed.

"Yeah," Jake said ruefully. "Ran into some difficulty when I was following up some leads on the green-card aspect of the case."

"And what would this 'green-card aspect' be, exactly?" Dickey asked as he sipped from his little plastic cup.

Jake looked at Siry and the captain nodded. Jake glanced at Sara and then launched into a somewhat edited version of his investigation, leaving out any mention of the abandoned subway station and what had gone down there the night before. He made it sound as if he'd run into a couple of heavies while running down info on the green card scheme, but although he'd gotten in a fight and been damaged he'd managed to escape. Or as he put it, they'd managed to escape him.

"So you think Guillaume Sam is behind this?" Dickey said thoughtfully.

"It seems like it," Sara offered. "Heard of him?"

Dickey shrugged heavy shoulders. "Of course. Everyone round the 'hood has. He's a big man with big influence in the community."

"Does it surprise you that he'd be mixed up in something like this?" Sara asked.

Dickey turned his dark, soulful eyes on her. "Detective, nothing on this job surprises me any more. Nothing."

I bet I could show you a thing or two, Sara thought, but kept quiet and only nodded.

"Sounds like it's time for an old-fashioned door-kicking raid," Siry said. "I'll get a judge to issue the papers. Dickey, can you supply uniforms from your precinct?"

The lieutenant started to nod, but Sara suddenly spoke. "Captain, maybe it'd be better if we used our own uniforms. Like Dickey said, Guillaume Sam has big influence in the Cypress Hills community."

"You suggesting that one of my men might tip him?" Dickey asked sadly.

Sara shrugged. "Like you said. I'm not surprised at anything anymore in this job."

Siry looked steadily at the Brooklyn detective. "It's your call, Carl."

The big detective drained his coffee cup and tossed it, empty, into the basket by the side of Siry's desk. He sighed, seemingly from the bottom of his shoes.

"All right," he said. "We'll use Manhattan men." He stood. "I've always wanted to see the upper crust in action."

"Mind if I smoke?" Guillaume Sam asked the uniform who was rummaging through Sam's desk drawers as Sam sat behind it. He had cigar and end-clipper ready to put into action.

The officer glanced at him. "I do. I'm allergic."

"Besides," Sara said, "it's bad for you."

Guillaume Sam grinned, showing rows of even, white teeth. "I'm not going to die of lung cancer," he said. "I've been assured of that."

"By Baron Samedi?" Sara asked with raised eyebrows.

"Oh, yes, Baron Samedi himself," Guillaume Sam assured her.

"How *are* you going to die?"

Guillaume Sam laughed. "I'm not," he said. "I'm going to live forever."

"Uh-huh."

The search team from Sara's Manhattan precinct had been at it for hours, but besides confiscating a couple of computers for detailed analysis at HQ, they'd found nothing remotely incriminating. Or even remotely interesting. Guillaume Sam had been so accommodating that Sara figured there was nothing dirty on the premises to find. Clearly Club Carrefour was and had always been clean as a whistle, or Guillaume Sam had been tipped and he'd hustled any evidence of illegal activity out the door.

He put the unlit cigar in his mouth and rolled it around zestfully.

"Tell me," he asked Sara, "how's your partner?

McCarthy, I believe his name is? I heard he ran into a little trouble yesterday."

"He's fine," Sara deadpanned. "He's checking out some rooms downstairs, I believe. Tell me. How's Jean and Gene?"

For a moment Guillaume Sam's face darkened in a frown, then it lightened and he laughed aloud.

"You *do* like to play rough, Ms. Pezzini." He took the cigar out of his mouth and studied it carefully. Finally, he said, "Jean had to leave my employ. That was unfortunate. She will be missed. Gene, however . . ." Guillaume Sam shrugged. "We shall see about Gene. We all shall see."

Intrigued, Sara was going to try to push him further, but one of the cops looking at the altar that dominated the rear of Guillaume Sam's office picked up an opaque lidded jar, held it up to his ear, and shook it.

"What's in here?" he asked.

Guillaume Sam looked at him and sat straight up in his chair, the frown back on his face. "Careful with that, fool! It is a *pot-de-tete*. It contains my soul."

"Sure," the cop said laconically, and put it back down on the altar.

"Okay, boys," Sara said. "I think we're done here. Let's go collect Detectives McCarthy and Dickey and the rest of the team."

"Finished so soon, Ms. Pezzini?" Guillaume Sam asked.

"We've seen enough." Sara paused. "By the way, where's your rat?"

"Possum, Ms. Pezzini. Baka is a possum. Being nocturnal, he's having his afternoon sleep." Guillaume Sam grinned widely. It wasn't a pleasant grin. "But you'll see him again. Soon. I promise."

CHAPTER TWELVE

From the outside St. Casimir's rectory looked shabby. The stone was grimy with accumulated city grit. The shingled roof was obviously in need of repair. Even the welcome mat was so worn that you could no longer read the large WELCOME imprinted on it.

The battered outer door had a brass knocker. No newfangled electric doorbell for St. Casimir's, no sir. Father Baltazar answered the door after Sara rapped—not too hard, because she was afraid that a solid blow would bring it down.

"Come in," he said, gesturing Sara inside the vestibule with a welcoming wave.

From the inside, though, the rectory was charming.

The furniture was old, but old furniture is often well-made and costly when in good repair, as Father Baltazar's was. Sara couldn't tell Chippendale from Louis XXIV, unless they were dancing barechested before her in collars and cuffs, but she could tell quality when she saw it. The desk, chairs, glassed-in bookcase, and even the old sofa in the cozy office-library that Father Baltazar ushered her into oozed quality. The room was filled with dark wood and old books and was well-kept, well-dusted, and extremely neat.

"Who's your maid?" Sara asked, looking around. "I could use her around my place. I have about a fifth of the stuff you do and my apartment is five times as messy."

Father Baltazar laughed. "I am," he said. "I'm afraid that I've always been excessively neat. It's one of my character flaws."

"It must be your only flaw," Sara said, sinking into what turned out to be a most comfortable sofa, "as you're brave, reverent, and cheerful. I'd guess you're thrifty as well, or else you wouldn't have accumulated all these books on a priest's salary."

"I don't have to pay rent," he said, taking the end of the sofa. "That counts for a lot in this town."

He was, Sara saw, trying to keep things light, but that wasn't what she wanted. She was afraid to admit to herself what she really wanted, but she knew that she longed for more than light-hearted comradery from the handsome–and brave, and loyal, and cool headed; God, she could go on and on–young priest.

"I meant what I said," Sara said. "About your flawless character."

"I'm blushing," Father Baltazar said, though he looked more troubled than embarrassed. He leaned forward and took Sara's hands in his. "You're a remarkable woman, Sara. Beautiful, terribly tough, brave, yet oddly vulnerable. I'd back you in damn near anything–and I already have. I'll stand with you against anyone–and, before this is over, I fear that I will. You have to realize one thing, though. I'll be the best friend to you I can be. But that's *all* I can be."

His hands were warm and strong and felt good on hers. She wanted more from them.

"I know you're a priest. I know you have vows—"

"I do," he said solemnly. "I live with them every day and have never broken them. But, Sara, even if I weren't bound by my vows what I just told you would still be true."

She looked into his deep dark eyes and saw the truth there.

"You understand?"

She nodded reluctantly, feeling like a fool. Of course, he would be gay. The best man she'd met in years. Handsome, brave, intelligent... She tried to pull her hands away, but he wouldn't let her go.

"Do you forgive me?"

Suddenly she felt ashamed at the flash of anger she'd felt. "Forgive you? Father—Baltazar." Suddenly she didn't know what to call him. "Father" seemed way too formal, "Baltazar," way too cumbersome. "There's nothing to forgive."

"How about a hug, then?"

She came into his arms and they hugged fiercely. The voices were disapproving, but she ignored them. At least for a while. It felt good to be in his embrace, as chaste as it was, and Sara realized that perhaps she needed a friend even more than she needed a lover.

"Call me Caz," the priest said. "All my friends do."

"All right," Sara said. "Caz."

"Good." He let her go."Now tell me what's been troubling you since you ran from the confessional that day we first met."

Although they separated, Sara realized that from that moment on they'd never be totally apart. There was a bond between them, a bond not only of shared experiences, but of understanding and of emotional closeness such as she had with no one else. Not even her sister. Not even her partner. She had to hide things from both of those people. With Father Baltazar—Caz—she could discuss those very things she had to hide from others. He'd understand. He might even be able to help.

Despite the voice's warnings she told him about the Witchblade, at least the little she really knew about it. She told him how she'd acquired it, seemingly by accident but actually, as she'd come to realize, by some sort of strange cosmic design. She told him what she'd done with it. Of the men and women she'd killed, of the strange menaces she'd faced, of the battles she'd fought and not dared tell anyone lest they think she was insane.

As she spoke Sara was surprised to realize how little concrete knowledge she had of the Witchblade. She told him about the reservations she had, of how it often acted against her will, how sometimes it even tried to trick her into doing something bad like killing Sandro, which had not only been against her wishes but also without any conscious warning.

Father Baltazar was fascinated by the story. "I've certainly never heard or read of anything exactly as you describe, though there are obscure writings and even more obscure legends about such a thing . . . Paul Narcisse may know more. He's much more of an expert on the occult than I am. I'm just a dabbler, really." He stared thoughtfully into the distance. "There are obvious parallels between what happens to you when the Witchblade takes control and what happens when a *voudon* initiate is 'mounted,' as it's called, by a *loa*. Though nominally at least you seem to have more control over the object known as the Witchblade, clearly there is some kind of force lurking in it that can take control if you're not constantly vigilant, if for some reason it feels it really wants control."

"I noticed the parallels myself," Sara said. "In fact, I was wondering if you or Paul could help me. Could–I don't know–give me some kind of guidance to help control the thing."

Father Baltazar shook his head. "Paul's the expert on possession. I'm just an interested observer." He checked his watch. "He should be here soon. We can either consult him, or set up some time to talk about your, uh, problem, privately." He looked at Sara speculatively. "I don't suppose you could give me a demonstration of this Witchblade in action?"

Sara shook her head. "I don't think that's a good idea. I call upon it only when I feel I must. Otherwise, I'm afraid that I'd lose even more control." The voices in her head chuckled, and Sara grimaced. "The voices are laughing. That's a pretty good indication that my fears are valid."

Father Baltazar frowned in disappointment. "I suppose you're right. In any case, it seems that this Witchblade is nothing to fool around with for trivial reasons. We may need it in the fight against Guillaume Sam, but I guess you're right to call upon it only when you feel it's absolutely necessary. Still," he said, his gaze turned inward, "it would be something to see."

"Be careful of what you wish for," Sara muttered.

As if on cue, the knocker boomed loudly against the front door, making an impressive percussive sound that reverberated through the cozy rectory.

"Excuse me," Father Baltazar said, and went to answer the door.

He returned with a troop of visitors. A serious-faced Paul Narcisse led the way. He nodded solemnly to Sara. Behind him were Alek and Kris Gervelis. Father Baltazar had mentioned that Alek was going to be present at the gathering, but Kris's attendance was something of a surprise. Neither brother looked particularly happy, but Kris was especially uncertain.

"Well," Father Baltazar said, "we're all here. Please find a seat. Make yourselves comfortable."

Alek nodded, smiled at Sara, and sat down next to her on the sofa. The others distributed themselves around the room, the priest taking the chair behind his desk. The five of them pretty much filled up the room. Sara had thought about bringing Jake, but ultimately had decided against it. She'd decided that the less Jake knew about such matters, the better. He wasn't one for mystic conspiracies. She hadn't even considered inviting Lieutenant Dickey.

Paul Narcisse took control as they all settled in. "I'm sure you all know why we're here," he said, looking at each in turn.

Kris Gervelis was patently uncomfortable. "I'm not. Not really. Alek has told me some pretty wild stuff. Stuff I think the police should investigate. Or maybe the Church. I don't know anything about such things."

Everyone looked at Alek, who grinned a little weakly. "I had to tell him. Kris has to know what's going on with Mountains. He's not only in charge of us business-wise, but Roger and Jerry were our friends, for Christ's sake."

"No one's saying you shouldn't have told Kris what's happening," Father Baltazar said. "But, anyway, what exactly did you tell him?"

Alek shrugged. "You know. About that cat or whatever it was called Sandro, and the boys disappearing with Sara thinking they were dead, and Gene and Jean getting shot and killed, and Guillaume Sam being a *bokor*–"

"Crazy stuff," Kris said, looking down at the floor as if unwilling to look the others in the room in the eye.

"Maybe you're right, Kris," Paul Narcisse said softly. "Maybe it's all crazy stuff. But it's all true, just the same."

He looked up, anger in his eyes. "Are you telling me the boys are dead, Paul? Is that what you're saying? Because they can't be dead. They can't be!"

Paul looked at him. Everyone looked at him.

"Why not, Kris?" Paul asked in a gentle voice.

"Sam, he wouldn't–" Kris caught himself, and finished sullenly, "They can't be. That's all."

"Sam wouldn't what, Kris?" Paul asked again. "He wouldn't hurt them? Have them killed? What kind of deal did you make with Guillaume Sam, Kris?"

Kris Gervelis looked at him stubbornly. "Deal?"

Paul nodded while everyone looked on, silently. "You seem unwillingly to believe that the Sterns were hurt, maybe even killed. But you don't deny that Guillaume Sam is a *bokor*, do you?"

Kris glanced around the room, then laughed weakly. "Of course he's not. Who'd believe such a thing?"

Alek sat back heavily on the sofa. "You were always a bad liar, Kris," he said in a low voice. "Always."

Kris turned on him angrily. "Do you know what it takes to launch a band nowadays? Huh? Do you? Of course not. No, for you it was the music. Always the music. But what about paying for the instruments? The sound system? Demo records? A tour? Drugs for those goofball Sterns? Where do you think that money came from, Alek, huh? The two-fifty a night we got playing local gigs? Do you have even the slightest conception of what it took? *Do you?*"

Alek, not looking at him, shook his head. "No, Kris. No. I don't."

Kris snorted. "Of course not. You just expected it to be there when you needed it. And I made sure it was."

"At what cost?" Father Baltazar asked quietly.

Kris sat back in his chair, his defiant gaze back on the floor. "Not much," he said. "I let Sam do the band's books."

Sara knew instantly what that meant. "You were letting him launder money through the band," she said.

Kris shrugged, but the defiance was gone out of him. "The band—we were doing okay, but maybe not as well . . . not as well as Alek and the others thought. Sam let us keep some of the money we ran through our accounts, for expenses. He said we could pay him back when we hit it really big."

"My God," Alek said, closing his eyes.

Sara could hear the pain in his voice. She put a comforting hand on his arm, but he didn't react. He didn't even look at her.

"It's not like we were doing badly, Alek," Kris said, a pleading tone in his voice. "We've doing better, really. It's only a matter of time. We're getting there. Soon we'll be able to do without Sam entirely. Then we can pay him back."

"That's why you say he wouldn't hurt the boys," Sara said.

"Of course," Kris said eagerly. "He has as big a stake in Mountains' success as we do."

"Except," Paul Narcisse said quietly, "he is riding the

lightning. He thinks he controls it. He might even control it sometimes, for a little while. But sometimes he must feed it, even when he doesn't want to."

"What do you mean?" Sara asked.

"Bakula-baka has needs of his own that must be satisfied. Even the *marassa*, the Twins that Guillaume Sam employed had to be paid in more than money."

"*Marassa*?" Alek asked. "You mean Gene and Jean?"

Paul Narcisse nodded. "They've worked for Guillaume Sam for years. In the beginning they just had a reputation as sadistic killers, but under the *bokor*'s tutelage they walked far on the left hand path. Twins, you see, are sacred. They can have great powers. They can switch bodies, enjoy an inhuman vitality that allows them to survive terrible wounds that would kill anyone else. But to stoke the fires of their magic, they must drain the powers of others—preferrably twins such as themselves."

"Rog and Jerry," Alek whispered. He looked at Paul Narcisse with an agonized expression.

"So you think they're dead. You really think they're dead."

Paul Narcisse looked at him as if gauging how much he could really take. "I don't know," he finally said quietly. "But I fear their situation may be even worse."

"Worse than death?" Alek asked incredulously. "There is worse than death?"

"Oh, yes," Paul Narcisse said. "Much."

There was a protracted silence that no one seemed willing to break. Sara could feel an emotional vortex running through the room threatening to snap out in unspeakable violence between brothers and friends. But she sensed that they hadn't plumbed the depths of revelation yet. And they had to. They had to get everything out in the open.

"But," she said into the pregnant silence, "all of this doesn't explain why Kris isn't surprised that Guillaume Sam is a *bokor*. Does it?"

"No," Father Baltazar and Paul Narcisse said simultaneously. Alek just looked at his brother, who glanced wildly from face to face.

"Well . . . " he said. "Well . . . we did have some talks."

"What did he promise you?" Alek asked. "What did he offer you for the soul of Mountains of Madness?"

"It's not like that!" Kris Gervelis protested, but everyone could see that despite what he said, it was indeed exactly like that.

"I know," Sara said quietly, again breaking the awful silence.

Everyone looked at her, except Kris, who in his agony looked at nothing.

"Magda Konsavage."

The look on Kris's face, his awful silence, confirmed her suspicions.

Alek sighed as if all the life had gone out of him. Even Father Baltazar slumped in his chair. Paul Narcisse wearily rubbed his eyes.

"He said," Kris said thickly, "he said that she would love me. Love me as I loved her. He would give me this when we paid him the money we owed."

"He lied, Kris," Paul Narcisse said softly. "He can't make her love you. Not really. It would be a hideous simulacrum of love that wouldn't have fooled you for a second."

Kris began to cry. Tears ran down his face, although it was hideously blank of emotion. He made no sound as he wept, but said in a voice as blank as his face, "I knew that. I think I always knew that. I just couldn't help myself."

With that admission he covered his face with his hands and broke down into great wracking sobs wrenched from the bottom of his heart and soul. Alek broke also. He slid off the sofa to his knees and lurched to the chair where his brother wept inconsolably, gathering him into his embrace, weeping and murmuring, "My brother, oh my brother."

Sara wept herself, wiping away tears, surreptitiously glancing at Father Baltazar and Paul Narcisse. Father Baltazar was grim as an Old Testament prophet. Only Paul Narcisse wore a trace of a smile, a sad smile burdened by the grief that had been loosed in the room, but a smile just the same.

"The bonds snap," he said, almost to himself. "One by one he loses his allies. He weakens—yet becomes all the more dangerous for it."

"Guillaume Sam?" Sara asked, wiping the tear tracks from her cheeks.

Paul Narcisse nodded. "Oh, yes. Weep not, friends, for we have sundered another cord of the *bokor's* power, weakening him ever more."

Emotions spent, the Gervelis Brothers slowly regained control. Father Baltazar tossed them a box of tissues, and Kris blew his nose and rubbed his eyes.

"A good cry cleanses the soul," the priest said. "Too bad our society frowns upon it."

Paul Narcisse leaned forward and put his hand on Kris's arm. "You've done nothing that's irredeemable. But if you move to our side, Guillaume Sam will grow desperate. We sit here in the eye of the hurricane, my friends, and when we pass through it into the storm again, it will blow upon us like a wind from hell."

"Do we wait for this wind to blow," Sara asked, "or do we take it to the source?"

"We have to know where to strike," Paul Narcisse pointed out. "Your search of Club Carrefour turned up nothing," he said. "The abandoned subway station belonged to Gene and Jean. It was their headquarters, not Guillaume Sam's."

"That means," Father Baltazar said, "that his *hounfort* is probably still hidden. Could he have held his ceremonies at the Club or the subway station?"

"Hmmm." Paul Narcisse considered the matter. "No, probably not. The club is too open. Anybody could find their way there. The subway station is too limited, the cars are too small to host ceremonies of any size. Besides, there was no *poteau-mitan*, no sanctuaries. Only the one altar to Baron Samedi."

"We can call on Papa Legba again," Sara said. "He owes me a third boon. I can ask him to send Sandro to lead us to Sam's *hounfort*."

Paul Narcisse frowned. "Papa Legba's boon is not an advantage to be used lightly. I'm not saying we shouldn't call upon Papa Legba. I'm saying we should hold back from using that card as long as we can."

"And if we don't play it before the game ends?" Sara asked.

"Then it's wasted," Father Baltazar said.

"We don't have to waste anything," Kris said quietly. "I've been to Sam's *hounfort*. I know where it is."

They all looked at him. His face was set, his expression that of a man who had made up his mind after a long period of uncertainty.

"Excellent!" Paul Narcisse said. "If we can destroy his *hounfort*, Guillaume Sam will be greatly weakened. He may be panicked into a desperate move. Do not underestimate his powers. They still are great. But if we can strike quickly, while he is off-balance, that will certainly be to our favor."

"What kind of resources would he have at the *hounfort*?" Alek asked. "What can he do there?"

Paul Narcisse shrugged. "There's no telling for sure. Perhaps, though, you will learn that there can indeed be a fate worse than death."

Sara nodded. She knew that that was true. And so did the bodiless, soulless voices twittering in her head.

CHAPTER THIRTEEN

They assembled in the back office of The Serpent and the Rainbow: bookstore owner, priest, police officer, musician, and Goth Rock band manager. It was, Sara thought, an unlikely and motley group with which to storm the gates of hell.

Sara thought for about a second of bringing Jake along. He had a steady nerve and a cool head and God knows he owed Guillaume Sam personally, both for the death of Juliette and the beating he'd taken at Sam's orders, but ultimately she decided to leave him out of this party. He'd come along willingly, but he'd be confused by the utter weirdness of the situation and any confusion on his part would probably cost him his life. Sara couldn't have that on her conscience. She couldn't live with Jake's blood on her hands.

"I'll have to ask you to look the other way, Detective," Paul Narcisse asked.

"Why?"

He gestured at the closed box that rested on the top of

his desk. "You're armed," he said. "But the rest of us shouldn't go to that place emptyhanded."

Sara sighed. He was right, of course. Their lives, and perhaps even more, were on the line. But once you started to compromise your vows, Sara wondered, where did it end? Of course, she hadn't *just* started compromising her oath to the police department. She started long ago when she first picked up the Witchblade and slid it, gauntlet-like, over her right hand. But now was not the time to get squeamish. Now was not the time to stop compromising, either, though someday, she realized, that time would probably come.

She only hoped that she'd be able to stop when she really had to.

"Are you two familiar with guns?" Paul Narcisse asked the brothers.

They glanced at each other and Alek shook his head.

"I'm a city boy. I played with guitars when I grew up, not guns." He jerked a thumb at his brother. "His weapon of choice was a pocket calculator."

"Better take these, then." Paul Narcisse lifted the lid of the box and removed two firearms and handed them to the brothers.

"Jesus," Sara said. "Where'd you get those?"

Alek looked at them, took the one Paul Narcisse offered him, and turned it over in his hands like he was uncertain which end the bullets came out of. "What the hell are these things? They look like props from some Italian after-the-holocaust movie."

"They're Jackhammers," Kris said. "Twelve-gauge automatic combat shotguns. Ten round plastic magazine placed behind the trigger. On automatic the full magazine will empty in two and one-third seconds with a Cutts-style compensator on the muzzle brake off-setting barrel jump and also acting as a flash eliminator." He looked at the others, who were all staring at him in surprise. "What? I read an article about them in *Soldier of Fortune* magazine once."

"Have you ever fired one?" Paul Narcisse asked.

"No."

"Better select single-round fire then. And stick to it."

Kris tried to hide his disappointment. "All right."

Paul Narcisse turned to Father Baltazar. "What about you? Are you armed?"

The priest patted his windbreaker's side pocket. "I have everything I need right here."

"All right then." Paul Narcisse gazed at the small band. All looked solemn, all looked determined. "There's no doubt that this will be dangerous. Perhaps even deadly. Some of us–" and here he looked right at the Gervelis brothers "–are not exactly trained for this sort of thing. Damballah knows I'm not, particularly. But if we stay alert, have faith, and listen to Detective Pezzini, we might all come back in the end. And in the end we all might have done the world some good."

Not a bad speech, thought Sara. She only hoped that she could live up to her part of it.

We hope so, too, the voices chorused in her brain. *We hope so, too.*

Paul Narcisse drove them to the *hounfort* in a battered old Volkswagen van that looked to Sara as if it had survived, though just barely, more than one previous foray into urban warfare. Or perhaps those holes in the body were just rust spots.

Indian summer had finally broken. There was a distinct chill to the air. Everywhere across the city people were sitting down to dinner and looking forward to a movie or a Mets game to round out their evening. Or perhaps they were just planning a long, quiet night at home with their loved ones.

Meanwhile, she and her companions were facing the promise of violent death. Not that Sara loathed the adrenaline-laced excitement that was already warming her stomach with a nervous energy that belied her calm exterior. But sometime it would be nice, she reflected, to see what that quiet evening at home would feel like.

She found herself looking at Alek Gervelis. He looked up and met her gaze.

"You're probably used to this sort of thing," he said.

"Maybe too much so."

"Well, I'm just hoping that I can get through this without peeing my pants."

She put a hand on his forearm and squeezed it gently, reassuringly. "You'll be okay."

He leaned toward her and put his head close to hers.

"If we get through this," he said in a soft voice, "how about we go somewhere quiet, just the two of us? Have a nice dinner. Maybe a few drinks. Then just relax and get to know each other a little better."

Sara smiled, amazed at how his thoughts seemed to parallel her own. "Sounds good," she said. "It's a date."

"Good." Alek leaned back against his seat. "Now just make sure I live through tonight so we can actually make good on it."

"I'll do my best."

"That's it," Kris said. He was in the shotgun seat in front, guiding Paul Narcisse through the streets of Brooklyn. They had moved from residential neighborhoods to a blasted industrial warehouse zone made up of huge block-like stone and brick structures of a peculiarly ugly neo-penal style of architecture. None seemed to be the centers of particularly successful industries or businesses, and many looked abandoned.

The building that Kris indicated was well up the block and across the street. Paul Narcisse guided the VW into an adjacent sidestreet that was actually more alley than street. He maneuvered the van so that they could watch the front of the building through the windshield while they themselves were hidden by the darkness of the unlit street.

Paul Narcisse made a sound of disgust deep in his throat.

"This is a vile place to have a *hounfort*," he said. "There are no trees, no grass, no plants at all, no clean running water. Only concrete, cement, and dirty brick. There is nothing to nourish the *loa*, or their people. Such a place would only find favor with those like Guillaume Sam, who worship death and decay."

He spit out the van's open window.

"Someone's going in," Father Baltazar said.

Two figures scurried from the dark side of the street to a door in the center of the warehouse's front facade. They paused there for a moment, then apparently were admitted. They disappeared inside.

"Perhaps there's a ceremony tonight," the priest said.

"I think we can count on that," Paul Narcisse replied. "I think we can count on the presence of Guillaume Sam and many of his *zobops*–" he turned to glance back at Sara and Alek, in the back seat "–those are the low-level cultists in his *bizango*, or secret society, probably recruited from all over the city and beyond."

They watched for a few minutes as seven or eight of what Paul Narcisse had termed *zobops* entered the structure, alone or in small groups of two or three.

"Is there a password?" Paul Narcisse asked Kris.

He nodded. " 'We meet at the crossroads.' "

"Right," Paul Narcisse said. "Let's split up. Caz, you go with Detective Pezzini. I'll go in with the brothers. You and I had best keep our faces hidden as much as possible, because we're the most likely to be recognized by those guarding the doors. Remember. 'We meet at the crossroads.' "

"All right," Sara said.

"Let's do it," Alek said. Quickly, he leaned over and kissed her lightly on the lips. "For luck," he said.

She smiled at him, her pulses already hammering wildly, the voices singing in her brain. She put her hand on the back of his head and twined her fingers in his long, thick hair.

"We'll need more luck than that," she said, and pulled his mouth back down to hers.

Their mouths met and opened and Sara kissed him hard, as if it might be the last kiss in her life. She was breathing heavily as she broke away and so was Alek. The voices laughed at her, thinking she was foolish. She knew what they thought and she didn't care. For a moment she put the palm of her hand against his cheek and he caught it and bought it to his lips, then they followed the others out of the van.

Alek and Kris and Paul Narcisse sauntered down the street. Alek, who wore a black duster that reached down to his ankles, had both his and Kris's Jackhammers, as well as a selection of extra ammo cassettes, secreted in the voluminous folds of his great coat. Sara and Father

Baltazar waited until they'd crossed over the *hounfort*'s side, then exchanged glances and followed. As expected, they were challenged at the door. Sara gave the ritual password. Father Baltazar kept his face averted and in shadow as much as he could.

Security was about as lax as they could hope for. The two guards waved them through almost disinterestedly. They were wearing ceremonial outfits that consisted of long flowing robes and pointy red caps with cheek flaps on either side that hung down to their shoulders. Despite the caps Sara could see crosses tattooed on their cheeks and the back of their hands. They were members of Guillaume Sam's private gang, The Saturday Night Specials, the bangers who were the foot soldiers for his various illegal enterprises.

The Gervelis Brothers and Paul Narcisse were waiting for them in the anteroom where the initiates donned their ceremonial robes. Alek was having a difficult time finding one large enough to fit over his tall frame, and that served as an excuse for them to mill about until they were all reunited.

Once properly enrobed they left the anteroom under the not-so-watchful gaze of another pair of bored Specials and followed other recent arrivals into the ground floor of what had obviously been a warehouse of some sort. Fifty or sixty *zobops* had already assembled.

The building had been gutted some time in the past, leaving a huge open space that encompassed nearly all of the structure's first floor. Clearly, Guillaume Sam didn't care about the place's aesthetics. It was post-industrial-depressing: bare concrete floor with piles of trash heaped randomly around the edge of a great open space supported by bare steel beams and columns badly in need of paint. The area was lit poorly by naked bulbs strung on wire. Some of the bulbs dangled from the ceilings, others from wires twisted around the pillar-like supports running from floor to ceiling. The light cast by the bulbs was fitful and distorting, throwing odd monstrous shadows that seemed to jump and jerk like inhuman marionettes. It was, Sara thought, vaguely unsettling even when nothing much was happening. She couldn't imagine what it would look like during the chaotic dancing of a *vodoun* ceremony.

The peristyle had been reduced to a *poteau-mitan* set in the usual circular concrete support whose surface doubled as an altar. The great pole was the only bit of color in the *hounfort*'s concrete and steel environment.

Sara and the others kept to the margins of the crowd, watching as a higher-level initiate drew the ceremonial *veve* around the dancing pole. A couple of small chambers serving as sanctuaries, *caille mysteres*, as Sara remembered they were called, were clustered behind the pole along one of the warehouse's interior walls. They were the size and general shape of office cubicles, roofed with thin, sagging, black plastic sheets. She could see flickers of movement in the chambers, but the sanctuary wasn't well lit and she couldn't quite make out what was happening inside the tiny rooms.

"What do we do now?" Alek whispered.

"Wait," Paul Narcisse said, "for the ceremony to start. Once the dancing and drumming begins we should start to work our way around the fringes of the crowd to the sanctuary. What we're looking for will likely be found before the altar in one of them."

They didn't have long to wait. The *houngan* finished creating the *veve* on the bare concrete floor and disappeared into one of the *caille mysteres* behind the dancing pole. After a moment the lights dimmed even lower and the chamber took on a murky, almost underwater-like darkness. Sara became abruptly aware of the concrete and steel smell of the place, underlain with an unpleasant musk of sweat and spoiled food. It was unpleasant, but so then was the *hounfort*'s overall environment.

The drummers came out of the *caille mysteres* when Sara wasn't watching. One moment the chamber was empty, the next it was reverberating like a concrete and steel amphitheater to the pounding of the *voudon* drums. The *houngan* led a line of dancers out of one of the sanctuaries and they began to make their way around the *poteau-mitan*, much like the dancers that Sara had seen at the ceremony in the Cypress Hills National Cemetery.

The drumbeats echoed in Sara's ears. There was, she realized, a qualitative difference between this ceremony and the previous one she'd witnessed. Everything associated with this ceremony was unpleasant. The surroundings were depressingly trashy. They smelled bad and looked even worse. Even the drumming, which had been thrilling and invigorating at the outdoor ceremony, was reverberating painfully in her skull. The voices complained of it to themselves. All and all it was a disagreeable experience promising even more disagreeable results. She could well imagine that evil would result from what was happening here tonight. She felt the Witchblade tingle at the edge of her consciousness.

The *bokor* leading the dance suddenly jerked about, flailing his arms oddly. It was clear that he had been mounted by a *loa*. He disappeared into the *caille mysteres* and came out with the cane and hobbled walk of Papa Legba. He cried out in *langage* as the dancers continued to whirl around him. There was no immediate response, but the drumbeats became so loud, so wildly arrhythmic that Sara's head began to ache.

The pounding force of the drums drove her to her knees. She wasn't the only one so affected. All around the room people were going down, a total of half a dozen or more. Some were rolling on the floor and moaning as if in the grip of brain seizures. The affect on her was less dramatic, just a weakening of her knees and a sudden inability of her legs to support her weight. When she went down, Alek bent over her, a concerned look on his face.

"Sara, you okay?"

She found that she couldn't speak, but she nodded and leaned on the arm he offered. She used it to pull herself up to her feet. When she looked back toward the *poteau-mitan* she saw Baron Samedi standing before it.

He was an awesome figure in top hat and coat, bigger than Alek, bigger than anyone present. He had a gigantic cigar in his mouth and was wearing a pair of sunglasses which was missing one of the lenses. His exposed eye shone like the eye of one possessed, which, of course, he was.

"Rum!" he roared in the voice of an angry bull. "Rum and food!"

He was as imperious as a king. When one of the female initiates offered a full bottle of white clairin rum, a raw, powerful drink potent enough to intoxicate a god, he pulled the cork with his teeth, spat it out, and then downed half the liquor in a single gulp. Another initiate approached him with a bowl of chicken and rice. He shoveled the food into his mouth while juggling bowl and bottle both, alternately gulping down mouthfuls of food and rum. He finished both in seconds, and threw the containers down on the floor where they smashed into dozens of sharp shards. He strode through the dancers, rubbing his crotch suggestively as he passed attractive female initiates.

The chamber's atmosphere was charged with a sudden sexual heat that Sara realized was flowing directly from Samedi. She looked at Alek, fighting the desire to throw herself upon him and rip away his clothes. He looked at her uncertainly, seemingly not as susceptible to the psychic suggestions floating in the air as she was.

Baron Samedi roared out an order in *langage*. The words struck Sara's ears like bullets. She could almost understand them. She felt she would understand if the voices weren't badgering her, if Alek, standing so close, wasn't such a smouldering pillar of masculine sexuality.

Torn by conflicting sensations and needs, she clung to his arm like a drowning person would cling to a buoy. She couldn't conceive of what might have happened next if two teams of four *zobops* each hadn't brought two wooden crates out of the *caille mysteres,* creating a new focus of attention. They were rough-hewn, long and narrow, and Sara suddenly realized what kind of boxes they were.

They were coffins. The men carrying them, two in the front, two in the back, set them down carefully against the circular cement altar around the *poteau-mitan* so that they leaned nearly upright. They were uncovered. Sara could see that they contained the bodies of Roger and Jerry Stern.

The Sterns looked no worse than if they'd been sleeping. Their faces were relaxed, their arms hung naturally and loosely at their sides. They didn't look at all like day-old corpses—at least, no more than the Sterns did when they were alive.

At her side, Sara heard a painful intake of,breath as Alek recognized them. He made half a move toward them, checking it when he realized that Sara still leaned against him with most of her weight. She straightened, feeling strength returning to her legs, but was loath to release Alek. There was nothing, she thought, that he could accomplish by going to the Sterns' side.

Kris Gervelis moaned as he, too, realized who lay in the coffins. Probably until that very instant he'd believed that the boys were okay, that, sure, they may have gotten themselves into a bit of difficulty like they so often did, but it was nothing that he or Alek couldn't fix. It was nothing irreparable . . . except, this time it was.

Baron Samedi strode up to the coffins. A collective gasp went through the onlookers as he planted himself before the Sterns, and began to speak again in *langage*.

"We must stop him," Paul Narcisse said in a low, urgent voice. "It's the ceremony for zombification. We must stop him before it goes too far."

But Paul Narcisse's warning came too late.

Baron Samedi shot his hands out. He placed one large palm over the heart of each corpse, and the *loa* cried out an impassioned order in *langage* that Sara felt she understood all too well. He was commanding them to rise, to open their eyes and walk from their coffins, and as they all watched, too frozen by horror to move, the brothers' eyes popped open.

Alek moaned at Sara's side. Even from where they stood they could see the awful emptiness in the twins' eyes, the utter lack of intelligence and will. But that didn't stop the walking corpses from stepping from their coffins.

Alek turned his head away from the awful sight. Sara

gripped the sleeves of his cloak, holding him now as he'd just held her. Only the strength she willed him from the sheer force of her personality kept him on his feet.

Then Kris, standing between them and the two priests screamed like a dying animal and all hell broke loose in the *hounfort*.

Ignoring Paul Narcisse's earlier advice, he thumbed his Jackhammer, which Alek had passed to him in the cloakroom, to full automatic and emptied the ammunition cassette into the ceiling.

His memory of the article in *Soldier of Fortune* had been accurate. It took two and a third seconds.

It made a sound like a series of nearly simultaneous bomb blasts, partially overlapping, each blending into a roar that seemed to last for a hell of a lot longer than two and a third seconds. The stench of gunpowder smothered the air. Screams of sudden panic came from the initiates both watching and participating in the ceremony as fragments of the ceiling rained down like cement hail, knocking some initiates off their feet while dust swirls kicked up by the blasts blinded others.

You couldn't have a more thorough panic, Sara thought, if God Himself had stepped out of the pages of the Old Testament and in a voice compounded of booming thunder and blazing lightning condemned everyone in the room to eternal damnation in the lowest, foulest pits of hell.

"I've got to reach them," Father Baltazar shouted, reaching into the pocket of the windbreaker that he still wore under his initiate's robes.

Baron Samedi whirled about to face the source of the confusion. His gaze met Sara's and for the first time a bolt of recognition ran through her. The body the *loa* inhabited was Guillaume Sam's. Of course. She should have recognized him earlier, but somehow he seemed larger, more regal, and even more powerful then Sam did in normal life.

The *loa* pointed a finger at them and purred in a low, laughing voice, "Kill them. Kill them all."

Roger and Jerry Stern—or rather, the soulless animated corpses that they had become—took slow, shuffling steps forward. They were an awful parody of humanity. Their faces were stiff, devoid of emotion, their eyes were blank, devoid of will. As they made their way through the panicked crowd, their movements became more fluid, surer, and stronger, though they never totally lost their inhuman stiffness.

Father Baltazar was the first to reach them—or, they him. His face was heavy with anguish, as was his voice.

"What have they done to you, my sons?" he asked, overcome by the emotion of the moment.

Of course, neither could reply either vocally or emotionally. Impassively, one of them reached out his arms—at this point, Sara still had no clue as to which Stern was which—and tried to grab Father Baltazar by the throat. The zombie's movements were still inhumanly slow and the priest dodged his clumsy embrace with ease.

But in that same instant the other zombie lifted his fist and swung it downward, stiff-armed. It was an awkward blow, but Father Baltazar didn't see it coming and it caught him right where his neck and shoulder met, driving him to his knees.

He grunted in pain. Paul Narcisse, lips moving in a silent prayer, drew an automatic from a shoulder holster and pumped three shots into the Stern who towered over Father Baltazar, looking down at him, devoid of pity or any other human emotion.

The zombie didn't even grunt or stagger. The shots punched through him with no visible effect. He reached out again and this time the priest couldn't evade his grasp. The zombie fastened his hands around the Father Baltazar's throat and began to squeeze.

By this time several of the *zobops* who had kept, or regained, their heads, had drawn their own guns and began to return fire. Bullets zinged about the warehouse like angry bees. Baron Samedi put his hands on his hips and laughed insanely.

"Find cover!" Sara shouted, and then ignored her own order.

She could see that Father Baltazar was really in trouble. The priest had dropped the little golden box he'd taken out of his windbreaker and gripped the zombie's thin arms with his own powerful hands, but wasn't able to break the creature's stranglehold. His face was turning red, his eyes were starting to bulge from their sockets.

Sara ran to his side and hurled herself against the other zombie who was also maneuvering to get his hands around the priest's throat. In an awful flash of memory, the movements of the dead Sterns reminded her of the time they'd both slipped their arms around her waist in Club Carrefour. This time, however, their faces weren't plastered with goofy smiles and their intentions were much more deadly.

She struck the Stern in his side with her shoulder at full running speed. It was like ramming a sack of cement, but the zombie couldn't absorb all her inertia and he crashed down on the concrete floor, still reaching out with his hands and opening and clenching them in strangling gestures. His legs also moved aimlessly as if he were still upright and walking.

The creatures, Sara realized, were apparently as slow of mind as they were of body. She leapt to her feet and turned to the one who was slowly strangling the priest. Father Baltazar had given up his futile efforts to break the zombie's hold and was scrabbling around on the floor trying to pick up the small golden box that he'd dropped. He couldn't see where it was, so he wasn't even coming close to retrieving it.

Sara bent down swiftly and picked it up. It took a moment for the word to come out of the mist of her almost-forgotten Sunday School education, but finally she recognized that it was a pix, the small container in which sanctified communion wafers were kept.

She quickly opened it and saw that it contained a small stack of the white circular wafers. She remembered when receiving communion as a child she'd take them on her tongue and they'd stick to the top of her mouth and tastelessly melt away.

What the hell? she thought. She looked at them blankly for a moment, then figured, *Well, Father Baltazar must know what he's doing. Obviously, he'd brought them along for one reason.*

She took a wafer from the container. The voices scolded her and for a moment she felt guilty as the realization hit that perhaps she shouldn't be handling a sanctified object with her unblessed hands.

No time to worry about finer theological points, she told herself, and stuffed the communion wafer in the zombie's mouth.

It was easier than she'd thought it would be. The thing

could only focus on one problem at a time, and strangling Father Baltazar occupied what little was left of his mind. He was also slack-jawed, with his mouth hanging open idiotically, so Sara was able to pop the wafer right in.

Automatically, his mouth closed on the morsel of food and he chewed like a cow working on its cud. He swallowed and, as if he were a living thing hit in the forehead with a killing hammer blow, immediately went down.

Father Baltazar tore free from the zombie's suddenly loose fingers. The creature's knees lost all strength and he slipped bonelessly to the floor. His expression relaxed as he fell and for that fraction of a moment Sara saw the man that the zombie had once been on his suddenly tired-looking features. And then his eyes closed and he was lying in a sad, dead heap, his arms still outstretched, almost beseechingly.

Father Baltazar choked, his hands gently probing his own nearly crushed throat. He tried to talk, but couldn't. Instead he pointed at the other zombie who had just clumsily regained his feet, and was coming towards them menacingly, not cognizant of his brother's fate.

Still on his knees the priest pointed, waving his hands. Sara understood what he meant. She took another wafer from the pix, and, ducking under the zombie's reaching hands, deftly placed the wafer in the zombie's mouth.

The result was the same. The zombie automatically ingested the morsel and reacted as quickly and as thoroughly as his brother had. He collapsed upon his brother's corpse, embracing him with his open arms.

Perhaps fitting, Sara thought, *but a terribly sad sight.*

She turned to Father Baltazar, helping him up to his feet. "How did you know the communion host would kill them—or whatever it did to them?" she asked.

The priest shook his head.

"It wasn't the host, " he said. "Probably not, anyway. Salt breaks the bond between the zombie's body and whatever is left of their soul still animating it. I figured it wouldn't hurt to use something blessed to bring the salt into the zombie's system, so I salted down a stack of communion wafers. But maybe now isn't the best time to speak of this."

The priest was right. Although only seconds had elapsed, the firefight had grown exponentially in volume. Alek, Kris, and Paul Narcisse were all pinned down behind metal beams and structural supports, along with forty or fifty unarmed cultists who were cowering and screaming. Sara's faction had the superior firepower with the Gervelis brothers' Jackhammers blasting away at the more than a dozen armed Specials who were returning fire with handguns.

Sara and Father Baltazar were trapped in the open, halfway between the area where Alek and the others were making their stand, and the Specials, who were firing from cover behind similar girders on the other side of the *poteau-mitan.* Baron Samedi, who had been standing right at the center pole, observing the developing firefight with more than slight good humor, was now casually strolling back to the *caille mysteres*, ignoring the bullets whizzing by him as if they were so many stingless bees.

"We've got to stop him," Father Baltazar, crouching now next to Sara said. "God knows what he's up to."

"Right." She turned to look back over her shoulder. "Suppressive fire," she called to the Gervelises, hoping that they at least had an inkling of what she meant.

One of them came through. She suspected that it was

Kris, whose *Soldier of Fortune* addiction had apparently not been a complete waste of time. After he'd emptied his first ammunition cassette on full automatic, he'd switched back to the more manageable single-fire option, the efficacy of which was pointed out by several Specials lying in pools of blood behind their inadequate cover.

Now Kris switched to full auto again and laid down a suppressive arc of fire, aimed, Sara hoped, above their heads. She scurried after Baron Samedi, who had already disappeared in the warren of small rooms that was the sanctuary.

Sara serpentined over the open ground. It took Father Baltazar a moment or two to realize what was happening, and then he took out after her. Paul Narcisse was at their heels as Alek joined the barrage with his Jackhammer, wisely taking the single shot option.

The reverberations from Kris's first ammunition cassette hadn't yet died as Sara reached the sanctuary, running through little or no return fire. The gangbangers kept their heads down as Kris's barrage echoed throughout the warehouse. She did have to pass one support that covered a crouching Special. He reached out to try to stop her, but without breaking stride she slapped him against the side of the head with her automatic, and he went down in a heap.

The voices laughed, calling for his head.

"Finish him–"

"–send his damned soul to hell–"

"–where it belongs."

She ignored their bloodthirsty urgings, concentrating on reaching the *caille mysteres* right before her. The chambers were poorly lit and small, although not without cover that could conceal, well, just about any crazy thing, from armed Special to undead zombie to angry *loa.*

She flung herself into the small room. An altar was set across the back wall, and crouching under the altar was someone or something.

"Get up!" Sara ordered. "Let me see your hands!"

A frightened squeal came from under the altar, and one of the female dancers scuttled out into the open, her hands up and empty, her expression terrified, as Sara threw down on her. The cultist ran out into the open area, evidently figuring her chances would be better out there, and almost bumped into Father Baltazar as he blundered into the small room and threw himself against the wall, panting with exertion.

"Find Samedi," he said when he could get his breath. "Try to get him out of Sam's body."

"How do I do that?"

The priest shook his head. "Not sure," he said, still short of breath.

Great, Sara thought. *The expert doesn't know, but he expects me to figure it out.*

There was a doorless opening on the wall against which Sara leaned, leading into yet another sanctuary room that was darker than the one they were in. She took a deep breath and rolled into the next room, keeping low.

Another altar stood against the back wall of this cubicle, but with even less light Sara was less sure of what it contained. Stuff. Piles of stuff, with no time to examine any of it. No Baron Samedi, though. Apparently.

She pushed herself through to the next room, thinking that this was like hunting poisonous snakes in the dark. Only maybe a little more dangerous. But there was nothing to do but go on and trust to her skill, and, maybe, that the voices would warn her in time if she was going to run into anything terribly dangerous.

She went through several of the rooms, flushing a couple of cultists who had no fight in them. She heard sounds coming from behind her, but when glancing back saw that Father Baltazar had been joined by Paul Narcisse. Both were following her as the firefight still raged.

She prayed that Alek and Kris were holding their own, that they wouldn't run out of ammunition, that their blood wouldn't be on her hands when this was all over. She prayed that they would find what they were looking for, that somehow she'd figure out how to chase Baron Samedi from the body of Guillaume Sam, that they'd find a way to end this all here and now without any more blood being shed.

Suddenly, her prayers were answered, though not all were granted.

She reached what seemed to be the last sanctuary room. Light shone through the open doorway in the back wall of this room, indicating that it was last in the warren of *caille mysteres*, and that it opened into the space of the warehouse's first floor.

She didn't need the voices to tell her that danger lay beyond that doorway, but they did so in no uncertain terms. She hesitated. Father Baltazar and Paul Narcisse joined her in the small chamber. She looked at them and realized that they knew the danger inherent in going through the doorway. But they couldn't stay in that empty little room forever. She gestured right, pointed to herself. Gestured left, pointed to them. They nodded, and Father Baltazar made the sign of the cross in the air before them all.

Before Sara could do anything he went through the door with a yell, unarmed, leaping to the left. She and Paul Narcisse followed, going right and left themselves, but a single shot cracked, catching the priest and slamming him against the outer wall of the sanctuary, blood suddenly running down his face.

Sara looked up to see Baron Samedi, laughing aloud, holding Guillaume Sam's pet possum in his arms, stroking it. Next to him stood Gene, smiling, pistol in his hands. Father Baltazar lay in a growing puddle of blood.

Baron Samedi calmly dropped the possum to the floor. It landed lightly, staring at them with its beady little eyes.

"Kill them!" Baron Samedi said, and the possum started toward them.

CHAPTER FOURTEEN

As the possum came toward them, it changed.

Sara had never thought it a particularly cute beast, but now it was downright ugly. It had always seemed more intelligent than it could possibly have been, but now its beady little eyes gleamed with a malicious understanding that seemed more than animal. As it scurried toward them the air shimmered around it, as if it was pushing through heat waves thrown off desert sands. And like a mirage viewed through distorting waves, the possum's outline rippled as it grew taller and bulkier, metamorphosing into something either a little more or a little less than human. Before Sara realized it, the Machete Murderer was shambling toward them, dragging his chains behind, armed with his favorite weapon and more than ready for action.

"Bakula-baka," Sara whispered.

"Damballah preserve us," Paul Narcisse prayed.

"Get Çaz out of here!" Sara screamed, and moved, waving her arms, trying to attract the thing's attention.

Of course, there was Gene as well as Baron Samedi himself to worry about, but right now they were beyond Sara's consideration. If she didn't figure out a way to neutralize the creature that called itself Bakula-baka, it would all be over, quickly and horribly. She remembered their meeting in Guinee with little fondness and even less hope.

Her half-conscious plan seemed to work. She attracted his attention and he went toward her, away from Paul Narcisse, who was running to the fallen priest. That was the good part. The bad part was that she had attracted his attention and he was coming toward *her*.

And it was clear that he recognized her.

"You escaped me in Guinee," Bakula-baka said, missing flesh slightly slurring his words. "Tonight you will not."

He waved his machete emphatically and grinned skeletally.

Sara knew she was no match for him physically, but she did outgun him. She fired, quickly and accurately, and hit him three times in the chest and abdomen.

To absolutely no effect.

The slugs penetrated Bakula-baka's massive frame, but didn't even slow his advance. He bore down on her with murderous glee, machete held high and ready for a decapitating blow. Her gun was useless against his supernatural defenses. She couldn't out fight him with her hands. She couldn't outrun him. She had no choice.

She surrendered to the voices. They'd been slavering in her brain like chained attack dogs demanding to be freed. So she let them go.

Bakula-baka was almost upon her as she calmly holstered her weapon and stood quietly facing him, her arms open as if to embrace him. Her unusual behavior penetrated even his rather thick skull and he stopped, staring suspiciously at the serene expression on the face of his intended victim.

Sara's mind exploded in a fireball of white heat, as it always did when she was enveloped in the Witchblade, and the cold metal appeared instantaneously upon her body, encasing her thighs, breasts, and abdomen in its chilly embrace. She shuddered at its touch, yet part of her welcomed it, like the caress of a lover whom she half-hated. Her mind danced in the incandescent blaze, her senses expanded to an inhuman degree. Every nerve, every fiber of her being felt more alive and vibrant than it did when she was outside the Witchblade's embrace. She felt invincible.

Bakula-baka was wary of the sudden change in her appearance. He advanced tentatively, impressed by the armor that Sara suddenly wore. But the Witchblade was more than mere armor.

Sara laughed aloud and pointed at him imperiously.

The Witchblade ran down her arm to her hand and to the tip of her extended finger, and it didn't stop there. It flung itself across the open space between Sara and the killer, extruding a razor-sharp tentacle.

The *loa* was astonished, but, reacting with more than human speed, brought up his machete with exquisite precision and parried the Witchblade's thrust before it could pierce his chest. The Witchblade's tentacle shrieked off the machete blade and the strangest battle in Sara's career began.

Sara had never before faced an opponent with such supernatural strength and skill. Bakula-baka looked big and clumsy, but in reality he was big and quick and handled his butcher's blade with all the finesse of a master fencer. She found herself in a back-and-forth struggle as she and her opponent circled each other like dancers in a graceful yet deadly minuet, thrusting and parrying, each probing for that crucial weakness, each looking for that moment when they could strike true and end the dance in a shower of blood.

Seconds ticked by. Despite the Witchblade's fury, Sara found herself having trouble focusing on her immediate problem: Bakula-baka. She had too many other things to worry about. She couldn't help but wonder how the Gervelis brothers were doing in the ongoing firefight, a situation so alien to them and so dangerous. Just on the edge of her peripheral vision she could see that Paul Narcisse had reached Father Baltazar. He had half-lifted the fallen priest in his arms and Baron Samedi was shouting to Gene, who was staring fixedly at the fencing match between her and the demonic *loa*, his gun ready, just waiting for the opportunity to revenge the death of his sister and his earlier wounding at Sara's hand.

She couldn't believe that Gene was still alive—*Damn!*

Bakula-baka had snuck in under her defense as she'd lost her focus. Not even the Witchblade could prevent him from landing a machete blow that slashed across her ribcage. The mystic armor pulled itself together in time to protect the area of her body where the blow landed, but it could only cushion. It couldn't soften the tremendous blow.

Sara grunted as the blade whipped across her, flinging her to the ground. Her head snapped down on the concrete floor with enormous force and a shower of bright lights exploded in her brain. She blacked out.

It must have only been for a moment because when she opened her eyes again Bakula-baka still hadn't reached her. She couldn't breathe. Her huffing lungs were struggling to draw in air.

And the Witchblade was gone.

It had vanished when she'd lost consciousness, leaving her virtually naked, protected only by her tattered clothes. Her breasts shuddered as she tried to focus her mind to draw a breath and call back the Witchblade.

She caught Gene's smile from the corner of her eye as he realized that he finally had a clear shot at her, and the hideous smile on Bakula-baka's half-face as he loomed over her, stinking of death and the grave. She desperately tried to summon the Witchblade in time to save her from the simultaneous attacks.

Gene's features suddenly blurred as if he were looking through radiating heat waves. When they settled again less than a second later he was still grinning widely, but his upper lip was missing its pencil-thin mustache.

Sara thought, *Jean?* and suddenly Baron Samedi roared in his great bull-like voice and Paul Narcisse fired two shots almost simultaneously.

The first hit Gene, or maybe it was now Jean, in the throat. A geyser of blood erupted from the wound, spraying in a fountain through the severed jugular. The second blew off the top of his, or her, skull, and Sara knew that he, or she, wouldn't recover from this wound.

A stricken, almost angry expression washed over Jean's face. It blurred again for an infinitesimal moment. By the time the body hit the floor it was wearing Gene's face once again, and both twins were finally, irrevocably, dead. At least, Sara hoped so.

Bakula-baka responded to the urgency in Baron Samedi's voice. He turned to see Paul Narcisse pointing his weapon at the *loa*'s mount. Sara still couldn't breathe and couldn't even draw in enough air to shout a warning as Paul Narcisse pulled the trigger and Guillaume Sam's body staggered at the impact of the slug tearing through it, just as Bakula-baka reached the *houngan*'s side.

Sara tried to scream but her lungs still weren't drawing enough air. Her voice could only croak so quietly that only she could hear the pitiful sound it made as Bakula-baka swung his machete and with one blow neatly took Paul Narcisse's head from his shoulders.

It flew away like an ugly, misshapen football. Sara felt almost as if she had been struck, not Narcisse. She watched in horror as Bakula-baka roared in glee and grabbed the headless body as it swayed drunkenly on its feet. The *loa* opened his mouth wide and clamped down upon the neck stump, making greedy sucking noises as it drained the spurting blood from Paul Narcisse's corpse.

Bakula-baka released the body, letting it fall over Father Baltazar, then whirled, turning his mad, staring eye on Sara. He started to lurch toward her as she still fought for her breath, fought to call the Witchblade back and direct it upon him, but Guillaume Sam shouted again, this time in his own voice. Samedi had apparently fled back to Guinee.

The *loa* answered Guillaume Sam's summons. He went swiftly to the *bokor*'s side and scooped him up in his powerful arms. Together they disappeared among the maze of the *caille mysteres*.

Sara suddenly realized she was breathing again, though the entire right side of her body felt as if it were on fire. She looked down and saw a great bruise already darkening her skin from her right breast down her ribcage and across her waist to almost the top of her thigh. In the center of the dark bruise was a dead white line an inch across, directly where the machete blade had struck her. Only the mystic armor of the Witchblade had kept her from being chopped through from chest to groin.

But that wasn't important, now.

She couldn't get up. She couldn't walk, but she dragged herself across the concrete floor to where Paul Narcisse's corpse lay over Father Baltazar. It took what seemed to be a long time. Right before she reached the pitiful bodies the gunfire from the other area of the floor ceased, and Sara knew she had to hurry. If the Gervelis brothers had been outgunned, if they were lying dead or wounded, her own life would be measured in minutes.

But first she had to see about Father Baltazar.

She pulled Paul Narcisse's headless and bloodless body off him, and laid it aside as reverently as she could, though she hadn't recovered enough strength to keep it from dropping the last foot or so to the hard concrete floor. Holding back tears, she turned the priest's face toward hers, so that she could see his features. She tore a scrap of cloth from the tatters of her shirt, not noticing that she nearly bared her chest, and wiped away the blood flowing down the side of his face.

Gingerly, she probed the wound on the side of his skull, feeling through his hair clogged with blood, and then had to fight back tears of relief. The bullet had only creased the side of his skull, tearing his scalp. Like most scalp wounds, this one was bleeding like a mother, making it seem much more serious than it actually was. She probed the area of the wound gently with her fingers, feeling around his skull. As near as she could tell, it wasn't broken. His wound wasn't fatal, or probably even particularly serious. She tore another strip of cloth from her tattered raiment and bound his head loosely to help ease the already slowing flow of blood.

Sara then realized that someone was calling her name. She recognized Alek's voice and shouted back.

"Here! We're here!"

It took the brothers a couple of moments to find her, but they finally tracked her by the sound of her voice. They burst through the warren of the *caille mysteres* disheveled and a little bloody. She was damn happy to see them.

She managed to get to her feet and started to hug a startled Alek Gervelis, but gasped in pain as they met in an embrace. *This time*, she thought, *something is broken.*

He looked down at her, still a little wild-eyed because of the adrenalin running through his system. He had shed the initiate's robe and his duster was tattered by bullets that had come uncomfortably close, but he seemed unwounded. Kris was bleeding from his right arm, but the wound was already bound and didn't seem to be troubling him half as much as the scene he now gazed upon.

"What happened here?" he asked in a small voice, his eyes wide at the sight of Gene's body, and Paul Narcisse's. "And—?"

He looked at Sara, who made no attempt to hide her near nakedness. Now wasn't the time for false modesty. She was too tired, too sore, too mentally exhausted. Wordlessly, Alek stripped off his duster and put it around her shoulders. She draped it around herself, grateful for his silent chivalry, grateful that his garment still retained his human warmth.

"What are we going to do?" Kris asked, as they heard approaching sirens in the distance. "What are we going to do?"

Sara shook her head. She had run out of ideas.

CHAPTER FIFTEEN

There was only one thing to do. Run.

It wasn't the first time since Sara had acquired the Witchblade that she'd found herself running from her fellow officers like a common criminal, but maybe it was the most painful time. She wasn't alone. She was with others who depended on her. Some of them needed medical attention, and she had no real idea of what to do besides bolt like rats from a burning building.

Fortunately they were able to exit the building before the police arrived in any appreciable numbers. Their presence at the *hounfort* was not something she wanted to explain to anyone in an official capacity. Not only would her career be over, she and her friends would be looking at serious jail time if their participation in the night's activities was ever discovered.

Although they all hated to do it, they had to abandon Paul Narcisse's body. There was simply no way they could take it with them and hope to avoid capture. It was difficult enough to drag Father Baltazar along, but fortunately he revived as they were making their way out of the building, and was soon able to walk under his own power.

He took one look at their faces as they stepped into the chill of the late September evening, and Sara knew that he didn't have to ask about Paul Narcisse. He knew his friend was dead. His expression hardened, as if he simply refused to let himself grieve at this time.

"Where are we headed?" he asked.

"I'm glad you're conscious, Caz," Sara said. "I want to go to your place—but not without your permission. We can't go to Paul's. The police will be there soon. And my apartment is too far to be our bolt-hole."

"That's a good idea," the priest said. "You can tell me what happened when we get to the rectory."

Sara nodded and they set off down the alley, one step ahead of the cops, who were still arriving by the car-full. Ironically, it was Sara herself who now slowed them the most. Her side ached at every step, as if a red-hot poker were lodged between her ribs. But she gritted her teeth and kept walking.

Alek Gervelis was a welcome presence beside her. She leaned into him and he helped her along as best as he could. He was smart enough to stay silent, secure enough to keep his thoughts, worries, and doubts to himself as they made their way across the borough back to Cypress Hills.

They kept to the dark as best they could, avoiding streetlights and crowds and all forms of public transportation. They couldn't afford to take a cab or bus or subway. Father Baltazar's clothes were soaked in blood from his creased scalp. Kris had an obvious gunshot wound. It was pretty clear that Sara had been in a serious fight. Anyone taking a long look at them would call the cops just on general principles. They looked like the aftermath of the climactic battle in a cheap gang movie.

It took longer, much longer than the trip out, but, bleeding and wounded, they finally got back to Cypress Hills and St. Casimir's, exhausted in body, mind, and soul. Father Baltazar's cozy study felt like a little bit of heaven as Sara flopped down into the comfortable old chair by the sofa.

The priest sighed. "Let me wash the blood off my face. Then I'll check everyone else. You can tell me what happened after I lost consciousness."

Father Baltazar saw to their wounds after he came back from the bathroom with a clean face and a gauze bandage wrapped around his head. Alek Gervelis was the only one to escape the raid on the *hounfort* essentially unscathed. Kris had taken several wounds, but they all were rather minor, the worst occurring when a bullet passed entirely though his upper right arm without hitting bone or anything vital.

Sara's injury appeared to be the most serious. She winced as the priest opened the duster and gently probed her ribcage.

"Follow me," he ordered, leading her to the bathroom. He detoured for a moment to his bedroom, coming out with a pair of sweatpants and an old shirt for her to wear, and then took her into his tiny bathroom to examine her more closely. She sucked in her breath as he ran his hands lightly up her ribcage. He nodded seriously.

"Looks like at least one rib's broken. I can tape them for now, but you'll have to see a real doctor soon to make sure nothing's floating around loose in there." He looked up at Sara. "In the meantime," he said quietly, "you can tell me what happened to Paul."

Sara did so, gasping a couple times as the priest put a little too much pressure on her ribcage. She finished the story just as the priest finished bandaging her.

"I'm so sorry about Paul," she said. "I feel so bad to have gotten him into this mess."

Father Baltazar shook his head. "Paul was involved in this long before you realized that it even existed." He sighed. "He loved the people of Cypress Hills. He'd give anything for their welfare–up to and including his life. But there's one thing he must not lose."

"What's that?" Sara asked.

"His soul," the priest said.

"His soul? But, surely, on his death–"

"It's not that simple for those who believe in *voudon*–certainly not that simple for initiates of the religion. Paul has already had his soul stripped from him. And, so to speak, put aside for safekeeping."

"Is that possible?" Sara asked incredulously.

"Certainly. At least Paul thought so," Father Baltazar said. "Voudonists call the soul the *gros-bon-ange*–the great good angel–and believe that with the proper ceremony it can literary be taken from the body and placed in a *pot-de-tete*, a small jar which is then kept for safekeeping on the *houngan*'s altar."

She remembered the confrontation Guillaume Sam had had with the cop searching his altar. But the whole idea still seemed crazy to her.

"Safekeeping from what?" Sara asked.

"From getting stolen and placed in a zombie's body, or an animal's body. From being trapped after the death of the body and not allowed an existence in the afterlife. Which is exactly what I'm afraid Guillaume Sam will try to do with Paul's soul."

"How–" Sara started, then stopped. She realized that she had no business questioning someone's supernatural beliefs, considering her experience with the Witchblade. "What do we have to do?" she asked simply.

"One of us has to go to the altar in Paul's office and retrieve his *pot-de-tete*," Father Baltazar said.

"I'll do it." Sara said.

Father Baltazar looked at her gratefully. "You'd be the best choice–but even so, you're hurt. Tired."

"I've been hurt worse in my life, and been more tired," Sara said, though truthfully she wasn't sure of the latter. "If you think the fate of Paul's immortal soul rests on whoever has control of this pot, we can't let it fall into Guillaume Sam's hands."

"You're right," Father Baltazar said. He took a ring of keys out of his pocket and extracted one, handing it to Sara. "This is to the back door of the bookstore. The *pot-de-tete* is on his altar. You can't miss it. It's a round earthenware jug about six inches high stoppered with a cork. Plain brown color, but with a rainbow painted in a horizontal arc on the front–or back, if he turned it around the last time he dusted."

Sara could hear the sudden catch in Father Baltazar's voice and for a moment she thought he was going to cry. She took him in his arms and held him as hard as she could with her sore ribs. He responded, hugging her tight enough to cause her to gasp.

"Sorry," he said.

"Nothing to be sorry about, Caz," she said. "I wouldn't be anywhere near stopping Guillaume Sam without you and Paul. Now it's just you, but we'll get him yet. We'll take him down together, no matter what it takes. For Paul. For all the helpless people of Cypress Hills whom he's preyed upon for years. We'll get the bastard. Don't worry."

The priest released her and stepped back, smiling.

"Go with God, Sara," he said.

Though unhappy about going out dressed like a refugee from a gym class, Sara knew she didn't have much of a choice in the matter. She couldn't waste time going back to her apartment to change clothes, and at this time of night, or morning, no stores were open.

She went back into the study and holstered her piece in the snug of her back. Kris was off making coffee in the kitchen. Alek watched her worriedly.

"What are you up to?" he asked.

"Just a little errand to run," Sara answered as lightly as possible.

"I'll go with you," he offered.

Sara shook her head. "No need."

"Still–"

"No need," she said again, with a little more emphasis.

They looked at each other silently for a moment.

"All right," Alek finally said.

She nodded, went to go by him. He touched her arm lightly and she stopped and looked into his eyes. He bent his head down and, mindful of her injuries, took her gently in his arms and kissed her softly and lingeringly.

"For luck," he said.

She smiled back at him and walked out of his arms.

"Come back to me in one piece," he called after her.

"I'll do my best," Sara said.

* * *

The Serpent and the Rainbow was shuttered and dark. Looking in, Sara thought it seemed a sad place. She wondered what would happen to all the books without Paul Narcisse to shepherd them. She hoped they wouldn't end up in some big garage sale priced at a quarter each. She hoped they'd all find a home someplace with someone who would love and cherish them as much as Paul Narcisse had.

She went past the store on the dark and empty street, into the nearest alley and headed for the rear entrance. She took the key that Father Baltazar had given her and silently unlocked the door and silently went into the building. The rear door opened into the receiving room where Paul Narcisse had unpacked his book shipments. She went into the corridor beyond, past the restroom, and finally to the office with the old, comfortable furniture that she remembered from her first visit.

She flicked on the lights as she entered the room, heading toward the altar. There was a slight creaking sound behind her and the voices in her head screamed a sudden warning. She whirled, drawing her weapon in the same motion, and found herself staring at Lt. Carl Dickey, who sat in the comfortable old chair behind Paul Narcisse's desk.

"You're pretty fast with that, aren't you?" he observed mildly.

"You're an eighth of an inch from dead," Sara said, "which is exactly how far I have to move my finger to pull the trigger. Let me see your hands."

Wordlessly, the lieutenant took his hands from his lap and placed them, palms down, on the desk. They were empty.

"What are you doing here?" Sara asked.

"Same as you, I imagine. Looking for the *pot-de-tete* with Narcisse's soul. Only, I don't have a single damn idea what it looks like and there's only about two and a half dozen jars on that damn altar to choose from."

"*Pot-de-tete*?" Sara asked. "How do you know about that?"

They stared at each other wordlessly for a long second, and then Sara nodded her head.

"Of course," she said. "When you've been at this job long enough, you're not surprised at anything."

"That's right," Detective Dickey said.

"How long have you been Guillaume Sam's man?" she asked.

The detective sighed from the depths of his soul. "Long as I've known what he's been doing in Cypress Hills."

"Why?" Sara asked with gritted teeth. She hated criminals who preyed on the helpless, but most of all she hated those who took their salary, hid behind their badge, and *helped* criminals feast on the helpless.

Lt. Dickey shrugged. "I wanted to go on living."

"You're saying he threatened you?" Sara asked.

"'Course he did. Just like he threatened you." Lt. Dickey looked at her with pursed lips, considering her as if she were some kind of odd bug he'd just discovered. "But *you*. There's something strange about you, girl. People around you turn up dead. Or worse."

"You've got something to say about me," she said, "say it."

Lt. Dickey shook his head. "Nope. Got nothing to say. I can keep my mouth shut. That doesn't mean others aren't talking. You got something strange going on. That partner of yours, and your Captain, they can't cover for you forever."

"Is that a threat?"

"Lord, no." Lt. Dickey frowned. "I already got one son of a bitch oddball on my ass. I don't need another."

"I see," Sara said, suddenly understanding the gist of their conversation. "And you don't know which oddball is going to win this particular confrontation, me or Guillaume Sam?"

"I never bet against Guillaume Sam," the policeman said, "but, like I said, people around you seem to end up dead. Or worse. He ends up dead or worse . . ." Lt. Dickey shrugged. "No meat off my bones."

"And I end up dead? Or worse?"

"I'll be sorry. Real sorry. But I'll still be here."

"Uh-huh. I suppose you were the one who warned Guillaume Sam about the raid of Club Carrefour," Sara said.

Dickey heaved one of his patented sighs. "I suppose I was," he said.

Sara shook her head and went up to the altar, keeping her gun out and an eye on Dickey at all times. She scanned the neatly cluttered tribute to Paul Narcisse's protector, Damballah, and wondered with a pang, *Who will lovingly take care of the altar with Paul gone? No one*, she thought sadly. *It'll all just go to the dustbin.*

She spied the *pot-de-tete*. Much like Paul Narcisse himself, it didn't occupy a place in the spotlight. It was tucked behind a pair of votive candles in glass containers dedicated to Aida-Wedo, Damballah's wife, the rainbow. She took the pot and turned back to Lt. Dickey.

"Here it is," she said. "You want it?" It wasn't an offer. It was a challenge.

Lt. Dickey shook his head. "You can have it."

"You're letting your boss down."

"Guillaume Sam may have a mortgage on my soul," the policeman said, "but he don't own it outright."

Sara sidled toward the door, gun in one hand, *pot-de-tete* in the other. She stopped in the doorway and looked at the cop, who had swiveled in Paul Narcisse's old chair to keep his eyes directly on hers.

"We'll talk again," Sara told him.

Lt. Dickey nodded. "I'm sure we will. Maybe on this earth, maybe in hell." He sighed again, sincerely enough that Sara believed in the sadness that seemed to course through his system. "You probably won't believe this. But good luck."

She turned the light off and left him sitting there in the dark, in a dead man's chair.

That night Sara found herself in the priest's bed.

She had brought the *pot-de-tete* to the rectory. After thinking it over she'd decided to keep quiet about Lt. Dickey's secret allegiance to Guillaume Sam, at least for the present. She recognized that she'd made the decision partly because of her secretive nature, which had become all the more secretive during her association with the Witchblade, but also because for now it would do no good to share such a confidence. Certainly things could change, and if she'd have to rat him out for the safety of her fellow conspirators she would. But for now, she'd hold it among the other secrets she was forced to live with on a daily basis.

Sara, Father Baltazar, and the Gervelis brothers held a brief strategy session despite the weariness that hung over them like an impenetrable fog. But the only strategy they could come up with was to have a good night's sleep and see what the next day would bring. Their battle against Guillaume Sam was like a heavyweight fight reaching its final rounds. They'd spent most of the first rounds slugging it out toe to toe and both sides had suffered grievous losses. Neither side could allow the struggle to go on much longer. Both had to go for the decisive knockout, and deliver it soon.

They decided that it'd be best if they stayed together, not even separating for the night. Safety lay in numbers, and they weren't going to make the mistake common in bad horror movies of splitting up to search the house. Sara, despite her protests, got Father Baltazar's bedroom, while the priest took the sofa in his study, and the brothers lay down on cushions on the floor in the adjoining living room.

Father Baltazar's bedroom, located at the rear of the house, was as quaint and cozy as his study. Other words to describe it, Sara thought, would be small and cramped. There was a single bed with an old handmade quilt, a nightstand, an ancient trunk at the foot of the bed, and more bookshelves crammed with more books, prints, icons, and other small *chackas*.

She would have stripped down to her underwear and tumbled into bed, but she had no underwear left. She unbuttoned Father Baltazar's shirt and draped it over the trunk at the foot of the bed, unbuckled her holster and set it on the night stand that held a small lamp and the earthenware pot that, according to Father Baltazar, held Paul Narcisse's soul. She unknotted the drawstring of the priest's sweat pants and let them fall in a pile about her feet, then slipped into bed and pulled the sheet and quilt over her.

She had never been so tired in her life, yet also never

so far from sleep. Her mind was awhirl with the day's happenings, and speculation as to what the next day would bring. They were headed, she knew, toward a final confrontation with Guillaume Sam, and they'd lost the one who knew best how to fight him. Without Paul Narcisse they were going into battle blind. No one else in the community could replace him. There were lower-ranking *houngans*, but Father Baltazar was reluctant to bring them into the conflict, reluctant to risk more lives in what might be turning out to be a hopeless cause. Still—tomorrow he might have to face that reluctance, and overcome it, just as Sara might have to overcome her reluctance to bring Jake into the fray, if they wanted to have the barest hope of winning.

She was grateful to hear a low tapping on her door, grateful for anything to take her mind off the roller-coaster of fear and anticipation that was making it impossible for her to sleep.

"Come in," she said in a low voice at the tentative sound at her door, and it opened a crack. A tall, broad shouldered form slipped into the room. She recognized the dark silhouette immediately.

"Alek."

"Sara."

He stood by the side of the bed, hesitant. "Sorry if I woke you up," he said.

"You didn't. I couldn't sleep."

"I couldn't either. Mind if I come in?"

"If I did, I wouldn't have said come in, would I?"

Alek laughed lowly. "I guess not."

He only had to take a couple of steps to reach the edge of the bed. Sara sat up against the pillows, holding the sheet up to her chest. She looked at the arm holding the sheet. She was almost surprised to see that it was flesh, not covered by the metallic sheath of the Witchblade. The voices were suspiciously silent in her mind. Almost distractedly, she wondered what they were planning.

"I just felt that I had to see you. Alone. To talk to you. To–"

Sara lifted the edge of the quilt, and Alek quickly slid into the bed next to her. It was a small bed. Just lying there, they were actually embracing, her arm under his neck, their legs pressed together from thigh to calf.

"I had to tell you," Alek said, "that these have been the most amazing days of my life. They've been awful, yet somehow exhilarating. You know the music we've been doing. Gothic. Dark. All that stuff." He shook his head. "Christ. What did I know about darkness, until this? What did I know about cold, soulless evil? Or pure valor?"

He reached out and touched her cheek gently. "This is just some crazy down-the-rabbit-hole adventure I've wandered into. But you–this is your life! How do you do it, day after day? How to find the courage to face this evil, nasty shit like Guillaume Sam and his creatures?"

Sara shook her head. "I don't know," she said simply. "I don't think about it. If I did, I suppose I couldn't do it."

"Yeah," Alek said, "but how do you keep from thinking about it? I mean, I know we have to face Guillaume Sam again. We're all hanging on a highwire suspended over a bottomless pit leading down to hell. And one of us–either Guillaume Sam's group or our group–is going to fall down into it and never come out. Probably tomorrow. How do you keep from thinking about it?"

"Here's one way," she said.

She leaned over him, her hair fluttering down upon his face like the wings of a dove, and kissed him.

It was a kiss that fulfilled the promises of their earlier embraces. It lasted a long time and, soft and sweet at first, grew harder and more insistent. She felt his hands discover that she was naked. Gentle as his touch was, she flinched when his hands brushed her taped ribcage.

"Sorry," he said into her mouth and, in concert, they maneuvered so that no weight or pressure would be brought upon her injured side.

Either the voices left her or she forget they were there. Afterwards, looking back at it, she couldn't tell which was true. All that she knew was herself and Alek Gervelis, holding back the fear, holding back the promise of the future, losing themselves and finding themselves in each other.

It was the sweetest, most human experience she'd ever had.

When it was over he fell asleep in her arms. He was too serious to smile, but she was happy enough to see his simple contentment. She held him close for his warmth, for the beating of his heart, for the blood coursing through his veins, and the sheer human electricity running on the network of his nervous system.

He slept, but she didn't.

She still couldn't, because she knew that she couldn't subject him or his brother or Father Baltazar to any more of what they'd experienced this day. They were not meant for it. They were not meant to face evil, whether coming from the barrel of a gun or the whisper of a *bokor*'s curse.

She was. It was her job. She carried the Witchblade, but, more importantly, she carried a badge.

She would see this thing ended. One way or another. Alone.

CHAPTER SIXTEEN

In a sense, Sara thought, it had all begun here. And perhaps it can end here as well.

Guinee was as peaceful and tranquil as ever. The weather was perfect, the scenery breathtaking. It seemed, Sara thought, like a great place to retire to, but she figured that at this rate it was unlikely she'd be around long enough to get a pension check. A nice headstone was probably the best that she could hope for.

She was at the crossroads. She sat down and waited, enjoying the feeling of the warm night breeze scented with tropical aromas playing over her nakedness, as the old man hobbled up the road toward her.

He shook his head and whistled at the sight of her.

"You are a vision," Papa Legba said as he reached her side. "It's a good thing you've called the old man to you, not one of the younger spirits."

Sara smiled. "Would they help me like you, Papa?"

"Maybe," Papa Legba said, leaning on his crutch. "Maybe for your smile, maybe for your favors, depending on who you called."

"Why have you helped me, Papa?"

"Maybe for your smile," the old man said, his face wrinkling into a hundred creases as he smiled himself. "Maybe because you're polite and need my help. Maybe because you seek my help only to help others. Maybe because a favorite son asked me to."

"Paul Narcisse?"

"Aye," the old man said, nodding. "He was a good boy. Respectful to his elders. Always ready with a proper sacrifice. Even sacrificed himself in the end."

"I know," Sara said, tears wetting her cheeks.

"Don't cry, child," Papa Legba said gently. "This is Guinee, land of the *loa*. All things are possible here. Speak from your heart, girl. What do you need?"

Sara looked down at her nakedness. "Well, I'd hate to go where I have to go tonight like this. I could probably use some clothes."

"Probably," Papa Legba said, and she was suddenly wearing a typical outfit of boots, jeans, and a pullover loose enough to move comfortably in, tight enough to show her lithe curves. "Just where do you have to go tonight, child?"

"You know." Sara gestured up the road to where the dark and forbidding cemetery lay. "I want to finish this. I want to finish it tonight, here, where no one else can get hurt."

Papa Legba nodded. "That would be good."

"I just want to know that I have a chance," Sara told him, suddenly desperate. "I just want to know that I'm not going to throw my life away and that my friends will continue to suffer at the hands of Guillaume Sam."

Papa Legba laughed. "Would it comfort you to know that Guillaume Sam is asking the very same thing of his benefactor, right now?"

Sara was surprised. "He is?"

"Would it comfort you further to know that you don't have to go on this journey alone?" he asked.

"Yes," she said.

A small head popped up from the *macoute*, the straw tote bag slung over Papa Legba's shoulder. It was covered with white fur and, like Papa Legba, had eyes the color of blood. It climbed out of the sack, and sat on the *loa*'s thin, frail shoulder.

"Sandro!" Sara exclaimed.

The spirit guide *meow*ed a faintly distant greeting. He was kitten-sized, perhaps in concession to his patron's apparent frailness, but with the same intelligence, the same fierceness underneath his placid surface that Sara remembered from their past encounter.

"Can he go with me?" she asked Legba eagerly.

But the old spirit shook his head.

"We cannot take sides in the battle between right and left. We partake of both, though my sympathies most often lie with the good and respectful. Besides," he grinned, "I'm not sure Sandro trusts you—or rather, that which rides you like a *loa* rides his mount. But do not worry. I am the opener of the door, the guardian of the gates. I allow the spirits to descend. Or, sometimes, ascend. Look, child, at who comes down the road."

Sara followed his steadily pointing finger to see someone trudging up the road the way Papa Legba himself had come. It took Sara a moment to realize that it was Paul Narcisse, whole and alive. Apparently. He seemed as serious as ever, and was dressed as neatly, as conservatively, as ever.

"Paul . . ."

Sara went to embrace him, but stopped before they

touched. Viewed from close up, he was ethereal. The moonlight shone through his eyes, making them dark pits in his skull. His legs faded into uneven nothingness at his ankles. This wasn't Paul Narcisse after all, Sara realized, but just part of him. His *gros-bon-ange*.

"Are you all right?" she asked. "I mean—"

"I'm fine," he said. "Thanks to you my *gros-bon-ange* was saved from Guillaume Sam. It rests safely in the *pot-de-tete* by your sleeping form as our spirits walk and talk in Guinee."

"You're the one who asked Papa Legba to watch over me?"

"It was the least I could do for someone willing to risk her life, her immortal soul, for my people."

"What do we do now?" Sara asked.

"Your instincts were good," Paul Narcisse told her. "The final confrontation could be fought on Earth, where many might die, or here in Guinee where it will be limited to those occupying this plane."

"But," Sara said, "in Guinee I lack my most potent weapon."

Narcisse shook his head.

"You only think you do," he told her. "Father Baltazar told me of your . . . situation. You have allowed this thing which mounts you to take possession of your body on its terms, when it wants to, so that it can further its own agenda. But you are stronger than that. You can bend it to your will. You have to stop being in awe of it. And being afraid of it. It needs you as you sometimes need it. You will never be able to control it entirely, but you can partner with it on your terms."

"How?"

"By being yourself, Sara," Paul Narcisse said gently. "It

chose you. It doesn't want you to know that it needs you more than you need it. Before it came along you were doing just fine. Before you came along it was in limbo, looking for someone like you.

"You're a rare person," Paul Narcisse told her. "You're a born warrior, full of strength and pride. But, rarer yet, you are a warrior with compassion. You don't fight for glory. You don't fight for financial reward. You fight to protect the weak and innocent." He smiled. "You're a rare commodity, Sara Pezzini, and the Witchblade knows that."

"But it can't even come into Guinee," Sara told him. "Every time I've come here it's been silent."

"That's because subconsciously you haven't allowed it to accompany you. You've been seeking a sanctuary from it, and you've found one in Guinee. But Guinee isn't preventing it from following you here. You are. Open your mind. Reach out for it. You will find it."

Sara found it hard to believe that she'd been exerting that much control over the Witchblade without realizing it, but there was no reason for Paul Narcisse to lie to her. He was the expert on such matters, she—despite the fact that she hosted the Witchblade—the novice.

She closed her eyes and concentrated. The silence around her was as perfect and as deep as the night. She reached out, questing with her mind, and after what might have been minutes or might have been hours, touched upon the familiar voices that were her omnipresent company. They were complaining grumpily to themselves.

"—left us again—"

"Where does she go—"

"–that we cannot accompany her–"

"What does she do–"

"–that we cannot see–"

"Miss me?" she asked, and caught the sudden tinge of startlement in their essences. "Then come and join me."

They did. Instantaneously. She was surprised to find them somewhat fearful of Guinee, as if it were a foreign land not suited to their taste. It was clear they didn't like this realm. Their uncertainty, oddly enough, made them seem more human, perhaps easier to deal with. She would certainly test Paul Narcisse's theories thoroughly before this sojourn in Guinee was over.

"You see?" he asked, as if he could read her mind.

Sara nodded. "Now for Guillaume Sam."

"You know where to find him?" Papa Legba asked.

Sara gestured down the road to the waiting cemetery. "Will he be there?"

"He will," Papa Legba said. "His presence is the third and final boon that I grant you. Of course, he will not be alone."

"Neither will Sara," Paul Narcisse said.

"Farewell, then," the *loa* said, "and good luck. Remember your old Papa from time to time."

Sara leaned over and hugged him. He felt as thin as the wind, but a strange electricity ran through his form and it seemed to impart some of itself to her. Suddenly she felt stronger than she had for weeks, mentally rested and ready for anything.

She looked at Sandro. He condescended to allow a swift pat on the head and scratch behind the ears. Sara smiled, feeling that perhaps they had at least gone some way toward making up.

"All right." She turned to the *gros-bon-ange* of Paul Narcisse, who stood wavering before her in the night wind like a mirage. "I hope you're not afraid of cemeteries," she said.

"A cemetery will hold my body," he said. "Nothing can hold my soul."

"I hope so," Sara said, and they started down the road together.

There being nothing more to say, they walked in silence, dead man and possessed cop, to the home of the Guede Family, of which Baron Samedi was the head.

Someone was waiting for them at the entrance to the graveyard. Paul Narcisse seemed to recognize him.

"Ah, Captain Zombi," he said. "How good of you to meet us."

For an evil spirit, Captain Zombi seemed a cheerful, even comical sort, with his trousers rolled up above his knees, a fat cigar in his mouth, and a half-drunk bottle of rum grasped by the neck in one hand.

"Not at all," he said sunnily. "We don't get such distinguished guests very often, and my lord, Baron Samedi, did not want you to lose your way among the tombs."

He gestured backward into the cemetery. Even with the full moon shining like a soft and gentle sun, it was a dark and disturbing place. Gravestones and monuments and crypts crowded closely together. Funeral statuary seemed to move like living things as clouds glided across the moon or the wind shifted the shadows of overhanging trees.

"This way, if you please."

The *loa* led them up a crooked pathway between the

graves. It was cold inside the cemetery. The night breeze was no longer warm, nor sweet. There was a chilly edge to it, and it smelled of wet earth and things that had lain in graves inside rotting wooden caskets for a long time. Darkness could be tasted on the air, and mysteries that Sara didn't want to know the solutions to.

They were waiting for her atop the hill that loomed in the center of the cemetery. Paul Narcisse named some of them for her. Just the important ones, for there were far too many for him to name in the time that they had.

There was the trinity of Baron Samedi, the head of the Guede family, in his top hat and sunglasses, alongside his brothers—or maybe other aspects of himself—Baron La Croix and Baron Cimetiere. There was Samedi's wife, Big Brigitte, goddess of black magic and ill-gotten gold, dressed in a flowing purple dress, and their three sons, General Jean-Baptiste Trace, General Fouille, and Ramasseur de Croix, Collector of Crosses.

Below them on the hillside were the lesser spirits, Guede Souffrant, Erzulie of the Black Heart, Marinette bwa Chech—Marinette of the Dry Arms—and Criminelle and the one-legged Ti Jean, and too many others to name or even remember.

Below them all, in a small open space in the graveyard at the foot of the hill was a man. He seemed almost small and insignificant among the gathering of *loa*, but Sara knew he was as powerful as many of them and more evil than most. It was Guillaume Sam. Chittering on his shoulder was the beast he called Baka, short for his real name of Bakula-baka.

Baron Samedi roared forth a welcome, and all the *loa* joined in with cheers and jeers and catcalls. The cemetery sounded like Pandemonium, the demon city of hell. Samedi threw his arms wide, and his sons called for quiet and the chaos melted into silence.

"No, my spirits," he said. "We should be kind to our guests. Never has Guinee seen such rare entertainment. A policewoman and a dead man on the right hand. A *bokor* and our own Bakula-baka on the left. Who will prevail?" Baron Samedi shook his head, chuckling with evil mirth.

"The Guede!" he shouted.

The assembled spirits took it up as a chant: "Guede! Guede! Guede!" until Sara could no longer hear the voices in her own head. She fell to her knees, covering her ears as the *loas'* voices speared into her brain. Paul Narcisse tried to help her rise. He shouted into her ears but she couldn't hear a word of what he was saying. He pointed and she looked and saw that Bakula-baka was charging at them.

"Tonight I drink your blood, *blanc*," the *loa* roared, machete held high, his horrible face rent by the thing he called a smile.

Guinee was the land of the spirits. Her body was back on the realm of earth, sleeping in the arms of Alek Gervelis, but somehow she knew that if her spirit were defeated here, she would never awake. Her flesh would turn cold and stiff and Alek would wake up with a corpse in his arms.

That horrible realization brought her to her feet to face the charging *loa*, made her reach deep into the abyss of her being and call forth that which she knew as the Witchblade, a thing of cold metal and razor edges, to armor her frail human flesh.

For a moment there was no answer to her summons,

no sudden, familiar embrace. But she did not panic. She called out again, imperious in her desire to protect those whom she loved, as well as the innocent and weak whom she didn't even know. To shield them from the rapacious maw of Guillaume Sam and his band of cutthroats and killers. And certainly love was stronger than mere greed, or how could the world survive at all?

The Witchblade came to her, arriving with Bakula-baka. Sara fell to the left, Paul Narcisse to the right, as the spirit, confused for a moment, deliberated over his target. He picked Sara and swung his machete in a great decapitating blow, but she had already moved and his thrust met no resistence whatsoever. His momentum yanked him forward and he fell, thudding face first into the rich Guinee soil.

Sara sprang upon his back with the lithe grace and ferocity of a jungle cat. She wrapped her arms around his neck and squeezed, as if trying to hug him to death.

Bakula-baka roared. Even from behind him she could smell the grave-stench on his breath. She could smell it emanating from his body in waves of gagging putrescence.

Can you kill that which has no life? Sara thought, then answered her own question. *I guess we'll find out.*

The spirit bucked and wrenched and Sara grimly held on. She wrapped her legs around his chest, gripping with her knees and heels. He shook like a mastiff trying to throw off a flea, yet Sara still grimly held on.

The Witchblade grew razor edges and quills and spikes that bit into Bakula-baka's flesh, but the flesh of a *loa* is not that of a human. It's stronger, harder, more resilient. But Sara gritted her teeth and pulled harder until the tendons and ligaments stood out like iron bars on her arms and neck, and she felt as if she herself were going to break.

Suddenly the *loa* had no more breath to waste bellowing in anger and growing fear. He flung himself backward to the graveyard earth and Sara felt the weight of a mountain slap down upon her. The weight of the *loa* was crushing her, the chains that dangled from his limbs dug into her flesh. At least her broken ribs didn't hurt. That would have given Bakula-baka an edge she probably couldn't have overcome. Still, she couldn't draw her breath, and for a moment was on the verge of passing out. Darkness clouded her vision and the stench of the Bakula-baka filled her mouth and nostrils.

NO! she screamed, or thought she did. Perhaps the sound came from the voices clamoring in her mind.

"NO!"

"NO!"

"NO!"

"NO!"

She didn't know how long she screamed, but suddenly she realized that the weight pressing her down into the earth was dead weight. Bakula-baka was no longer moving, no longer trying to dislodge her. She felt wetness upon her face and chest and she realized that it was the blood, or the life essence of the thing, running back down upon her.

She heaved with all her strength and rolled the gigantic body off of her. She kneeled in the dirt next to him as he lay unmoving. She panted like a dog, her body crying for oxygen, as she looked down at him. The razor edge of the Witchblade had nearly hewn through his bull-like neck. Bakula-baka's head was attached to his body by only a thread of dried flesh.

An awful scream made her look up from the body. Guillaume Sam, his face twisted into a demented mask, was running toward her like a maniac. Like Sara, he didn't seem to feel the sting of his earthly wounds, or perhaps Paul Narcisse's bullet hadn't done him any real damage. He bent over and scooped up the machete that Bakula-baka had dropped. Sara had only time to lift her arm up as he swung it at her, and the machete hit the Witchblade and shattered into dozens of dull iron shards.

Guillaume Sam looked at the broken blade, dumbfounded, and suddenly Paul Narcisse grabbed him by the shoulder and whirled him around. Narcisse grasped his cheeks and put his mouth on Sam's, tight and hard, and kissed him long and deep, but without passion or love.

It was a spirit duel of will power and mental strength as each strove to absorb the other's *gros-bon-ange*.

In the end, Guillaume Sam tried to pull away, but the spirit of Paul Narcisse was too strong. Guillaume Sam made an awful moaning sound and started to shrivel. First his legs and arms were sucked up into his body, then his abdomen and chest started to wither. Soon his entire body was just a flap of wrinkled skin hanging from his head, which still remained in Paul Narcisse's deadly grasp. Then that too began to shrivel like an apple in a hot oven and finally Paul Narcisse was kissing nothing. Guillaume Sam had vanished.

Paul Narcisse looked down at Sara and put out a hand to help her to her feet.

"What happened?" she asked.

He took a small earthenware jug out of the *macoute*

that he carried over his shoulder and showed it to Sara. "I was no longer using my *pot-de-tete*. I thought Guillaume Sam's *gros-bon-ange* might find it comfortable."

"That means–" She couldn't articulate the words.

Paul Narcisse nodded. "His soul has been captured. His body lies empty." He smiled at her. "Yet Guillaume Sam will waken this morning. And my body will rest easy, knowing I have a new and interesting home."

"But–"

"Hush," Paul Narcisse said gently. He wiped Bakula-baka's blood from Sara's cheek and neck. "We can talk about this later. Now we have to pay our respects to Baron Samedi, his family, and allies."

"Respects!"

"Certainly. They are most deserving of it. They are great and powerful *loa*. And if they live in the darkness, do they not therefore help to define the light?"

They approached their audience, which had been deadly silent during the latter stages of the duel. Paul Narcisse kneeled and put out his arms in supplication while Sara, still clad in the Witchblade, stood by his side.

"Great Baron Samedi," Paul Narcisse intoned, "Baron La Croix, Baron Cimetiere. Madame Brigitte, and other spirits high and low, accept our sacrifice to your greatness, and our thanks for our soujourn in Guinee."

"Hmmm," Baron Samedi harumphed. "A poor enough sacrifice, as it turns out. Do you know how long it will take to mend our brother, Bakula-baka?"

"At least you can fix him," Sara observed. "Unlike those humans he killed on Earth."

Baron Samedi laughed his earthshaking laughter. "Defiant to the last, eh, girl?" He shook his head and sighed.

"Well, it shows how little you know if you think that. Still, you'll find out soon enough."

Sara didn't like what Samedi implied, but decided it would be better if she didn't question him any more closely.

"And you," Baron Samedi asked. "Will you sacrifice to us as well?"

"If it'll keep you off my turf," Sara said.

Samedi laughed, and his brothers joined in. "Go, *blanc*," he said, waving his hands at her in a shooing gesture. "Go home. You are needed there, and here, after tonight, I think we all need a rest."

Paul Narcisse touched her shoulder and together they turned and walked out of the cemetery. The air, she noted, was again warm and sweet. She could hear night birds singing in the trees as they walked down toward the crossroads and the old man waiting for them there.

"It's funny," Sara said, "but Guillaume Sam told me once that Baron Samedi promised him he'd live for eternity."

"Oh, he will," Paul Narcisse said, shaking the *pot-de-tete*. "It just won't be a very exciting eternity."

Sara sighed.

"Unlike our next couple of days," Sara said. "How are we going to explain all this to my Captain? We need a fall guy to take the blame, or you'll have a much too exciting twenty-to-thirty in Attica."

"We have a fall guy. Two, in fact: Gene and Jean. Give the police their underground headquarters. We can put enough information there to pin dozens of killings on them–killings they did indeed commit. The green card scheme will come to an end. I'll see to that. The money laundering is more problematic, but we can always blame it on an amuck accountant. Guillaume Sam will gladly pay back taxes and restitution. Don't worry. It'll work out."

Sara sighed. She was paid to solve crimes, not cover them up. This was another fine mess the Witchblade had gotten her into. Or at least complicated, once she'd gotten herself into it.

"It is not our fault–"

"–we did nothing–"

"–no blame–"

Oh, shut up, Sara thought.

And they did.

EPILOGUE

It was an unusually warm and mild spring, flowers and birds arriving early and abundantly.

Sara had little time to visit Cypress Hills, but she went to St. Casimir's whenever she could. Father Baltazar was always glad to see her. The church was clean and neat, freshly sandblasted, and well lit by a new electrical system donated by Guillaume Sam. Carl Dickey had retired from the N.Y.P.D. He was running a bookstore that had recently come on the market, and seemed happier, though he still had his deep, sad voice, and suits that were two sizes too big.

Club Carrefour was still the neighborhood's most popular club. Little had changed there, unless you were privy to the back office, where the altar that had once been there had been taken down and replaced by another whose main attributes were snakes and rainbows.

Magdalena Konsavage had retired from the music business. It seems that she had fallen in love with the manager of her old band, Mountains of Madness, and they had married and moved far away from Cypress Hills. Father Baltazar thought they'd opened up a travel agency in Miami, specializing in tours of the Translyvanian Alps.

The drummer from Mountains of Madness—Sara never did learn his name—had become a priest, but had not retired from the music business. Father Baltazar said you could hear him play quite frequently in Cypress Hills National Cemetery, if you wanted to.

Alek Gervelis disappeared for a while, then released a solo CD that garnered a small but intense critical and popular following. It was introspective, lyrical, almost mystical in nature. The most popular song on it was called "Sara Seraphim."

Sara got postcards from him from Kathmandu, Casablanca, Lhasa, and Leng. They said that he had learned much, but there was still much to learn. Someday, they always said, he would find his way back to New York City, and her.

Sara tucked each and every postcard into a painted tin box she'd taken as a keepsake from Paul Narcisse's altar. And each time she did so, the voices in her head were blessedly silent.

ABOUT THE AUTHORS

JOHN DeCHANCIE is the author of two dozen books—both fiction and non-fiction—and his novels in the fantasy and science fiction genres have been attracting a wide readership for more than fifteen years. His humorous fantasy series, beginning with *Castle Perilous*, became a bestseller. He has also written in the horror genre, and for publications as widely varied as *Penthouse* and *Cult Movies*. His short fiction has appeared in *The Magazine of Fantasy and Science Fiction* and in numerous anthologies, including *Castle Fantastic* and *Spell Fantastic*. DeChancie's most recent book, *Other States of Being*, is a collection of some of his acclaimed short fiction.

JOHN J. MILLER is the author of more than a half-dozen novels, including *The Twilight Zone, Book 1: Shades of Night, Falling*. He has also written a number of short stories, including ten in the *Wild Cards* shared-world series edited by *New York Times* best-selling fantasy author George R.R. Martin. His non-fiction has appeared in magazines as diverse as *Tropical Fish Hobbyist* and *Baseball Digest*. His most recent work, "Something Robotic This Way Comes," appeared in *Transformers Legends*, a prose anthology based on Hasbro's giant robot toy line. Among Miller's upcoming projects is the novel *Wild Cards: Five Card Draw*, the latest entry in the series, to be published by ibooks, inc. Miller lives in New Mexico.